Rev

This is a great read, a real page-
deep-rooted hatreds, as well as tribal rivalries that dog the composition of the Middle East, and preclude a possible resolution.
From the start, the author draws the reader into a world where
modern and historical animosities are twisted together in a knot
that seems impossible to untangle. The author also has an excellent eye for visual detail to paint the picture of different environ-
ments for the reader. This is a must for lovers of political thrillers.

Readers' Favorite

Books by Stefan Vučak

General Fiction:
Cry of Eagles
All the Evils
Towers of Darkness
Strike for Honor
Proportional Response
Legitimate Power

Shadow Gods Saga:
In the Shadow of Death
Against the Gods of Shadow
A Whisper from Shadow
Shadow Masters
Immortal in Shadow
With Shadow and Thunder
Through the Valley of Shadow
Guardians of Shadow

Science Fiction:
Fulfillment
Lifeliners

Non-Fiction:
Writing Tips for Authors

Contact at:
www.stefanvucak.com

CRY OF EAGLES

By

Stefan Vučak

Dedication

To Jaye … when things get difficult

Acknowledgments

Information on properties of sticky labels, my thanks to Mark Gower, Adrian Van Drunen and Andrew Norman of Avery Dennison Materials Pty Ltd. Any liberty taken in the use of those facts was done on my initiative.

Cover art by Laura Shinn.
http://laurashinn.yolasite.com

"Where no counsel is, the people fall, but in the multitude of counselors there is safety."

Proverbs XI:14

Mossad motto

Glossary of Terms

Action officer : The case officer designed to perform an operational act during a clandestine operation in hostile territory.

Agent : A person who has been recruited by a staff case officer from an intelligence service to perform a clandestine operation.

Al Jazeera : Meaning 'The Peninsula', an Arabic television and Internet news network headquartered in Doha, Qatar, sympathetic to extremist Islamist movements.

Al Qaida : 'The Law'—a militant Sunni Islamist organization, with the stated objective of eliminating foreign influence in Muslim countries, eradicating those they deem to be 'infidels' and reestablishing the caliphate, rulers descended from Muhammad.

Avoda : The Israeli Labor Party, formed in 1964 as center-left social democratic and Zionist party, but is now a centrist party.

Bang and burn : A demolition and sabotage operation carried out by an intelligence service.

Black operation : Clandestine or covert operation not attributable to the organization carrying it out.

Burned : When a case officer or agent is compromised.

Burqa : An enveloping outer garment worn by Islamic women to cloak the entire body. It is worn over the usual daily clothing and removed when the woman returns to the sanctuary of the household.

Case officer : An operations officer serving as an official staffer of an intelligence service.

Chametz : Leavened grain products. Must be burned or sold before Passover begins.

CIA : Established in 1947, the Central Intelligence Agency is the U.S. foreign intelligence service providing human source information (HUMINT) and analysis.

Clandestine operation : An intelligence operation designed to remain secret as long as possible.

Collections Department : Department in Mossad responsible for foreign espionage operations.

Compartmenting : Various ways information is held by those

who have a 'need to know' and withheld from their superiors or colleagues.

CTAPS : Contingency Theater Automated Planning System—a computer system that supports a carrier-based strike planning process.

Cutout : A person who acts as a compartment between the members of an operation, but which allows them to pass material or messages securely.

Department of Homeland Security : Established in 2002, DHS is a Cabinet department responsible for protecting U.S. territory from terrorist attacks and responding to natural disasters.

FEMA : Federal Emergency Management Agency is an agency of DHS responsible for coordinating a response to a natural disaster within the U.S.

FIG: FBI Field Intelligence Group, one in each of the 56 field offices, tasked with analyzing data to forestall a criminal activity or provide input to solving a crime.

Hamas : Harakat al-Muqawama al-Islamiyya or Islamic Resistance Movement is a Palestinian Sunni Islamist organization and is a majority party in the Palestinian National Authority. Its charter calls for the destruction of Israel and its replacement with a Palestinian Islamic state.

Hezbollah : 'Party of God' Shi'ia Islamic militia and political organization based in Lebanon. Its objective is the transformation of Lebanon's multi-confessional state into an Islamic regime and the complete destruction of Israel.

IDF : Israeli Defense Force.

JTTF : FBI Joint Terrorism Task Force, a field office group charged with surveillance activities, electronic monitoring, source development and interviews to prevent a terrorist act or apprehend perpetrators.

Keffiyeh : A red-checkered headdress tied by a black rope circlet, the *agal*.

Knesset : The legislature arm of the Israeli government. The Knesset sits on a hilltop in western Jerusalem in a district known as Sheikh Badr before the 1948 Arab-Israeli war.

LAP (Lohamah Psichologit) : Department in Mossad responsible for psychological warfare, propaganda and deception operations.

Legend : A complete and verifiable cover identity developed for an operative working in a foreign country.

MIIDS/IDB : Military Intelligence Integrated Data System/Integrated Data Base—a set of integrated computer databases that support a carrier-based strike planning process.

MOIS : Iran's Ministry of Intelligence and Security, also known as VEVAK.

Mossad : Israeli foreign intelligence service, headquartered in Tel Aviv's northern suburb of Herzliya, formed in 1949 by Prime Minister David Ben-Gurion.

Pesach : The festival of Passover celebrating the legend of Exodus when the Israelites fled Egypt.

National Security Agency : The National Security Agency/Central Security Service (NSA/CSS) is the U.S. cryptographic intelligence agency, created in 1952, responsible for collection and analysis of foreign communication and signals intelligence (SIGINT).

Office of the Director of National Intelligence : Established in 2005, the ODNI serves as the head of the U.S. Intelligence Community, overseeing and directing the implementation of the national intelligence program.

Pasdaran : Islamic Revolution's Guards Corps (*Sepah*), a branch of Iran's military, but separate from the mainstream army, the *Artesh*. The IRGC was formed following the Islamic Revolution in 1979 which overthrew the Shah.

Political Action and Liaison Department : Department in Mossad conducting political activities and liaison with friendly foreign intelligence services, and with nations whom Israel does not have normal diplomatic relations.

Research Department : Department in Mossad responsible for intelligence synthesis.

Sakr-18 : Egyptian manufactured Multiple Rocket Launcher, a derivative of the Russian BM-21 *Katyusha* MRL, mounted on a 6x6 wheeled truck with a crew of five.

Shahab-4 : A two-stage Iran liquid-fuel missile, based on the North Korean *Taep'o-dong-1*.

Shi'ia : A branch of Islam who believe in the ascendancy of imam clerics as true interpreters of the Koran.

Shin Bet (Shabak) : Israel's internal security and counter-espionage service.

Special Operations Division (Metsada) : Department in Mossad responsible for conducting assassinations, sabotage and paramilitary projects.

Stage management : Managing the operational stage in a deception operation to ensure that all conditions and contingencies are considered.

Sunni : A branch of Islam dedicated to reestablishing the caliphate, rulers descended from Muhammad.

Taliban : A fundamental Sunni Islamist religious and political movement, created by Pakistan's Inter-Services Intelligence agency in the early 1980s to counter corruption, brutality and fighting among Afghan warlords.

TAMPS : Tactical Automated Mission Planning System—an interactive, graphical computer system used as an aid in planning a carrier-based air strike.

Technology Department : Department in Mossad responsible for developing technologies to support Mossad operations.

Tefillim : Two black boxes worn by orthodox Jews. One is strapped to the forehead and the other is tied to the right arm. They contain extracts from the Torah written on parchment.

The Institute for Intelligence and Special Operations : Mossad's official name.

Prologue

Northern Israel, 1979
Town of Kiryat Shmona *on the Lebanon border*

Low clouds, gray and fluffy, rolled down the gentle Golan
Heights slopes, obscuring the Hulla Valley in creeping shadow.
Somewhere in their depths lightning flickered, followed immediately by a muted rumble of rolling thunder. A patch of clear deep
blue sky still hung above the city. Warm buttery sunshine bathed
the sprawling settlement and the checkered pattern of green and
yellow fields surrounding it. A cool breeze gusted among the
curbside trees and made the leaves whisper in alarm.

Dressed in a dark red cotton T-shirt, blue collar fluttering
around his neck, black sweat pants and green-striped Asics,
Matan leaned into the turn when the bike rounded the corner.
The old Vespa sputtered, then surged down the street as he
shifted gears. It might be old, battered and scarred, but it served
him faithfully, and he would not trade it in for the plastic things
they made these days for anything. With the hot, stuffy and
smelly stores of the town center and its milling traffic safely behind him, he welcomed being back in the residential district. The
last-minute shoppers gave him a pain; everyone wanting to finish
the necessary chores before tomorrow evening's festivities. Why
leave it all until the last minute? The cool shaded street looked
infinitely more preferable. He fancied he could smell cut hay,
probably ketchup from his last hamburger.

A group of youngsters playing hopscotch on the sidewalk
looked up when he approached and waved as the worn-out little
scooter, trailing a thread of blue smoke, roared past them. Matan

waved back, not stopping this time. Sometimes, when feeling mellow and generous, he would give the kids a treat and take them for a spin around the neighborhood, the distinctive thrumming of his Vespa a familiar sound to everyone in the area. Today, he was in trouble and not feeling particularly mellow or generous. It wasn't as though he had actually done anything *wrong*. But try explaining that to his mother had gotten him nowhere. She simply didn't understand him or where he saw his future taking him. Buried in Israel's 'glorious past', as she put it, that was her problem. He had lived through that past: the deprivation, missed meals, sweating in the kibbutz fields, ritual and prayers. It held little glory for him.

He slowed down as he approached his house, waved to the frail old lady next door picking up her mail from the gatepost letterbox, then gave a long sigh. Sickly, Milaka lived alone, was kind to him mostly, except when he and the guys trampled her flowerbed tearing down the sidewalk. His mother used to beat him up for those antics when he was a kid, but what could he to do? It is not like they did it deliberately. The old lady should not have planted along the fence in any case; an open invitation for mischief. Anyway, he figured her to be a goner before Hanukkah. There would be mourning, tears, wailing and other unpleasantness. And he would have to stoically endure the whole miserable business, like anybody actually cared, and no one did, but the dreary observance of due form had to be obeyed, no matter how banal. Inertia, the thought came to him unbidden. And those who had gossiped the most would wail the loudest. It was all so irrelevant and hypocritical.

He pulled into the driveway, killed the engine and took off his helmet. With a quick squint at the clouds, he hung the helmet on the left handlebar. Across the street, Eben, a retired investment banker from Tel Aviv, leaned against his spade, looked at him and the Vespa, then shook his head in disapproval. Matan could clearly imagine the old relic's thoughts: 'That the boy would be working on the eve of Pesach. No respect anymore, that's what it was, and no discipline. Now, in *his* day such transgressions would not be tolerated.' Matan had heard it all before. Clearly, Eben saw no inconsistency that he was digging up his own garden on the eve of this most revered festival. Nevertheless, when Matan climbed off the scooter, he nodded politely to his neighbor. Standing behind his rough-hewn limestone fence, Eben's frown only deepened.

What made the crabby man come to this place, Matan could never figure out. The acerbic hypocrite clung to his shield of orthodoxy like a drunkard clutching the edge of a bar, assured of the superiority of his outdated convictions, refusing to acknowledge the danger of his extremist position. An investment banker? More likely a collection agency hitman. Matan smoothed back a shock of thick black hair with an unconscious gesture. He should have a haircut, he mused ruefully, *another* thing for his mother to complain about.

"Shalom, neighbor Eben!" he shouted good-naturedly to make sure the old dotter heard him.

The old man supposedly had hearing problems. Sometimes Matan wondered whether the gambit was simply a ploy to gain attention. He had seen that gag pulled by oldsters before, and it always felt pathetic.

"Joyriding again, eh, Matan?" Eben ventured, his voice filled with veiled accusation.

"At school," Matan countered, not in the mood to argue.

The old man's sour demeanor hung over him like a dark blanket, cutting out the sunshine of life. They lived in two different worlds and Matan could not bridge them. He didn't care to meet the old duffer halfway anyway. As a young impressionable kid, he liked listening to Eben's stories, his life in Tel Aviv, the world of high finance and political intrigues, the Yom Kippur war and the never-ending lamentations on the degenerating morality of the young.

Kiryat Shmona being a stone's throw from the Lebanese border, Matan had first-hand experience of the 1973 war, saw and heard the crash of artillery in the hills. He and his family had spent too much time in smelly bomb shelters for the adventure to be amusing. But it was exciting in its way, not understanding what all the fuss was about, not having to go to school. That was the best part. While Eben became increasingly conservative and cantankerous in his outlook, Matan's world had expanded when education and travel, admittedly only within Israel, broadened his horizons. He found the old man's dogmatic and pontificating pronouncements increasingly hard to digest, and moreover, extraneous. In his opinion, the guy was a senile relic who should confine himself to a rocking chair. But as a dutiful son, he nevertheless paid the man respect due an elder.

Eben raised his head and lifted an admonishing finger. "At school? Today? You're a good boy, Matan, most of the time, but you mock the Lord with your sins."

"He shall judge, old man," Matan said impatiently and strode toward the front door, ignoring the cool breeze ruffling his T-shirt and Eben's displeased stare. He looked up at the gray clouds and hoped it wasn't going to rain tomorrow.

Built of typical white sandstone, the double-story house had a balcony bordered by wrought iron railing from which hung potted flowers on black chains. Flaked paint gaped along the white railing and rust streaks marred some of the support rods. Looking at them, Matan grimaced. He needed to sand and repaint the things, but the arduous and exacting task didn't altogether fill him with eagerness. Sooner or later though, he knew his father would take him to task over it. Probably sooner than later, he thought glumly. How can he keep up with his studies if they kept piling chores on him? But did that get him any sympathy? Hardly. According to his mother, the sooner he started 'honest work' the better. That meant working in a factory or being a field hand;

both options were outside Matan's life plan and a source of ongoing irritation for his mother. Who was going to maintain the kibbutz tradition? But there, at least, his father was sympathetic, for which Matan was extremely grateful. His father understood that Israel's future lay in industry and commerce; the kibbutz was part of a romanticized past.

He opened the door and walked into the cool, shadowy interior of the entrance corridor. He shook off the runners and slid his feet into a pair of slippers parked next to an assortment of shoes on a small square of carpet as the door clicked shut behind him.

"Matan? Is that you?" His mother's shrill voice echoed from the kitchen and he flinched, knowing what was to come.

Little Raya stuck her head out from the dining room doorway and grinned with gleeful anticipation.

"You're in trouble," she pronounced comfortably, clearly relishing the coming scene.

He stuck out his tongue at his younger sister. "Am not."

"You are," she said and promptly stuck out her own tongue.

He took a step toward her and raised his right hand. She gave a shriek and vanished.

"Mommy! Matan was going to hit me!"

Peri emerged from the kitchen, wiped her hands on a somber black apron tied around her waist and glared at him.

"Where have you been? You were meant to help with the cleaning. If I find any chametz tomorrow, I'll be blaming you."

Clinging to her mother's dress, Raya beamed in expectation and made a face at him.

Matan's shoulders drooped, knowing he could never explain it to her. Why did she put him through this torture every time?

"I had an assignment to finish, Mom, and—"

"And being at Tel Hai is more important than preparing for the Pesach?" she demanded, her voice deceptively mild whenever her anger spilled against him, and he recognized the danger signal.

"Of course not," he said defensively. "But if I didn't get the thing finished, it could affect my whole semester's grade."

"You should have thought of that before. Instead, you spend all your time with those traitorous friends of yours and leave your work until the last minute. Doesn't your family mean anything? Don't we come first?"

Matan winced, stung by her words, the cut worse for being partly true. Not wishing to talk about it, he walked to where she stood and hung his head.

"I'm sorry, Mom, that you don't understand. My friends are not bad, even if two of them happen to be Palestinians."

Her clear chocolate eyes regarded him with seething fury. "That's exactly what I mean. Those people want to destroy us and you besmirch the family name by associating with them. Your father and I raised you to respect our country, and if necessary, to fight for its freedom from those who would destroy us. Like your friends! And to have you hanging around them, well, it's a disgrace. That's what it is."

"Let's talk about it some other time, okay?" Mati countered sharply, having heard the old arguments many times before. "If you want me to help, tell me what you want done."

"We'll talk about it when your father gets home," Peri promised and wiped a trace of flour off her left cheek. "And you keep a respectful tone, you hear? You children have it too easy these days. When your father and I settled here—"

Here it comes, Matan thought with a silent groan.

"—life was harsh, but we endured, and we endured for a good reason. We had a country to fight for—"

Matan looked around. "Where is he?" he countered to break up her tirade.

"Selling chametz," his mother snapped, "and don't interrupt."

During Passover, no chametz—leavened grain products—

could be held in the house. Anything found had to be either burnt or sold, usually to a local rabbi who acted as an agent, or directly to a non-Jew. A family gentile friend on the other side of town regularly bought their leftover and unused chametz, and as such transactions took a bit of time to conclude while the hospitality rituals were played out, Matan didn't expect to see his father until evening.

"And Janina?" he demanded, having got his mother distracted.

"Unlike you, you ruffian, your sister knows her duty. She's out shopping. Should be back any minute."

Apart from kosher cakes, cookies and cereals, the treats were expensive and overly fattening, but very good to eat. Right now, that part did not even hit his list of concerns. Despite the weary ceremonial and dull ritual, Matan liked Passover and the feasting. It was celebrating a fable, he knew that, but a country needed roots. Anyway, it should take his parents' minds off him and his list of misdemeanors, at least for a while.

They just didn't understand.

* * *

Shrouded entirely in low fog, the scarred Tatra 815 truck rattled and bounced gamely along the dry, rocky riverbed. Nothing stirred along the empty terrain, far removed from prying eyes, ideal for the task at hand. The hard seats, worn out even before the Egyptians had handed over the rocket launcher, did nothing for the two occupants' humor. However, judging from the driver's rapt attention and glazed eyes, the discomfort didn't seem to matter. A deep throbbing clatter filled the cab from the worn engine, mixed with groans from the twisting truck chassis, stinking petrol fumes, burnt oil, sweat and stale cheese. Garbed in the traditional *keffiyeh*, the bearded occupant in the right seat looked up from his map and shouted. The driver didn't hear him.

Exasperated, he grabbed the driver's right arm and shook him.

Khalid jerked his head around in surprise as though he had wakened from a deep sleep. In a sense, he had been, his concentration on driving total. He relished the coming operation and a chance to unleash a volley of death against his people's enemies and those who had wantonly murdered his family. The thought of Israeli bodies torn to bloody shreds, plastered along the walls of their devastated homes, like his mother, two sisters and a brother had been when the Mirages attacked their border village, filled him with holy joy. This was payback time and war he understood. Allah was great and Khalid was the god's servant, exacting retribution against a decadent and hated invader.

"We're there!" Rashid shouted and tapped the smeared, stained map. His cell leader had chewed him out for not keeping the map properly clean and in its plastic folder, but Rashid treated the reprimand with scorn. Getting new maps didn't concern him. Besides, that was woman's work, not a fighter's.

The battered vehicle slid to a stop as Khalid pumped the brake pedal. He really should top up the brake fluid, if he could find some. Despite his cell leader's brave rhetoric about the need for courage and sacrifice, it was lack of logistics that hampered their operations, not lack of courage. A wall of red dust flew into the cab and momentarily obscured the dry gorge before them. Hands still on the steering wheel, Khalid cleared his throat, twitched his *keffiyeh* into place and glared at Rashid.

"You're sure this time?" he chided, his thin mustache and beard caked with a film of grime. "I'm not in the mood for another of your childish blunders. Last time, you had the map upside down."

Rashid winced at the painful memory. His error cost the supply convoy an additional two hours of shaky night driving and bouncing on hard seats. His cell leader had not been very understanding, although the mistake was easy to make. Half the roads in southern Lebanon didn't appear on any map at all. The excuse had not gained him any sympathy from the other men either.

"I didn't have the damned thing upside down," he snarled. "I simply took a wrong turn, okay? And you shouldn't be riding me over it. We got there in the end, didn't we?"

"Fool! Give me that." Khalid snatched the folded map from Rashid's hands and spent a minute peering at it. Satisfied, he grudgingly thrust the mangled paper into his brother's lap. "Looks okay. Right, let's get on with it."

Leaving the engine running, he opened the door and jumped down. The dust had cleared and he looked up, scrutinizing the shallow walls of the gorge. The air smelled of rain and he hoped they would miss it. He didn't relish the idea of driving the old truck through cloying mud. A clammy wind swirled around him, making him wince at its bite, reminding him that he did not want to hang around longer than absolutely necessary. He tapped his stained jeans, brushed dust off his face, unclipped the bulky walky-talky and pressed the transmit button.

"Unit two in position," he said on the preset frequency and waited. The set crackled and he heard the familiar rough voice of his cell leader.

"You're late! Fire on schedule. Out."

Abrasive and insensitive, that was his cell leader. No sense of humor whatsoever, Khalid mused wryly. An idiot. He clipped the set to his belt and clenched his fists. He was prepared to put up with lots worse than his cell leader, as long as they kept letting him fire the rockets. With a last look at the heavy clouds above him, he grimaced and climbed back into the truck.

"We are 'go'. Let's get set up."

Rashid grinned, switched on the electric generator powering the launcher and unclipped the remote fire control unit mounted where the glove box would sit in a normal car. Trailing a finger-thick black cable, he climbed from the cab.

Khalid stared after him, shook his head and wondered why the merciful god had paired him with such a simpleton. The fact that they were brothers did not even occur to him. Before blowing his brains all over the ruins of their bombed house, taking the easy way out, his father entrusted him with the burden to look after his younger brother, and he could not get away from it. With a patient sigh, he lowered the rear chassis support jacks, switched off the engine, slid along the seat and climbed down.

Standing behind a slab of red granite that had rolled down the steep slope, Khalid watched as the Multiple Rocket Launcher assembly rotated a few degrees southwest and tilted back. This version of the Egyptian built Sakr-18 MRL, a Soviet BM-21 *Grad* variant, carried up to twenty-one 2.95 meter-long rockets with a range of some twenty kilometers. Each 122mm diameter *katyusha* missile delivered a twenty-three kilogram high explosive fragmentation or cluster munitions warhead. Due to its large circular area of probability (CEP), the *katyusha* could not be used against point targets, but against a sprawling settlement, it was an ideal urban terror weapon. The launcher normally required a crew of five to serve it. However, there would be no reloading this time around. This was strictly a one-shot hit-and-run proposition, which suited Khalid just fine. He wasn't ready to be a martyr yet.

Right now, the launcher carried only six of the deadly missiles. It would simply have to do. Although adequately funded and provided for by Syria and Iran, the PLO did not stock an unlimited supply of the things. As Khalid's cell leader had explained in his tiresome monologue, today's raid consisted of three launchers spread behind the Menara Cliffs, designed to frustrate any immediate Israeli retaliation. This was not a set piece battle, he pounded into his drivers, and he wanted no heroics. Keep to the objective: strike quickly and melt away before enemy Mirages or attack helicopters could get to them. Given that tomorrow was the infidel's celebration of Passover, Kiryat Shmona would be packed with people and ripe for slaughter.

Khalid had grinned. Sometimes even the PLO had a good idea now and then, only mildly wondering why the strike had not been planned for tomorrow.

"All set," Rashid announced as the whine of machinery stopped and he looked expectantly at Khalid. His brother grunted.

"You sure we're safe here?" Khalid demanded and Rashid nodded.

"Safe enough." He preferred using the remote control rather than firing the rockets from the truck. Two of their colleagues had met with a gruesome death when a malfunctioning round exploded on launch, setting off the others in sympathetic detonation, ripping the truck and its occupants to bits. Their cell leader lamented the loss of valuable equipment, acknowledging with surly reluctance the martyrdom of its crew. A hard man, Rashid mused.

"Okay, let's check the connections," Khalid said and started walking toward the launcher.

Rashid muttered a soft curse and followed his older brother. What could they check? Once the rocket was seated in its boxy cell, it was ready to go. Not like there was any wiring to clip, but before a launch, Khalid insisted on checking the few connections from each launch box to the cell platform. Well, it did no harm, Rashid allowed generously, but he still considered it a waste of time. Khalid was an old woman and worried too much. *Enchala*, what the god willed.

Apparently satisfied, Khalid returned to the relative safety of the boulder and crouched. He glanced at the wristwatch on his right hand and nodded to Rashid. His brother grinned and armed the firing circuits. Two minutes later, Khalid looked up at the sky.

"Allahu Akbar min kullisay," he muttered, and Rashid pressed the large red firing button on the boxy remote. *God is greater than anything*.

A javelin of searing fire and white smoke billowed from the launcher as the first missile ignited. Each launch tube was grooved to impart a slow rotation to the rocket. Primarily fin-stabilized, the rotation ensured accuracy at close range, and the target this time was only fourteen kilometers away on the other side of the hills.

Every three seconds the launcher spewed out one slim missile in a loud *whoosh*, imparting a velocity of 600 meters per second. Booming echoes and choking exhaust fumes filled the dry wadi by the time the last rocket arced over the cloud-shrouded hills.

When the launcher was exhausted and silence descended, heart racing, ears ringing, Khalid laughed, clapped his brother on the back and scrambled toward the truck. They could not waste time idling about, since the hated Zionists were sure to mount a mortar counterattack, backtracking along the *katyusha's* trajectories. He planned to be well away from here before that happened. He might even get away.

* * *

Clearing the Menara Cliffs, the entire northern Hula Valley lay invitingly open. Across the valley, a bare five kilometers wide, rose the Golan Heights range and Syria. It was a terrible tactical position.

The first missile had already arced into its 350 meters per second terminal descent, having covered the range in thirty-four seconds by the time the Israeli border listening posts issued a warning. When the sirens began their wail, it was far too late to react. Silent, its engine dead, the *katyusha* arrowed down and slammed into Matan's Vespa. The HE fragmentation warhead detonated, sending out a hail of steel shards, accompanied by a devastating shockwave.

Caught in the open, Eben hardly had time to look up when he heard the familiar low whistle from the descending missile. He didn't hear the explosion nor feel the shrapnel as it cut through him. The blast ripped his stone fence into fragments, which cut him into bloody ribbons before he could react. The front of his house and the houses around him were blasted apart, their remnants hurled spinning into the air.

Carrying a plastic bag of groceries in each hand, Janina had stopped at the entrance when the expanding wall of destruction slammed her body into the solid wood door before both were torn to shreds. Pushed by a giant's hand the walls of her house dissolved into their constituent blocks, ripping some into lethal fragments. The missile's shaped charge ensured maximum horizontal devastation. What was not flattened was flung into the air, causing wide area damage as debris crashed onto surrounding homes.

Standing behind the kitchen sink, Matan watched Janina walk up the driveway. She glanced at the Vespa and shook her head, setting her black bangs swaying. A small smile lit her oval face as though she understood. Matan liked his older sister, but this time, he knew her sympathies would not be with him. He took a few steps down the corridor, ready to open the door for her when he heard the anonymous whistle. For a vital second, he stood frozen and blood drained from his face.

"Mom!" he shrieked and made a desperate lunge to push her away from the window. "Under the table!" She stared at him, not moving, her eyes reflecting shock and disbelief. He grabbed her wrist and yanked her down as he dove for the table. "Raya!" he shouted in horror, knowing he could do nothing.

Thunder and smoke shook the ground and the front wall dissolved before him. Unbearable pressure squeezed his chest. Heat enveloped him and something heavy slammed into his left side. He fell into darkness and there was relief and silence.

Chapter One

Tel Aviv
Present Day

"In defiance of recently imposed UN trade sanctions, President Hamadee Al Zerkhani announced yesterday that Iran would not bow to illegal international pressure to cease what he termed is Iran's peaceful development of nuclear power, designed to promote an alternative energy source for his people. When asked why three weeks ago, another three hundred gas centrifuges were commissioned, technology not required for civilian-grade reactors, President Zerkhani stated that Iran wished to ensure an energy supply that would guarantee his country's independence and continued economic development. The fact that Iran already enjoys significant reserves of gas and oil seems to have escaped him. The president added that any interference with his country's legitimate exploitation of nuclear technology would incur the gravest consequences for the United States, and Western economies in general.
"The weather forecast for Tel Aviv today—"

Namir Bethan casually stabbed one of the preset radio channel buttons and the car filled with the haunting strands of Beethoven's sixth symphony. He relished the second movement, its subtle complexity and nuances, easily overlooked in the seemingly simple melody. The density and texture of the composition filled his soul with contentment and satisfaction. The piece was one of his favorites. Noting the turnoff, he slowed and eased the black BMW into Harav Kook Street. Nondescript office buildings lined the street, some modern, showing their reflective black or copper windows, glittering bright in early morning sunshine. Others were more conservative, built out of traditional white and yellow sandstone. A relatively new suburb of Tel Aviv, Herzliya dared to experiment with alternative architectural styles.

Tall trees lined the broad sidewalk, casting dark shadows along the street. Early starters, briefcases and bags in tow, hurried along, sometimes turning to walk into one of the buildings. Mildly curious, he wondered what their day would be like; a distraction while his brain did the driving on automatic. A sparrow made a startled dash across the street, vanishing among the thick foliage of a tree.

As the car whispered down Shival Hekochavim Street, he could see the familiar loom of an eighteen-story building, the sidewalk protected by a three-meter stone wall. Namir brought the car to a stop in the double driveway, climbed out and slid his black passkey into the security pad slot. Closed-circuit cameras mounted on each side of the wall stared down at him with intimidating curiosity. The heavy steel gate slid back without a rattle. He gave an involuntary glance up the sheer facade of the gray building, now outlined against the rising sun. With spring in the air, the days were getting warmer and his thigh didn't bother him as much. This early in the morning, the air was still crisp. He climbed into his car, slammed the door shut and drove through the courtyard.

"Welcome to the Institute for Intelligence and Special Operations," he muttered with wry amusement as he slowly drove toward the underground parking entrance. Not openly advertised, those who wanted to know where Mossad was headquartered could find out easily enough. The dashboard clock read 7:30, and had read that for a while now, he noted ruefully.

Since his wife's death two years ago to a brain tumor, undetected until far too late to do anything about it, his comfortable two-bedroom Tel Aviv apartment held nothing to keep him there. Fatalistic, the loss and guilt still hit him hard. He should have spent more time with her, valuing what he had. But as with such things, perspective came when one was powerless to undo what years of neglect had wrought. He made up for it now by burying himself in work. At least his country's needs were not being neglected—a poor consolation nonetheless. It did nothing to fill the lonely echoes of his empty apartment.

Unconsciously, he swept his eyes over an array of cars already parked in the lot, low-grade officers not entitled to an underground parking spot. He slipped his key into the security portal and waited as the heavy doors rolled up. Still not fully open, he drove into the dark maw. The underground parking lot had four levels, but his executive position allowed him a spot on the ground level. He parked the car, switched off the headlights, stepped out and leaned back in to pick up a slim brown calf-leather briefcase from the passenger seat. The parking and brake lights flashed when he automatically set the security lock. Given where he worked the action caused him to smile. Pocketing the keys, he slowly walked toward the foyer entrance. He dragged out a biometric badge from his coat pocket and pressed it against the door sensor. Satisfied, his electronic master unlocked the door with a heavy click. Inside the spacious cool foyer the security guard, sitting behind a curved reception station, looked up and nodded sternly.

"Morning, sir," he said with formal dignity.

"Shalom, Jaron," Namir replied heavily as he did each morning, walking slowly toward the middle of three entrance portals, his footsteps echoing against the marble floor. He passed the badge over the sensor. The red-lit panel turned green and gave a sharp beep. He walked through, stopped before the polished steel of the left elevator that ran through the building's core and pressed the dark access triangle. It turned soft amber. A few seconds later came a blunt chime and the double doors opened. There wasn't much of a demand this time of day. It took a moment for the elevator to surge to the seventeenth floor—his department. Light gray carpet muffled his footsteps as he made his way between glass-fronted offices, most of them with their privacy curtains drawn. He could not hear anyone else on the floor.

When he hobbled to the left corner office, he passed his badge against the lock and the latch gave a little click. He opened the door and closed it softly behind him. Heavy beige carpet covered the rectangular room floor. A wide, brown executive desk stood tucked against the far corner; bare, except for a standard keyboard, optical mouse, an 18" rectangular LED screen and a multi-function phone terminal. A round glass coffee table filled the empty space in the center, surrounded by four soft easy chairs. A floor-to-ceiling bookshelf occupied one wall, cluttered with bound volumes and paperbacks, magazines and various periodicals. The windowpanes were standard double-glass, designed to defeat vibration and laser voice intercept devices.

Namir placed the briefcase on the desk and sat down. He clicked open the two side latches, lifted out a slim blue folder, closed the briefcase and stood it against the desk drawers. He toggled the mouse and the screen lit up with the Mossad logo and motto. The desk did not mount a processor or workstation. His connection, like everyone else's, was provided through a secure shielded cable to high-speed servers on the fourth floor. The other equipment in the room was a color printer and a document shredder that ripped up to twenty-four pages at a time into three-millimeter square flakes.

The airconditioning sighed softly from two grilles mounted in the false ceiling.

A sharp rap on the door interrupted the thick silence. It opened and he looked up. Holding a steaming mug of coffee, two sugars, a young woman, dressed in a severe gray business jacket and pants, dark hair cut short, walked in and placed the mug next to the closed folder.

"Shalom, Mr. Bethan," she said primly and gave him a tight-lipped smile.

"Thanks, Mira," he growled and reached for the cup.

17

He gave an appreciative sniff and took a tentative sip. Black, hot and sweet, the way he liked it. His doctor told him to cut down on his sugar intake, but damn it, there were limits.

"Anything I should know?" he demanded, eyeing her over the rim of his cup.

She frowned and her pleasantly round face clouded. Pencil-thin black eyebrows added to her severe expression, highlighting her large brown eyes. A hint of red lipstick gloss softened her otherwise stern poise.

"Nothing that demands your immediate attention, sir. Unless you consider Iran's latest bout of histrionics an issue," she allowed with a trace of wry amusement and waited, knowing full well her boss was spending time in idle conversation. He knew everything of importance that went on around the world without having to be reminded. But it was a ritual they played out every morning and she didn't mind.

"I do, but that's an ongoing headache." Namir passed a gnarled hand through his receding shock of gray hair refusing to stay combed.

"Yes, sir." She frowned and bit her lip. "I cannot understand why the United States doesn't do something. And the UN is just as lame, fulminating and impotent. Somebody should bomb *them*!"

"I'll suggest it to Director Doron Kameer, but it's complicated," he mused, largely agreeing with her.

When the great powers did eventually reach an acceptable consensus, the original intent was so watered down that the final UN resolution held little meaning or potency. He took another sip, placed the mug down with a soft tap and spent a moment studying his ruthless-looking assistant.

Recruited from Shin Bet, Israel's internal security and counter-espionage sister service—inter-service poaching was rife, even though strictly frowned upon, but nevertheless a lively industry—the one-time Army captain's feminine exterior masked a

18

hard no-nonsense professional. At twenty-eight and one of his star case officers, she filled a vital function by being his personal assistant. In his view, secretaries were a luxury and potential security risks. Namir indulged in neither. Capable, disciplined and dedicated, he intended to continue mentoring her, provided he himself lasted the distance. In his game it only took one unguarded step and his brother colleagues, jackals more likely, would be baying and snapping at his heels. Then again, he had a job to do and Mossad didn't operate like the UN. To advance, she needed to round off her experience by working in other departments. He would hate to lose her.

Looking through her, thinking about things, he made up his mind and squared his shoulders, but was unable to suppress a flutter of unease in his stomach. The action he contemplated would be way over authorized limits. Sometimes though, such things were necessary. He wondered whether history would agree with him.

"When Matan Irian comes in, ask him to see me, will you?" he requested in dismissal.

"Of course, sir."

As the door closed behind her, leaving a whiff of lavender in her wake, Namir cracked his knuckles, reached for the keyboard, logged in and tapped out his search parameters with quick, efficient strokes. A number of messages waited to be opened in his Inbox, but he ignored them. The server immediately retrieved and displayed his search document. It had no classification attached to it, Namir's logon already providing the necessary access levels.

Sitting back, sipping his coffee, he quickly scanned the salient points outlined in the paper. He knew them off by heart, but the task helped him to think and reflect on what he contemplated. Written more than four years ago when Iran's uranium enrichment program was already well advanced—it never would have, had vital gas centrifuge designs not been provided by Pakistan between 1987 and 1991 by Dr. Abdul Qadeer Khan, to be precise—the document outlined a remarkably prophetic dissertation. In his opinion, Israel should have acted as soon as Iran's fledgling enrichment program was unearthed. However, the then Mossad director, Ephraim Halevy, was foremost a politician and wary of adverse repercussions should an operation to disrupt Iran's march toward a nuclear capability somehow backfire. Not that Namir could exactly blame the director, but he missed the old days, like in 1981 when Israel bombed Osirak, sending Iraq's nuclear ambitions into the stone age.

A wry smile of grim satisfaction lit his face at other successes as he recalled the assassination of Fathi Shaqaqi in 1995, founder of the Palestinian Islamic Jihad, by two of his agents right in front of the Diplomat Hotel in Sliema, Malta. The scum *deserved* to die. But the single wet ops which gave him the most satisfaction was having Izz El-Deen Sobhi Sheikh Khalil, head of Hamas, blown sky high, car and all, in 2004 while the guerilla fighter was in Damascus.

He understood and appreciated that type of direct action. Today, murky diplomacy and conforming to delicate international sensibilities were the norm, while Hamas terrorists targeted Tel Aviv and Jerusalem's citizens on buses and restaurants. Still, it was not as though Israel had not given them cause, he contemplated equitably. He would never say so aloud, but in his opinion the notorious wall building program, an attempt to fence off the occupied territories and stem the flow of suicide bombers, was an asinine political decision, compounded by another equally asinine decision to exploit the moment and annex additional Palestinian land. The effort failed abysmally and only served to harden international condemnation. It did nothing to placate illegal settlements, and tactically, did little to stop the bombings. Then again, how else could the Palestinians respond? Without a standing army to field in battle, terrorism remained the only weapon left to them. The old adage about a terrorist being a freedom fighter had a rather apt ring. Israel itself had used similar tactics against the British occupation after the Second World War. History was replete with lessons of failure, to the unheeding care of those who strove to repeat the mistakes.

Sometimes everything seemed so futile.

If he had his way, he would eliminate the politicians. That would solve everybody's problems. Prime Minister Sharron Ibrahim had the capacity and the will to act, but his Kadima Party coalition was hamstrung into inaction. Not that Labor or the minor parties such as Gil and Shas were any better. And Ibrahim's often imperious and forceful attitude had not helped to push through unpalatable policies. To hold power, successive governments had sacrificed their ability to formulate and execute initiatives by catering to extremist and radical single-issue coalition partners. Lately, Israel changed governments like he changed socks, an ominous symptom of fragmented ideologies and loss of vision. In the long run, that led to internal disintegration. But knowing what to do and having the will to do it, whatever the cost in personal careers, were the hallmarks of good government everywhere. In his view, Israel seemed doomed to pursue a fatalistic course of internal appeasement, incapable of realizing that placating the ultra-orthodox elements in its ranks simply to hold onto power left no one room to reach a workable settlement. Fortunately or unfortunately, depending on one's point of view, the Palestinian National Authority with its hostile Hamas government fared even worse. Sometimes a lot could be said for the value of a dictatorial regime.

Personally, he echoed Shimon Peres' sentiments that, *'Israel has no real option of turning to the political sphere in order to obtain a compromise that would constitute a genuine breakthrough—no compromise could ever satisfy the Arabs.'*

The inevitable consequence of that policy was the reinforcement of a concept that there could never be a political option on which Israel could base its security, which gave rise to a general psyche of interventionism by the Israeli Defense Force establishment in the political decision-making process. Since the military were perceived as the sole instrument capable of defending the country, any criticism or curtailment of its power was interpreted as a direct threat to national security. Namir admitted that lack of public debate on the automatic application of force as the sole mechanism to solve his country's problems had managed to derail every peace initiative to date, even if Israel's own religious extremists were willing to entertain the initiative—which they were not. Growing militancy between Fatah and Hamas, and disintegration of the Palestinian National Authority, might encourage the military to take matters into their own hands. That, of course, was but a single step from fascism, the worst of all possible outcomes.

Well, he might not be in a position to solve all his country's problems, but staring at the screen, he had no qualms about jump-starting the process. Viewing the proposal, it had all the classic elements of a military deception: a specific objective, playing to the enemy's preconceived assumptions, a clear method selection and simple execution. At least he hoped it would be simple. The exploitation component was missing, but in this case, hardly relevant. The tricky bit was that Kameer also had access to the proposal and could conceivably connect the dots, a bridge to be crossed later. He pressed the print icon and the printer immediately began to hum as it spat out the report. He picked up the still warm pages, tapped them together against the desk and reached into his drawer for a stapler.

He was still reading when the phone went off.

"Yes?"

"Mr. Irian to see you, sir," Mira announced.

"Send him in." Namir placed the report on the desk, face down, as his tall visitor walked in, military bearing clear despite the tastefully cut dark gray suit, and closed the door behind him. It was nothing specific that marked his visitor, more a collection of small subtleties: clear penetrating eyes, aura of complete confidence, economical body movements, and that something that said 'command presence'.

"Ah, Matan, take a seat," he said warmly.

"Thanks." Matan nodded, glanced at the coffee table and settled himself into the nearest chair, his legs stretched out before him.

Namir folded his hands and leaned forward. "How is Sarah these days? Still beautiful as ever?"

"And I'm still very much in love with her," Matan declared, his voice crisp and determined.

"How about that! And Admina?"

"Growing up too fast."

Namir chuckled. "She is going to break some hearts along the way."

"As long as some slick city kid doesn't break *her* heart."

"She's lucky to have you and Sarah looking out for her."

"That's a matter of opinion. Sometimes I just don't understand her."

"The same way she feels about you, I'm sure."

"I don't doubt it. Anyway, why don't you come around some evening and straighten her out. She'll listen to you."

Namir lifted his hands and laughed. "No thanks! I'm happy to leave that problem to you. I've had my time. But talking of problems, any further developments at tracking down that Hamas cell?"

Two weeks ago a twelve-year-old Gaza girl had walked into a Tel Aviv restaurant near Old Jaffa and blown herself up, taking eleven patrons and bystanders with her, and eighteen others injured, some seriously. Recovered from the debris were nails, nuts and roller bearings—a vicious combination to make a statement. The incident caused an outcry and much breast-beating by everybody. The Collections Department suspected that a single Hamas cell had orchestrated the attack, having carried out a similar atrocity a week earlier. That time, it was a fourteen-year-old boy. To brainwash children…

Matan stared at the Special Operations Division director and wondered why the sudden concern. It was not something that could be solved overnight, if at all, like incidents of indiscriminate roadside shooting, spraying cars and two cabs with AK-47 fire. Namir's leg had to be acting up again, he thought comfortably, although he wasn't showing it. The old codger looked fit and would probably outlast everybody.

As far as Matan knew, the director was only fifty-eight, but the thick gray hair, hard chiseled features, prominent nose and dark complexion, made him appear older; except for the eyes, deep green and lively. Despite the apparent external decrepitude, the eyes revealed an indomitable spirit, one that ruled his department with a rod of iron. Special Ops did not always follow the strict interpretation of its charter, earning a degree of enmity along the way not only from its sister departments, but from the Knesset as well. However, it did get things done, most of the time. In his book, that made up for everything else. Politicians did not need to know what their intelligence organs were up to—until it failed them. Namir made sure that his department did not fail. Matan liked that kind of thinking.

From what he knew, the Metsada chief had always been involved with intelligence, taking over the Special Operations Division in 2002 after a stint in the Political Action and Liaison Department. A former Mirage pilot, Namir was a rising star in the Air Force Intelligence before being recruited by Mossad into the Collections Department. His organizational and administrative abilities, coupled with a flair for the innovative, ensured that he gravitated through Mossad's operational sections as quickly as possible. Running Metsada seemed to have given him a home. But he worried about the chief, especially after the sudden death of his wife. Work was the only thing that seemed to matter to him these days.

"I wouldn't mind seeing some of those holier-than-thou Hamas leadership strapping on a bomb themselves for the cause," Matan muttered sourly and Namir grinned.

"You and me both. Maybe we should send them a memo. How about that!"

"Something to think about. Anyway, the Research Department has given us a couple of leads, but we're not moving fast anywhere."

"The Director is looking closely at this one, Matan."

"Kameer?" Matan looked incredulous. "He's got nothing better to do than be bothered by a suicide bombing incident?"

The corner of Namir's mouth twitched in sympathy. "I wouldn't be too critical. The prime minister is giving him a hard time and we must do our duty as we see it," he deadpanned. "Sharron Ibrahim's niece was injured in that blast."

"It's an internal security matter," Matan protested. "Shabak are handling it."

"Apparently not well enough. That's why we are involved. Just keep an eye on things, will you?"

Namir regarded his senior case officer with deliberate scrutiny and no small measure of fondness. A reserve colonel, having enlisted in the Army for officer training following the death of his mother and two sisters in 1979, forty-two, wife and a daughter, Matan had proved himself to be an exceptional analyst. Recruited from the Army into the Political Action and Liaison Department, it did not take long for the hierarchy to spot a rising talent. Less than a year later, working for the Research Department, Matan had produced a number of analyses and action proposals deemed controversial even by Mossad's progressive standards. Namir had one of them on his desk now. Two years later, with his help, Matan wound up in Metsada, the Special Operations Division; Mossad's action arm dealing with assassinations, sabotage and covert paramilitary projects. The dirty tricks department, he reflected with satisfaction and a measure of pride. As a case officer and stage manager, Matan had no equal. His operations to date were planned and executed with faultless precision and total deniability. No loose ends, simply painstaking attention to minutiae and detail. And right now, for his scheme to work, Namir desperately needed that skill.

Despite the years, Matan carried himself with confident ease, his lips pressed permanently into a thin line. Some still called it arrogance, but in reality, it was a reflection of his capabilities, exaggerated perhaps by his officer training and automatic authority. Colonels always acted like they were one rung below God. Hair still black, Namir noted, marred by a hint of white at the temples. Long face, dark complexion, square jaw, Matan could easily have passed for an Arab and spoke Farsi without an accent. The dark mahogany eyes, sunk deep into the skull, were bright with amusement. They were also eyes of a man who had suffered much and managed to survive and thrive. Namir knew that Matan yearned to be out in the field, but he was far too valuable to risk losing on some gutter-crawling ops, being groomed for a deputy's position in the Collections Department. That had rankled at first, but in the end, Matan accepted the inevitable exigency of the service. This should be especially sweet, Namir thought—bittersweet, perhaps.

"Be that as it may," he allowed, "but I didn't call you in to talk about the Hamas or Shabak's incompetence. I want to broach the possibility of a bang and burn black ops. You would be the team cutout and action officer."

Matan sat up and the small hairs on the back of his neck bristled with anticipation. A bang and burn usually involved demolition and sabotage, invariably in foreign territory. That meant *dangerous* territory. The two years spent with Metsada had been, in the main, soul-fulfilling experiences, but with little personal excitement. Namir had allowed him two opportunities to conduct a field mission, one in Lebanon and one in Jordan. Both went well and eliminated their targets cleanly—Syrian agents who were providing Hezbollah with advanced tactical training. The operations left him physically taxed and he knew that his field ops days were numbered. He'd had a taste and it was enough, content now to be a planner and organizer, the invisible man who pulled the strings. What had changed that Namir would now want him out there?

"Sounds, ah, like a challenge," he ventured cautiously, looking for traps.

Namir chuckled. He couldn't help it. The dangled bait was sniffed, but Matan was too good an operative to snap at the obvious.

"You'll enjoy this one. It's something that you dreamed up yourself."

"I've put up lots of screwy proposals," Matan muttered acidly, "which you and the Director never tire of telling me." Only one person was spoken to or referred in the third person—Doron Kameer, head of Mossad.

"Someone has to restrain your youthful enthusiasm," Namir said dryly, then cleared his throat. "Seriously, though. This time, there will be no restraints, no half measures. On this one, we're playing for broke."

"Okay, my curiosity is aroused." They had known each other long enough to be on first-name basis. Besides, Matan had sufficient seniority not to be overawed by silly bureaucratic protocol.

"What I have in mind might save us from a confrontation with Iran."

"What will save us is to simply bomb the place," Matan said evenly, perfectly serious. "Waiting for the UN or the U.S. to hammer out an acceptable solution is an exercise in futility, and you know it. A surgical strike will set them squawking, but it would also eliminate the threat."

"Not a novel idea, and something your military colleagues would love to do. Politically though, it is not an option. However, we could get someone else to do the job for us and wear the heat.

How about that!"

Matan sat back in shock and his eyes darted to the overturned papers on Namir's desk. He couldn't be considering...

"You want to bring the United States into direct conflict with Iran? That's crazy!"

"Your report didn't read all that crazy when you wrote it," Namir said mildly and smiled at Matan's expression of amazement and confusion.

"When I wrote the thing, I was tossing up ideas, scenarios."

"Perhaps. Did you listen to the radio this morning?"

"Yeah, I've heard the latest."

"Hamadee Al Zerkhani has now made your scenario more than just an idea. He has made it viable. And if you think about it, it's not as crazy as it may sound. You sketched out the tactical and strategic agenda pretty well yourself. Iran develops a nuclear weapon, mounts warheads on its Shahab-4 missile inventory and holds a trigger to our heads, to everybody's head. The next step is economic blackmail, forcing Europe and the United States into policy changes designed to make us give up the occupied territories and recognize an independent Palestinian state, or risk an oil embargo by shutting off the Strait of Hormuz. Of course, Israel would never agree, no matter how sensible the solution, because it would be an imposed one. Even if the government of the day wanted to, its single-issue coalition partners would derail any such move. Forcing the issue would cause a revolution."

"Holding onto the occupied territories is half our problem," Matan remarked sourly. "As is our continued expansion in settlement building throughout the West Bank in clear violation of the Roadmap. But the major problem is our refusal to acknowledge the Palestinian's right to a state of their own, as much as they are refusing to recognize us. We'll never move forward until everybody gets over that."

"Agreed, and that's a political dimension. I must deal with today's reality. A nuclear capable Iran would give it political and religious levers to rally all the Shi'ia in the region to their standard, and in the process making them the dominant force in the Middle East. To keep their Sunni regimes in power and the oil flowing, Saudi Arabia and the Gulf states would be forced to share some of that power with their Shi'ia minorities. But it would be a fragile peace. In the end, there would be open sectarian unrest, which in turn would lead to an inevitable confrontation."

"I don't believe that anymore, and neither do you," Matan said bluntly. "There is no Shi'ia insurgence in Saudi Arabia or any Gulf state. It's a beat up perception."

"Perception or not, Iran's Council of Guardians could use the pretext to try and neutralize Israel."

"What they want to neutralize, Namir, are the Pakistani Sunnis and the emerging extremists who seek to impose a Taliban-style Islam on everybody in the region."

"What Iran wants to neutralize is Israel's extended nuclear deterrence," Namir snapped, getting rather tired of Matan's defeatist attitude. "Our ability to threaten the Arabs with annihilation, should they get out of line, would vanish. We would be threatened as well. As a military officer, it is something that you, of all people, should appreciate. How about that!"

Matan chuckled, ignoring the implied rebuke. "That's the first bit you said that I fully understand."

"I'm glad that you *do* understand," Namir said dryly.

"I also understand something else. As a military officer, I fully sympathize with the Army's frustration at being held back from cleaning up the Hamas by politicians who are more interested in preserving their hold on power than solving the country's problems. Beating their heads against the Wailing Wall and sticking notes in the cracks may be good publicity, but doesn't achieve anything."

"Perhaps, but our problems cannot be solved by application of more military force," Namir said coldly. "At least not by our military. Iran's current posture of belligerent defiance has given us a window of opportunity to take affirmative action that could prevent a future holocaust."

"I don't know that sabotaging American oil infrastructure and drawing them into a response would necessarily solve our problems," Matan murmured, and a sudden chill filled the air. Namir wasn't kidding when he said that on this one they were playing for broke, and playing with big chips indeed. "The political landscape has changed since I wrote that proposal, you know. Keep in mind that we're not dealing with a homogeneous enemy here. Just because Iran, Syria and the rest are Islamic states, they're not all Arabs."

"To the average Israeli on the street, it's a moot distinction," Namir corrected him. "The threat is still the same."

Matan sighed and shook his head. "You're not swallowing the apocalyptic panic-mongering drivel spouted by Benny Morris at *Jerusalem Post*, are you?"

"Morris might be a rebel rouser and a pain, but he reflects the view of a significant portion of our population."

"I'm not so sure about that. At best, I would say it's a radical minority. But, okay, let's say we get away with it, consider the repercussions. If Iran is destabilized, the Sunnis and the Shi'ia will be at each other's throats for sure. The entire Middle East would degenerate into open factional warfare that would make Iraq look like a street brawl. Well, more than it already is, with President Walters having pulled out U.S. troops. Without a stable energy supply the Western economies would take a savage hit. Tactically, you might achieve your objective, but strategically the solution sucks."

Namir pointed a finger at Matan. "A bit dramatic and oversimplified, but this time, I think you're wrong. There will be some inevitable economic repercussions, I agree, but I doubt on the dire scale that you paint. Iran's population has become better educated, better fed and housed, and are starting to enjoy decadent Western luxuries decried by the hardliners. The Council of

Guardians may be fanatics in our eyes, with a God-given right to subjugate the infidels, but they're not fools. They want to stay in power. To do it, they must ensure the people do not rise up in another revolution. A strike by America against their nuclear installations might be damaging to the Council's sensibilities, and there will be the expected protests, marches and breast-beating against the Great Satan, but business would go on. After all, a strike would not be targeting population centers. The UN, the French and the Germans will fulminate at what they would call unrestrained American aggression, but secretly, they would be relieved. They don't like the idea of a nuclear Iran any more than we do."

Namir's words were soft, calm and measured, and Matan suspected, backed by enormous research. Still, his training told him that research counted for little in the face of actual experience. Something else he needed to consider, something Namir might not want aired. The problem was that Israel itself had contributed in no small way to the current mess when it supplied nuclear material to Turkey. What happened next was inevitable.

Everyone in the international community knew that since the 1980s, Turkey had sought to develop its own nuclear fuel capability and an indigenous reactor design. It also pointed to a possible nuclear weapons development, which was conveniently ignored by everybody. Provided adequate monitoring was set in place the U.S. did not object to the idea. After all, Turkey was a strategic NATO ally and a secular bastion against the more radical sectarian regimes in the south. Israel apparently did not have a problem with Turkey being a nuclear balancing counter against Pakistan and Iran either. How could it know that Turkey would actively traffic nuclear material directly to Pakistan, a nominal enemy. In Matan's view, it should have, especially after the overthrow of Prime Minister Nawaz Sharif in 1999 by General Pervez Musharraf. With a large neighbor suddenly under military control and a predominantly Sunni population, Iran became understandably nervous and resumed work on its heavy-water reactor at Arak and the uranium enrichment plant at Natanz. Despite these warning signs, Israel continued to supply Turkey with information and technology.

It all came to a head in 2003, a case where Mossad stumbled badly.

One of the Collections Department agents was caught trying to sell two hundred triggered spark gaps to a Pakistani with known military and radical Islamic links. As it turned out, the CIA was on top of it and allowed the transaction to continue in order to trace the whole supply operation. The spark gaps were to be procured from a Massachusetts company, Perkin-Elmer Optoelectronics, who were prepared to make the delivery once the required end-user certificates were provided, detailing that the switches would not be sent to blacklisted countries like Pakistan. The Mossad agent knew he could not obtain such certificates and approached the head of a Mossad front company in New Jersey, Giza Technologies, which had previously supplied nuclear components and weapon designs to South Africa.

What followed could have been taken straight out of a spy thriller: rerouted shipments, front companies and multiple handoffs through a number of countries before the switches eventually wound up in Pakistan. The CIA sting exposed a smuggling network that linked Israel, South Africa and Turkey, and compromised Giza Technologies. Despite the evidence to prosecute, the U.S. State Department quietly quashed the matter to protect its Turkey interests, but Israel had to wear the embarrassment. Although the Collections Department conducted the operation without full authorization, and its director had gotten the chop, Mossad bore a lot of heat from the ensuing fallout.

What Namir proposed now could be a case of misguided zeal, a piece in a tangled web of conflicting international and domestic interests, or genuine patriotism. Matan couldn't tell. A report outlining a possible tactical scenario was one thing. Acting on it and against the United States, might not be the wisest course of action. Should the operation fail, Mossad would not be the only one feeling the heat. Whatever his doubts, it wouldn't be career-enhancing to voice them now.

"Even if we pull it off, there is no guarantee that America would blame Iran and commit to a retaliatory strike against their nuclear installations. They could hit anything."

Namir nodded. "Agreed, but the current U.S. administration is looking for an excuse to go after Iran's enrichment plants. Our action will give it to them. The President is young and inexperienced, bound to be influenced by Congress and public opinion. He'll deliver. Even if he strikes some other target, Iran should get the message."

"You hope. Still, it could work," Matan said with objective professionalism, mulling over the tangle of practical obstacles standing in the way of such an operation. "However, you know what could happen should the United States ever find out that we were behind this."

"You don't have to remind me. You now know why I want you to be the team action officer. The mission must remain compartmented…forever."

Matan understood perfectly. He did not need to have that part spelled out.

"This will entail some loss of American life, not counting likely environmental effects."

"Worth it to neutralize Iran's threat, but charges can be placed to minimize significant damage. After all, we want to sting America into action, not actually create an environmental disaster."

Matan pursed his lips and gave a reluctant nod. "In theory, that's true, and doable. Who knows about this?"

Namir's eyes were expressionless. "No one."

Matan stared. "This has not been authorized?"

"If you take this on, Matan, it must remain the blackest ops ever. No one can know and no one will be pinning any medals on you. However, you'll have my grateful thanks and the ignorant gratitude of your country. How about that!"

And probably a bullet in the head at the end of it, Matan mused. He had been around long enough to know by now how the grownups played.

"That makes up for everything," he said without humor.

"You also know why the Director can't know, or the Prime Minister."

"Yeah. CNN would have it on tomorrow morning's news and Israel would be dead. And *we'd* be shot the next day for treason. Or maybe something not that nice." Matan sighed and pulled at his chin. "Why me? You have a dozen tame action officers who are far more qualified. Doing field work is different than directing it behind a safe desk."

"Tell me about it." Namir grunted and rubbed his right thigh, result of a Lebanon ops. Not exactly a failure, but it did cost him three men. "The reason I want you is that every operation you ever handled has gone off without the smallest flaw. That cannot be said for all our ops. It was before your time, but you recall the bungled attempt in 1997 to assassinate the Hamas leader Sheikh Khaled Maskal? I wince at the thought even today. Then in 2004 we had that New Zealand passport fiasco."

Matan nodded. "It wasn't exactly your best day."

"There were others. In each case, I saw to it that heads rolled. Just goes to show you, my boy, never take a holiday in the middle of an ops. But this time, there cannot be even a hint of a loose thread or more than heads would roll."

"There is always the random element."

Namir's eyebrows dipped in a frown. "Nothing must surface. Nothing!"

"I got it, all right."

"Good. There is one other thing. Given the nature of the operation, there will be one departure from your original proposal."

"Oh?"

"Despite what your report recommends, I cannot endorse the use of one of our *Dolphin*-class submarines to attack Galveston Roads."

"I agree, and I was going to make the same point myself," Matan said evenly. "Although attractive, involving the Navy could never be contained. Sooner or later, someone would blab and we'd be compromised."

"Exactly."

"Unless you were prepared to sink the sub with all hands on mission completion." Matan meant it as a joke, but Namir wasn't smiling.

"I considered it, but as you pointed out in your own risk assessment, too many people would be involved, and after the event, there would be the inevitable questions. Besides, how would we explain the loss of the submarine? There are also some serious logistical problems associated with that option. No, too many cracks through which we could all fall." Namir paused, his green eyes probing his senior case officer, liking what he saw. "There is one other reason why I want you. An important reason, although you might not agree with me. It is your high level of personal ethics."

Matan stared at the director and snorted. "My personal level of ethics?"

"All your psychological profiles demonstrate that. You left the Army because of ethics."

"I left the Army because I didn't see how bombing helpless Palestinians contributed to our security," Matan growled, unwilling to have the scabs over that wound probed. He was also irritated at Namir's theater psychology and the fact that it was working.

"My point exactly. The decision cost you a star, but it is clear to me that you didn't want it badly enough to continue as a tank commander."

"A man has to live with himself."

Namir nodded in sympathy. "That's right. It is one element that runs consistently through every one of your proposals. They were all honorable."

"My halo does have some ragged edges, you know. Anything else?"

"Yes. I want your assessment on conducting a strike against a Sorush offshore platform connected to the Kharg Island terminal."

Matan stared. "You're looking to create a retaliatory trigger against Galveston? Why?"

"Easy. Having attacked their platforms before, Iran would not hesitate to accuse the Americans of conducting this raid as well."

In 1987, asserting that Iranian oil platforms were used as staging facilities for attacks by the Revolutionary Guard against tanker shipping in the Gulf, the U.S. attacked and destroyed two Iranian offshore oil production installations in the Reshadat complex. In 1992, Iran brought an Application before the International Court of Justice against the U.S. for attacks on its facilities. In 2003, the Court at The Hague ruled the U.S. attacks were unlawful, but did not violate the 1955 commerce treaty between the two countries and the matter was dropped. Understandably, Iran had never accepted that decision.

Namir tapped the desk with his finger. "So far, Al Qaida, probably under instructions from Iran despite the fact that Al Qaida is a Sunni front, has refrained from making direct attacks against American oil infrastructure. Both sides are too vulnerable to such acts and notwithstanding Iran's histrionics, shutting down its oil output would hurt them far more than it would the United States, provided OPEC does not retaliate in kind by curtailing production and raising prices even more than they already have, which they could do in any case."

"That's your bureaucrats talking, Namir, and they're way off the mark here."

"Oh? Enlighten me."

"With pleasure. Hitting Sorush makes the Americans out to be the bad guys. Galveston would be retaliation that everyone can understand, and more importantly, sympathize with. The objective here is to generate world empathy for America, not Iran."

"The thought *had* crossed my mind, you know," Namir said patiently.

Matan grinned, unabashed by Namir's sarcasm. "If that weren't enough, I will give you another reason—injection and extraction. Sorush is in the middle of the Gulf, out in the open. International naval forces, including Revolutionary Guard gunboats, constantly patrol the area. Unless you came in by submarine, a surface approach is bound to attract unwelcome attention. Take it from me, it's an awful tactical scenario. I wouldn't want my sorry ass hanging out there on some dhow pretending to be fishing while loaded to the gunwales with high explosives. Even if we somehow got in, chances of getting back in one piece would be marginal at best."

Namir shrugged. "It was just an idea."

"Then put it out of your mind. If you leave out Sorush, the mission is doable, but the economic backlash could be severe for everybody should this backfire. Our own providers, Mexico, Norway and Egypt to a lesser degree, could cut off supplies if pressured by America. Even if that doesn't happen, Israel would be an international political and economic pariah."

"Israel would weather it and we will have removed a Damocles sword hanging over us. How about that!"

Matan made a face and rolled his eyes. "Damocles sword, my ass. Israel isn't worried about a military threat. Like you said, with a nuclear-armed Iran, we lose our bargaining chip with the Arab states, based on the fact that right now *we* have the bomb and they don't."

"You *do* believe in the necessity?" Namir asked pointedly, somewhat unprepared for the impersonal dissection of his idea.

"If I didn't, I would not have proposed the scenario," Matan said testily. "But please, don't sell me propaganda. Save it for the politicians."

"I'll keep that in mind," Namir said acidly and his eyes clouded. "I promised that you would be the action officer, and you will be. Stage management will be critical and your team's effectiveness cannot be distracted by having to worry over administrative details. In case you harbored any melodramatic ideas of playing a dashing agent, you will not be part of the actual strike team."

Matan grinned and his eyes brightened. "It never occurred to me."

"I'm sure. Seriously, you're not a field operative, and having you blunder around in a wetsuit and balaclava would endanger not only your mission, but the lives of your team."

"You don't need to spell it out, Namir. I know my limitations."

"I'm tempted to lock you in a safe and burn the combination. Unfortunately, that option is not available to me," Namir remarked, his face stern. "When you have your ops plan done, we'll go over it. In the meantime, offload any small stuff on your plate to young Ritchie. A bit of pressure will do him good."

"Does that include tracking down that Hamas cell?"

"Absolutely. It's routine work which he should be able to handle on his own." Namir stared hard at his protégé. "One more thing. I don't want you making calls or referring to this mission in any way to anyone. No paper trail or emails. Nothing. Whatever you want, you talk to me. No loose ends."

"You're acting like this mission has already started and I agreed to run with it," Matan said with a tight smile, suddenly not sure he wanted any part of this.

Their eyes locked. "It has and you are, aren't you?"

"I guess I have," Matan said slowly, then sighed and stood up. "At least it should be warm in Galveston, and I need to build up my tan."

"Just don't spend *all* your time building it."

"Talking about spending…"

"Already taken care off. You'll get a notice of a special slush account later today."

Matan liked this side of Namir's setup. The director realized that fighting their own bureaucracy was sometimes half the problem and made sure the bean counters did not get too inquisitive. He kept a number of alias 'floating' bank accounts created for black ops, untraceable and closed on every mission completion. Matan had used the system before and found it infallible. However, there were other ways to cover his butt and he had resources of his own.

He paused as he reached for the door handle. "I'll talk to you in a couple of days," he said with a nod, opened the door and stepped out. It closed behind him with a soft click.

Namir stared at the door for a few seconds, then picked up his mug and took a sip. The coffee had gone cold and he put the cup down. He grew aware of muted voices from outside as his senior staffers filtered in. The airconditioning whispered in the background.

When he mentioned to Matan that this operation must be completely black, he had neglected to state the obvious corollary: how to ensure that Matan and his team were never burned. There was a way, but he didn't want to pursue that solution. Not yet, anyway. What was Mossad coming to when they could not even trust one of their own? But Mossad wasn't in the trust business. What he meant was that *he* was not in the trust business, which was saying the same thing. Personal feelings or not, he could not afford to get sentimental.

The necessary steps would be taken.

He swiveled the chair, locked his fingers into a pyramid and watched the sun come up, wiping out any last minute second thoughts as the shredder chewed through the report.

Chapter Two

Beneath a copper sky, heavy breakers broke over golden sands with rolling booms that sent silver spray arching up through frothy foam. In the distance, whitecaps marched across a mercury sea as the sun, shrouded in a cloak of reds and browns, dipped into its embrace.

Not noticing the taste, Matan sipped his bourbon, shielded from the violence outside by heavy floor-to-ceiling lounge windows. Dimly lit, fitted with dark wood paneling, modern, softly contoured leather chairs clustered around small square tables. The place smelled of expensive brandy and fine cigars. Half a dozen men in their sixties, wearing conservative dark suits preferred by senior corporate executives, provided the crowd. Two were alone, reading local tabloids. The others were evenly split between two groups. Subdued noises drifted into the lounge from the bar outside.

A gusting wind swept the deserted beachfront with driving sand. Protected by a curved stone quay from the worst of the weather, tall masts of moored sloops and ketches nevertheless swayed and jerked in the roiling sea. It made him seasick just looking at them.

He had not wanted to come today, planning the operation preoccupying his time and thoughts. Perhaps too much time. He had been concentrating on technical aspects of his mission, choosing for the moment to sidestep the trickier problems of insertion and extraction. His father had not been interested in lame excuses, insisting that their regular fortnightly rendezvous be kept. Lighten up, he said. Maybe he had a point, Matan mused. But this meeting was drinks only, no dinner. His old man wanted to keep an appointment with a theater later in the evening. Usually, they had repast at Matan's place, giving his dad an opportunity to taste real cooking in a family atmosphere. His father knew how to take care of himself, and Matan had sampled some of his Dad's culinary experiments a number of times, but there was something different having a woman prepare a meal. Given that quirk, he wondered why most professional chefs were men. Just one of those things. Besides, when she wasn't being an accounts manager at Price Waterhouse, his Sarah loved to fuss over her two menfolk. He absently patted the soft fold leaning over his belt in testament to that care. Still, he couldn't blame his emerging bulge on his wife. He needed to exercise more, hating the thought of turning into one of those sagging, repulsive, greasy men who lounged around him. Sarah had kept her fine, trim figure, and they enjoyed the good things that life offered. The least he could do was keep his end of the unspoken agreement.

The surf boomed against the shore to the echo of fond memories.

There was no denying the technical challenges surrounding his mission and the chilling prospects of its success, or failure. He knew all too well, just as Namir obviously did, that random factors could unravel even the best planned and faultlessly executed ops. It was impossible to account for the random element that *always* reared its head, and critically, the elusive human dynamic. Painstaking attention to every fiddly detail helped mitigate the risks, but could not entirely eliminate them. And the single major risk facing any ops? Complexity, of course. His military training had pounded that one into him from his first day as an officer candidate. Given its string of recent failures, it is something he felt that Mossad had forgotten or neglected to apply along the way.

Okay then, to get the job done and walk away with skin intact implied no fancy maneuvering of clever plots; get in, cause hell and get out. That meant no clandestine entry into Houston or wiping his tracks. Instead of trying to be invisible under a cover of fake identities, always difficult to achieve, he and his team must move within an established and unquestioned pattern of routine behavior. After a moment, he had it and smiled. As usual, when he allowed his mind to gnaw at a problem, things invariably sorted themselves out.

Regardless of the outcome, he knew that through this act, Israel would be changed, and changed irrevocably. But even if successful, would it necessarily be in the best interest of his country? The supposition being, of course, that he knew what that actually meant, seeing how the concept was underpinned by layered assumptions and conflicting points of view. If Israel would only establish a recognized Palestinian state. That one move would neutralize Hamas, Hezbollah and Iran, surely in the best interest of Israel. However, his personal view didn't count, no matter how sane the outcome. Tragically, the multiplicity of conflicting single-issue coalition partners all but guaranteed that any meaningful effort by the Kadima-led government, or any government, for that matter, to implement an outcome acceptable to the Palestinians would be doomed to failure, regardless of any well-meaning U.S. sponsored summit talks. Then again, he recognized that U.S. Middle East policy served American interests, not Israel's. Six years into the Bush administration and nothing. Then, just before the elections they get busy trying to hammer out a deal to crown Bush's time in office. Simpletons!

If Israel could not accommodate a Palestinian state, in the long-term, what was the point of his mission? It would do nothing to curb Iran's support for the terrorists, or bring Hamas to the negotiating table. On the contrary, it could accelerate the very meeting engagement Namir feared. And if the mission was compromised? There was only one way for the Metsada director to ensure that the human end of the ops remained totally secure, and Matan wondered if he would survive his moment of hubris.

It was ironic to be confronted by indecision, now that his proposal had come to haunt him for real. But when he wrote the thing, it was an intellectual exercise, not something he ever expected to be implemented. Too late for second thoughts now, he mused wryly, his sense of ethics getting a squeezing.

He saw his father walk into the lounge and looked up. The entrance caused others to survey the intruder before resuming whatever business was being transacted. His dad noticed him, gave a quick smile and walked purposefully toward him, eating up the distance with long strides.

"Shalom, my boy. Sorry to be late," Ravid said gruffly, fondly patted Matan on the shoulder and sat down.

"Just admiring the scenery, Dad," Matan replied indifferently and lifted a finger to attract the waiter's attention.

"Horseshit. Nothing much to admire around here," his father quipped.

Garbed in a white coat and black trousers, the starched individual walked to their table and nodded.

"Sir?"

"Glen Livett on the rocks. No water."

"Very good, sir."

"A nasty day to be outside," Ravid added when the waiter retreated. "Again, please extend my apologies to Sarah and Admina, but I simply couldn't miss that Joshin play."

"Admina is going to hate you," Matan told his father cheerfully, forefinger raised in warning.

"I'll make it up to her."

"Beats me what you see in a boring play anyway," Matan said, which produced the usual predictable reaction. His father reared up his head and glared.

"To a straitjacketed, brainwashed Army type like you, culture is a waste of time and I shall not dignify your ignorance with a rejoinder."

Matan waves a hand. "Forget it. Go and enjoy yourself. I must say, for a sixty-four-year-old man, you cover a lot of territory."

The elder Irian raised bushy gray eyebrows, his black eyes alive with amusement. The hair at the temples may have been white and the thick hair a bit grayer now, but the dark face, firm mouth and high forehead were strong with purpose and character. A senior production manager at Lion Electronics Ltd., having joined the organization shortly after its formation in 1984, Ravid's work threw him into the company of many government busybodies. Chosen to be the exclusive Farnell electronic equipment distributor for Israel's defense forces accounted for the relationship. Matan knew that Mossad's own Technology Department dealt with Lion on a regular basis. He had no idea how long his old man would keep working and he seemed to relish the pressure. Never having remarried after losing their mother, Matan guessed his father spent little time in his comfortable one-bedroom apartment. He did not mind. The loss of his mother had hit him hard, had hit both of them hard. For him, the loss was dulled somewhat by weeks of convalescence lying in a hospital while his ribs and pelvis healed. His father, on the other hand, returned that evening to smoke, fire, ruins, flashing lights, wailing ambulances and ogling curiosity seekers, to find his house gone and family already buried in the pyre. They had endured, but life had changed irrevocably for both of them.

Waiting for the casts to come off, Matan turned away from a future in engineering and building, taking a road that led to more death and more destruction. He had not forsaken his Palestinian friends, but it had never been the same afterward. In the end, even they had drifted away as their attitudes hardened and only his father remained—until Matan met Sarah. She had lit up his days and given him a future worth pursuing. He hoped to live long enough to enjoy it.

"You waiting for me to croak so you can lay your greasy, capitalist hands on that inheritance of mine?" Ravid mused and Matan snorted. The socialist influence of the kibbutz in his youth still dominated his father's thinking.

"I'd be eating pretty thin slices of old bread if that were the case."

His father laughed. "Better believe it. The cupboard is bare."

The waiter brought a tumbler of amber liquid on a silver tray, supported by a cork coaster. Ravid nodded, picked up the glass in a salute and took a sip. He winced as the stuff went down.

"I see that I'll have to start bringing my own, seeing how you persist in buying me cheap booze."

Fiddling with his own tumbler, Matan's grin faded. "Dad…"

Seeing the concern on his son's face, Ravid leaned forward. "Something the matter?"

"I don't know. Could be."

"If it's work, I don't want to hear it. You know how I feel about what you're doing with your time. You had a brilliant career going for you in the Army, son—"

"And do what with it, Dad?" Matan demanded, annoyed that he needed to explain himself again. "Shell helpless Palestinians in the Gaza Strip? Is that your idea of a brilliant career?"

"At thirty-eight, you were in line for your first star. And you blew it! God above, what were you thinking joining those hoodlums?"

"I believe that fighting for Israel's survival has some value, and not necessarily behind a tank gun tube."

"But at what cost?"

"We've been over that, Dad. The work I do helps our country as much as, and maybe more, than me commanding an armored brigade."

"So you say," the older man muttered, but a conspiratorial twinkle lit his frank eyes.

The truth of it was that he had serious misgivings when his boy decided to leave the Army and join Mossad's shadowy world. He wouldn't say it, but he was also a little proud. Mossad only picked the best, at least they used to. From what Matan said, the field fodder these days was lamentable. Why does an organization, any organization, whether military or civilian, go to pot as it matures and the bureaucrats and bean counters take over? Consolidation and loss of direction, that could be it. He could read the signs at Lion and didn't like it. Maybe it was time to give it away. And do what?

He took a sip and sat back. "Okay, my boy. What is it?"

It needled Matan that his old man held such a dim view of his second career. He forced himself to stay focused, not wanting to argue. He swept the lounge with a quick glance. If anyone was shadowing him, they would not be obvious enough about it to be spotted. Anyway, it didn't matter. He leaned forward and stared at his father.

"Remember the contingency we talked about once?" he said softly, hating to do this, but he had no choice if he wanted to protect his family.

Ravid's eyes clouded, instantly serious. "They'd go after you? I knew it! They're soulless bastards."

"It's their job to cover all angles, and maybe I'm being paranoid, but this time..." Matan trailed off, not having to state the obvious.

"You're a desk jockey, for crying out loud. Or are you? What's going on, son?"

"No questions, Dad. And I couldn't tell you anything in any case. Should something happen, there is a package in our drop point. You'll know everything then. But only if something happens, otherwise don't be tempted to peek. And I mean it. If something *were* to happen, you'll know what to do."

Slowly, Ravid nodded and his eyebrows lifted. "If they go after you, they'll be coming after *me*!"

"No, they won't. It's just insurance, Dad."

"Some insurance. You think a bunch of papers or photos, or whatever you got in that tin box, will keep me safe?"

"No guarantees. Not in this business, but it's the best I could do."

Ravid didn't like this, any of it, but understood the need. In Matan's line of business being paranoid was an occupational prerequisite. What could be so important that his son felt in danger of his life? He sighed and shook his head.

"You've started me thinking and now I won't be able to pay attention to Joshin's play. Damn you."

* * *

Namir pursed his lips, shook his head and gave a rueful smile. He tapped the sheaf of papers on his desk with a stiff finger, his eyes fixed on the bemused features of his guest and chuckled. He couldn't help it. The situation was that absurd.

"You've certainly stretched the envelope on this one, my boy. I don't mind telling you, when I first read the thing, I was outraged and disappointed. What outraged me was your blatant disregard and flouting of every known conventional tradecraft procedure, and I was disappointed that the best man I had couldn't cut it. I figured young Ritchie could have done a better planning job. I wanted to see a covert penetration that was completely untraceable, an extraction equally slick and mayhem on the ground, with the Americans running around in little circles. Just like the movies. And then I read your crap, because that's what I thought it was. But once I cooled down and boxed my emotions, I read your proposal again and was able to appreciate the brilliance of your plan. And it is brilliant, my boy. Damn me if it's not. Goes to show that you cannot believe what you see in the movies. By the way, I said no paper trail."

Matan relaxed a tad and allowed himself a small smile of satisfaction, tinged with relief. The director's reaction was predictable in every respect. Still, he would have loved to be a fly on the wall when Namir first read his proposal, minus the fly spray, of course. It took him four days of research, planning, drafting and re-planning before he was satisfied the scheme would work. The hard facts had been relatively easy to obtain; Mossad kept an extensive information database. It was putting all the pieces together, making sure they all fitted into a watertight plan, that part took time. His smile broadened.

"For your eyes only. And my server directory is secure, a matter of a little encryption algorithm I happen to use." There was security…and then there was security. In his line of work, he played the craft inside and outside the office. It was simply a game, but deadly nonetheless for the loser. The pointy end of Mossad had no sense of humor.

"Proof even against my IT guys?"

"Especially against your IT guys."

"Mmm. Disregarding the fact that you committed a technical security violation, you wouldn't by any chance be willing to share, eh?"

Matan simply laughed. "If you want to hide some skeletons, dig up your own."

Namir raised a quizzical eyebrow, gathered the loose pages and shoved them into the shredder. Nobody said anything while the machine did its business. When the thing was done, he leaned back into his chair and tapped the empty desktop.

"You've done well, my boy. I would never have thought of it; open, transparent and untraceable. Your Washington tours will certainly pay off now, and Ellis and Tabor are both known couriers. You cannot be compromised if there is nothing to compromise. Very neat. Attending the Department of Homeland Security symposium against counterterrorism was a master touch. But I expected nothing less from you. And I like the cost profile, covered as legitimate field trips."

"I thought you would," Matan said dryly and Namir cocked an eye at him.

"The bean counters are always baying at the door, my boy. Will you be ready to go in two weeks' time?"

"It's a bit tight, but doable, provided you can put me on the Israeli team."

"Shabak will be pissed at having one of their men bumped off, but leave that with me," Namir declared and pulled at his chin. "I noted that you left me holding the bag with Al Jazeera and the Iranian government website penetrations."

"Can't be helped, since I won't be here to do the job myself. Somebody's got to supervise Ronel…and finish cleaning up after him."

"I suppose. I see that you'll be using TWIC badges?"

Namir was referring to the new tamper-resistant biometric Transportation Worker Identification Credential tags, administered by the U.S. Transport Security Administration, designed to prevent unauthorized entry into secure port facilities. It wasn't a bad idea in theory, but in his opinion, of questionable practical value. But Americans loved their layered bureaucracies, as though a building full of public servants on Pennsylvania Avenue constituted a solution.

"Valero is using them, even though the system is yet to be fully implemented. Lack of sufficient card readers, I think. The Technology Department has a whole boxful of the things, something our station desks acquired, including some for the Port of Houston Authority. Badges or not, I cannot see how the Americans can hope to make such a huge place totally secure."

"Their problem and a good thing for us." Making up his mind, Namir pursed his lips and nodded. "Very well. Your plan is approved. How about that!"

Matan leaned forward a fraction. "Approved in every respect?"

How does he select a man, three men actually, ask them to lay it all on the line for their country, then quietly dispose of them like they never existed? The ethical implications had troubled Matan, even though as a military officer, he accepted a level of attrition as a matter of course. But this was not a battlefield. Or perhaps it was, even if somewhat different, but nonetheless equally lethal. Hiding it all under a banner of patriotism, was he? Matan closed off that part of his mind. He could not afford to start questioning himself or get sentimental, not now. Focus on the big picture, he admonished himself and part of him sneered. The big picture had always been a convenient shield for those who relished trampling on the individual. But he wasn't doing that. Was he?

The Metsada director looked hard at his protégé. "Ellis and Tabor are valuable operatives and I will hate to lose them, but I recognize the necessity. No loose ends. Pity about Ronel. He's the best Internet sabotage specialist we have."

"He would be a loose end and you know it. If any of them talked…"

"You're right," Namir grated and gave a thin smile. "To answer your next question, I never thought of you as one of those loose ends. In case you were wondering."

Matan didn't believe a word of it and he wasn't hatched yesterday. *Any* loose end was a direct threat to Namir.

"As a matter of fact, the thought *had* crossed my mind," he responded candidly. "Being naturally hardboiled and suspicious, you know."

"Fool! I don't work that way. If I went around cleaning up everybody after every mission, Metsada wouldn't have anyone left."

"This ops is a bit different, Namir, and we both know it. No hard feelings. Just covering my ass so I can enjoy being deputy boss of the Collections Department."

Namir grunted and shook his head. He had nothing to grumble about, having anticipated this move. Nevertheless, there were ways of evening things out—should the need arise. As Matan said, this ops *was* different. A pity really, but he needed to keep the broader objectives in focus. There was far too much at stake for sentimentality…and morals. But morals were the first sacrifice on the altar of expediency.

"Ellis and Tabor? Should either of them have a similar suspicious idea…"

"They're still trusting, but you can take the necessary preventative measures," Matan replied without emotion. "I understand that your special sweeper team has done this once or twice before."

The director showed no reaction that his senior case officer would know about that side of Metsada's operation, but was not displeased. In his line of work, protecting his organization from itself and the oversight mechanisms of his own government rated in priority with steps he had to take against foreign intelligence services, friendly or otherwise. Mossad had many enemies and not all of them were outside the country.

"They have, and preventative measures will be taken."

"I thought they might, not that I want to know all the gory details. I won't be nagging you with progress reports and shit like that. Unless things go wrong or I want something."

"Acceptable."

Matan nodded, stood up and slowly walked to the door. He clasped the handle and turned, his eyes searching.

"Last chance, Namir. Do we really want to do this?"

Namir looked back, his eyes hard. "Only death is a certainty, my boy."

"If death were the only thing waiting for us," Matan said softly, opened the door and walked out. The click as the door closed had the fatal sound of finality.

* * *

Ariel Ronel lifted his startlingly large pale brown eyes and stared at the senior case officer, not believing what he had heard.

Matan could almost hear the sharp questions going through

the young man's mind despite the slack-mouthed expression of incredulity. His clean Scandinavian features were easier to read than a book. But the boy was a professional and could not help mull over the problem, no matter how crazy the idea. Despite his youthful and casual appearance, Ronel was a man. At twenty-six, the Web expert was an honors graduate in computing from Tel Aviv University. He held a master's degree in Network Topology from MIT and was one of three key Internet specialists in the Technology Department. He could have picked any position he wanted in the private sector, but instead chose to give something back to those who arranged to bomb a bus in Jerusalem on which his sister was taking a ride to Bethlehem before the Palestinians closed off all travel to the town. Mossad and Shin Bet were full of people who wanted to 'give something back'. Well, this was the boy's chance, even though, this time, he was going to be giving back everything he had. For the good of the many? Matan wondered about that one and was still to come up with a satisfactory answer. Life was shit.

Ignoring the cup of coffee on the colonel's desk, which had gone cold some time back, Ronel absently smoothed back a shock of blond hair above his right ear.

"Let me get this straight. You want me to hack into the Al Jazeera's website and plant an information page in the news section of their site. Then you want to do the same thing to the Iranian government site. Both sites to be penetrated using a trigger to simultaneously insert pages at a time of your choice without leaving a trace."

"That's the idea," Matan agreed.

"Can I ask why—"

"You don't have the need to know, yet."

"Yeah, that's what I thought you said…sir," Ronel murmured and brushed his hair again. He pursed his lips and sighed. This was some serious shit. "Penetrating Al Jazeera shouldn't be much of a problem. The site's security protocols are rudimentary at best. I've had a chance to look at it some time back," he said with an engaging smile. "The Iranian Ministries of Culture and Foreign Affairs will be a little harder to crack, but not too much so. There are ways to bypass the firewalls without leaving a trail. As for planting your pages without anyone knowing how it was done—"

"Not how it was done," Matan interrupted. "Without—"

"Being traced, I know. It shouldn't be too difficult if I use an input or help prompt to gain entry. You're talking about semi-public Web servers and neither are really secure sites. At least the partitions that hold the news releases are not. This trigger you want, though. That part will be a pain."

"In what way?"

"We'll have to—"

"Nobody on your team. Just you," Matan said softly, but the meaning was clear.

Ronel nodded. Just him, eh? Something heavy was going down, that was clear.

"Okay, only me. The problem is, I must write all the instruction code, package it as an executable and hope it all works when the time comes."

"You would test the thing first, of course."

"Sure, but it's not like downloading a Microsoft patch…sir."

"Are you telling me it cannot be done?"

"I'm saying it would be far simpler to insert your pages in real-time. A blind download is insensitive. Despite all my tests, I could miss something and an abort in any step could alert their security protocols and you've blown the whole mission, whatever it is. Trust me. This is better done hands-on when doing it for real."

Matan had hoped to execute a sterile penetration, but he also appreciated the potential pitfalls. The temptation to be too clever had sunk more than one operation, the action officer in charge thereby committing a cardinal sin—losing focus of his mission objective. As a military officer, it was something that was drummed into him at the National Defense College, and he learned that lesson well, having his ass hammered during a rotation tour at the U.S. Army's National Training Center at Fort Irwin, California. That was merely an exercise of Israeli armored cavalry doctrine against the NTC OPFOR, where only pride was hurt. In this case, losing focus of his mission would cost more than just his pride. This was not a sandbox evolution with toy tanks. Ronel's approach meant an increased security exposure, but Matan would mitigate that risk and he was not about to argue with a specialist. He studied the IT nerd and nodded.

"Very well. Hands-on it is. Get to work on it."

"When do you want this done?" Ronel queried. "I've got a few things in the hopper already."

"Have everything ready to execute in ten days' time. You will coordinate with the Metsada Director."

Ronel's eyebrows climbed. This was some *real* serious shit, then. "And the Web pages text? That must be integrated into existing display formats."

"The text will be provided when you do the penetration. Set up appropriate Web templates, or whatever those sites use, and I will have the text ready as attachments that you'll be able to cut and paste."

"Fair enough. I'll scout the sites and let you know what formatting will work best."

"One more thing, Mr. Ronel. This is compartmented. No one is to know what you're doing. No one. Are we clear on that?"

Ronel nodded and grinned like a kid caught with his hand in a cookie jar. "I do have Top Secret Blue clearance, Colonel."

"And I don't care if you have a dialup line to God! He doesn't get to know about this. Your superior doesn't get to know about this. Your sweetheart doesn't get to know. No records, no paper, no emails. If anyone asks what you're doing, refer them to me. You will open a directory on the test server to which only you, the Metsada Director and I, will have unrestricted access under

Level Five entry protocols. That means no automatic backups of any kind. Anyone attempting to open your directory will wish they had never been born. And if you violate security, you will be shot. Am I getting through?"

Ronel had gone somewhat pale, wondering what he had walked into. Colonel Irian had not raised his voice in any way, and he didn't have to. Ronel had gotten the point, all right. Messing with this thing would not be healthy. But the technical challenge still made his skin prickle with anticipation.

"Everything is quite clear," he said, subdued and not at all sure he wanted anything to do with this, whether his career benefited or not.

"Good. I didn't mean to jump down your throat, son," Matan relented and smiled. "Enjoy yourself, but remember, a slip could cost lives. Right now, I cannot tell you more."

"I understand, sir." Ronel stood up, gave a single nod and walked from the office, deep in thought, his mind already working the problem.

When the door closed, Matan chuckled and reached for the phone. He had put the fear of God into the boy, perhaps going a bit over the top, but he was certain the message was received. The problem with all techno geeks was that they assumed security applied to someone else. So smart in one way, yet still so ignorant and innocent. His next collaborator was far from innocent.

He tapped in an extension number and waited. It only took two rings.

"Nadar Kaleen," a crisp voice announced, generating an image of cold efficiency and a can-do attitude.

"So formal this early in the morning? Not even a shalom?" Matan chided his friend and heard a fruity laugh, making him recall a craggy face, eyes that had seen too much death and a steely determination never to give in.

"Well, if it isn't my old tank buddy Colonel Irian! What do

you want? I'm too busy for shaloms."

Matan chuckled. Kaleen was in charge of Metsada's equipment and special stores, meaning all the nasty devices and dirty tricks used by field operatives, including explosives. He either procured them or made them up as needed. An ex-Army bomb disposal specialist, Kaleen had quit the service still in his mid-thirties citing 'diminishing returns'. He knew that one day, statistics would catch up with him if he continued in his current line of business, and retiring in a cedar box wasn't part of his game plan. Metsada gave him the best of both worlds, minus the scary shit. Kaleen made sure that Metsada appreciated his talents by getting to know everything about every demolition package and ordnance piece made and used by just about every foreign country and the intelligence community in general; an encyclopedia of covert destruction. And he had little time for fools, which Mossad was capable of collecting as anybody else.

"I need some packages," Matan said, referring to demolition charges. "Five, to be exact."

"Hah! Blowing things up, it's better than sex. Take it from me. After a while the gal just isn't interested."

"Your cynicism is showing again, Nadar."

"Just telling you how it is. Specifications?"

"I want fifty gram Composition-4 with timers manufactured by Iran Electronic Industries."

"IEI, eh? Very interesting, but I won't pry into your skullduggery."

"Better all around. You have the stuff or not?"

"Testy, aren't we? I've got some on hand. Anything else?"

"I want one timer set to fail, but it cannot be obvious. Cook the circuit board or whatever it is you do to those poor things."

Kaleen laughed. "Cook the circuit board indeed. What do you think I run here? A basement operation? We're a bit more sophisticated than that down here. When do you want the stuff?"

"Next ten days would be fine."

"Can do. My curiosity is tickled."

"I thought you said you wouldn't pry."

"I'm naturally nosy."

Matan smiled. He couldn't say anything, of course, but it was a game they always played. "I've got roaches in the cellar."

"Must be bloody big roaches to need C-4 treatment."

"Better believe it. One more thing, Nadar. The packages must be clean." That meant no fingerprints or attached material that could be traced to Mossad.

"Got it. And take care, Colonel. That's some nasty shit you're playing with."

"I know. Always a pleasure doing business with you," Matan said cheerfully and gently placed the receiver into its cradle. If only he could have Kaleen on the mission…

Now for the hard part.

* * *

Humming some tune he'd heard on the radio the other day, Nadar Kaleen lightly sprayed the two halves of the timer assembly with freon, then carefully wiped the casings and seals with a cleaning rag. He did not 'cook' the circuit board as Matan so jokingly suggested. His friend had an odd sense of humor, but what could he expect from an ignorant tank driver? It hadn't been such a bad idea, but if someone were to run some simple tests, which he figured was the objective here, they would quickly find that the board failed from application of heat—a deliberate act. There was no way to hide charring and scorch marks on the circuit elements, no matter how carefully done. This, then, must be made to look like a normal post-manufacture fault. His curiosity was itching to know what the colonel wanted with the packages, but knew better than to pry. Given they were Iranian, it was nothing good. It wasn't his business and it was healthier not to worry about such things too much. Nosing into someone else's fun could end up being terminal.

Still humming, totally absorbed, ignoring the two technicians at the other bench, he mated the casings and replaced the six star screws in the back plate using a small battery screwdriver. He should be using new screws, but he didn't have any, and the ones he did have were not the right color. Wearing gloves, he sprayed the entire assembly and wiped it down. Holding the timer in his hand, he flipped the 'On' toggle switch and watched a row of zeros flicker in the amber display, then clear. He typed in the timer sequence to make sure it all worked and pressed the commit switch. A small red LED began to blink twice a second in the top right corner of the unit and the numbers started to cycle down. They reached zero and the light went off. He had run tests against the board itself, but he never took chances. Satisfied, he switched off the unit and nodded.

Amazing what a drop of liquid nitrogen can do to a resistor or two. Of course, the fault could not be induced just anywhere. It had to prevent the surge of current from the nickel-cadmium battery reaching the detonator. He had tested that as well. It would not look good had he fried a wrong component.

He picked up the ready-sealed fifty gram pack of C-4 and mated the timer assembly to it. The finished product was indistinguishable from the four packages already sitting side by side on the bench. With only a casual glance at the overhanging shelf filled with assorted containers, wire bundles, boxes of electronic components and plain junk, he peeled a green circular sticker off a standard office stationery roll and slapped it against the demolition charge. Matan should now have no trouble identifying the faulty pack, provided, of course, his old buddy didn't lose the patch. But that wasn't his problem.

He placed the marked pack next to the others and slowly removed his gloves. A professional job and another satisfied customer. Admiring his handiwork, Kaleen resumed humming.

* * *

When the overhead down-lights dimmed and faded to a sullen orange glow, the two tall men sitting behind the oval conference table instinctively straightened as they peered at the full color aerial view projected on the screen: green water, harbor facilities, two moored oilers, tank farms and what looked like clusters of refinery fractionation towers. It could have been anywhere. The two men exchanged puzzled glances. Were they going on a cruise?

"What you're looking at," Matan spoke briskly, drawing attention to himself, "is the Valero Texas City Refinery." He waited for them to comprehend what they were seeing, then said simply, "Our job is to blow it up, a bit of it at least." He calmly ambled to the door and flipped three switches. The room flared with white light. Showing no expression, he took a seat opposite the two men and waited.

Kiva Ellis leaned back, folded his muscular arms over the table and, after a glance at the screen, chuckled.

"Okay, I'll bite. Some Louisiana freedom fighter is pissed at Texaco for ripping people off at the pump and hired us to do something about it, right?"

His voice was deep and resonant, matching his heavy, intimidating frame. Sitting beside him, slightly shorter, Teman Tabor grinned. He had narrow features supported by a wiry body that belied his considerable physical strength. A martial arts expert, he wasn't someone to tangle with. But sitting there, relaxed, he looked tame enough.

Matan allowed himself a sympathetic smile. The boys were taking it well, but they did not know the half of it. "Nobody is pissed off at Texaco, Mr. Ellis, as you so colorfully put it, although they deserve to be. We are the ones pissed off…at Iran."

They stared at each other. Tabor whistled in comprehension as the wheels clicked and his eyes widened. "We attack America and you want to make it appear like Iran did it? Wow. Will that cause a row."

"What we want to do is provoke America into a retaliatory response."

Ellis looked hard at Matan. "You aren't kidding. Let me guess. The uranium enrichment plants?"

"Or their reactor. If Iran develops nuclear weapons, Israel is screwed. Plain and simple. The UN and the U.S. are sitting on their hands and that makes it our move."

"I like it," Ellis murmured after a moment, his smile grim. "It's about time we took the fight to those nutty Ayatollahs. Bastards. While the Americans are at it, they might as well bomb the Knesset as well. Just another bunch of self-serving morons. They'd be doing everybody a favor."

Matan wagged a finger in friendly warning. "That's treasonous talk, Mr. Ellis."

Ellis shrugged. "They are as much of a problem as the Palestinians and you know it. The National Union and the United Torah parties are the worst. Religious bigots, that's all they are."

From their personnel jackets, Matan knew that both men were somewhat right-wing in their orientation and not very pious, but it was also a quality that got them picked. He wanted someone willing to force action rather than intellectualize about it. Tabor was twenty-nine, no family ties or relatives, an F-16 pilot until a landing mishap forced him to eject, which damaged his spine and ended a promising career. The man was thorough, reliable and dedicated. Metsada did not hesitate to recruit him.

Ellis, on the other hand, was only twenty-six and a seren in the Navy, equivalent to a lieutenant. No personal ties and both parents still alive. His problem was, he had shot off his mouth once too often regarding lack of retaliatory action by Navy command against Hamas and Fatah—a foolish thing to do in any service. A negative fitness report, citing views not consistent with naval policy and doctrine, effectively torpedoed any possibility of advancement and the boy resigned his commission. Mossad kept an eye on most Israeli Defense Force officers as potential recruits as a matter of routine. Ellis did not have to wait long before he found a new home where his views were more appreciated, or at least not frowned upon. Matan knew the boy missed sea duty, but international travel seemed to make up for it.

Something else he had observed. Although older, Tabor appeared content to defer to Ellis without resentment. Perhaps it was merely a case of not forcing an issue playing the alpha male gambit. Nevertheless, Ellis had an air of confidence and purpose that transcended mere age. Under different circumstances the kid would have made a powerful stamp in Metsada. Although a once-off, this mission should make him happy.

"Leaving out the Knesset option, let me lay it out for you," Matan went on. "In April, the U.S. Department of Homeland Security will be hosting a symposium on counterterrorism. It will include representatives from the EU, Australia, Japan and—"

"Israel," Tabor finished for him, making the connection fast.

"That's right, Israel. It will be my cover to get into the country. The conference will be held over two days, after which I will spend a day at our embassy briefing the Ambassador, including the Mossad station chief. I will then make my way to Houston for a seemingly routine update of our consulate. That's where you two come in.

"You are simple couriers, already tagged by the FBI and CIA. I've been to Washington twice and our presence should not be seen as anything but ordinary, which it will be. As couriers, you will be carrying confidential papers for our consulate in Houston, using a standard Continental Airlines flight Tel Aviv to Newark. You'll also be ferrying demolition charges in sealed diplomatic pouches immune to x-ray probing and chemical detection in case U.S. Customs want to be nosy. Once your official business has been concluded, we'll meet, pick up a consulate car, drive to the refinery and survey the layout."

"Why not use a rental car?" Tabor demanded. "FBI forensics—"

"Won't get near our car. If the job is done right, they will have no reason to suspect our involvement. Even if they were to suspect something, they wouldn't be able to touch it without going through diplomatic channels. A rental car, on the other hand, would leave a document trail, something we don't want. Everything we do must appear normal. But we won't be using a conspicuous limo either, if that's what's worrying you. Okay?"

Tabor mulled that over and nodded. Matan cleared his throat.

"Good. You'll pick up a regular pair of white coveralls at Newark and I'll supply the TWIC badges in case you're intercepted. But while we are talking about forensics, Mr. Tabor did raise a good point. Although the FBI will not suspect a consulate vehicle, you must avoid contaminating the car. Use plastic sheets on the seats and floor for that. Now, about our target. Apart from a few chain-link fences, the place is practically wide open. Despite the apparent lack of visible security, we'll do an on-site visual. The following evening you two will go in, place the charges at designated points and you're out of there. Extraction will be via a normally scheduled Air France flight to Paris from George Bush International leaving at 2210. We'll be half-way across the Atlantic by the time the charges go off and there'll be nothing to link us with the mess."

Ellis pursed his lips and frowned. "Galveston is way across town. Doesn't leave us much time to plant the charges and make our way from Texas City all the way to IAH."

"It's tight, but doable," Matan declared. "You must be at the airport by 2100 to check in. Texas City to IAH is fifty-seven miles, one hour and ten minutes if you take I-45 and US-59. Add another four miles to the industrial complex, which makes it about one hour twenty minutes. Allowing for contingencies, you need to get the job done by seven p.m. and clear the area. Part of our on-site visual will be to confirm travel times to make sure.

Study your maps. I don't want you guys getting lost."

"Sounds simple enough, provided we don't get stuck in traffic," Ellis muttered darkly.

"You'll be hitting the place on a Sunday evening. Traffic shouldn't be a problem."

"Okay, I'll bite. And the car?"

"Leave it at the airport. Somebody from the consulate will pick it up. And wipe it down for fingerprints before you leave it. Another thing. I don't want you guys picked up for speeding and having to answer fool questions from some nosy cop, diplomatic immunity or not."

Tabor nodded. "Got it. What if site security is not as soft as you anticipate? Do we abort?"

"We cannot pull this scenario again. Not in this format anyway. You must hit the target first time out. Should the penetration start to fall apart for whatever reason, you bug out. If the charges are already planted, you recover them first."

Ellis glanced at Tabor and shifted in his seat. "We are going in unarmed?"

"You have a problem with that?"

"We are going all the way there just to be scared off by some security guard?"

"Mr. Ellis, if you're in an abort situation, killing someone won't help. If you're discovered carrying a weapon on your way to Valero or during egress, you've blown it. Leaving somebody behind with a hole in their chest would be just as bad. This has got to go down clean or not at all."

Ellis clearly didn't like it and Matan wondered if he made a mistake picking him. The man was too eager to blow someone away.

"What if that somebody wants to check out our TWIC badges?" Tabor said, trying to relieve the sudden tension.

"Remember, it will be dark, and the fact that you're wearing them should be enough protection. If not, you do what is necessary and extract. But we don't leave any bodies. Clear?"

"Why are we suddenly squeamish about whacking a guard?" Ellis protested. "Once the place goes up, you'll have bodies all over the place."

"That's accepted collateral damage and you'll place charges to minimize loss of life. But think it through. If you kill somebody or knock them out, you must hide the body. Sooner or later, they'll be missed and you'll have a search on your hands. The search window will be a maximum of six hours if they start looking at say, eight p.m., detonation time being two a.m. Within that timeframe, if you leave the charges in place, can you guarantee that they won't be found?"

Ellis sighed and hung his head. "I guess not."

"I thought so. If they find the charges, the Americans will be alerted and you would have scuttled any hope of us carrying out the mission later on. Therefore, killing someone would be plain murder. Do you understand the difference?"

"Yes, sir."

"Okay, let's say we pull this off," Tabor persisted, trying to ignore the family fight. "Why should the Americans think this was done by Iran? They're more likely to blame Al Qaida."

Matan tore his eyes off Ellis, sorely tempted to let him go. But he would be an added security risk, one that would have to be dealt with immediately, which could make Tabor suspicious. He kicked himself for not interviewing the two men before picking them. Always the details.

"They could, but they won't. The charges are Iranian made and one of them has been set to fail. FBI labs will have no trouble identifying the source. We'll also be planting news clips in the Iranian websites claiming responsibility."

"Neat, and we can rely on the Americans to do the rest. You hope."

"There is always that," Matan agreed. "But that's a political dimension and not our concern. Our job is to make sure nothing does goes wrong. No matter what, you cannot afford to get caught." He looked at each of them in turn. "Both of you are seasoned professionals with two covert missions under your belts and you know how to handle yourselves in the field. That's why I picked you. But what's needed here is subtlety, not a frontal attack. Naturally, you don't breathe a word of this, now and forever."

"Naturally," Ellis said and a wry grin distorted the right side of his face. There was no need to belabor the point. He'd been around the block and knew how the game was played.

He glanced at the now pale image on the projection screen. "It's doable and has the minimum of cute. The devil is in the detail, as always. But I guess that's your department."

"Correct. Let me show you how we'll get this done." Matan stood up and switched off the lights.

Chapter Three

Sarah reached up with her slim arms and hugged his neck, her large brown eyes soft and misty with tenderness. Matan bent down and kissed her yielding lips, oblivious to passing onlookers, the general noise in the departure lounge, PA announcements and watchful Army personnel brandishing Uzis.

"I wish I didn't have to go, sweetie, but it's only a week," he murmured huskily, holding her tight, feeling her tremble against him. She pulled back and searched his face.

"It might as well be an eternity, and this time it's different, I can tell. You've been moody, preoccupied…"

He sighed and cupped her face in his hands. The thing was, she could read him like a TV screen, sensitive to his every emotion. It was the same with him, of course. Only to be expected after years of living together, and that's what made this so tough.

"I've had a lot to do at work and you worry too much. Anything you need, call Dad, and I'll have my cellphone."

"I want you, not your cellphone." She pouted and sniffed.

She wasn't going to cry, although her heart ached. Matan did not mind her crying or displaying affection in public, but she also understood that he liked to see her in control, not just another blubbering female.

Wearing a wistful smile, he smoothed back her short hair and pecked her forehead. "Love you," he said softly and picked up his briefcase. He felt lousy, like he were leaving her forever. The problem was, he *had* been moody and preoccupied. There was a reason, but he should not have taken it out on her. "I've been neglecting you and I'm sorry. I'll make it up to you when I get back."

"Just come back," she murmured, her eyes bright.

He turned suddenly and marched toward an open security portal queue. He quickly emptied his pockets into a small gray plastic tray and took off his watch. When his turn came, he pushed the tray and briefcase into the dark maw of the x-ray scanner and stepped through the body sensor portal. The airport guard, portable sensor in left hand, waved him through. Still picking up his belongings, he turned, but Sarah was gone. They both hated goodbyes, but she always drove him to the airport when he had to go away. He hoped that she wouldn't fret too much, knowing she would.

He hated to leave her, especially now. For the first time since he joined Mossad, tiny cracks of doubt were starting to appear in the wisdom of his career choice. He believed in what he was about to do, that remained unshakeable. It was the aftermath and the lives to be tossed away that gnawed at him. Something else entered the equation, and with it a new realization. He was a soldier fighting a war. Perhaps not a shooting war, but deadly nonetheless. And in war, someone had to die. It was his job to make sure those lives were not wasted. Reassured, he straightened his shoulders, raised his head and proudly marched toward the glittering shops.

The duty free area of Ben-Gurion Airport was bright, noisy, and filled with people gawking at colorful merchandise, hugging packages, spouses and children. It was pathetic. Ignoring the temptations, he walked briskly to the King David Lounge, picked up a magazine and ordered a Crown Royal whiskey on the rocks. He had twenty minutes to kill before they started the scheduled boarding, if the flight was on time. His mind cleared and he focused on the job at hand.

Half-way through an article on the latest unrest between Greek and Turkish Cypriots, a lush voice from hidden speakers calmly announced the departure of El Al Airways 10:40 flight LY7, Tel Aviv to New York. *"Would all passengers please make their way to gate six for immediate boarding. Thank you."* Matan tried to picture the face and figure that went with the voice, then shrugged. It was a harmless diversion.

The Boeing 747 was a large aircraft and a long queue of harried, anxious, excited faces waited to board. Many were still sitting in the gate lounge, belongings on lap or floor, staring vacantly at nothing, waiting, already tired. For Matan, it was like taking a bus. He walked past the queue and presented his passport and business class boarding pass to the pert attendant at the check-in stand. The action attracted a share of hostile stares from the coach class passengers. He couldn't have cared less. She flashed him a toothpaste commercial smile, passed the ticket through the sensor and handed him the stub.

"Have a pleasant flight, sir."

He nodded and walked down the boarding tube, a shadow among other shadows.

* * *

Fading sunshine glinted off the Capitol building from a clear blue twilight sky as the cab made its way downtown along the brightly lit Pennsylvania Avenue. It was early evening, but traffic was still in rush-hour mode, fortunately for him, going the other way. Looking out the window from the back seat, Matan stared vacantly at passing buildings, gaudy displays, pedestrians, bums sleeping on the sidewalk, and streams of SUVs. Given the cost of oil these days, he could not figure out why people here still persisted at driving such monsters. The enormous cultural differences between America and Israel always struck him hard. It was a fleeting observation, something to amuse his mind, and he was tired. Even in the business class section the ten-and-a-half-hour flight to New York had started to become weary. There was only so much he could drink or eat, and the in-flight movie selections were not enough of a distraction to last the distance.

By the time the flight arrived at JFK, the time zone differential only compounded his weariness. Despite his diplomatic status, clearing Customs and collecting his luggage took time. Having his picture and fingerprint taken as an entry formality added to his fatigue. The Washington hop to the Ronald Reagan Airport was mercifully short, only fifty-five minutes. When he finally touched down, he was heartily sick of airplanes and travel and crowds. What he needed was a shower and ten hours of sleep.

The cab pulled quietly into the brilliantly lit reception circle of the JW Marriott Hotel. A bellboy hurriedly extracted Matan's bag from the trunk, placed it on a polished brass trolley and disappeared through the revolving entrance. Matan paid off the driver and followed the boy, giving an involuntary shiver in the crisp air. Mid-April or not, Washington was cold. Traffic noises were loud behind him and his nose wrinkled at the stink of petrol and diesel exhaust fumes.

The Marriott lobby was luxurious, refined and modern, reflecting the class of clientele frequenting the halls of power in downtown DC. Ordinarily, he would book something closer to the Israeli embassy in International Drive, and cheaper, but the Homeland Security conference was held at their headquarters in the St. Elizabeth campus in South Washington. It meant catching a cab to either location, but at least the Marriott was in the center of things and he was not on a budget. It gave him an evil sense of satisfaction to be reveling at government expense.

He checked in, allowed the bellboy to take him to his room, tipped him and stood for a lonely moment surveying the spacious apartment. The airconditioning whispered in the background and he could just hear the city noises from below. After unpacking, took a bottle of Wild Turkey from the bar fridge and had a slug, not even temped to have dinner. Showering quickly, he turned off the lights and crawled into bed.

Although only a diversion, he looked forward to the coming two days.

Despite initial misgivings, Matan found himself enjoying the antiterrorism sessions. American experts were gathered from a number of government areas: FBI, CIA, National Counterterrorism Center, Departments of Justice, State and Defense. Curiously, the National Security Agency was poignantly absent, which caused some raised eyebrows. But then, NSA had always been a close-knit, secretive organization. The presentations were professional, stuck to the point and, more importantly, were realistic and relevant, something the international visitors clearly appreciated. Matan certainly did. The symposium also gave him an opportunity to glad-hand some people and gauge the caliber of his opposition when the time came for the Americans to apply their procedures. He admitted that he faced a formidable array of expertise and technology, but critically, it was fragmented across a number of government agencies who were not always willing to share knowledge or provide cooperation, still jealously protecting their patch of turf. The moderator wryly admitted that lack of information sharing allowed 9/11 to take place, even though all the pieces were there to be seen beforehand, which was not altogether a revelation to anybody.

Progress had been made to address that deficiency by creation of the Department of Homeland Security in 2002, and in 2004 establishment of the National Counterterrorism Center under the Office of the Director of National Intelligence. In the event of a domestic incident, the Director, National Operations Center, responsible to the DHS Director, Office of Operations Coordination, had the authority and jurisdiction over all national agencies in the detection, identification and apprehension of any terrorists. The remark generated a ripple of good-natured ribald comments from rival agency presenters, particularly from the FBI, who considered this their bailiwick. Although intended to be humorous, it confirmed to Matan that there was still a serious undercurrent of inter-agency rivalry. No one particularly liked the DHS and the bureaucratic monster it had become, or the threat it represented to the survival of other bodies.

Despite the infighting and the ponderous nature of their apparatus, he did not doubt at all that the United States would mobilize all the vast resources at its disposal to track and burn his team. He wondered whether the mechanisms he had put in place to forestall that eventuality would be adequate to keep his ops black. But second-guessing himself now was a soul-destroying exercise in futility. He had either properly stage-managed everything, or he hadn't. It was not so much the prospect of a bullet in his head that bothered him, but the resulting fallout against Israel, should the operation somehow fall apart. As Namir had pointed out, they were playing with big chips indeed.

He did not recognize any of his EU colleagues, which was not a bad thing—there'd be less speculation regarding his presence, given Israel's internal problems. There had been little opportunity to talk to his opposite number in Shin Bet who made up the other half of the Israeli team prior to the conference, both of them having different itineraries. But during coffee breaks, Matan sensed a degree of coolness from the man. Because his presence had bumped off the other Shabak agent? Well, screw him. In many ways, the in-between sessions provided more constructive feedback and ideas than the formal presentations, made as they were from actual field experiences. After all, America had only suffered one major foreign terrorist attack, albeit an extreme example of the type.

When they eventually met, the Israeli ambassador knew who Matan was, of course, but not the substance of his mission. General chitchat, updates on home events and the DHS debrief took a couple of hours. Following a working lunch in the embassy canteen with three senior staffers, and later a meeting with the Mossad station chief, Matan still managed to make it to the Marriott by dusk, which gave him enough time to shower and change for dinner. The hotel had an excellent restaurant and he decided to eat there rather than cruise around looking for something else.

Besides, a fresh breeze had sprung up and he only packed light-weight suits. If that were not enough of an excuse for not venturing out, he knew all the city sights and didn't want to play the tourist. All in all, it hadn't been a bad three days.

The next day, he woke committed.

It must have rained during the night as the air had a clean, washed smell that left the morning sky blue and clear, marred by two dissipating contrails high up. He did not think much about anything as the cab drove him to the airport. After calling Sarah when he got up around six, which made it about 1 p.m. in Tel Aviv, telling her that all was well and asking how Admina was, the conversation left him feeling momentarily nostalgic. The gravity of what Israel was about to do was staring him hard in the face. But he could not afford to think like that, not now. Composing himself, he cleared his mind and his eyes turned hard. Time enough for sentimentality later—he hoped.

The three-and-a-half-hour flight to Houston's George Bush International was smooth and the service efficient. Being dumped into a hot and sticky afternoon that waited for him outside the domestic terminal spoiled the day somewhat, but he expected that; hence the summer suits. It was after 3 p.m., the sun beating down with pitiless glare, when he reached the Holiday Inn Select Greenway. The only nice part of the setup was that he could almost see the Israeli consulate down the street. From his ninth floor suite, he spent a moment observing the stream of traffic along the Southwest Freeway. Far on his left, the downtown skyscrapers were hardly visible through the pall of brown smog. Houston was flat, functional, uninteresting—somewhere to do business, not live.

He called the consulate and confirmed his appointment with the Consul-General for 10 a.m. the next morning, despite the fact that it was a Saturday. He also reminded the receptionist about dinner tonight with the Mossad station chief.

"Tell him I'm looking forward to having some genuine hot

Mexican chilies," he demanded and heard her easy laugh.

He confirmed the availability of a car and was assured that a vehicle would be waiting for him. All the arrangement had already been made from Tel Aviv, but he took nothing for granted. Like as not, some consulate staffer could have taken the damned thing for a joyride. With Ellis and Tabor arriving tomorrow afternoon, he did not want to be left scrambling for transport. It was always the details.

* * *

Two hard knocks shattered the comparative silence of the suite. Matan looked up from the desk, glanced at his wristwatch and nodded: 4:30 p.m. exactly. Precision, he liked that. It showed that the boys could be relied on to be equally precise when executing their mission. Pushing back the chair, he stood up and stepped to the door, paused, then opened it. Despite the long flight, the two men looked relaxed and comfortable; advantage of youth, Matan mused dryly, but without jealousy. He did not begrudge them their vitality. They would need it. Ellis wore a dark green Lacoste T-shirt, cream trousers and white runners, while Tabor seemed content with a brown short-sleeved shirt, black trousers and shoes. Matan instinctively glanced up and down the empty corridor and motioned them in.

"You guys are obviously none the worse for wear after your trip," he remarked with a smile, closing the door behind him.

"Piece of cake, as the Americans would say," Ellis replied with a shrug.

Did the colonel think they were over the hill? During the flight, he flirted with a Continental Airlines cabin attendant and things could have progressed had he stayed in New York. As it was, she was on a schedule and so was he. Still, it helped pass away the time.

"Good. Your business with the Consulate concluded?"

"All done," Tabor said. "Although the Third Secretary did grumble at having to wait for us on a Saturday. I told him to put in a letter of complaint."

Matan snorted. It was always the same; don't disrupt the normal flow of bureaucracy.

"The packages?"

"In the room safe," Tabor added, casually scanning the room. It could have been his, stamped from the same mold. "It's a calculated risk, I know, leaving them there, and if I'm burgled, we're in the shits."

"They're still sealed and timers checked?" Matan demanded sharply and Tabor nodded. It would be more than embarrassing to have the things fail because of a faulty timer. "Remember, when you handle them, use gloves and make sure you wipe the things down before attaching them. And for God's sake, don't throw away the damned gloves. Dispose of them in some public trashcan and wash your hands thoroughly. If airport security runs one of their sniffer dogs past you, I don't want you tagged for explosives because you were careless, diplomatic immunity or not."

"Don't worry, boss," Ellis said and smiled. "We've been over that."

"I know, but it's always the little things that trip you up. Keep that in mind and you'll live to enjoy your retirement. Got the coveralls?"

"Bought them while waiting for our Houston flight," Tabor said patiently. "And we removed all the identifying tags."

Matan nodded. "Good. Remember, gloves when putting them on or taking them off. And get rid of them like we discussed; stash them in a dumpster at some supermarket along I-45 or US-59. *Don't* do it at the airport. Use a gas station for the plastic seat and floor covers, or when you have the car washed. As for the TWIC badges, I'll take them off you once we're in flight. Right, if there is nothing more, let's get on with it."

As they piled into the corridor, Ellis figured Matan was an old fusspot, but appreciated the attention to detail. Something could always go wrong and it was important to break the chain of evidence in case any one item was intercepted. A smooth operation meant a smooth extraction and that was always desirable.

The elevator took them to the basement parking lot that felt like a steam bath. Road noises could be heard from the outside. Fluorescent tubes provided enough light to see, but not enough to dispel the feeling of gloom radiating from dark support columns and naked concrete walls. The place smelled of petrol and burnt rubber.

Their footfalls echoed forlornly on the hard floor as they made their way between rows of motorcars. Although not full, there were enough vehicles to keep them from feeling lonely. Matan guided them to a late model Toyota Camry, switched off the electronic alarm and tossed the keys to Tabor.

Traffic was light along the Southwest Freeway, and it only took some ten minutes to reach the I-45 S on-ramp. The afternoon sun glared at them as they headed toward Galveston. Sitting in front, Ellis switched on the radio, fiddled with the stations and settled for some light jazz.

Thankful for the airconditioning, Matan absently watched the flowing traffic and the surrounding suburbia to the whispering hum of the engine and background music. Strictly speaking, there was no compelling reason for him to be here, but he wanted to see the refinery complex for himself. He also wanted to make sure that Ellis and Tabor knew their way around and could handle the car in a strange environment. That might irritate them, but it was something he could live with. So far, Tabor was driving like he was born here, but tooling along a broad freeway was easy.

Houses, neat lawns and regular streets, slowly gave way to stretches of open greenery as they left the city. Patches of thin cloud glowed red low in the western sky. Bands of darker cloud hugged the ocean beyond Galveston. When they neared the neatly marked Loop 197 North off-ramp, Matan glanced at his watch—thirty-five minutes since they took the I-45. It seemed that his worst-case scenario of two hours to the airport had plenty of slack in it. Ahead, he could clearly see the brightly lit refinery stacks and the outlying POL (petroleum, oil, lubricants) tank farms.

It was 5:45 p.m. when they rolled past the Industrial Canal Road and into the complex itself. He could see two moored tankers tied to the wharf, riding high. The entire place seemed deserted, although he knew that over five hundred individuals worked on the 290-acre site. Most of the refinery on their right was a tangle of fractionation towers, venting stacks, holding tanks and running feeder piping. Tendrils of white steam rose from several towers. There was a certain geometrical beauty in the neat lines of white piping as they branched, reconnected and disappeared among tall columns of steel. It seemed almost a blasphemy to destroy such sculpture.

The air held a distinct smell of crude oil and gasoline, but not oppressively so. As they neared the railyards, they passed a large three-story building on their right, presumably an administration block, surrounded by a parking lot. Matan could see about two-dozen cars. What he was interested in were signs of any obvious security. A heavy chain-link fence bordered the complex along the Industrial Canal Road to the 14th Street South entry, but from there the place was wide open. Tabor didn't slow down when they took 14th Street and drove past the admin building, now on their left. The rail siding was packed with tanker and freight cars. A background hum of machinery filled the air. Looking hard at the refinery complex on his right, Matan imprinted the layout in his mind, amazed at what he was seeing. Anyone could simply walk in and do whatever they wanted. He couldn't believe it, but wasn't about to question his luck. There *had* to be more security.

Tabor rejoined Loop 197 North at the end of the rail siding

and drove uptown toward Texas City. After ten minutes, he pulled into a side street and parked opposite a convenience store. Next to it was a coffee shop with chairs and tables laid out on the sidewalk. A young couple nursed tall drinks, eyes only for each other. Directly ahead of them the sun had grown large and orange, about to sink below the horizon. Tabor switched off the engine and turned his head.

"Too easy, boss."

"Looks that way," Matan tended to agree. "Easy or not, it's no reason for us to get slack, and lack of security is a worry."

"Maybe they have cameras on all those towers?" Tabor ventured and Matan gave a shrug.

"Possible, but I doubt it. Let's grab some coffee and wait for dusk." His watch read 6:10 p.m.

It was still warm, but a creeping freshness promised a cool night. They snagged a table and a pretty Latino waitress took their orders. The young couple hardly gave them a glance, and there were enough customers inside to keep their presence unremarkable. An occasional automobile driving by broke the peaceful silence. After twenty minutes of idle chatter, having finished their drinks, Matan paid the bill and they walked across the lit street to their car. Although the sun had gone down, it was not yet fully dark. Ellis took the wheel.

By the time they returned to the refinery, the western skyline was a purple swathe. Dazzling floodlights illuminated the complex in harsh monochrome. In the fast fading light, the sounds of machinery seemed unnaturally loud. Driving down Loop 197 North, the place still appeared unoccupied, which was, of course, merely an illusion. *Someone* had to be around to run things. Matan realized that automation probably accounted for lack of people, but it was somewhat eerie to see such an enormous complex operating without human beings scurrying about.

With the garish lights fading behind them, Ellis took the I-45 on-ramp and smoothly accelerated toward downtown Houston.

Nobody said anything much. After all the planning, it was some-what sobering to be faced with the cold realization that they would actually destroy part of this place. The drive to IAH was a non-event, taking only an hour and twenty minutes even though it was Saturday night. The traffic was understandably heavier along the approaches, but easy enough to follow into the airport itself. By the time they returned from the airport and reached Greenway Plaza, it was 8:40 p.m. Matan suggested dinner, but wearing broad smiles, Ellis and Tabor announced that they had plans. What action was available in Houston that would be of any interest, Matan was not sure, but he could not resent them their freedom. He left the car with the boys, reminding them to thor-oughly wipe it down and clean it before the ops.

After a quiet meal at the hotel restaurant, Matan retired to his room. Nursing a tumbler of Elijah Craig, he ran over the day's events. He was uneasy at the apparent lack of site security. It couldn't be that simple, he told himself, looking for a catch. But if that was the way the Americans ran things, he was happy to take advantage of it. Replaying the drive in his mind, checking for anything he might have missed, he finished off the bourbon, sat-isfied that he had it covered. All that remained to be done was confirm where to plant the charges and run through the extrac-tion. Oil and gasoline fires were not something to mess with lightly. But that's what tomorrow's meeting was about. He just needed to figure out what to do with himself for the rest of the day. Visit the LBJ Space Center, perhaps? There weren't that many palatable choices available.

Lounging in bed, he scanned the TV channels and, for some reason he couldn't explain, settled on an episode of CSI Miami. It was corny and shallow, but he admired the technology. If only real cases could be solved so easily.

* * *

The Camry rolled into the parking lot without attracting attention. It was also convenient, as parking along the road would make them conspicuous. Tabor switched off the ignition and the lights, and waited. Heavy clouds drifted slowly toward Houston, making the surrounds darker than normal. The complex was fully lit and black shadows lurked everywhere. After two minutes, with no one coming from the building, he and Ellis climbed out of the car and retrieved the carry-on bag from the trunk. Pinning on the TWIC badge to their coveralls, they casually crossed 14th Street like they belonged there, and made their way toward the processing plants and five huge storage tanks along the Industrial Canal Road. A strong breeze swirled through the complex, ruffling their hair and clothing. Just as they got among a tangle of piping and humming machinery, a sleek blue cruiser, orange lights flashing on top, slowly drove down 14th Street. It stopped and somebody directed a high-powered floodlight at the refinery, the beam tracking between towers, piping and holding tanks. The light blinked off and the cruiser slowly moved on, turned into Loop 197 and accelerated toward the railyards. Tabor and Ellis exchanged glances and grinned.

Placing charges against the two central holding tanks was easy. They simply walked to them, set the timers and slapped the packs against the steel wall at ground level, away from any direct light. In shadow, it was unlikely that anyone would see them without a detailed inspection. A charge was attached to a pump station and what appeared to be a generator plant. It took them five minutes to walk to the fractionation towers themselves. Yellow flames hissed from thin venting stacks. Ellis had suggested that the job could be done quicker if he and Tabor worked alone, but Matan vetoed the idea. If someone saw them, it would look better if they were together, and they could support each other in case of trouble. Although not completely convinced, Ellis did not consider it worth arguing the point. Besides, the boss could be correct.

Tabor fixed the last pack under a feeder pipe leading to a storage tank, well away from other charges, and peeled off the green sticker from the dud package. He set the timer and, without thinking, crunched the tab and threw it on the ground. Ellis spun him around and snarled.

"Idiot! Pick it up."

For a second, he stared at Ellis in astonishment, then comprehension dawned. Sheepishly, he bent down and picked up the innocent wad of paper.

"Sorry," he mumbled and grinned.

"Fool!" Ellis shook his head and sighed. "Let's get out of here."

They had to lie low for three minutes as two men in white coveralls engaged in an argument, ambled along a gravel path between the refinery proper and the tank farm. Alone again, they sauntered casually toward the 14th Street entrance. The wind hissed around them, unfriendly and cold. No one saw them as they walked to the Camry and slowly drove off.

"Hear O Israel, the Lord our God, the Lord is one," Tabor muttered irreverently, peeling off his gloves.

Somewhere along I-45, after a rueful glance at Ellis, he wound down the window a bit and allowed the slipstream to whisk away the crunched wad of green paper. He sat back, satisfied. The impact of what they had done would be far-reaching, but the operation itself had been slick and smooth. Matan had style. He had to give the man his due.

At 10:25 p.m., only fifteen minutes late pushing out due to a delayed passenger, Air France Airbus A340 flight AF31 lifted off from George Bush International Airport and headed across the Atlantic.

* * *

At 2 a.m. the timers in the charges counted down to zero and a little microprocessor chip sent a small voltage to the detonator imbedded deep within fifty grams of C-4 plastic explosive. The detonator flashed into incandescence and the resulting pressure wave set off the white mass of the main charge.

The two central storage tanks along the Industrial Canal Road blew apart in a spectacular flash of light and noise that sent flames shooting three hundred feet into the air. The constituent plating was hurled spinning within the column of burning gasoline. Liquid fire rained around the tanks, which engulfed the small storage farm across the road. One of the two tanks was almost empty, preventing the container next to it from brewing up. A fractionation tower, piping and power generation machinery were flung into the air amid the roar of flaming gas and petroleum products as the remaining charges cooked off. Blazing gasoline fell on the rail yard, setting everything alight. Secondary explosions rocked the site as rail tankers detonated like incendiary bombs, adding to the conflagration. Across Loop 197 several small storage tanks succumbed to fire and went up in successive eruptions. Spillage control systems automatically kicked in, spraying the burning tanks with a special suppression foam mixture.

Sensors imbedded throughout the sprawling complex were either destroyed or failed due to heat overload, but those that remained faithfully transmitted their signals to the control room computer. Noting extensive damage along feeder pipes, storage tanks and fractionation towers, the computer initiated emergency shutdown of two main crude oil input units and flow-on pumps to the eastern network. With loss of feedstock the vacuum distillation towers, distillate hydrotreaters and the naphtha reformer automatically closed down. Using manual overrides, crews closed feeds to other pumps along the line and Valero's capacity of 245,000 barrels per day suddenly went off-line.

Flame and billowing clouds of toxic black fumes surrounded the admin building, its windows blown in by initial blast overpressure. Workers scrambled into cars or simply ran along Loop

197 away from the horror behind them. Where burning fuel fell, some cars didn't get away. An easterly wind pushed a roiling column of partially burned hydrocarbons and pollutants now rising to more than three thousand feet across Texas City and Houston's southeastern suburbs.

The Valero refinery emergency management plan swung into action and resources were marshaled to first assess the extent of the damage, the threat posed to the remaining plant infrastructure, and initiate containment measures. An automatic Level III alert went out to the Texas City Fire Department who immediately dispatched mobile units to the site. The alert also activated the Emergency Operations Center (EOC) and a siren warning blared into the night directing the public to stay indoors. Cable Channel 16 and radio 530 AM bulletins were immediately broadcast, details pending.

As per procedure, EOC notified the police commissioner, the local FBI office and the Department of Homeland Security.

* * *

At 9:45 a.m., on the fourth floor computer and network center of the Mossad building, not having received an abort signal, Namir glanced at the young man beside him and nodded.

Ronel grinned, cracked his knuckles and started typing into the keyboard, staring all the while at his 21" LED screen covered with layered display windows. Breaking into somebody's website wasn't such a big deal. The trick was to do it without anyone knowing it had been done. For that, he was using a derivative of the CIA's Triangle Boy software, originally produced by SafeWeb of Oakland. What Safe Boy did was route his commands through several innocuous server addresses before being routed to the actual site of interest—effectively muddling his trail.

Namir watched with interest as Ronel broke into the Iranian Ministry of Culture Web server through a help page, avoiding the thorny part of having to worm through firewalls and security traps. There was a poisonous fascination seeing all the elaborate access protocols bypassed so easily, which made him wonder about the security of Mossad's own closed server network. Were its secrets secure from their own network specialists? The prepared HTML extract was inserted using script from a coded file, the process repeated with the Ministry of Foreign Affairs server.

Ronel was startled when he first saw the news pages, understanding immediately the magnitude of the operation being conducted and the impact on Israel. Once over his shock that Mossad had even dared do this, he felt proud to be singled out for such a critical assignment, and vowed that nothing would go wrong with the penetration. And it sure beat the hell out of boring system programming and Web content management. This was payback time.

The servers and other machines around him whispered among themselves as he worked. He had the floor to himself and the equipment did not need supervision unless a fault was detected within the network or tangle of physical comms links. Otherwise, hardly anyone came here.

"Two down and one to go," Ronel observed with satisfaction and started typing again.

Breaking into the Al Jazeera server only took a couple of minutes. He planted the HTML page and got out seemingly without attracting attention. Exhilarated, he leaned back against his seat and sighed. It hadn't been a bad piece of work if he said so himself. It wasn't like breaking into Q-Tel, Qatar's telco. That one had been a challenge.

"It's done," he declared and reached for his mug of coffee. "The pages are linked and visible to anyone browsing the sites," he said as he scrolled through the websites, displaying the pages.

"Excellent," Namir said warmly and patted him on the shoulder.

The boy had tried to explain the PHP and SQL code used to

infect the sites, but it was black magic as far as Namir was concerned. Still, he understood enough to appreciate the skill involved.

"One thing left to be done."

"Right."

Ronel opened the secure test server directory listing and highlighted his working directory used to trial the penetration scripts. He pressed the delete button and confirmed the action on computer prompt. Accessing the system utilities menu, he activated the drive defragmentation routine and looked up.

"People don't generally know that deleting a file or directory doesn't actually wipe the information itself. It merely removes an ID tag in the drive's table of contents. With the right software, I could reinitialize the tag and be back in business. But once the drive is defragged and the Recycle Bin cleared, no one will be able to reconstruct the physical files."

"Good job, Mr. Ronel," Namir said warmly and stood up, not caring how the potentially incriminating data trail was removed, as long as it was removed. "You have done well. Take the rest of the day off. I'll square it with your supervisor." Of course, he had no intention of telling anyone anything.

Ronel looked startled, then a pleased smile lit his face. "Thank you, sir. I appreciate that. My plate is pretty clear and I could use the time."

"You're making a great future for yourself here, my boy." Namir patted the youngster again. "Remember, this is completely black."

"Got it."

"Good man." Namir stood up and let himself out, giving an involuntary shiver when he stepped into the warm corridor. The computer room was decidedly too chilly for his liking.

He walked toward the men's toilet, stepped into the empty room and wrinkled his nose. The air had a pronounced whiff of urine and harsh deodorizer, unlike the refined perfume that lingered in executive restrooms. Ignoring the smell, he calmly stepped into the nearest cubicle and locked the door. Reaching into his coat pocket, he took out a small vial and a plain envelope. He removed the stopper and placed the vial into the envelope. Holding it against the wall, he drove his left elbow against it. There was a satisfying crunch of breaking glass. He emptied the broken fragments into the toilet bowl and pressed the flush button. The swirling water swept the mess down the drain. When the cistern refilled, he flushed the toilet again, placed the stopper into the envelope and pocketed it. The stopper was made of hard rubber and could conceivably surface in some toilet—not a desirable thing. He would dispose of the envelope later. In the meantime, the slow poison he had slipped into Ronel's coffee while the boy was preoccupied would do its untraceable work. It was too bad, for the kid had potential.

Outside, he waited for the elevator to take him back to the seventeenth floor.

* * *

Humming, Ronel finished his coffee, washed the mug, logged off and closed the screen. Happy, he took the elevator to the ground floor, waved to Jaron at the security desk and walked toward the parking lot. What a day. He looked forward to seeing how the local and world media would treat the events unfolding even now in America. He did not doubt that the next few days would make for an exciting time. And being singled out like this by the Metsada director himself would not do his career any harm at all. *You can't keep good talent down,* he told himself. He climbed into his battered old Renault, not bothering with the seatbelt, and drove out with the reckless confidence of the young.

He entered Arlozorov Road, heading east for Giv'atayim, thinking about things to be done during the day when a spasm clutched his chest, the pain sharp, stabbing through his heart. He instinctively clutched at his chest and screamed as another wave of fire constricted his heart. Without realizing it, he released the steering wheel and his right foot jammed down on the accelerator as his back arched. Suddenly out of control, the car veered across the busy boulevard. Oncoming traffic scattered before him to squeals of smoking tires and blaring horns.

A concrete light pole stopped Ronel's car as the vehicle slammed head-on into the obstruction at ninety kilometers per hour. The engine block and transmission were driven into the passenger compartment as the front crumpled, breaking both his legs. Blood gushed from severed arteries and torn flesh. The steering wheel tore into his chest, crushing it, even as he was thrown forward by the collision. His head was propelled against the window and jagged glass cruelly lacerated his forehead and scalp, the wounds bleeding profusely. Still moving forward and down, his head hit the dashboard and the impact cracked two vertebrae in his neck.

Ariel Ronel was dead before his mangled car finished wrapping itself around the light pole.

Chapter Four

As the heavy dark Pontiac rolled into Loop 197 North, making its way past parked cars and gawking citizenry, two police cruisers, their lights flashing, barred the road. Glass littered the sidewalks where warehouse windows were blown out. A state trooper waved his glowing yellow baton, directing the car to pull over.

Thomas Meecham sighed and pursed his mouth in frustration as he steered the long car to the curb. All those people, like it was some kind of picnic or genuine reality show. Morbid, that's what they were.

Christ!

It was going to be one of those days, he could tell. It certainly started like it. The rolling explosions from the refinery must have woken most of Houston. If they hadn't, they certainly should have, he mused grumpily. Since he had to be awake, there was no reason why everybody else should not share his misery. He'd been in bed by 11 p.m.; early by his standards and he fully expected a quiet night—a number of quiet nights after his breakup with Malena. Not that she was possessive, or tried to smother him or anything. She needed more than he could or was willing to give right now, and didn't want to share him with another mistress any longer. He could still hear her cutting snarl of scorn as she stormed out of his house. Pick one, she demanded, her or the job. But she knew his job meant everything to him. Besides, all the girls liked a dashing investigator. Didn't they? At six foot one, lean and muscular, hard jaw and flowing black hair, his penetrating blue eyes had cut quite a swathe. At first, she also admired his stylish smile and casual roguishness, but unfortunately, the glamor quickly wore off after relentlessly long days, some-times longer nights and all too frequent absences. The Bureau was a demanding taskmaster if he wanted any kind of career. In the end, that's what did it. Both saw it coming, and being what they were, apart from tearing each other up, could do nothing about it. Then she told him: when he was prepared to grow up and make her his life's priority, she would be there for him. Until then, he could take his job and shove it, long days and all. What was a man to do?

He sighed as the Pontiac stopped. Still, it had not been all bad, and they'd had some good times together, in and out of bed. A smile creased his face as fond memories chased each other. Christ, what a body she had! Made your eyes water. Stop fanta-sizing, Tom, he told himself sternly. A gal wants her man to be around and not just for a romp. She wants somebody to chew out, to cry on and take care of her. The bottom line: he loved his job more than he loved her. At least for now, he did. Well, he had made his choice and now had nothing to complain about. It may have cost him a relationship, but the Bureau had also paid back. A senior special agent, he had done well.

Goodbye, Malena. It's been fun. Maybe we'll bump into each other some-time. And for your information, babe, I am *all grown up.*

The state trooper walked to the car as Tom wound down the window. A roar like an approaching freight train bashed his ears and he crinkled his nose at the sharp chemical stink of burning oil and gasoline.

"Road closed, sir," the trooper announced coldly, all business. "Nobody goes through."

Tom glanced at the flames and billowing smoke climbing into tortured clouds overhead. "Yeah, tell me about it," he said and pulled out his badge. "FBI."

That didn't seem to overawe the trooper, but he did relax somewhat. "Any more of you guys coming?"

"My forensic team," Tom said, staring at the roaring flames.

"Anybody else here?"

"Captain Travers, downtown police."

"Houston?"

"Nah, Texas City. But you can expect Houston to send some-body along pretty soon. Apart from the fire department and am-bulances, there is also a FEMA guy nosing about."

"Already? Christ! What's he doing? Handing out relief pack-ages?"

"Don't know, sir."

On reflection, maybe that wasn't such a bad thing after all. Given the New Orleans fiasco after Katrina, he figured that FEMA wanted to be on the ball and be seen doing their job. Spreading PR bullshit, more likely. Still, he didn't want the fellow underfoot, no matter what his intentions.

"If TV or wire services show up, no one goes through, even if escorted by the President himself. Clear?"

"That's what Captain Travers said, sir. They won't like it," the trooper added equitably and stepped back.

"Like I care." Tom put the car into gear and slowly drove to-ward the fire. Having a pissed off TV crew was the last thing on his mind. His dashboard clock read 3:55.

A helicopter clattered overhead, its pencil searchlight plying over the scene below. He wondered whose it was, probably CNN or some other network not wanting to miss a chance to upstage the sitcoms for ratings. In one way or another, this was going to be front news for some time to come. Well, they can keep the sky, but there was going to be no messing on the ground until he scraped off every piece of evidence there was.

Along the railyards on his left, fire tenders were mopping up. White foam clung to half-blown tanker cars, almost burying some of them. The entire complex was a contrast of garish blacks and whites, lit by powerful floodlights attached to a forest of towers. Across the road on his right, a single storage tank billowed twist-ing flames and thick smoke. Tenders directed streams of foam into the roiling hell. Beside it, two tanks were a tangle of shriveled melted steel.

He could sense the heat through the rolled-up window. As far as he could see, the refinery complex on his left looked okay. There was no fire and he could not see any destruction, probably obscured by fractionation towers and running piping. Farther down along the Industrial Canal Road, a volcano of flame roared from a huge storage tank, shooting high into the night sky. Tom marveled how anybody could put out such a mother, hating to be the sorry bastard on the scene.

"My, my, my, what a mess," he muttered and gave a long sigh.

Police cruisers, fire tenders, ambulances and Valero-marked cars clustered in the admin building parking lot. Several cars were burnt-out black shells and the building itself bore extensive scorch marks. Foam still dribbled down its sides, but the fires seemed to be out. Dark windows gaped at him in silent agony. Despite the destruction, Tom was impressed. In less than two hours, most of the secondary fires had been put down.

He parked his car where it was unlikely to be run down by a tender and climbed out. He slammed the door shut behind him and took a deep breath. The sharp petroleum smells helped to steady him, to focus. No one paid any attention as he walked toward a group engaged in heated discussion. When a burly firefighter threw down his helmet, he figured the discussion was more than heated.

"You guys can go and screw yourselves!" the firefighter declared in no uncertain terms. "I'm not sending any more of my boys near those tanks."

"And why not, Chief?" Tom demanded calmly. Heads snapped around and stared at him. A police officer pushed back his visored cap and glared.

"And who the hell are you? This is a restricted area, Mister."

"Never was," Tom said, measuring the guy, deciding he could take him. "Otherwise whoever set up this little party would not have gotten in. The place doesn't have any security." He waited for his words to sink in. "Captain Travers, I presume?" He glanced at the fire chief and grinned. "I always wanted to say that." He fixed a cold stare on the cop. "I'm Special Agent Tom Meecham, FBI, Houston office."

"Okay, FBI, Houston office," Travers snapped, hands on hips, not looking at all happy. "You are telling me this was deliberate?"

A smallish man wearing neat jeans, polo shirt and alligator loafers, pushed through. His hair was graying around the temples, but he carried himself with authority.

"*I'm* telling you this was deliberate," he announced with a scornful smirk at the captain. "And I've been telling you the same thing for the past half-hour."

"Damn right!" The fire chief nodded and spat on the asphalt. "You just have to look at the fire pattern, and employees at the site reported explosions. No way this was an accident."

Travers was no fool and knew when he was on the losing side of an argument. But to believe that somebody would deliberately sabotage the Valero refinery was unthinkable. Unthinkable or not, if this *was* a criminal act, it meant an investigation, forms, Feds crawling all over the place, finger-pointing, ass covering and a general disruption to his peace-loving lifestyle. *Shit!* But Travers was a professional and carried out his duty as he saw it—well, most of the time. Had he been a front-line cop the Commissioner would not have dumped him to the Texas City precinct.

Well, hell! It wasn't his fault that Galliano and the Sigani brothers had gotten off on a technicality due to inadmissible evidence. The young DA bastard wasn't up to it and was outmaneuvered by a high-powered attorney who knew his shit. The fact that someone on his team fumbled the evidence trail had not helped his cause.

At least Laraine liked Texas City and the easy hours that now filled his days. They were close to Galveston and the beaches, and managed to do some touristy things they previously had no time for. His two boys were in college and didn't bother him as long as he paid the bills. What they did in their spare time, he didn't want to know. The deal would continue until they graduated. If they failed to keep up their grade points average, they were on their own.

He studied Meecham's hard features, unwavering eyes, hint of an amused smile, and decided not to mess with the guy. FBI would have sent down their best and Meecham seemed the type able to handle himself. He could tell. Travers had looked like that himself not so long ago, when he thought he walked with all the answers. *Ah, shit.*

Tom saw something fade in Travers' eyes and nodded as the cop capitulated. He looked down at the executive.

"I'm Richard Selek, General Manager," the man announced and automatically held out a business card. Tom pocketed the thing without looking at it.

"Glad to meet you, Mr. Selek. And I'm pleased that you agree with my assessment."

Selek shrugged. "It's simple enough. Like the Chief here said, look at the damage pattern. No single ignition source could have caused this level of unrelated destruction. Too many safety devices in place for that to happen. But whoever did this didn't know what he was doing."

"In what way?" Tom demanded.

"We lost some storage tanks, pumps, piping and a fractionation tower. It's bad, don't get me wrong, but if someone really wanted to put us out of commission for keeps, they should have hit the control room. As it is, we have this section isolated and we'll be back online within hours. Admittedly at reduced capacity, but we're still in business."

"I see."

"I heard your comment about security. Do you have any idea how much it would cost to make 290 acres impenetrable?"

"I don't know, but how much is it going to cost you now, Mr. Selek?" Tom turned to the fire chief without waiting for a reaction. He had come across this attitude time and again. The bean counters calculated risk profiles and figured they'd get by, hoping shit wouldn't happen. "And why are you so upset?"

"Selek here has two three million-liter storage tanks smoking along Canal Road. Maybe you've seen 'em on the way in. One was full and flaming gasoline has crossed the road, infecting the tank farm on the other side. They're small stuff and we're handling it. But some burning gas has gotten into the water and the tide is carrying it toward the shipping channel. The second tank was almost empty, thank God, only 120,000 liters of distillate. Selek wants me to contain the fire to those two tanks. If holding tanks on either side of them light up, I've got nothing to fight them with. We're shooting up to 12,000 gallons of foam mix per minute at those things, but I don't know how long I can keep that up."

Selek held his mouth pursed, but his clenched fists clearly highlighted his frustration.

"We're pumping the adjacent tanks out, but if they go, it'll be like an atomic explosion going off. The flames will spread across Loop 197 into the tank farm on the other side. I'll lose half my plant and you're looking at a major disaster scenario."

The fire chief sighed, weary of the whole business. "Mr. Selek, I'm doing the best I can with what I've got. Until additional support tenders and foam tankers get here, there is nothing more I can do. I've got my boys fighting one of your three million-liter tanks across Loop 197 already and we think we've got the situation contained. Your automated suppression systems are helping, for which I'm grateful, but I don't have anybody spare to put on Canal Road. It's simple as that."

"Okay, Chief, I know you're doing your best," Selek conceded resignedly.

There was no use arguing with the man and he knew it. Everybody was doing their best. Valero had a nice emergency disaster plan, all neat and bound up, but it hadn't provided for a terrorist contingency. Meecham's comment did not escape him and he wondered how much the cleanup *would* cost. The Board would be looking for heads to scalp and he hoped one of them wouldn't be his. After 9/11, he had urged the Board to beef up security, but was voted down. If there was any finger-pointing over tonight's disaster, he would bring that item up, only mildly wondering if it would make any difference.

"Driving down the road, the refinery itself didn't look all bad," Tom ventured.

Selek's smile was grim. "The fires may be out, Mr. Meecham, thanks largely to our suppression systems and spillage controls, but that's not to say things aren't grim. There is considerable infrastructure damage. Like I said, they should have hit the control room."

"Has anybody contacted DHS?" Tom asked.

Travers nodded. "When I called you guys, I also called the Director, Office of Operations Coordination, as per SOP. They'll be sending someone down."

Tom smiled with approval. "So, you figured all along that this could be a terrorist attack?"

"I might be a backwater cop, Mr. Meecham, but I do know my business."

"I never doubted it, Captain. My forensic team should be arriving shortly and I guess that means I'm assuming jurisdiction."

"If the Feds want this, you're welcome to it, Mister," Travers said with feeling.

"By the way, has anybody seen a FEMA guy who's supposed to be around?" Tom asked, looking at each of them.

A somewhat portly, balding individual stepped out of the gloom and proffered a pudgy hand.

"Ray Klent. I was just waiting for everybody to run out of

things to say," he announced in a high-pitched voice, clearly enjoying himself.

Tom stared as Klent pushed back his glasses, which had slid down a bulbous nose, not bothering to take the offered hand. The man carried himself with annoying confidence, his dark suit out of place a little, but that didn't seem to bother him.

"Mr. Klent, I would appreciate if you didn't wander about until my team has had a chance to examine the scene," Tom said politely, clearly irritated.

"I'm simply doing my job," Klent replied urbanely and smiled.

"That right? This is not a disaster scenario and there is no immediate threat to the population at large—"

"The pollution aspects are of concern, Mr. Meecham," Klent interrupted smoothly. "And the shipping channel is threatened by burning gasoline flowing into it."

"Which the Port of Houston Authority is capable of handling," the fire chief retorted hotly. "All the emergency services are fully integrated, including medical care and evacuation."

"That may be the case, but—"

"As far as I know," Tom snapped, "the Governor has not declared a state of emergency or made a formal request to the President for FEMA to be involved. In other words, you've got no business being here."

"That's technically correct—"

"In that case, you're in the way and I would appreciate if you could please remove yourself from the scene," Tom finished for him.

"You have no authority—" Klent started, but Tom raised his hand to silence him and turned to Travers.

"Place this man into custody and hold him for twelve hours. I don't care what you do with him after that."

"Hey! You can't do that," Klent protested, realizing the situation had gotten out of hand, and after all the trouble he'd gone through to be here. Instead of being proactive, his boss could interpret this as needless meddling in order to shine his own ass.

Travers grinned, some of his good humor restored, and motioned to two of his men. "Take him away."

Kent was still spluttering his protests and threats as two uniformed cops, wearing wry smiles, led him to their car. Doors slammed and the cruiser rolled off. Travers watched it go and shook his head.

"Never liked the pushy son of a bitch."

Tom's cellphone went off and he reached into his coat pocket to drag it out. "Excuse me," he muttered to the others, turned and took a few steps back. "Meecham," he said briskly into the palmed handset.

"Mr. Meecham, this is Assistant Director Bruce Wellard, Counterterrorism Division, Washington. Are you in a position to talk?"

Tom looked nonplussed, wondering what the hell was going on. "Yes, sir."

"Good. It appears that you have a foreign terrorist incident on your hands…Iran. Al Jazeera and the Iranian Ministries of Culture and Foreign Affairs posted news pages on their websites claiming responsibility for the attack on Valero."

"Christ!"

"I've alerted the Houston office Joint Terrorism Task Force and the Field Intelligence Group. They'll be in touch once you get back to your office. Are your men on the ground yet?"

"My forensic team is due any minute, sir."

Tom did not much enjoy group multitasking or interagency involvement. Everybody merely got in each other's way or fought for jurisdiction. And what the hell was he going to do with a FIG? The horse had already bolted.

"Good work. As the point man for this investigation, I want you to coordinate all local and FBI activities, and cooperate in every respect with Director, National Operations Center, Mark Price."

"Price? Former CIA Deputy Director, Operations?"

The way he heard it, Price was destined for great things in the CIA, but a sudden falling out with the Director, National Clandestine Service just as he was about to take up his appointment, ended it all. But DHS had snapped him up before Price had time to start feeling too sorry for himself. He happened to know this because the Bureau had been after him itself.

"The same. I've spoken to your boss and he concurs. For the duration of this assignment, you will hold the rank of Supervisory Special Agent. Get to the bottom of this, Mr. Meecham," Wellard snapped and cut the connection.

"Thanks for nothing," Tom muttered and pocketed the phone.

Everybody giving orders, like that solved everything. Still, his new rank would be useful if he needed to cut corners. He palmed his chin and gave it a good rub. Iran, eh? Christ! His life had suddenly become extremely complicated and he wasn't sure whether that was such a good thing. He hoped Price had all his shit in one bag. If they fumbled, both their careers would be in the crapper. Malena wouldn't mind.

Tom walked back to the group and cleared his throat. "Gentlemen, we have a situation."

* * *

While the onions sizzled, Mark Price finished cutting the bacon and scraped the finely diced squares into the frying pan. He gave the mess a quick stir with a wooden chopstick, nodded with satisfaction at the wafting aroma and squirted in a dash of barbecue sauce. A barbaric practice, he knew, but didn't give a damn. Humming, he broke two extra large eggs into the pan and worked the mixture into a paste. A single tomato, also finely chopped, was thrown into the steaming concoction. Pepper, salt and more sauce were added while the eggs congealed. With an expert twist of a chopstick, he neatly folded the mixture, turned off the glass hotplate, allowing the omelet to brown on one side, and poured himself a second cup of coffee. A touch of sugar and a final nod, he used the remote to switch on the 42" LED screen. The CNN logo was coming up for the 5 a.m. news. With the coffee safely on the dining table, he picked up the frypan and neatly slid the omelet onto the waiting plate.

Sitting down, he suppressed a yawn; not enough sleep. It wasn't as though he was tired or overworked, just one of those things. Then again, being wakened early hadn't helped things. Absently watching the TV, he flipped the napkin across his knees and took a sip of coffee. The screen showed soaring flames and billowing black smoke climbing into a dark sky. Glaring flood-lights lit the refinery complex, highlighting crowded towers and a jumble of running piping. He cut a piece of omelet and brought the fork to his mouth. Chewing, he waited for the commentary.

"Good morning. This is CNN five o'clock news, live from New York center. Your hosts, Ralph White and Sharyl Knight."

Looking important, Ralph straightened a stack of papers before him, then stared at the camera with solemn dignity.

"At approximately two a.m. Central Standard Time, the Valero Texas City Refinery was rocked by a series of explosions, which caused extensive damage to processing facilities and associated storage tanks. Two refinery workers are known to have died in the initial event and subsequent firestorm. Four are badly injured or burned." Ralph turned to his pretty co-host. *"Sharyl, can you give us the latest update on this tragic situation?"*

The woman was suitably grave as she nodded, her flaming mane of golden hair seemingly set in concrete. Mark wondered if she was that frigid in bed. Those self-starters these days wanted it all, power *and* control. Then again, why the hell not?

"Thank you, Ralph," she said demurely and turned to the camera. *"As reported in our news-breaking bulletin an hour ago, what you are looking at are camera shots of the initial devastation taken from our helicopter at the scene."* A small window overlay popped on the screen

showing the complex as the helicopter panned the ground below. *"The local fire department has contained the situation and there is no danger to Texas City or the Port of Houston waterway."* The scene shifted to concentrate on the storage tanks. *"As you can see from the live feed, several holding tanks are still ablaze and every effort is being made to prevent burning fuel and oil spreading to associated tanks and the remaining plant infrastructure. For the moment, all media are banned from the site for safety reasons. We can only wish the brave men down in that inferno luck and success in containing this disaster. This is CNN at twelve minutes past the hour. Back to you, Ralph."*

Mark snorted. *Goodnight, Sharyl.*

Studying the screen, it did not look like the situation was going to be contained anytime soon. What interested him was not the scale of damage, but where that damage had occurred.

"Thank you, Sharyl."

Here it comes, Mark thought, taking another mouthful. So far, this had been an identical feed from an hour ago. From here on, it was going to get serious. A good presenter, Ralph waited for tension to build before proceeding.

"We are now in a position to reveal that this was not an ordinary industrial accident, but an orchestrated and deliberate attack against the United States by the Islamic Republic of Iran! Almost immediately after the attack taking place, Al Jazeera and the Iranian Ministries of Culture and Foreign Affairs websites claimed responsibility for this unprovoked atrocity." The overlay window showed the websites and the offending English language bulletins. *"We can only surmise that this was done in response to increased American sanctions against Iran in protest of their ongoing nuclear program, whose sole objective is the acquisition of nuclear weapons and destabilization of the entire Middle East region. To analyze the international impact and the likely American response, we are joined—"*

Well, crap! It was out in the public domain, not that it could have been contained. Mark reached for the remote and shut off the TV. He didn't need the situation analyzed. It was grim any way he cut it and Ralph's emotion-laden dialogue would do nothing to soothe wounded public sensibilities.

When the lid blew off, Colin Forbes did not allow grass to grow under his feet, calling Mark at 3:20 a.m., allowing for an hour's difference with Texas. The Director, Office of Operations Coordination, had been informed about the damning Web pages and calmly proceeded to set into motion the vast resources at his disposal. He hadn't demanded that Mark climb out of bed and rush off to Houston. It was far too early for that and they had nothing to work with. He would simply be another bureaucrat gumming up the works, something the FBI probably didn't want right now. Web pages were one thing, but before the White House could even start formulating a measured response, they would need evidence, proof. That was going to be the kicker as always, especially if Iran was involved. With the FBI on the ground, they would hopefully come up with something useable. Mark knew Tom Meecham and trusted how the man operated. What he didn't trust were Houston's JTTF and FIG, more busybodies underfoot doing the same damn thing—being experts after the fact.

Forbes wanted Mark to get his team activated ASAP and coordination put into place with the FBI, CIA and the National Counterterrorism Center, in that order. They needed to start sniffing out trails and identify possible precursor indicators. That's the bit that bothered Mark a lot. There had been no warning at all on this one. All covert operations he had ever been involved with generated *some* warning flags. The increasingly strained dialogue between Iran and the new administration had placed all the intelligence services on heightened alert for that very reason. Did somebody drop the ball? Maybe the NSA or the CIA were hoarding some signals intelligence and were too dumb to recognize it for what it was. It wouldn't be the first time. He had come across that often enough in his past life as a CIA spook. Whatever. He only hoped this wasn't going to degenerate into another finger-pointing and blame allocation exercise. There was going to be enough crap over this as it is when the President got out of bed, if he wasn't up already.

Still, it would be sweet having that Zardwovsky shit under his command. The National Clandestine Service Director had managed to derail Mark's career at the eleventh hour, but that's how things went. The rest of the blame game, he could handle. The problem was, when the old Soviet Union collapsed, the CIA lost a familiar enemy and found itself floundering in the new world order, undecided where to pour the billions in Congress appropriations, and afraid that they'd be chopped off at the knees if they didn't produce. The entrenched management mindset could not cope, and the agency had degenerated into squabbling power factions, dropping the ball on several serious intelligence cases. The classics, of course, were 9/11 and Iraq's lack of weapons of mass destruction. If you didn't have hard HUMINT evidence, manufacture it. The CIA was good at that kind of shit. Still, Mark couldn't blame the CIA entirely for the Iraq fiasco. The Bush administration and Vice President Cheney in particular, had to wear some blame for the ensuing mess.

These days, CIA careers were made through sucking up and office subterfuge. To a certain extent, it had always been that way and Mark had learned the rules well. But when the job became merely playing the office politics game, he could see the writing on the wall. In that atmosphere, getting shafted by Zardwovsky was inevitable. When Colin Forbes invited him to join DHS, he figured this would be his chance to shape an operations department that would have a clear focus and mission statement, unencumbered by the weight of stifling history and ingrained self-serving behavior. He had done just that, but hadn't figured on the parasitic bureaucracy that had grown around core operational DHS departments, threatening the organization's capacity to act through sheer weight of mindless procedures; Under Secretary for toilet procurement and Assistant Secretary of office color schemes. And all the other agencies acting scared like DHS was the government. Maybe Walters would cut through the bullshit and clean out the parasites. Anyway, he was too old to start somewhere else and too young to retire.

Well, crap!

Mindless procedures or not, Valero was NOC's first real test and he would make sure it passed with honors, procedures be damned. If anybody got in his way, they'd get trampled, simple. He was certain that Forbes would back him up. At least he hoped so.

Andrews was alerted and a Gulfstream V prepped and waiting for him. By the time he arrived at Houston, Meecham might be in a better position to talk to him. His quandary was whether to fly to Scholes International, a stone's throw from Texas City where he could survey the site for himself, or head directly for the George Bush main airport, which was closer to the FBI offices in East TC Jester. Anyway, looking over piles of tangled metal wouldn't tell him anything. He was not a specialist and would just be in the way. Best thing would be to call Meecham once he was in the air.

But first, he had to finish his omelet. After all, breakfast was supposed to be the most important meal of the day, and he figured it might be a while between omelets.

* * *

Namir Bethan signed off the last requisition slip and placed the document on top of a neat pile of other completed paperwork. He hoped the building foundations were up to the load. The endless flow of forms, updates, directives, authorizations, newspapers and periodicals would someday surely sink the place. No wonder Mossad was getting to be a screw-up. The bean counters were starting to act as though everybody else worked for them. In his view, the paper shufflers were foreign saboteurs whose sole objective was to paralyze Mossad with governance regulations.

The phone rang, loud in the general silence of the office. Outside, warm sunshine beckoned, but Namir was not going to be given time to enjoy it. He glanced at the gray LED display above the keypad and read off the caller's name. Speaking of the devil…It had not taken long for the Mossad machinery to get activated, but given the gravity of the situation, he would have been hugely disappointed had the call not come. He picked up the receiver and sat back.

"Doron, what can I do for you?" He pitched his voice just right, friendly and unconcerned.

"We need to talk, Namir," the Mossad chief said briskly and cleared his throat. "There's been a development. Can you come up?"

"What's going on?"

"Just get up here, okay?"

"Of course. Be there in a minute."

This was it…

The elevator took him up to the eighteenth floor. He had to pass his key card against a sensor before the thing would take him up. Sometimes he questioned whether internal security was taken a tad far. If somebody came in with an AK-47 and wiped out the floor, it would probably leave Mossad far more efficient. Cool, soft green carpet muffled his footsteps as he strode past glass-walled offices, the layout very dissimilar to his own floor. Here, legal and Kameer's own executive staff lorded over the agency.

He paused, absently rubbed his right thigh and walked into a spacious office near the west corner. Kameer's personal assistant looked up and flashed him a warm smile. Her clean Nordic features, framed by a mane of platinum hair that cascaded past her shoulders, topped a tall, trim figure. Her eyes were dark blue, which tended to lighten when she was happy, and turned almost black when her mood swung the other way. They had always been friends, even before his wife's death, but since then, Rinah hinted she was willing to have that friendship blossom into something more. He'd been tempted, despite a difference of fifteen years between them. But it was complicated at many levels. In that, he envied the impetuous daring of the young. In many respects, life was very simple for them, driven as they were by the irresistible urge to procreate. He admitted, were it otherwise, the human race would have died out.

Then again, a date or two wouldn't cause any harm, would it? He wondered if she was free for dinner.

He returned her smile and inclined his head at the closed door on his right.

"He's expecting you," she said softly, her eyes laughing at him, and got up to open the door. "Mr. Bethan, sir."

"Show him in," Namir heard Kameer's grave voice, sounding tense and uncertain. Namir sympathized. This was going to be a long day for his boss, probably for everybody.

As he walked past her, Rinah's scent enveloped both of them and he allowed himself a moment of distraction. Her eyes held his in bold invitation before the fires in them faded. She waited for him to walk in, then closed the door with a click. He squirmed. Dangerous woman, that.

The office looked like his own, except it was far larger, accommodating an oval conference table that now seated four solemn men dressed in dark, conservative suits. This high up, they had a grand view of Herzliya and Tel Aviv shrouded in brown smog. In the center of the table, gold-bordered cups sat neatly arranged around a silver tray, which held a slim carafe of coffee, sugar and cream. No one had reached for the coffee as yet.

At the head of the table, Kameer looked up as Namir entered, giving him a penetrating look.

"Ah, all together at last. Take a seat."

Namir returned the gaze, nodded to his colleagues and sank comfortably into a contoured leather chair. The material squeaked as his weight came down.

Of German descent, Kameer was of solid build, black hair parted on the left side, with a pencil Clark Gable mustache and clear, searching eyes. A political appointee, not a professional intelligence operative, he concentrated predominantly on procedures, governance and accountability. That was not necessarily a bad thing, but Namir wondered whether in the process to streamline the internal machinery the director had forgotten, or overlooked, Mossad's mission, threatening to turn the organization into another bloated government bureaucracy. To be fair, he did listen to his department heads and sometimes acted against the prevailing political breeze, which, of course, did not always sit well with the government or the Knesset. Despite all that, Namir was able to work with him and the director didn't interfere too much in the operational workings of his department. As long as that continued, they'd be fine.

Kameer placed the tips of his fingers into a pyramid shape and cleared his throat. The soft chatter faded and everyone turned to focus on him.

"This is a briefing for your information only. Ten minutes ago, Segan rang me saying that Iran has carried out a bang and burn operation against the Valero Texas City Refinery in Houston."

"Shit!" somebody said. Namir thought it was Joakim.

"My God, they must be insane!" Joshin, Director of Collections, gaped and exchanged incredulous glances with the others.

"We know it's Iran," Kameer plowed on, "because the Ministries of Culture and Foreign Affairs posted bulletins in the English language part of their websites, claiming responsibility. Al Jazeera is carrying the same bulletin."

"Why just in English?" Joakim, Director of LAP, the psychological warfare department, demanded with a heavy frown. "I'd have thought they would be trumpeting this coup in Farsi."

Kameer shook his head. "I don't know, and right now, that's

not the issue. Given the fact that Iran *had* posted the bulletins, the American intelligence services will undoubtedly focus on establishing an evidence trail. It's only four a.m. in Washington and the American administration will only now be getting over the initial shock before considering likely response scenarios."

"I'll tell you what they'll be considering," Segan, Director of Research, declared, his coal black eyes and blocky features severe. He was Navy and a hawk, and relished the frontal approach. Hawk or not, he always backed his actions with solid planning. "How to hit Iran's nuclear facilities. Those ragheads have given President Walters a perfect excuse to go after them."

"Segan's right. And if they do that," Sanvel, the diminutive plug-shaped Director of Political Action and Liaison, added softly, "it is something we should have taken care of ourselves years ago."

"Just like when we hit the Syrian reactor at Al Kibar," Segan said with obvious satisfaction. "We should have dealt with Iran in the same way."

Joakim shook his head with clear disapproval, his jowls trembling. "Syria is weak and cannot retaliate. If America had not given us the nod, we wouldn't have gone in at all. Iran is a different matter altogether. They are far more capable, and if they wanted to strike at us, their Shahab-4s can do the job easily. They don't need nuclear warheads."

"It's the potential capability and what they would do with it that worries me," Sanvel snapped.

"Always the reactionary, eh?" Joakim sniped, his voice coming deep from a full chest and ample belly.

"And you analyze things too much!" Sanvel declared contemptuously. "What were we supposed to do? Allow the Syrians to build their reactor on the Golan Heights?"

Joakim wagged a warning finger. "If you would only stop and think, you'd realize it's not that simple. We should not have bombed Syria at all. Our preemptive strike policy simply reinforces international perception that we are intransigent and don't believe in the diplomatic process."

"The diplomatic process is a hollow reed with no substance," Sanvel retorted. "What has diplomacy done for us with the Palestinians? Push them out of the territories, I say, and end it once and for all!"

"Your naivety would be pathetic if it were not so dangerous," Joakim remarked sadly. "Attacking Iran would have far-reaching repercussions. At first glance, an attack might be seen as a desirable thing for us, but the situation would quickly go into meltdown were Iran to retaliate. And they would. For one, they could blockade the Strait of Hormuz and stop the flow of oil, or attack tankers. The effect on Western economies would be catastrophic, including ours."

Sanvel simply smirked and pointed a stubby finger at LAP. "The Americans will act and do us an invaluable strategic service, whatever the economic fallout."

"You're assuming a knee-jerk reaction. President Walters may be young and untested, but during his campaign, he proved himself to be knowledgeable and cool under pressure. Despite the latest sanctions against Iran, his overtures to Arab countries signals a major shift in foreign policy, something not necessarily in our best interest."

"With Houston in flames, he won't have a choice but to strike."

Kameer gave Sanvel an irritated glance, then looked hard at Joakim. "You examined scenarios to neutralize Iran's enrichment plants. What's changed your mind?"

The ex-Army general leaned toward the table, his olive face tense. "I'll tell you what's changed my mind. The mess in Iraq, Hamas winning government, Israel building a wall along the West Bank and growing militancy of Sunni extremists in Pakistan. Failure of America, Europe and the UN to secure a brokered deal for a recognized Palestinian state, that's what's changed my mind. Not that we've helped along the way."

Sanvel sat appalled as Joakim's voice hammered the room. "You're a traitor to start talking about giving up our sacred lands to the Arabs!"

"And you don't know your history," Joakim replied coldly. "Our problem with the Palestinians is that neither party is prepared to accept the other's right to national existence. The plain truth is, there will never be peace with the Arabs until hardliners in our own religious and military ranks are marginalized, and Israel becomes a genuine secular state."

"Blasphemy!" Sanvel pounded his hand against the table.

"My point exactly." Joakim nodded, his smile grim. "It is reactionaries like you who keep us from achieving peace."

Kameer cleared his throat. "Let's stick to the subject at hand, shall we? Joakim, I still want to know why you have a problem with Iran's attack."

Unfazed by Sanvel's outrage, Joakim slowly looked at the stony faces around him. "My problem is this. When you strip away the veil of superficial propaganda value, I've got to ask myself, why? Why would Iran attack America now, knowing that a response would certainly follow, one that would be endorsed by the entire world? Because America imposed sanctions of its own?"

"President Zerkhani did warn of consequences if anyone interfered with Iran's nuclear program," Joshin pointed out and Joakim nodded.

"Granted, but American sanctions don't constitute internal interference. I don't get it. Iran has spent billions on their nuclear infrastructure. And we are being asked to believe that they're willing to risk that by blowing up one small American refinery? What is their objective and what do they hope to gain? I cannot believe this is blind retaliation simply because of American sanctions.

The Council of Guardians is not that fanatical. Attacking Houston is against all military principles. We are missing something."

There was momentary silence before Kameer turned to Namir. "This is a briefing, but I am willing to entertain some discussion. What is your reading on all this?"

As the second-most senior department in Mossad, Collections being the largest, Namir's position carried with it enormous prestige and respect, albeit sometimes grudgingly given. Sanvel for one would not mind seeing him stumble. The little shit was only 160cm tall, but that in no way diminished the man's huge competence, ambition and capacity to irritate. Sanvel was also orthodox in his religious leanings, as he demonstrated just now, which tended to color his thinking, making him doubly dangerous. Too dangerous for the position he held.

"Without probing into possible Iranian objectives, operationally speaking, it appears to be a slick job and I agree with Segan completely. America is likely to hit Iran's nuclear facilities, and that, gentlemen, would be a good thing for us—whether we want to admit it or not. Joakim has raised some probing questions, which I am sure he will explore fully. The answers may be important for all of us. We can speculate on the likely political and economic fallout, but that's about it. We'll just have to wait and see how America reacts." He paused and looked directly at Kameer. "Apart from sharing this news with us, what's Mossad's position?"

The director frowned as every eye turned on him. Sanvel was an ongoing problem, as his reaction proved, something he would take up with the Prime Minister. He needed his director's objective or Mossad would become extremist, destroying its effectiveness as a rational instrument of national security. And Sanvel had demonstrated his proclivity for extreme responses once too often.

"We don't really have a role in this. If the CIA want our help, we'll give it to them. But it's not our operation. The ball, as they say, is in their court. However, I do want an assessment statement that I can take to the Prime Minister. Joakim, you've got two hours."

Joakim rolled his eyes in exasperation. "Give me a break! Sharron Ibrahim has a staff. They'll feed him what he wants to know."

"But maybe not what he needs to know," Kameer said softly and cleared his throat. "I want an objective assessment: threat scenarios, response options and likely impact on Israel, political and economic. How the PM uses that information will be up to him. Got that?"

"Okay, you'll have it," Joakim growled in resignation, irritated at having his department used for what he considered to be trivia.

"Fine. In the meantime, like you, I am keen to see the media reaction and analyses from the armchair pundits. If you ask me, we face some interesting times ahead of us."

Namir could not agree more as he stood up, giving Joakim a surreptitious glance. It would not do to underestimate the portly LAP director. The man had cut through the rhetoric and gone right to the heart of the issue. In the end, no matter what the psychology department director thought, Namir felt completely comfortable. Public opinion would exert enormous pressure on President Walters to strike, and whether he wanted to or not, his hand might be forced. Iranians, after all, were religious fanatics, not subject to logical analysis. He was sure this fact would frustrate everybody, including the Americans.

As long as that frustration did not prevent them from bombing Iran to hell, and that, Namir thought, was precisely what his plan relied on.

He was about to walk out when Kameer motioned with his hand for him to stay.

As the others left, they gave him curious glances, which would no doubt generate a stream of speculative gossip. Waiting outside, Rinah flashed Namir a look of encouragement before closing the door. He nodded to her and sat down, knowing exactly what was coming.

Kameer cleared his throat, evidently uncomfortable. He steeled himself and his eyes probed over Namir's emotionless features.

"I'll come straight to the point. What happened today is something we contemplated doing ourselves, in the same way we contemplate many scenarios. Ordinarily, I would not be concerned, but apart from some variations, Valero bears a striking resemblance to a scenario proposed by Matan Irian some time back."

"There is nothing wrong with your memory," Namir replied evenly. Nevertheless, his pulse picked up a bit. *Kraut bastard.* "We all produce scenarios, Doron. Most ended up shelved because they were impractical or would have resulted in negative consequences for Israel."

"Yes. Could be simple coincidence and the idea wasn't exactly novel. It's curious though, that Houston was hit at this particular moment."

"What's curious? American sanctions clearly irritated Al Zerkhani and he retaliated."

"It could be that simple, I agree, but Joakim has me thinking," Kameer said and cleared his throat.

Namir waited. *Come on, say it!*

Kameer shifted in his seat. "You know what I'm going to ask, don't you?"

"This is not my ops, Doron, if that's what's bothering you. But I'll tell you this. I would not have minded doing it myself. How about that!"

Kameer cleared his throat and nodded. "I know. You were vocal enough about it."

"That doesn't make me responsible."

The Mossad director's eyes remained leveled on him for several long seconds. "I needed to ask."

Namir stood up. "I know."

* * *

At precisely 6 a.m., President Samuel Walters walked down the stairs leading to the Situation Room, a floor beneath the Oval Office. An immaculately dressed Marine guard stood to and held the heavy wooden door open for him. Walters marched through without looking at him, eating up the distance in easy, youthful strides. There was a hurried scraping of chairs as everybody inside immediately stood up.

"Please, sit down," Walters invited amiably in his unmistakable radio announcer New England accent, taking his seat at the head of the long table. Opposite him, a giant LED screen, currently focused on Iran and the Persian Gulf, took up half the back wall. A smaller screen on either side showed the tactical disposition of U.S. forces around Europe and the Middle East. Behind the screens lay communications consoles, their solemn lights blinking occasionally. A faint whisper of airconditioning accompanied the silence as everyone respectfully waited for him to pour a cup of coffee, stirring in one sugar.

He had been in the Situation Room before, of course, but every time he came down into the dungeon, the place reminded him of a Radio Shack store. It had that same smell of electronics, large screens and background radio chatter. The place had something else, a pervasive stink of wood polish and shampooed carpet. He would speak to somebody about that.

Well, old son, he told himself, *you wanted to be the man in the White House and the Situation Room was an inescapable part of the package.* Quite a change from being a Senator, he chided himself. After four months into his presidency, the gloss and glamor was wearing thin alarmingly quickly. He didn't know which was worse, winning the presidency or having to move from Michigan. Cathy was still settling into life in the White House, his two girls as visitors, both already married, one living in New York and the other in Boston. Bush told him the novelty would never wear off. Cathy was getting more comfortable with the Secret Service protocols and he was yet to do the fun things like riding in Air Force One, holding ambassadorial functions and traveling abroad. But they didn't pay him to like it, he reminded himself, only to do it. *That's what you wanted, to change the world, didn't you?* He had no ready answer for that one. Still, he was only fifty-one, young enough to pick up the pieces even if he managed to get a second term nomination. But after eight years in the White House, would he want to play the lecture circuit? Still, Clinton seemed to be doing okay at it.

"Third cup of coffee and it's only six a.m.," Walters grumbled sourly after taking a sip. No one smiled. "Okay, let's sum it up. Manfred?"

Manfred Cottard, the White House chief of staff, blinked, marshalling his thoughts. After two harrowing years acting as Walters' campaign manager and political strategist, by the time the elections came around, he had enough. He should have stuck to running a Senate office. Fundraisers, buying votes, chartering the campaign through the primaries to secure the nomination, fielding dirty tricks, it all finally wore him out. It became worse when it dawned on the Democratic Party that with Walters, they could actually win. Election day was a letdown. All the exit polls showed Walters way ahead. That was when Cottard took Sam aside and told him the bad news. He must look elsewhere for his chief of staff. Cottard could not see himself lasting four years in the White House pressure cooker. He would go ragged. Walters listened, but the fact that Cottard *was* the chief of staff demonstrated Sam's skill as a negotiator and salesman. It hadn't turned out all bad, if you liked seventy-hour weeks. If things didn't work out, he could always go back to Wall Street on his own terms.

He rubbed the underside of his bulbous nose in a characteristic gesture and looked around at the assembled men. Absent were the National Director and the Deputy National Security Advisor for Combating Terrorism. In the previous administration, the National Director reported to the Assistant to the President for National Security Affairs. The National Director also reported to the Assistant to the President for Homeland Security on matters relating to global terrorism inside the United States. One of the first things Walters did when assuming office was to get rid of such layered bureaucracy—parasites feeding off each other.

"The local fire department has the outbreaks contained, with the exception of one three million-liter tank of gasoline. The surrounding storage tanks were pumped out and there is no danger of fire spreading. Burning fuel has entered the waterway, but the Port of Houston Authority is on top of it. FBI forensics are on the site. FEMA had a guy nosing around, but the FBI man on the ground threw him out."

"What's FEMA doing there?" Walters demanded. "Damnation! We don't have a disaster declaration."

"A case of overzealous enthusiasm," Cottard said with a wry smile.

Walters glanced at Patrick Marshal, FBI Director. "Give your guy a pat on the back." He looked at Cottard. "What else?"

"National Operations Center is in the loop and the director is flying down to Houston. Counterterrorism protocols are now in effect. However, as per your order, airport, rail and road services remain open."

"Mr. President," Marshal spoke quietly, which caused heads to turn, surprised at the interruption. "Was that wise? The perpetrators could still be in the country."

Walters returned the gaze evenly. "Tell me why I would want the transport system still running?"

The FBI director pulled at his chin, thinking about it, then nodded and looked up. "Target profile."

Vice Admiral Raymond Grant, CIA Director, looked confused. "What are you talking about?"

Marshal turned to Grant, examining him like a specimen in a petri dish, and finding him as uninteresting.

"Target profile. The attack on Valero targeted our infrastructure. Previous terrorist attacks on United States soil, namely the New York World Trade Center in 1993, Oklahoma City in 1995, the 1996 Olympic Games in Atlanta, and 9/11 in 2001, they all targeted civilians. With the exception of Atlanta, the perpetrators were willing to sacrifice themselves. That does not appear to be the case here."

"We don't know that!" Grant protested.

"No, we don't," Marshal replied equitably. "But I'll bet you my pension that we won't be finding any martyred bodies. Whoever carried this one out has flown." He looked at Walters and nodded. "Very good, Mr. President."

Walters shrugged and grinned. "It wasn't brilliance on my part, Pat. It's a case of being well briefed. Shutting down the transport system would have caused unwarranted disruption, chaos and panic. Definitely not in anyone's interest. Handling it this way transforms a seemingly terrorist industrial incident into one of united national outrage. Admittedly, the scenario involves a degree of political risk on my part if we fail to apprehend those responsible quickly, but that's something I can mitigate. And we do have a smoking gun of sorts. Okay, Manfred. What else?"

Cottard nodded. He'd had the same argument with Sam prior to the meeting, advocating a general shutdown, and lost. Then again, Walters was the President and he trusted Sam's political instincts.

"As of twenty minutes ago, Iran removed the news bulletins from their websites and are denying any involvement."

"I'll bet they are," Grant smirked and gave a heavy snort of disbelief.

Walters shot him a cold stare before turning to Manfred.

"Casualties?"

"Six refinery workers were caught in the initial explosion and subsequent fire. Two of them have died, including one fire-fighter. Two firefighters were burned, but they'll be okay. One of the injured workers isn't likely to make it. The others carry vary-ing degrees of burns. Apart from some blown windows, we don't have any civilian casualties." Cottard finished his brief and waited as Walters sipped.

Walters put down his cup and looked unflinchingly at his friend. "Well, that's something. The people that were hurt, what-ever they need, see that they get it."

"Yes, Mr. President."

"We'll cover all expenses, and that goes for the funerals. I also want you to start looking at compensation. I don't want this dragged through the bureaucracy. Another thing. I want the in-surance companies to honor all claims. I don't want another New Orleans on my hands. If those bastards start playing games with the fine print, I'll have the IRS nail their hides to the wall. See that they get the message. And arrange for me to talk to the vic-tim's families."

"Yes, sir."

So, the commander-in-chief *was* obeyed, Walters thought with sardonic amusement. But this was chipping away at the edges. Now it got serious. He turned his attention to Lieutenant General (Ret.) Colin Forbes.

"Ever since it was set up the Department of Homeland Secu-rity has come in for a lot of flak from everybody, including me. All that manpower and money, Colin, I want to see it work. NOC…Mark Price, isn't it?"

"Yes, Mr. President," Forbes confirmed. The man *was* well briefed.

"How good is he?"

Forbes lifted his chin, daring anyone to contradict him. "I re-cruited him myself."

Grant muttered something and shook his head. Walters frowned. "You want to share that with the rest of us, Admiral?"

Two small red spots appeared on Grant's cheeks. "The man is not a team player, Mr. President, and I don't tolerate insubordination."

"And that's why you got rid of him, I know," Walters finished for him, his voice frigid. "I don't tolerate insubordination either, Admiral. Whatever Price wants, he gets. Are we clear on that?"

"Clear enough." Grant obviously didn't like it, but was smart enough not to make it an issue right then. And Price was going to get precisely what was coming to him. In his opinion the man was a carry-outer, not a thinker-upper. Landing a job as head of NOC was simply outrageous.

"Good. That goes for you, too," Walters said, looking pointedly at Trent Bruster, Director, National Security Agency. Grant and Bruster were like flints, always striking sparks off each other. But then, there has always been an intense rivalry between the CIA and the NSA. Right now though, he had no time for that nonsense.

"I don't have a problem with that and I agree with Colin. Price is a good man," Bruster said evenly in his Texas drawl, trying hard not to look at Grant.

The CIA turd always gave him a burr up his butt. Grant had been an incompetent as a flag officer and he was proving to be equally incompetent managing the disparate factions within the CIA. He heard, everyone had, about the dustup Price had with that twitch Zardwovsky. The National Clandestine Service director was Grant's protégé and thought the sun rose and set on the fat little shit. Given such opposition, Price never had a chance. Well, one could only hope the new president would see through the smoke and mirrors and fire both their asses.

Walters nodded. "If I hear that we're turf fighting on this one, there are going to be some involuntary retirements. We have a test case scenario here, damn it, and I want to see everyone performing as advertised. You all know that I campaigned to streamline the intelligence services. There are too many overlapping organizations running around in the same circle and you guys are now in a rut. This is your opportunity to prove me wrong."

Walters noted the solemn expressions before him with satisfaction, certain the point had gotten home. If it hadn't, there was still his threat, which he fully intended to carry out. DHS for one would be coming in for a very close look. The previous administration somehow allowed that monster to get out of hand, wasting billions of dollars without producing any returns. He directed his gaze on the figure at the far end of the table.

"Okay, Graham, any indicators that I'm missing to suggest that Iran was about to hit us?"

Retired Vice Admiral Graham Stone, National Security Advisor, witnessed the altercation between Grant and the president with amusement. Grant was walking on thin ice, and if he wasn't careful, was going to fall through. He held the president's eyes without blinking. He did not like some of Walters' policies, domestic or foreign. In his view the Democratic Party was deliberately isolating the country from the world's stage, focusing America inward—a bad course of action given Chinese and Indian growing insurgence on the world's economic and consequently, political arena. In his opinion, that's what it was, a gladiator arena that encompassed the entire planet. America either carved out a place in that arena or started taking orders from somebody else, orders not necessarily in its best interest. Still, the president had economic advisors who would hopefully be telling him the same thing. But would he listen? The man was smart, but even the smart ones could be deluded.

"There is nothing on my board, Mr. President. Despite sometimes vitriolic rhetoric against the West and the United States especially, which I suggest might be aimed for domestic consumption more than anything, Al Zerkhani is a progressive thinker and a moderate; at least by their standards. He campaigned on that platform and enjoys considerable popular support, particularly from the younger elements of the population. He did bring genuine social and economic reform, something not always welcomed by entrenched interests, and the Council of Guardians seem happy to give him his head, for now at least. Only one thing stands out. Last month the UN authorized increased sanctions against Iran for refusing inspection of its nuclear facilities by the International Atomic Energy Agency. The United States went a step further when you announced unilateral sanctions. That could have been the trigger."

"And you argued against it, I know. Are you saying Valero was a message? Lay off or we'll cripple your oil infrastructure, is that it?" Walters demanded softly.

"It is possible, sir. As Marshal pointed out, civilians were not the target."

"They cannot be playing that game. They are far too vulnerable themselves. Their whole economy is oil based. We remove Kharg Island and a bunch of their platforms in the Gulf and they're history."

"I agree, sir, and that's part of the problem. We all know Iran's been playing us for suckers with their on-off IAEA inspections, while lobbying the Europeans to go softly or risk jeopardizing their commercial interests in the country. So far the tactic has worked. Every time we talk about sanctions in the Security Council, the Europeans howl, and any initiative that does get approved is so diluted, we don't get anywhere. Meanwhile, Iran continues to pursue its strategic objective to secure a nuclear capability. It is one of the arguments you used for imposing sanctions, meaning no disrespect. Lest we forget, it is also worth reminding everybody that it's the Russians who are building the Bushehr reactor for them."

"The Russians don't relish a nuclear Iran any more than we do," Bruster pointed out. "This could be a simple commercial venture."

"It could," Stone agreed. "And building an enrichment facility could be part of the same package."

"Your conclusion being?" Walters prompted, always ready to listen to Stone. The man could be irritating, even infuriating, but he could not fault the Admiral's incisive analyses.

"Let's face it, Mr. President. A nuclear industry has many flow-on effects, economic as well as military. Our sanctions merely reinforce the perception of a Western nuclear club, which Iran has exploited successfully. Because the tactic was working, it makes no sense for them to strike at us now. They were getting everything they wanted already. They might be concerned with the previous administration's rhetoric and preparedness to take unilateral military action against their facilities, but you campaigned against perpetuating any such policy. That must have given them a measure of reassurance. A strike against Valero is an open invitation for you to do that very thing. Even if I take into account the extremist position of the Council of Guardians, this attack simply doesn't make any tactical sense. Given the vulnerability of their own infrastructure, why provoke us into a retaliatory response? How does that further their strategic objective to develop a layered defense?"

"I'll tell you how. They want to trigger an open Shi'ia conflict throughout the Middle East and conduct a strike against Israel, their ultimate objective," Raymond Grant said softly, looking at the incredulous faces around him.

Walters allowed the silence to linger for several seconds. "You can't be that shallow, Admiral. Discounting their existing Shahab-4 inventory, your position demands that Iran already possesses nuclear weapons." His comment caused another stir.

Grant nodded, burning from the rebuke. "That's right, Mr. President. It does."

"And you have indication of that?"

Grant sighed and shook his head. "No, sir. I am postulating

that those weapons were not domestically produced. They don't have the capability, we all know that."

"Comments?" Walters glanced around the table.

Bruster snorted. "That's a ridiculous suggestion, Mr. President. NSA hasn't had a sniff of signals intelligence to suggest that Iran has acquired clandestine warheads. And there is only one place where such weapons could be sourced. With rising oil and gas revenues, the Russians are not scrambling for hard dollars anymore and are not crazy enough to sell old MIRVs to Muslims. Their Muslim-dominated eastern states are unstable as it is and a nuclear Iran would be a nightmare for them. I'm not saying that they haven't sold Iran MIRVs. I'm saying that there is no evidence to support such a proposition, unless Grant has HUMINT that he's not sharing, and it wouldn't be the first time."

Grant sat up and glared. "Now, just a minute!"

Walters raised both arms. "Hold it! If you guys cannot cooperate, those retirements can start right now. Clear?"

Grant cast a simpering look at Bruster before catching Walters' cold stare. "I apologize, Mr. President."

Stone tapped the table with long fingers. "We should consider another scenario, Mr. President. I maintain that Iran is not pursuing a nuclear capability to threaten Israel. They are probably more worried about Pakistan and the threat posed by installation of a Taliban-style sectarian Sunni regime. As you know, the Afghanistan campaign isn't doing very well. The Taliban are surging again and NATO is pulling back support. As are we."

Walters nodded. "I am not unaware of that problem, Graham, but how does that factor into Iran's attack on us?"

"The Iranian and Al Jazeera websites were telling me one thing and the Iranian government is telling us something else. I'm saying it might not be them at all."

The comment raised a babble of protest. Walters banged his palm against the table and silence returned.

"This is an open forum and I will entertain *every* scenario, however extreme. Given what is at stake, we cannot afford not to. Admiral Grant?"

The CIA boss squirmed, clearly not relishing the attention. "I acknowledge the possibility, Mr. President."

"Have someone research it. Manfred, how is Wall Street likely to react?"

The White House chief of staff frowned. "Hard to say, as we don't know what the trend drivers will be. Emotions will be running high, and contrary to popular belief, the market is emotion driven. Gold is likely to go up as are the oil futures. Everyone will be scrambling to top up their reserves, which could cause OPEC to raise prices. The dollar may take a hit as the market waits for us to take a position. Provided we don't say anything rash, I don't expect Dow Jones to dip all that much."

"You mean if I don't say anything rash," Walters said and gave a deep sigh. "I hope you're right. We are just getting out of the sub-prime mortgage debacle left by the previous administration. The economy doesn't need another jolt. Okay, let's sum it up. Valero is contained. The FBI are on site and hopefully will get us some evidence on which we can act. Iran has denied involvement. That could be a red herring or a genuine expression of innocence. Before I can move, we must determine which it is. Congress will reflect prevailing public opinion and demand that I respond militarily. I cannot blame them for that. And I *want* to slam the bastards responsible. So, this is what I want done.

"Manfred, get the Cabinet together for a nine o'clock brief. We'll use the Roosevelt Room. I want the Communications Director to draw up a statement for the Press Secretary to use in his ten o'clock gaggle. I will follow it with a statement of my own. We'll give them the facts as we know them, condemning Iran and committing to a strike if we find them responsible. Is that rash enough?"

"Sounds good, Mr. President," Cottard said with a wry smile.

"I want this handled nice and tight, and above all, we must project calm and avoid a feeding frenzy by lending credence to suggestions of a knee-jerk counterstrike; especially with everybody twitchy and ready to jump. Get Prichard in the loop. I want him pounding the table in the Security Council. Then get hold of the French ambassador. Request that they call President Hamadee Al Zerkhani. I want a no-bullshit meeting with someone from his government, and I want it today. Suggest Paris as neutral ground. That should stroke their vanity, and it's in their own interest that we get to the bottom of this. Zerkhani must be told in no uncertain terms that I'll blow his ass if he refuses. I'll put his country into the Stone Age. This could conceivably be an internal MOIS operation, unknown to the government, however unlikely. Either way, he must convince me that Iran had nothing to do with this."

"I'll get on it, Mr. President."

"To cover all bases, advise the Chairman of the Joint Chiefs to put *Nimitz* and the *Dwight D. Eisenhower* carrier groups on ready alert. *Nimitz* will hold the fort until relieved by the missile-guided carrier USS *Antietam*, due when?"

"Two weeks."

"More than enough time to settle this. There is to be no violation of Iranian airspace or their territorial waters. Apart from that, the carriers are free to exercise their air wings and covering fleets as they see fit. If the Iranians squawk, that's just tough, but under the circumstances, I don't think they will."

"I'll see to it," Cottard acknowledged.

"Good." Walters focused on Grant and Bruster. "I want the CIA and the NSA to sift through anything and everything that could conceivably have a bearing on what has happened, no matter how outrageous. If it's not Iran, somebody else could indeed be pushing our buttons. When you find something, Price and Marshal are in the loop and Graham is your point man to me."

The President stood up and everybody followed suit. "I want

answers, gentlemen, and I want them now."

Chapter Five

Tom gulped down the last of the tepid, bitter coffee, screwed his face in distaste and placed the Styrofoam cup on the '80s style pale green laminated kitchen table. The canteen, looking like any other canteen he had seen, was on the western side of the building, and although the air smelled of gasoline and burnt wood, it had escaped the fire itself. At one end was the usual serving counter, soda vending machines, glassed-off partitions that held hot food and a checkout. Two women served anyone who happened to want anything. Tonight, it was on the house, courtesy of Valero Refinery. Utilitarian tables held the usual salt, pepper, sugar, sauces and tissue dispensers. As a makeshift command post, it did the job, but he needed to get back downtown. He had spent enough time crawling around this godforsaken place, and if he saw any more piping and smelled more crude oil, it would break his heart. It was almost enough for him to swear off driving. The prospect of another long day and missed sleep did not exactly make him feel all fuzzy with enthusiasm either.

A couple of tables away, three firemen, bulky in their orange gear and air tanks, helmets stacked on the floor, quietly sipped their coffee, watching ABC on a large LED screen mounted on the opposite wall. It was the same stuff on all news channels: shots of the burning refinery, fire tenders milling about, and anchor experts on this and that providing one-liner solutions. All the fires were now out, with the exception of one three million-liter tank still blazing away gamely along Canal Road. The way he heard it, the flames were being smothered by a layer of suppression foam that slowly strangled the fire. Another couple of hours and it too would be out. Then it was simply a matter of mopping up the mess. At least none of the adjacent tanks had caught, for which everybody was extremely thankful, especially Selek. A fuel slick came dangerously close to a moored tanker in the fairway, but prompt action by the Port of Houston Authority emergency services and some strategically placed booms kept the situation in hand. Five hours and the disaster was contained. When Tom drove in, he would not have believed it possible. It went to prove his philosophy that people were generally mean bastards, but when it came time to pitch in and help, they came out shining. Go figure.

Tom's eyes lingered on the three firemen murmuring among themselves, their drawn, haggard, smudged faces telling their own tragic story. The worst was over, but the effort had cost two of their own. The fire chief walked in, helmet under his arm, and Tom waved. The older man's scowl cast a gloomy cloud over his face as he moved wearily between tables. He pulled back a metal-legged chair with a prolonged scrape and plopped himself onto it, giving a huge sigh. A middle-aged woman, wearing a dark green dress bearing the Valero logo on her left breast, hurried toward him holding a glass carafe of coffee and a handful of cups. Without saying a word, she filled one and handed it over. The fire chief nodded.

"Thanks," he said and took a thirsty pull without adding cream or sugar. Tom gaped at him. The coffee must be scalding. Before the woman could walk away, he held out the cup for a refill. This time, he took a slow sip and grunted with satisfaction. "I needed that."

"So I gathered," Tom said with a wan smile. "Everything under control?"

"Yeah, we're on top of it." The fire chief glanced at the retreating woman. "Got to hand it to Selek. He did okay for a pencil driver." He eyed Tom for one speculative second. "Your guys didn't let weeds grow under their feet either."

Tom figured that was about all the accolade he would get from the man and grinned. "Couldn't, even if they wanted to. I've got Washington burning fires of their own under my butt."

"Hah! What's to worry? Iran admitted to doing it. It's just a matter of creaming the bastards, right?"

"It's not that simple, I'm afraid."

"Yeah. You need solid evidence. So, your guys find anything?"

"We identified four explosion sites and that's about it. There are some metal fragments that could be remnants of control box casings, but we won't be sure until we analyze the stuff. I don't know what good that will do anyway. Whoever hit this place didn't leave an ID. They were pros."

"You're not expecting to catch anybody, then?"

Tom grinned. "Would you hang around after this?"

The fire chief snorted and sipped his coffee. "But you've got to go through the motions, I know," he muttered without much sympathy.

"I don't want bodies. I need evidence," Tom complained. "If these were normal explosions, my chances of finding something would be better. But this scenario sucks. Fire destroyed everything. Anything left has probably been washed away by tons of suppression foam. Not that I'm blaming your guys. Still, we could get lucky." His cellphone went off and he palmed the handset. "Meecham."

"It's Brian. I thought I'd cheer you up. We found an intact explosives package, timer and all."

"Christ!"

"We're trying to disarm it now."

Tom thought that over. Brian Peters was head of his forensic team and damn good at what he did. If he thought they could disarm the package without having to wait for bomb disposal, Tom wasn't about to blow smoke his way. He liked his people to use initiative and did not believe in giving unnecessary orders or making a nuisance of himself.

"Where are you?"

"Number three cracking tower. The thing was stuck under a feeder pipe. Would have brought the whole thing down had it gone off." Peters paused and Tom could almost see the grin on the man's face. "You'll like this. There is Arabic writing on the faceplate."

"I'll be right over." Tom snapped the lid of his phone shut and smiled broadly.

The fire chief looked at him and chuckled. "I gather you got lucky?"

"Big time. They found one of the charges and it's got Arabic writing all over it."

"No shit?"

"It appears a fault prevented the thing from going off. That's not to say it won't once we start fooling around with it."

"Hah! So, if I hear a bang, I'll know why."

Tom frowned and shook his head, not amused by the gallows humor. "You've got a cruel streak in you, did you know that?"

"Yeah, I've been told," the chief agreed cheerfully, playing with his cup.

Tom stood up and dusted off his trousers. "You better send somebody to number three cracking tower. Just in case."

"You got it."

Tom nodded and walked toward the exit. Outside, it was still dark, but the eastern sky was starting to color, the cloud layer a sullen yellow, reflecting light from the complex and the city. A thin wind gusted fresh from the sea and he rubbed his hands. As he crossed 14th Street, he spotted one of the forensic men waiting for him.

"This way, Mr. Meecham," the youngster chirped and hurried down a gravel path dividing the refinery from the still smoldering tank farm.

They turned off the path and made their way past running piping and small towers. A large fractionation tower loomed before them, lit by floodlights mounted at several levels. There was a squeal of brakes behind him and Tom turned. A fire tender was pulling up. Four men spilled out and started wrestling a long hose. One of them waved and began walking toward him.

"Mr. Meecham?"

"That's me."

"We were told that we have an explosive device situation here."

"That's right. Follow me."

"Don't we want to wait for bomb disposal or something?"

"We're handling it," Tom said briskly.

"If you say so. I just don't want to be around if that thing decides to go off. You hear?"

"Loud and clear." Tom turned and motioned to the forensic youngster.

Around more pipes and they were there. When Peters saw Tom, he said something to one of his men and hurried over. He stopped, smiled and held out gloved hands with two plastic specimen bags. One had a rectangular black metal box and the other looked like a slice of butter encased in a green wrapper.

"We got it," Peters announced with evident satisfaction. "Must have been a circuit short. We'll know more once I get it back to the lab."

"Good work," Tom said warmly, eyeing the bags. "I'm going back now myself. You're welcome to tag along."

"I'll do that, thanks. It will give me a chance to start looking more closely at other pieces we found. I don't expect much, but with this thing, we don't need more."

"If you found one, there could be others," Tom pointed out. "Maybe on delayed timers."

"I know. The rest of my team will keep sniffing until they've covered every inch of this place."

Tom turned to the fireman standing patiently behind him. "It doesn't appear that you'll be needed after all, but thanks anyway."

"No problem." The fireman nodded to the others and they

immediately went about hauling the hose back toward the truck. Tom watched them go and looked at Brian.

"Okay, let's go."

At the parking lot, he pulled up a police cruiser as it was easing itself out. The driver wound down the window and waited for Tom to catch up.

"Do you know the FBI offices at East TC Jester?" Tom demanded and the officer nodded.

"Yes, sir. Been there a number of times."

"Great. I'll want you to run interference for us, lights and siren. It's Monday morning and I don't want to get stuck in the crush."

"Ah, I'll have to clear that through Captain Travers, sir."

"While you're doing it, you can roll her out, officer." Tom ambled to his car and got in. Brian slid in beside him and pulled the door shut.

The heavy Pontiac moved behind the police cruiser and Tom waited. Suddenly the cruiser's blue and red roof lights came on and the car slowly turned toward the exit. He suppressed a yawn, eased into gear and followed. Price was due at the office by ten o'clock; plenty of time for Tom to go home, grab a shower, have some breakfast and be back in time to hold NOC's hand.

He was at a loss what to tell Price, but with a demolition charge in hand, he hoped Brian would have something solid for him to chew on by the time the man showed up. He also had a talk with the Joint Terrorism Task Force and Field Intelligence Group team leaders, but the guys were just getting their act together, still coordinating with NOC, the CIA and NSA. Knowing how those agencies operated, he did not expect much action for a day or so, no matter what heat Washington piled on. These things took patience and time. He knew. He also knew that in this case both would be in short supply for everybody. The TV and papers would be full of nothing else, with chair analysts pontificating learnedly, demanding instant retaliation regardless of consequences. That way, of course, they could have it both ways while the public tried to make sense of it all, stuck in traffic, listening to their radios, hoping that gas wouldn't go up at the pump.

Tom felt slightly sorry for Samuel Walters, new into the White House and still feeling his way, but not so sorry that he was choked up or anything. Still, the president would want answers and would want them fast. With everybody screaming to bomb the shit out of Iran, Walters would be damned no matter what he did or didn't do. Well, that's why the man got paid the big bucks.

It turned 7 a.m. when they took the I-45 toward Houston and the police cruiser switched on its siren. This early, traffic was still relatively light as they roared past the flow in the fast left lane, cars ahead of them obediently moving into the slower center lane. Cloaked in gold, Houston's jagged skyline stood sharp against a steel sky. The towers glared bright from reflected light, making driving uncomfortable and tricky. Tom reached into a tray behind the gear lever and pulled out his shades, then blinked with relief after slipping on the tinted glasses. His brain in neutral, he followed the wailing police cruiser, thinking about nothing in particular. A sudden craving for a bacon and egg sandwich made his mouth water. He glanced at his passenger, but Brian was dozing, oblivious to the world, head on his chest. He wished he had Brian's easy conscience. The soft drone of the engine and the soothing whisper of tires made Tom yawn again.

The I-45 skirted downtown and they headed northwest. Traffic thinned, most of it now on the opposite carriageway heading into the city. Indicator blinking, the cruiser slowed, pulled right into the I-160 off-ramp and cars scattered before its siren. I-160 was heavy both ways, taking a direct east-west route across the city. A couple of miles farther, the cruiser turned into East TC Jester Boulevard. Trees lined the left side, casting heavy shadows. On the right, residential housing crowded the edge. A block beyond the turnoff, the police car switched off its lights and siren and swung left into Pinegate Drive. Clad in reflective blue glass the saw-tooth three-story main FBI building threw a large shadow over manicured lawns. The two-story parking block beside it gaped with vacant spots. The police cruiser turned right into the circular entrance and stopped. Tom pulled up beside it and wound down his window.

"Much appreciated, officer. Thanks."

The cop waved at him and the cruiser moved off. Tom shook Brian's shoulder.

"Wakey, wakey."

Peters blinked and stared vacantly before recognition ignited a spark of life in his eyes. "We there already?"

"End of the road, pal," Tom confirmed brightly. "You go and do your thing while I zip on home for a few minutes to click my eyeballs back in. I'll be back by nine o'clock or so."

"Don't fall asleep in the shower," Peters quipped, climbed out and waved.

"And you don't talk to anybody, and don't flash those samples around," Tom warned as he shifted the gear lever into 'Drive' and moved off. It was asking a lot to keep the lid on this, but he did not want idle gossip or unsubstantiated rumors ending up in the media.

He drove east along Jester for a couple of blocks, then turned right into Ella Boulevard and a right again into West 18th Street. Three blocks down, he made a left and a right into the leafy Hoverhill Drive. Green lawns, mature trees, well-kept houses, clean sidewalks—an oasis of peace and quiet. He pulled into the driveway of his single-story weatherboard house, black tar shingles sparkling in morning light, and paused, hands on the steering wheel. With a weary sigh, he got out and slammed the door. Overhead the sky was a brilliant blue, unmarked by any cloud, a perfect day to be mowing the lawn or fixing that sagging gutter at the back. Mowing the lawn, he could do, but he reminded himself to call the estate agent again to have the gutter fixed. He was getting a bit tired having water sluice down the side every time it rained hard. He could do the job himself, but after all, the place was only a rental and he was not about to sink money and time into something not his own.

It was cold inside and the rooms echoed his lonely footsteps on the polished oak floors. With Malena gone, some of the warmth seemed to have gone with her. Christ! This wasn't the time to start feeling sorry for himself. He headed for the bedroom.

It was about 9 a.m. by the time he got himself cleaned up, fed and looking crisp again. He knew that by nightfall, the day would catch up with him, but he could face the prospect with a measure of equanimity. By the time he drove back to the office and parked the car in his reserved spot, the dashboard clock read 9:15. Not too shabby for government work, he thought comfortably. The FBI building was almost full, everyone buzzing with the latest news. When he stepped into the kitchenette for a cup, several of his colleagues waylaid him for information. After a while, he got tired of repeating himself and hosing down wild speculation, and fled to his second-floor office. He was logging on when the phone went off.

"Meecham," he growled.

"It's Charles," the voice on the line announced with a heavy rasp.

Charles Beltrain was in charge of the Houston Division office, a great administrator and liked to stick his nose into an interesting case from time to time. Tom didn't hold it against him; once a law enforcement officer, always a cop, unless you were turned and became a bureaucrat or political manipulator. In a gush of rare generosity, he acknowledged the need for both animals.

"I just got in," he announced, hoping the boss didn't want a meeting or something.

"I know, and I'll keep out of your hair, Tom. I've chatted with Bruce Wellard and I am happy with his recommendation to keep you in charge."

"Thanks, I appreciate that."

And Tom did. He did not particularly relish engaging in office politics, but he had learned the moves and played it with all the professional coolness he applied to one of his cases. It hadn't taken him long to understand that to get ahead, he needed to reach for any opportunity as it presented itself and grab it. No one would hand him anything for being a nice guy. These days, there was no a market for nice guys.

"I've also spoken to Dr. Peters," Charles went on, "but he wouldn't tell me anything. Your orders, I suppose. Don't worry. I'm happy to leave him alone. I understand that Mark Price from DHS is due here at any moment."

"That's right. I'm expecting him around ten."

"I won't pry, but bring him up when you've finished with him, will you?" Charles ordered and the line went dead.

Tom stared at the receiver and placed it in its cradle. "I'll do that," he murmured.

After taking a sip of coffee, he finished logging on. There was the usual list of emails, some administrative, technical updates, a reminder for him to change his access password, and one each from heads of the JTTF and FIG. That meant a meeting with both after seeing Price. And NOC would probably want to be in on that as well. Using Outlook, he booked a conference room for 11:30 a.m. and sent the invites. Acceptance acknowledgments came back almost immediately. He nodded with satisfaction and got stuck into cleaning up the email list, while his brain sorted through procedures he would want to apply to this case. It was complicated.

He jerked when the phone rang, startled that it was already past ten o'clock.

"Meecham."

"Security, sir. There is a Mark Price here to see you."

"Thanks. I'll be right down." He replaced the receiver and

stood up. "Well, this is it," he muttered firmly, exhaled loudly and strode from the office, making for the elevators.

On the ground floor, he faced four electronic entrance portals, a security desk on his left with two guards and a wall of tinted glass that was the entrance. The gray-tiled stone foyer was almost deserted. A nervous youngster sitting on a blue couch set against the right wall looked around, his fingers working themselves into a knot. A hopeful recruit, perhaps. When he saw Tom, he made to stand up, but the effort was stillborn when Tom looked away. Two dark-suited agents were walking toward the entrance, deep in conversation. Heavy glass doors slid out of their way.

Tom took in his surrounds with a single glance, his attention on the tall individual waiting beside the security desk. Lean, hard-featured, dark brown hair brushed straight back, powerful hands; the impressions portrayed a man who had seen action, faced death and walked away to talk about it. The tasteful dark blue suit, deep yellow tie and silver cufflinks, also showed the worldly side of the man. Competence and confidence was written all over him. Tom was tall, but this guy topped him by at least an inch.

The man turned as Tom walked between two access portals, his visitor badge pinned to his left breast, and smiled, showing even white teeth. The large, almost violet eyes lit up with genuine friendliness. But there was something else in those eyes that Tom recognized, a glint of hardness that only came after one was tested under fire. He ought to know. Malena also remarked several times, when snuggled together in pillow talk, that he had that same glint.

Tom stuck out his hand. "You must be Mark Price."

Price grasped the proffered hand hard and they shook. No one tried for the juvenile knuckle-crusher grip.

"And you must be Tom Meecham."

"Guilty," Tom said, returning the smile, liking Price immediately. The NOC boss definitely appeared like someone with a mission, for which he was grateful. He had dreaded the prospect of working with some bureaucratic, political hairsplitting Washington weenie. What he saw of Price confirmed his initial assessment. He nodded to the guards and pulled Price's elbow toward the portals. He slid his badge against the sensor. It beeped, turned green and he was through. Price repeated the procedure.

"We'll go up to my office first," Tom said, waiting for the elevator. "I've arranged a meeting with JTTF and FIG for 11:30. Once we're done, I'll take you up to see Beltrain. He'll want to glad-hand you and tell you that the whole thing will be wrapped up by tomorrow morning. But don't let it fool you. The man is sharp."

Mark chuckled in acknowledgment. He had done his homework on all Houston's key personnel, including Meecham. So far, the senior agent was living up to expectations. They were all straight shooters here, and on a job like this, that didn't bother him at all. They would get along.

"Like you?" he ventured, testing the waters of familiarity.

Tom looked up and raised a quizzical eyebrow. "Nobody is like me," he said and Price laughed with delight. They would *definitely* get along.

"That irreverent attitude must go down well in some circles."

"Christ! Like that keeps me awake."

On the second floor, Tom led his visitor to the kitchenette where they fueled up. A couple of his colleagues made to butt in, but he froze them with a glance. In his office, he invited Price to make himself comfortable, giving the NOC boss a close look.

"You haven't wasted any time coming down here," he remarked casually, implying with thinly veiled subtlety that Price was now playing in his sandbox.

Mark grinned, understanding the inference immediately and not resenting it at all. As far as the FBI was concerned, what could he value add that would make a difference?

"The President calls Colin Forbes and Colin calls me. You can add up the rest."

Tom rolled his eyes. "And I thought *we* were like that. How did you get here so fast?"

"They gave me a Gulfstream V to ferry me around."

"That must be comfortable. Okay, down to cases. I'm not going to play the good news, bad news shit. But before we get started, let's sort out the question of jurisdiction."

Mark nodded, expecting it. "Fine, go ahead."

"We have an apparent case of terrorism on United States soil—"

"You said 'apparent'?"

"Habit. The Iranians might have done it, but I'm not taking anybody's word for that until I have all the pieces spread out in front of me."

Mark didn't say anything, but he was relieved. Meecham knew what he was doing and would not allow whatever personal feelings or external opinions on the matter interfere with his professional approach.

"An apparent case, like I said," Tom went on, "which makes it FBI property. I'm in charge. As the overall coordinator between the FBI and other agencies, if you can smooth my way and field Washington, then I'm your eternal slave. I have operational authority and you have strategic—until we disagree. Strategically, our objective is the same, namely to catch the bastards, or at least pin the blame on somebody."

Mark's smile was broad, but his eyes were not laughing. "I gather you don't have much time for the Department of Homeland Security." He made it a statement.

"Internal security has always been the FBI's responsibility, Mr. Price."

"And no Washington weenie is about to tell you otherwise, right?"

"If you like."

Mark took a sip of coffee and nodded. "This is your case, Tom, and I have no intention of telling you how to go about sorting it out. My job is to see that it *does* get sorted out. It is also my job to help you in any way I can, which includes making sure that NSA, the CIA and anyone else gives you whatever information they have, no questions asked. If you run into a brick wall, I'm the man to tear it down. If something squeaks, I'll pour oil on it. Fair enough?"

"I like it," Tom said instantly and leaned forward. "Of course you know, to do our job, we'll probably end up rubbing some people the wrong way."

A happy smile lit Mark's face. "Yeah, ain't that a bitch?"

With the hard part out of the way, Tom allowed himself to relax. He understood the theoretical reasoning behind Bush's decision to set up DHS, but thought the approach created more problems than it solved. And so far, they hadn't solved anything. The FBI had the mechanisms, procedures and protocols already in place. With additional authority to cut across inter-agency bullshit, they could handle any terrorism or counterterrorism threat. If that weren't enough, Bush went and created the National Counterterrorism Center, everybody spinning the same wheels. With DHS, all he managed to achieve was to spawn another monster bureaucracy, hated by everybody. The first time it needed to perform, DHS fell flat on its collective face. Katrina showed FEMA to be a fumbling tiger, and by extension, the entire DHS. All that manpower, analyses, projections, reports and political point scoring down the gurgler when it came to the crunch. The organization simply wasn't set up to handle operational incidents. He sincerely hoped Walters would do away with that paper shuffling factory and allow the FBI to get on with the job, a view shared by many within the Bureau. Price seemed prepared to let him do just that, provided, of course, Meecham got results.

Why didn't Beltrain pick somebody else? Tom would have been happy chasing some interstate murderer or dope pusher. His inner self sneered at him for being a coward. If he wanted a soft job, he should have gone to Wal-Mart.

All right, let's see if he had the right stuff to play with the grownups.

"Having gotten that out of the way—" he began, but Price cut him off.

"Some background facts for you. NSA has started a SIGINT sweep for any domestic or foreign communication that might have a bearing on this. The CIA is in the loop, doing the same thing from their HUMINT sources. That will take time, and I don't know whether the President will let us have it. On the home front, airports, rail and bus services were asked to give us their weekend surveillance tapes. My bet is on George Bush International. If Iran did pull this off, whoever was on the ground would not want to linger. I certainly wouldn't. Langley will be running faces against their database trying for a match. It's a long shot, I know, but it's a start. Even if they fled the country, we'll be able to go after them and give them a package of our own."

"I would like to see that," Tom said and nodded with approval. Price obviously had not been wasting time either, something he appreciated. "And I've got an item of my own that should cheer up your day. The bad guys left us a present."

"Oh?"

"Yep. An intact demolition package."

"Well, crap!" Price pursed his lips in a silent whistle. "This is really good news."

"I thought that would make you all soft and gooey."

"From your smug expression, I gather it's got Arabic writing?"

"All over it. The lab downstairs are looking at it right now."

"Who knows about this?"

"Beltrain."

"By now, that means everybody," Price mused and Tom shrugged.

"Probably. It's not something we could have compartmentalized. Not in time, anyway."

"Okay, that's one piece of the puzzle, but there are still many empty slots."

"You got it. But like you said, will the administration wait for us to fill them before they act?"

"I'm just glad it's not my call," Price said with feeling. "Your JTTF and FIG teams. I want them plugged into all agencies. I'll set up the communications protocols they will need."

"You can brief them when we meet," Tom offered, "but they've started the ball rolling already."

"Good. I'll remain here for the rest of the day to make sure you're happy with the agency pipelines and the information taps are turned on. Press statements come from me, but if you get waylaid on the sidewalk, tell them the investigation is proceeding and to call my office for details. As for reporting back to me, I won't be breathing down your neck, but I will want to know what is going on: problems, issues or bottlenecks, in order to handle Washington and be in a position to help you. I'll also want copies of your evidence: photos, notes, the usual stuff."

"That's fair enough," Tom agreed. "I'll call or email. If I call, it will mean I want action pronto."

"No problem."

"Right! Let's go down to the lab for the latest." Tom stood up.

Price did the same, walked to the door and turned. "Your lab. Is there anything you need?"

"We have a pretty good setup here, but Dr. Brian Peters, that's my forensic point man, will tell us if he's short of anything."

Test stations, glassed sample cabinets, bubbling beakers over Bunsen burners and odd equipment took up half the first floor. Like all labs, it had a distinct whiff of chemicals and discharged ozone from the electrics. Garbed technicians moved silently between benches. Quiet conversation filled the background, mixed with the tinkling of glassware and the hum of machinery. Tom led Price to a corner bench where Brian, dressed in a white lab

141

coat, was peering at a green screen. No one paid them any attention. Tom tapped Brian's shoulder.

"Brian, say hi to Director, National Operations Center, DHS, Mark Price. He's here to see that we're doing our job."

Peters stood up and offered his hand. "A pleasure, Mr. Price."

Price shook his hand and looked at the screen. "Likewise, Dr. Peters. Found anything interesting?"

Peters pointed at the top right corner. "You could say that. It's an image of a detonator control box screw magnified two hundred times."

"What am I looking for?"

"Striation marks, parallel lines scratched into the screw heads."

"And that means…"

"I'm trying to figure out why the detonator failed. It could be a simple manufacturing fault, always possible. The unit works just fine, I've tested the timer. But when it counts down to zero, there is no current surge. I tested for that too. So, something inside—"

"Is stopping the current," Price finished for him.

"Right."

"Why don't you simply open it up and trace the circuit?"

"I intend to, but I'm the suspicious type, Mr. Price. I want to establish if the control box was opened since manufacture."

Mark thought that over. "If someone wanted to put in a new battery, he would have to open the box."

"Right again. But see those lines? This box has been opened at least three times."

"And how is that significant?"

Peters shrugged. "It might not be significant at all."

"But you're just suspicious," Price said and smiled. Peters smiled back.

"I used to watch CSI, you know. Lots of good pointers. Seriously, a battery for this type of charge lasts for quite a while, and judging by the lack of scratches, the detonator box doesn't look all that old. So, why would somebody want to pull it apart three times? And before I open it for the fourth time, I'm collecting all the information about it that I can."

"Any fingerprints?" Tom asked, not expecting any. The boys who pulled this off would have been professionals.

Peters shook his head. "It's clean."

"Have you found anything else?" Tom demanded.

"As a matter of fact, I did. It could be nothing, but when I tried to take the C-4 demolition charge out of the sample bag, the plastic was stuck to one of its sides."

"Some sort of adhesive residue?"

"Looks like it. Beats me what a bit of glue would be doing there, though. But I'll know more once we analyze the thing. There isn't much of it, and at first glance appears to be a contact adhesive. A microscope scan of the control box revealed part of an arc, something like a circular patch. I've got no idea what it means. It could be a dab of dried mayonnaise for all I know."

"But you're suspicious," Price said again and chuckled.

"The mass spectrograph should give us its composition and we'll keep digging until it all makes sense." Peters sighed and rubbed his eyes.

Tom was all concern. "You all right? Take a break if you want to."

Peters shook his head. "I'm fine for now and this thing has me intrigued. Don't worry. I'm not the only one working on it. We won't miss anything."

Studying the scientist, Mark believed him. The man knew what he was doing and wasn't taking anything for granted, or making shortcuts in procedure based on gut feel.

"Is there anything you need? People, equipment?" he offered, but Peters shook his head.

"Thanks, Mr. Price, but we're okay so far. If I run into trouble, Quantico has extensive labs."

"The writing…" Mark prompted.

"Oh, yes. A standard timer/detonator made by Iran Electronics Industries. They handle a lot of military supplies for the Pasdaran and the regular army. Our Washington office even has a sample." Peters grinned and picked up an 8" by 10" glossy blow-up. "The same model as our baby."

Mark nodded and nibbled at a fingernail. "So, it might be Iran after all."

"Seems that way," Peters agreed. "But like I said, I'm the suspicious type. I don't take anything at face value. If we can get hold of an Iranian demolition timer, someone else could have done it also. Iran has connections with a whole slew of terrorist networks, Mr. Price, and all of them are mad at Uncle Sam."

"Yeah. But only Iran had those Web pages," Mark murmured, wondering how the FBI managed to get their hands on an Iranian timer. Did he want to know?

Tom regarded Price with a heavy frown, not saying anything, and decided to give somebody at Cyber Division a little call. He was also the suspicious type.

* * *

Clear blue skies stretched from horizon to horizon. With nothing to focus on the eyes were drawn inexorably into the depths. An oily sea glistened like a vast pool of mercury, bright from reflected sunlight, making everyone squint in discomfort. That's how it was in this part of the world. No clouds for about eight months of the year, just relentless heat and humidity. At least on the water there was wind generated by the ship's motion. It helped a little.

USS *Nimitz* (CVN-68), Carrier Strike Group 11, plowed through the flat Persian Gulf waters at a steady twenty-five knots. Its 101,000 tons dead weight left a creamy white wake that faded into distant haze. A steady hum of machinery noise permeated the spaces, generated by four steam turbines, powered by two Westinghouse A4W reactors that turned the ship's four shafts.

On the black anti-skid deck, green shirts were directing F/A-18F 'Black Aces' ready alert Super Hornets, Strike Fighter Squadron VFA-41, to cat one and cat two forward steam catapults. Dressed in heavy flame-retardant clothing, helmets on, it must have been stifling in the oppressive heat and ongoing cacophony of noise. The towbar on the nose gear of each trembling aircraft attached to a slot in the shuttle and the jet blast deflector angled up off the deck behind the twin tailpipes. The yellow shirt for each Hornet twirled his right index finger in the air and the pilots wound up power, flames splashing against the JBD. Satisfied, the pilots saluted, pushed their heads back against the ejection seat and waited, right hand on the hatch handle to prevent jerking the stick back when the jet was shot off the cat. Both shooters extended their leg forward in a crouch and pointed down the deck. With a surge the catapults hurled the graceful Hornets toward the bow. Steam billowed in their wake from the cat slides. Once off the deck, they sagged, then climbed, one angling port and the other starboard. In seconds, they were merely glinting specks as they maneuvered to their CAP (Combat Air Patrol) position, as per orders for afternoon evolutions.

On cat three, an early warning E-2C Hawkeye waited to hook on, its turboprops whining impatiently, an odd sound among the high-pitched scream of powerful jet engines. Its flat twenty-four foot APS-145 rotodome, perched on top of the fuselage like a giant white mushroom, somehow oddly out of place. Astern, the Landing Signals Officer watched two F/A-18C VFA-81 'Sunliners' Hornets turn from final into the glide path for a trap. On the starboard side of the 1,092 foot carrier, in front and aft of the island, aircraft from CVW-11 crowded close together, their tails hanging precariously off the deck, like crows perched on a wire.

Sitting comfortably in his leather chair, the airconditioning keeping flag bridge a comfortable seventy-four degrees, Rear Admiral Ronald Vincent, Commander Strike Group 11, watched flight deck operations without actually paying attention. It was merely a distraction from events back in Houston. By now all the crew had seen the fires and destruction at Valero refinery on CNN or some other channel. It was not something that could be kept under wraps even if he wanted to, which he didn't. As a military man the strategic implications were immediately clear. What he did not know was how the National Command Authority would respond tactically. Walters was a new president and still to firmly pick up all the administrative and military reins as commander-in-chief.

The U.S. armed forces offered a staggering response potential, including nuclear annihilation. But that was a last-ditch effort when sanity was lost and everyone stepped off the brink. Even without deploying WMDs, Walters already had a formidable arsenal in the Persian Gulf theater to confront Iran. And confront them he must. Not responding would mean his political ruin, and from what Vincent had seen of the man, the President would strike back hard.

Walters was Air Force and saw action in the first Gulf War before entering Congress to conduct a different type of war. He should understand military doctrine and principles of power projection. America's prestige in the world hinged on what he did next. But strike at what? Iran was a target rich environment. Not counting the more dangerous inland installations, there were dozens of valuable and vulnerable oil platforms stretching all the way from Kuwait to the Strait of Hormuz. Then there was Bandar Abbas, with its strategic naval and air facilities. Juiciest of all though, and tactically the most valuable, were the uranium enrichment plants and the new reactor at Bushehr.

He waited all day for some kind of Word from Central Command, and getting frustrated at lack of action, until he remembered the time difference between Washington and the Gulf. It was 4:15 p.m. here, which made it only 8:15 a.m. down there. The president would probably be into his second cup of coffee, he mused irreverently.

The door to flag bridge opened and Commander Lee Garrett, Communications Commander, stepped in holding a writing pad. By the look on Garrett's face, Vincent knew that he was about to get some action at last.

Garrett stopped and saluted crisply. "Admiral, you have a FLASH from NAVCENT." His voice was even and measured, without a hint of tension as he offered the pink flimsy.

Vincent nodded and quickly read through the note.

161224Q APR
FLASH FLASH FLASH FLASH FLASH FLASH FLASH FLASH
FM: NAVCENT BAHRAIN
TO: USS *NIMITZ* CVN-68
SUBJ: READINESS CONDITION
SC1/TOP SECRET—OPERATION EAGLE
PERSONAL FOR COMMANDER CARRIER STRIKE GROUP 11 /
PERSONAL FOR COMMANDER CARRIER STRIKE GROUP 11
   //BT//
   1. MISSION RETASKING FOLLOWS IMMEDIATELY.
   2. SET DEFENSE READINESS CONDITION (DEFCON) THREE.
   3. PROCEED TO STRAIT OF HORMUZ FOR POSSIBLE STRIKE
   AGAINST BANDAR ABBAS/CHAHBAHAR NAVAL
   INSTALLATIONS AND PROVIDE PROTECTION FOR
   COMMERCIAL TRAFFIC TRANSITING SAME.
   4. AUTHORIZE ENGAGEMENT IN AGGRESSIVE SURFACE
   AND AIR EXERCISES.
   5. IRANIAN TERRITORIAL INTEGRITY MUST NOT BE
   VIOLATED.
   6. CURRENT ROE IN FORCE.
   VADMIRAL R. GALLERY SENDS
   //BT//

Well!

"Thanks, Commander." Without showing any emotion, he initialed a copy and watched Garrett leave, then his eyes sought out his Flag Lieutenant. "Please ask the CO and the CAG to meet me in flag bridge as soon as convenient."

"Aye aye, sir!" The youngster saluted and hurried out.

Vincent grinned after him and started to read the message again. At least it was straightforward, clearly a positioning move. But what about USS *Dwight D. Eisenhower* somewhere near Kuwait? Perhaps NAVCENT wanted to keep *Ike* up there, ready to strike the Kharg Island terminal and other facilities in the area. If the president wanted to hit Bushehr, *Ike* would be right on station. It didn't matter. *Nimitz*, 'Old Salt', with some eighty-six operational ready strike aircraft of its Carrier Air Wing CVW-11, supported by Destroyer Squadron 23, was up to the job.

Flight ops forgotten, Vincent waited for the ship's two senior officers. When the men arrived, CVN-68 bold on their baseball caps, he smiled and without any preliminaries, led them to his day cabin. Rich blue carpet muffled their footsteps as they shuffled around a teak desk, maneuvering padded chairs. Pale wood paneling adorned the bulkheads, glowing from defused light that came through the outward slanting square windows. A large watercolor of *Nimitz* adorned one wall, painted by Vincent's daughter. A grown woman with a family of her own, she nevertheless managed to find time to indulge her hobby. On another wall were the usual naval paraphernalia: chronometer, barometer, temperature and humidity gauges. The cabin was austere, and Vincent did not go for flashy displays, preferring results to speak for him, like the six rows of fruit salad on his chest that included the Navy Cross and Silver Star.

They were seating themselves when a steward—mess management specialist in current parlance—dressed in impeccable whites, quietly walked in and placed a silver carafe of coffee on the desk. Cups and add-ons followed.

"Thanks, Bill," Vincent said warmly and the steward nodded. "Admiral…gentlemen."

When the door closed, Vincent extended his hand at the coffee. "Before it gets cold."

Brent 'Chips' Roberts smiled faintly and reached for the carafe. The smell of rich coffee spread through the cabin as he poured. Finished, he handed the carafe to Mike 'Boomer' Ulesky, his CAG. Even though since the '70s, Commander Air Group had been designated as Carrier Air Wing, nobody was about to call its commander CAW—not if they valued their next fitness report. Asinine bureaucracy wins again.

"You must give me the secret of your blend, Admiral," Roberts complained, inhaling the odor like a connoisseur. "In the interest of the service, of course."

Vincent laughed at *Nimitz's* commanding officer. "When you get your own stars, Brent. In the meantime, all I can tell you it's how the beans are roasted. Bill won't go beyond that, and I don't ask. I just enjoy."

"I'll have to sign on for another tour, then," Ulesky moaned, "just so I can drink your coffee, sir."

Vincent grinned, regarding his two senior officers like a father watching his sons, and liking what he saw. At thirty-nine, Ulesky was young for a four-striper, but one hot Hornet and Tomcat driver. Getting the CAG slot on *Nimitz* was no luck. He was simply good, a good officer and leader who had ticked all the right boxes. The man bristled with all indicators for fast-track flag rank.

Roberts, on the other hand, was a senior captain. He needed to be to command a carrier. And he was one of those curious creatures who had given up pushing Tomcats through the sky with his hair on fire and transferred to a surface, black shoe, command. It wasn't that Roberts no longer wanted to fly, far from it. But time made little allowance for his likes and dislikes. Age was catching up with him and an ejection from a dead F-14 a few years back hadn't helped. Rather than wait to be grounded, a fate worse than death for a naval aviator, he did the only thing short of resigning, which never occurred to him—second-generation navy. After a CO slot in a *Ticonderoga*-class missile cruiser, exec of USS *George Washington* flattop, he was given *Nimitz*, and a spot on the Rear Admiral promotion list. Some said that Roberts was a future Chief of Naval Operations, something that Vincent would not argue. But the boy would have to wait his turn as he eyed that slot for himself.

He filled his cup and handed the message flimsy to Roberts. It took the captain a moment to digest the information. He shoved the paper at Ulesky, the gleam of battle glowing in his eyes.

"Aggressive exercises, eh? Well, we can accommodate that. Within the ROE, of course."

Vincent chuckled. "We cannot bomb Bandar Abbas or Chahbahar, Brent, if that's what you were wondering."

"Never crossed my mind, sir."

"Sure. But if they send out hovercraft or patrol boats our way, you send them to the bottom should they cross the ten-mile exclusion limit."

"Can do."

"Admiral, the way I read this, we keep Iranian fighters at the territorial limit line, right?" Ulesky queried and Vincent nodded.

"You read that right, Mike. As you know, their air force is nothing much by our standards, a gaggle of odd aircraft, mainly Russian and Chinese, with some of our old F-4s, F-5s and F-14s. They shouldn't be a problem for us. The rub is, they can saturate our defenses with land-based SAMs and SS-N-22 anti-ship missiles—if it comes to that."

"If it comes to that, Admiral, we'll cream them," Ulesky growled, allowing no room for doubt.

"You really must stop eating those nails for breakfast, Mike," Vincent chided and Brent grinned. Ulesky took it in his stride.

"I don't want anybody here thinking that CVW-11 are a bunch of pussies, Admiral."

"You should allow your admiral to have the last word, Boomer," Vincent said, wearing a broad smile.

"What's the plan, sir?" Roberts asked.

"Anything on the threat board?"

"CVIC reports everything normal, Admiral. No unusual air, surface or SIGINT activity."

Vincent nodded. Iran could be playing innocent or perhaps just waiting to see how America would react. Either way, he meant to be ready.

"I want the battle group steaming east and parked somewhere off Bandar Abbas by dawn. Then we'll start our exercise program; ASW with screening destroyers and helos, in case they want to sortie their Kilo-class diesels against us. I want missile defense, good guy/bad guy air maneuvers, and I want a four-plane CAP, the outer one covering the coast. One more thing." His eyes bored unwaveringly at his commanders. "We don't violate the ROE. If one of your hot sticks, Mike, thinks I'm joking and hangs out his ass, he'll spend the next twenty years in Leavenworth. I don't want anyone getting caught by an SA-5 Gammon or SA-10 Grumble because his hair was on fire. Make sure the boys get the Word. Understood?"

"You got it, Admiral."

"Until told otherwise, we are a message the United States wants the Iranians to get loud and clear. That's all. Right, let's start talking threats and mission specifics. We haven't received an Air Tasking Order, so I don't know what targets NAVCENT has in mind for us, but I want to be prepared. From now on, satellite downloads every hour until I know every lizard that's sunning itself around Bandar Abbas and Chahbahar, and every floating twig. I also want you two to start work with the strike intelligence analysis cell on packages to hit naval installations around those sites, including recommendations for optimum screening profiles of civilian water traffic."

"Do you want detailed mission plans, Admiral?" Roberts demanded crisply, all business.

Vincent nodded. "CTAPS, TAMPS, MIIDS/IDB, the works. Once we are tasked, I want to be able to respond within an hour."

Roberts glanced at Ulesky. The Carrier Intelligence Center (CVIC) would be a very busy place over the next twelve hours. Well, the job description did not require that he sleep.

* * *

Manfred Cottard watched as the president scrawled some corrections and handed the paper to the press secretary, marveling at the man's energy. Walters was a reactor running at 110 percent. It was as if Valero had been a shot of adrenalin and it was infectious. The entire White House staff caught it and were running around in seemingly disorderly confusion. However, looks were deceptive. This was the administration's first real crisis and Cottard took steps to make sure that the president had all the support necessary—from everybody that counted.

Alone again, Walters rubbed his temples and sighed. "How much time before the Cabinet meeting?"

"Twenty-five minutes, Mr. President," Cottard said gravely. They might be friends, but Walters was the president and nobody would persuade Cottard to stoop to first name familiarity, not even in private.

"This is going to be one ball busting day," Walters announced and placed his hands on the *Resolute* desk. He might be stretched, but his eyes gleamed in anticipation. "Grant and Bruster… There is too much friction between those two, and both of them are trying to score points."

"We must ease Vice Admiral Grant out," Cottard recommended immediately. "He's building empires and in the process is forgetting what the CIA is all about."

"Old school. Still, let's wait and see how he performs," Walters countered, "but I tend to agree. And I do want to let some air out of the CIA. They're not an intelligence service any longer, merely another bloated buck passing bureaucracy. I'm tired of getting glossy analyses after the fact. I want them *before* shit happens."

"That could be a big ask, Mr. President," Cottard murmured, "and not something that can be done overnight."

"Damnation! What good are they, then? If Bush can create DHS with a stroke of a pen, I can get rid of dead wood in the same way. And do something about those damned PDBs. It's strained baby crap. I want genuine threat projections, not ass-covering maybes."

Cottard grinned, sharing the president's revulsion at the sifted intelligence the CIA served as their President's Daily Brief input. It was supposed to be a critical analysis of world trouble spots that gave the National Command Authority a heads-up, but the content was mostly null. He got better information from CNN. Everybody worried about their career, afraid to tell the truth.

"I'll get on it. By the way, Ed Bishop was pissed that you left him out of this morning's brief and had Colin Forbes there instead."

"That's just tough," was Walters' cool reaction. "Forbes had a need to know and has immediate operational responsibility. I didn't want the DHS Director filtering my decisions. If he is pissed now, he'll be aggrieved even more when I ask him to justify his existence. The FBI is not a Cabinet posting and they are much more valuable to the country. Why should DHS be any different? I was appalled when I first learned that they've got an Assistant Secretary for Policy, for crying out loud! I make policy around here, damn it. It's gone too far, I tell you."

Cottard studied the president and rubbed the underside of his nose. "Are you serious about chopping up DHS?"

"Hell, yes. And Valero has given me a perfect opportunity to evaluate what goes. All that duplication and redundancy across the agencies, it's a waste of money and delivers nothing. I campaigned on this, at your urging, I might add, and I aim to deliver."

Cottard smiled. "You didn't need much urging, Mr. President."

Walters chuckled. "Perhaps not, but this horseshit has got to stop. Every time we have some disaster, we are paralyzed because nobody is accountable. And then we breed another agency to solve the mess. We've got to streamline things or the government will simply grind down. It will cost some jobs, but this nonsense is just a drain on the public purse."

His phone went off and he picked up the receiver. He listened, eyes widening in surprise. "Please ask Admiral Stone to step in, will you? I'll take the President's call then." He replaced the receiver and whistled. "What do you know? It's Hamadee Al Zerkhani himself, and he wants to chat."

"Not about the weather, I'll bet." Cottard pursed his lips and nodded thoughtfully. "I am officially impressed. For once, it didn't take the French long to act."

There was a knock and Walters' personal aide opened the door. "Admiral Stone, sir."

"Thanks, Unice. I'll take that call now."

"What's up, Mr. President?" the national security advisor queried as he walked confidently across the Oval Office carpet with its great seal plastered in the center of the room.

"I've got the Iranian President on the line," Walters said as the phone rang. He punched the conference speaker button. Stone glanced sharply at Cottard and sat down.

"President Al Zerkhani, sir," Unice announced formally.

"Mr. President, this is Samuel Walters."

"Good morning, Mr. President," the translator's voice came through clearly, his American accent unmistakable. Evil as though that might be, it was an unavoidable byproduct of their English language schools. And who the hell would want to talk with a clipped, stiff British accent *designed* to be condescending.

"It has not been so far, Mr. President," Walters countered firmly and waited for the translation. If the raghead sought to worm his way out of this one, he was barking up the wrong palm tree.

"A most tragic and deplorable incident, sir," Zerkhani's translator responded gravely. "However, I want to state categorically that my country had nothing to do with Valero. I anticipate your skepticism, Mr. President, and I don't blame you for it. I would feel the same way were our respective positions reversed. Despite the incriminating Internet evidence, something that we are investigating, I again stress that we are not responsible. In case you harbor suspicions if VEVAK might be involved, this is also being investigated. I have spoken to the French President and received your warning. On Muhammad's honor, sir, you have my word that we did not carry out this barbaric and unprovoked attack on the United States. We had no reason to."

Walters mulled that over for several long seconds. So far, he had heard nothing to make him change his mind, but swearing on Muhammad's honor? He wondered whether Zerkhani would lie through his teeth to throw him off the track. It was possible, but would he do it right now, given what was at stake? He simply wasn't sure.

"For the sake of peace, Mr. President," Walters replied, his brow knitted in concentration, "I would like nothing better than to accept your word. But I cannot get past those Web pages, sir. We both know that nothing gets posted on your sites without official approval, and Al Jazeera would never dare place something without sanction from your Ministry of Foreign Affairs."

"As I said, Mr. President, the matter is being investigated. We both know how easily such evidence can be planted, as could explosives. What do I need to do to convince you? Unless you accept my word that we are not involved, I understand you will be forced to act, and I will have to initiate an appropriate response, one that will have the gravest consequences."

Walters understood Zerkhani's diplomatically couched words, and what was more, he sympathized, but he couldn't read the man. He needed to stare him in the face and gauge his reactions, evaluate all the subtle nuances of facial expressions and body language, impossible to do over a cold phone. But then, Zerkhani faced with a similar dilemma. Could he trust the man? That's what the whole thing boiled down to, but past relations between both countries made that a hard sell, his own administration included. Yet, Zerkhani could be telling the truth. He admitted the possibility, however unpalatable the thought. If this were indeed an elaborate third party plot designed to bring the U.S. and Iran into open conflict, it was succeeding. Graham had hinted the same thing, damn him.

"Mr. President, are you there?" the translator prompted politely.

"I am here, sir," Walters answered heavily. "You're making this very difficult for me."

"Mr. President, we have our differences. I would be foolish to deny it. And if I may be permitted, given the situation in which we now find ourselves, some of those differences stem from your lack of understanding of us as a people, our history and our national objectives. Just because those objectives don't happen to coincide with yours, does not automatically make us enemies."

"I appreciate the frankness of your comments, sir, but your internal propaganda and support of terrorist organizations lead me to question your objectives."

"Have any of our affiliates perpetrated an attack against the United States, sir? Respectfully, I suggest that you're arguing from an invalid premise."

Walters almost laughed. The bastard had a point there. "I don't deny the possibility. If you followed my campaign, you know that one of my commitments is the review of our foreign policy regarding the Middle East. America has made mistakes,

Mr. President, but I aim to have them redressed."

"I am relieved to hear that from an American administration, sir, especially under the current circumstances."

"Mr. President, you must know that the American people will demand that I act. Unless compelling evidence is produced to the contrary, I will find it impossible not to act. Do you understand that?"

"I understand perfectly, Mr. President, but I would urge you to stay your hand until our mutual investigations are concluded. Premature action will only serve those who made this attack on your country. But should you decide to act, please ask yourself this question first. Why would I want to provoke the United States? And why now? I admit that your unilateral trade sanctions are hurting my country and are something that I deem a violation of international law, but that is hardly a legitimate reason for me to retaliate, and certainly not against an oil installation of minimal consequence to you. My country's nuclear program is a matter of economic and strategic national security, sir, which in no way threatens the United States."

"It threatens the stability of the region," Walters countered.

"It might threaten perceived Western political interests, Mr. President, including Israel's, but that does not translate directly to regional instability. Iran has enemies of its own, sir."

"Pakistan."

"That's right, Mr. President. They still refuse to acknowledge our territorial waters in the Arabian Sea and our ancestral right to rivers Hirmand, Parian and the Harirud, not to mention their disregard of the Paris Treaty of 1855, which gives us the right of supervision in western Afghanistan. You might argue that world events have abrogated that treaty, but Iran does not see it that way. And, if I may, American support of Pakistan's increasingly extremist regime as a bulwark against Taliban resurgence does not contribute to finding a lasting solution. Everyone seems to have forgotten, or ignores the fact, that it was Pakistan who created the Taliban in the first place."

"And it's gotten away from them, I know," Walters acknowledged quietly.

Pervez Musharraf created the Taliban as a mechanism to curb the growing power of Afghani tribal warlords. And he did it during his term as chief of the army by using the notorious Inter-service Intelligence Directorate. That Al Qaida had taken advantage of the situation was in hindsight inevitable.

"But Pakistan is not our only concern, Mr. President," Zerkhani pointed out.

"I am aware of disputes with your neighbors over the Caspian Sea coastline allocations and I understand your nervousness, sir. Political and religious extremism is a disease to be shunned by everyone. But your nuclear program threatens others as well."

"If you are referring to Israel, that is an unwarranted fear promoted by the Zionists and your Jewish lobby. If I wanted to destroy Israel, I don't need nuclear weapons, only an acceptance of Iran's own destruction. And that, sir, is something not in our national interest."

Walters tended to agree. However, possession of a nuclear capability provided strategic advantages as well as tactical options. United States had averted a hot war with the Soviet Union through the use of that strategic advantage. Would a nuclear Iran be necessarily such a bad thing? Israel would howl, they already were, but it could also force them to modify their oppressive policy against the Palestinians, which could eventually lead to a settlement. Nevertheless, he *had* asked himself the same question Zerkhani did. Why would Iran attack the U.S.? There was no clear political or economic gain. He wished there was a way to wind back time.

"President Zerkhani, confrontation between our two countries would be unsettling for everybody and bad for business. I shall not act until I am completely satisfied that Iran has indeed perpetrated this act of naked terrorism. For that's what it was. However, should further evidence emerge pointing to your guilt, I shall strike without hesitation. Furthermore, I am advising you that USS *Nimitz* and USS *Eisenhower* carrier battle groups are being positioned as we speak to carry out any action I might deem appropriate. I would urge your forces not to test my determination to act."

There was a prolonged silence, presumably while Zerkhani digested that threat.

"President Walters, Iran will take no provocative action, but I must warn you in turn that we will take steps to protect out territorial integrity. To do otherwise would not be acceptable to my people."

"I understand, and you have my guarantee that the United States will respect your territorial integrity at all times."

"Thank you, Mr. President. Your commitment will help my investigative endeavors. As a gesture of good will, I shall instruct my UN Ambassador to announce that Iran will provide unrestricted access by the International Atomic Energy Agency inspectors to all our facilities."

Walters raised an eyebrow and exchanged startled glances with Manfred and Graham.

"That is indeed welcome news, Mr. President."

"As I stated before, sir, every effort will be made to uncover the penetration of our websites in order to avert a catastrophic outcome. If there is anything I or my intelligence apparatus can do to assist your investigations, I offer you my full cooperation."

"Thank you. I shall keep that in mind," Walters acknowledged.

"In view of this discussion, Mr. President, do you still wish to engage in a personal meeting with your Secretary of State?"

"If acceptable to you, sir, I would prefer to maintain a direct dialogue between the two of us."

"I would enjoy that as well. Good day, sir," the interpreter said and the line went dead.

Walters switched off the speaker and stared thoughtfully at nothing, then looked directly at Graham. "What do you think of that?"

"This could be a clever case of misdirection on Zerkhani's part, and I hate to say it, but I believe him. In my opinion, Mr. President, despite public outrage against our sanctions, Iran simply doesn't have a strong enough reason to attack us. There just isn't any percentage in it."

"Then again, they could have used the same logic to hide an attack. But I keep coming back to the same old problem. To what end? Manfred?"

"I wish I could have seen his face, Mr. President," Cottard countered, clearly frustrated, and rubbed his nose. "I could tell if the son of a bitch was lying. He is certainly capable of it. But if it wasn't him, then who was it? It could even be Al Qaida for all we know. I wouldn't put it past them, but I doubt it somehow. This is too sneaky for their taste. They prefer a more direct, in-your-face approach. One thing is certain. We better find out before we make a horrible mistake."

"You guys are not making this any easier," Walters complained petulantly. "Of course, you're both right. What a mess. I wish I understood how those people think! All that historical and religious baggage they've been carrying around for centuries. I just don't get it. And when I boil it down, I'm not surprised. Our own history is only a couple of hundred years old. And what is worse, we are not a single people with a single religion, not like them."

Graham scratched his chin. "It's not that hard to get a handle on them, Mr. President. I am oversimplifying, of course, but until the mid-nineteenth century, the clerics claimed the right to exercise judgment over all matters religious as true leaders of Muslim communities, and resisted any form of secular control. You can argue the validity of that position, but you must keep in mind that our concept of democracy does not apply where Arabs are concerned. Anyway, our problems began when Russia seized northern Iran and the British took over the rest to protect their Indian empire. That intervention set off a wave of industrialization and reform, not to benefit the local population, but to further European interests. The clerics inevitably saw this as corruption of their national identity and a direct threat against Islam. When oil was found in 1908, the British gained control and paid Iran a pittance, which over time, generated increasing resentment. After World War I, everybody compounded the mess by arbitrarily redrawing centuries-old boundaries and created a Middle East as we know it today. As you know, in 1925 a military officer gained control over the army and proclaimed himself Shah, a dynasty that lasted until 1979."

"I get that," Walters said impatiently. "But how does it make us their enemy?"

"Easier than you might think, Mr. President. The Russians and the British effectively controlled everything, and oil revenues kept the Pahlavi dynasty in power through a succession of repressive regimes. After the Second World War, the United States supplanted the old powers by propping up the Shah as a front line bastion against perceived Soviet encroachment. We trained their army and supplied the weapons. The clerics became increasingly agitated when the Shah introduced secular schools and legislated against ulama authority. From his sanctuary in Iraq, Ayatollah Khomayni became a focus of unrest against the monarchy and what he saw as dilution of Islam by decadent Western ideas and values. In 1979 the lid blew off and the Shah fled. Iran became an Islamic republic subject to all the rigor of Shi'ia Shari'a law."

Walters studied his national security advisor with interest. "How come you know so much about them?"

Stone allowed himself a small smile and shrugged. "It's been a curiosity of mine, Mr. President."

"I can tell. So, this is what we have. At first, it was economic and political domination by pre-First World War Europe, then the British effectively stole their oil. After World War II, we stepped in to hold the Soviets in check."

"That's about the size of it, sir."

"And all the while, nobody gave a shit what the Iranians themselves wanted. They were simply pawns in a geopolitical power struggle. It's no wonder that they hate our guts. Still, I don't know if the average guy on the street has gotten a better bargain by exchanging the Shah for a bunch of conservative extremist clerics."

"Perhaps not, Mr. President, but understanding where they're coming from might alter how we view politics in the region. And for the guy on the street, there is no difference between religion and politics. For them, religion *is* politics."

"Yeah, if we don't blow them away first. But how does all this help me now?"

"I suspect it already has. You admitted to President Zerkhani that the United States made mistakes. I don't think anybody has said that before, and in his own way, he appreciates that."

"The IAEA inspectors?"

"Yes, sir. It's not going to make us pals, but right now, every gesture counts."

Walters pursed his lips, nodded and pinned Stone with a hard stare. "Possibly, but before I start feeling sorry for them, we must remember that the Ayatollahs control Iran, not Zerkhani, and they are extremists, bending the Koran for the purpose of maintaining personal power. Zerkhani might be more pragmatic and willing to entertain a dialogue, but will the Ayatollahs let him?"

Stone shrugged. "Nothing is certain, Mr. President, and we will not find out without testing the waters."

The President glared at his national security advisor. "What is certain is that I must be briefed in depth about Iran, the entire region's history and its fallout on today's situation. The CIA and State presumably have experts?"

"Including professionals who lived there, Mr. President," Cottard said.

"Good. Arrange a series of sessions for them to talk to me." Walters ordered and glanced at his wristwatch. Damnation! It was already past nine. "We need to hash this out some more, Graham. With Tanner. Right now, keep after Price. As soon as he finds anything, I want to be the first to know."

"Yes, Mr. President."

"Right! Let's go see the Cabinet and give them the bad news. One thing, we don't disclose that I have spoken to Zerkhani. Clear?"

"Tanner won't like it once this breaks," Cottard pointed out, referring to the Secretary of State. "And he should be involved."

"He will be involved," Walters said firmly and stood up. "I'll brief him after the Cabinet meeting."

Chapter Six

Dragging the suitcase on its two back rollers, Matan walked through the 'Nothing to Declare' gate and into the noisy arrivals concourse. Despite the fact that it was well past midnight, people crowded the terminal, waiting for loved ones, friends or enemies. Avis, Hertz and hotel reservation booths had customers queuing for service. Bored, tired-looking tourists, wondering what the hell they were doing here, surrounded the Information desk. Matan felt a bit like that himself. Two nightshift cleaners pushed floor-polishing machines, adding to the racket. An army type stood nearby, Uzi slung casually on his shoulder, suspiciously scrutinizing everybody. Speakers announced arrival times or requested Mr. So-and-so to report to airline such-and-such help desk, the sound sufficiently distorted to make it hard to understand. Israel built missiles that could launch a satellite, but could not manufacture clear PA systems.

He spotted Sarah waving at him among others looking for arrivals and his spirits lifted. Lord, she looked good, her welcome smile an island of sunshine and laughter, an oasis of safety and warmth. Seeing her, he realized how much he missed her, missed her voice, merriment and understanding. A weight that had gripped his heart suddenly lifted and he hurried, his footsteps light and eager.

He dropped his briefcase and she flung herself at him, her head pressed against his chest. Without effort, he swung her around and sought her lips as her eyes shone her welcome. Following a sweet moment, he pulled back and brushed her hair. After all the years, the old zing was still there. Passersby gave them amused glances. An orthodox, black-clad Jew, wearing the *tefillim*, frowned deep disapproval as he strode by. Matan and Sarah did not see him.

"Wow, tiger," she growled with contentment, holding him tight.

"I was hungry," he purred, the sound coming from deep within his chest.

"We'll have to get you some raw meat, then," she said and rubbed herself provocatively against him.

"How about right on that bench?"

She giggled, something he longed to hear. "That would just get us noticed, dear."

"To hell with them, but okay. Take me home or lose me."

Hand in hand, oblivious to the crowd, they walked toward the exit. Thick glass doors opened automatically and Matan shivered as crisp air cut through his lightweight suit.

"Damn! I can't wait for summer."

"Did you hear about that awful thing in America?" Sarah asked, her face clouded with concern. "All those lives lost. Why can't we stop doing this to each other?"

"I don't know, sweetie," he replied honestly, surprised at his reaction.

Now that it was done, he wondered whether it had been necessary. Israel's reaction to any crisis always tended to be a violent response. Sometimes that had been crucial, but now it had become automatic as though it was the only and correct thing to do. He had given up a military career because of that, and here he was, perpetrating the pattern in another guise. He sighed, wondering what the hell was the matter with him. You crushed an enemy any way you could or he would crush you, right? Basic Clausewitz.

"I guess we'll keep on doing it until men of good will on both sides decide that it's enough."

She raised a quizzical eyebrow at that. "And you're a romantic."

"There is too much bitterness and we keep passing it on to our children. They'll have much to thank us for," he mused, his voice full of irony.

"And now you're being cynical," she chided him.

He was tired, not thinking straight and had a long day. A long week, for that matter. Waiting at Bush International was a strain, worrying about all the things that could have gone wrong. Did the boys do it or were they even now in some room under harsh lighting with beefy cops working them over? But he had not received an abort signal, so things must be all right. When at last Ellis and Tabor walked casually into the Air France business class departure lounge, he pretended not to see them, but a palpable flood of relief coursed through his body. They walked to the bar without any indication of recognition and flagged an attendant, playing the game to the end. He gulped down the last of his Crown Royal without feeling the liquor's bite.

During the flight across the Atlantic, he was dozing when the cabin came alive with the chatter of excited voices. He glanced at his watch: just after 3 a.m. Houston time. Looking around, he overheard snatches of conversation in French and English. There was no need for an interpreter. Casually, he switched on the large LED screen that unfolded out of his comfortable seat and selected the English version of the CNN news channel. Flames, billowing black smoke, twisted metal, fire tenders and destruction. The helicopter view made the scene surreal, somehow detached, removed from reality. It was like watching a movie set. He wondered how much misery this particular movie had cost. He switched off before the commentary and dissections started. That part, he could fill in for himself. Reaction had set in and he was feeling fragile and moody.

Sleep eluded him, his mind replaying the scenes from a hell he helped create. By the time the flight landed at Charles de Gaulle, he was emotionally and physically worn out. The Airbus A340 touched down at 2:45 p.m., only five minutes late, but it took another ten minutes for the aircraft to taxi to the terminal. As he was transiting, he did not need to clear Customs, and he had some three-and-a-half hours to kill before the scheduled 6:40 p.m. flight to Tel Aviv.

After unobtrusively collecting the TWIC badges from Tabor, he had not seen the two agents and didn't care what they were up to. As far as he was concerned, their part was done and they were good as dead, or would be soon. He didn't know how Namir intended to remove them, even remotely. Keep it compartmentalized, he told himself. Despite his warning to the Metsada chief, he wondered if Namir would try something cute with him. He was being paranoid and knew it, but that didn't stop his subconscious from nagging him, and he'd been too long in this business without having learned a little. Even though he had covered himself, what kept gnawing at him, was it enough? He hoped it was something he would never have to find out.

Charles de Gaulle was an ultramodern, spacious, sprawling airport and the French had gone all out to ensure that transiting passengers were provided for. He booked a room at the adjoining Hilton, took a light meal, showered and sacked out. It was only for two hours, but he felt refreshed luxuriating in a proper bed and eager for news. Flight AF2220 boarded without fuss, his business class status steering him past the normal hassles. The Airbus climbed into an evening sky, engines whining at full power, banked and headed southeast. Five hours and twenty minutes to go before he got home again. The flight was comfortable and it could have been worse.

CNN was full of the latest from Houston and Washington. Matan watched with interest the replay of President Walters' statement after the usual 10 a.m. press conference. The man looked calm and unruffled by events, acknowledging the unprovoked terrorist attack on the United States and thankful that more lives were not lost. He admitted talking to President Al Zerkhani, but added that naval forces in the Persian Gulf were being positioned to take whatever action might be deemed necessary. Even as he spoke, FBI and other intelligence agencies were sifting through available evidence. Once he was satisfied that Iran had indeed carried out this act of naked aggression, America would respond without hesitation, using all the force at his disposal.

Listening, Matan frowned. What could Zerkhani have said to change the president's mind? Whatever it was, Matan did not like introduction of such a variable. The plan called for a swift response, not deliberation.

Watching the president, Walters looked fully in control, someone who was not about to be rushed into premature action. Graham Stone, the National Security Advisor, stepped to the lectern and handed Walters a note. Cameras captured every tense moment as the president scanned the note, his face slowly coloring with indignation and outrage. He looked up and his eyes coldly traversed the press gallery.

"I am informed that the FBI have recovered a demolition package from the Valero Refinery site."

An excited ripple swept through the press and Matan exhaled with relief. For a moment there, he wondered whether they'd failed to find the damned thing.

"It is understood that the device was manufactured by Iran Electronic Industries."

The comment generated a frenzy of questions. Walters raised his arms and waited for everybody to settle down.

"Given this development, I will be directing the Joint Chiefs to prepare an immediate strike package against selected targets in the Islamic Republic of Iran, and I challenge President Hamadee Al Zerkhani to deny any involvement. To the people of Iran, I say this: My anger is not directed against you, but at your leaders whom you should decry as common criminals. Justice will not be long in coming."

The press exploded, but Walters was not taking any questions, and marched out without looking back, his senior staff in tow.

Matan switched off, having seen enough. It was possible that within hours, even before he touched down at Ben-Gurion, that America would have responded. If that happened, it would be quick service indeed. But he never doubted America's ability or willingness to crush an irritating opponent. Thorny diplomacy, on the other hand, like the Israeli/Palestinian problem, seemed beyond their reach. The thought did not bring him any relief, only a cold feeling of foreboding. Namir had set into motion something neither of them could now control, and Matan wondered what kind of a world he would find himself in tomorrow.

When AF2220 landed, America had not struck and he was still wondering. The longer they held off, of course, the more likelihood that some compromising evidence would be unearthed damning Israel. He could not imagine what that would be, but after the DHS antiterrorism conference, Matan held profound respect for America's technical prowess when properly channeled.

Still holding hands, Sarah led him through the airport parking lot to their car. He stashed the bags in the trunk and she steered the Audi out of the lot onto Highway 1. Although it was late at night there was sufficient traffic to make driving less lonely. She had the heater going, for which Matan was grateful. Comfortable, enjoying Sarah's company, he felt fresh and relaxed.

"How is Admina?"

Sarah turned her head, an impish smile on her face. "Out on a date. Still out when I left for the airport."

Matan sighed. "That girl is growing up too fast," he lamented, something fathers had done for millennia. "Her latest conquest, have you seen him?"

"He seems a nice enough boy. He is at Tel Aviv University studying chemical engineering."

"If he hurts her, I'll have one of my hit squads bust him up," he warned, half serious, and Sarah laughed.

"I am sure he's got the word already. She likes to drop hints that her daddy is an important wheel at Mossad, just to see the boys squirm. A cruel streak she picked up from your side of the family, I might add."

"Nice to know that she's not all *your* daughter."

She turned into Ayalon Highway and headed north, following the Yarkon River, with Tel Aviv a blaze of lights on their left side. Several cars overtook them, impatient to get to where they were going.

"And Dad?" he asked after letting his mind wander for a while.

She chuckled. "You know Father, boss of all creation. But he hasn't been meddling, if that's been bothering you."

Matan smiled, the picture of his father issuing edicts at random while Sarah took it stoically in stride. It described their relationship clearly. She was fond of him, he knew that, but in her house, the older Irian was a guest and had to play by her rules.

"He seems worried about you for some reason."

He looked at her, keeping his face impassive. "What did he say?"

"He hasn't said anything. He's just evasive, like you. But I know him."

"It's Mossad again, I'm sure of it. You know how he is. I'll talk to him, but it's nothing."

After a moment of poignant silence, she gave him a quick glance. "How was Washington?"

"Cold! Like here. And I didn't get to do any of the touristy bits, in case you were wondering. And I wasn't carousing either."

She nodded and patted his thigh. "I don't know about that, dear. You used to be a fast swinger at one time."

"Used to be? You mean that now, I'm old and decrepit?"

She glanced at the slight bulge around his waist. "No comment. And the conference?"

"Actually, I enjoyed it," he said truthfully, smarting a little from her reference to his waistline. It was his fault really; definitely time for corrective action. "I wish we had a fraction of the resources available to them."

"But would it make a difference, you think?"

"Ah, sweetie, you've put your finger on it. Americans don't have Hamas and Hezbollah to contend with."

"Will America strike?" Sarah asked suddenly, looking at him, her eyes large with concern.

"I don't see them not doing it," he said slowly. "Especially after finding that explosive. It's pretty grim evidence. But I wouldn't worry. Iran is a long way off. We'll be safe."

"How can anyone be safe at a time like this?" she countered, her voice full of misery. "Hamas will use this as an excuse to stage more rocket attacks against us and more suicide bombings. There will never be peace as long as one Palestinian lives."

Matan was startled to hear her say such a thing. "You don't mean that, do you?"

She sighed and gave a shrug. "Why not? Let's face it. We've made a mess of things. Or our government has, which is saying the same thing."

"How?"

"You know how. The Palestinians must have a homeland of their own. You argued that yourself. They lived here for centuries before the UN gave us our independence. And what did we do? We used the event to forcibly drive them into Jordan and Lebanon. We denied their heritage while claiming our own. It's no wonder they're bitter, not only at us, but at Arab countries in general who stood by and did nothing. If only Jordan had ceded part of its western territory and the West Bank to them. Had they done that, the 1969 War of Attrition might never have happened and we'd probably be at peace."

He wasn't sure that she was right, but acknowledged the possibility.

After a moment of silence, she turned to look at him. "You

agree with me, don't you?"

"I know this; not releasing the occupied territories and expanding our settlements is a festering sore eating ever deeper into our national body. Now, it might be too deep to heal, I'll give you that."

"In the meantime, we simply muddle along, right?" The bitterness in her voice was unmistakable and he didn't know how to reach her.

"We can always hope that someone or some event will change our headlong rush toward destruction," he murmured and brushed her arm. And perhaps that event had already happened.

They were quiet as the car turned into Rakach Boulevard, crossed the Yarkon River and headed for Haifa Road and the Bavli suburb. It was dark and lonely on this stretch, street lighting providing the only relief from the blackness of night. Matan was almost home and didn't want to think about politics anymore. He reached with his left hand and squeezed Sarah's wrist against the steering wheel. She flashed him a smile, and for tonight at least, everything was right with the world.

"Love you," he whispered and her face flushed.

"You're not going anywhere for a while?"

"I'm yours for the duration."

"Good."

The raw meat she served after he showered was definitely worth the wait.

* * *

Standing beside the revolving carousel, waiting for his suitcase, Tabor noticed Colonel Irian pick up his bag and make his way toward the 'Nothing to Declare' exit.

"Lucky stiff," he muttered without resentment, hoping he would not be kept waiting long. The way it should work, if you checked in late your bags should be out first, but fates have a perverse streak and the truism was not always true. When his bag popped up from the handling conveyor below and slid down onto the carousel, Tabor was waiting to snag it.

"Bastard," Ellis commented beside him and Tabor grinned.

Ellis gave a satisfied grunt as his own bag came up. They collected their luggage and ambled toward the exit. A young Army segen mishne strode toward them, but Tabor was ready. He reached into his pocket and dragged out the diplomatic passport. The soldier looked disappointed, nodded to them and walked off in search of another victim.

"You still want to share a cab?" Tabor queried and Ellis grunted.

"As far as Nahlat Yitshak."

"Deal."

Once outside, clutching their light jackets more tightly, they walked to the cab rank, waited a minute in the short queue and piled into the next cab, both taking the back seat. The cab drove off, accelerating past the brightly lit terminal.

Nobody saw the heavily dressed individual standing near the exit, black hat deep over his eyes, speak quickly into a cellphone. When the cab rounded the corner and vanished, he pocketed the phone and slowly walked toward the parking lot.

As the cab took the Highway 1 on-ramp, a dark Citroen followed four cars behind it. Close to the airport, the highway was lit from high poles on both carriageways, but they thinned out quickly to one every fifty meters or so. Two kilometers out, the poles were reduced to single stands along the median strip, long arms hanging out over both carriageways. The cab picked up speed, unaware of the Citroen. After two kilometers the Citroen driver picked up his cellphone and spoke briefly.

Behind an embankment lining the curve in the highway, Ben-Gurion a blaze of lights in front of them, the tall light pole mounted on the central nature strip providing excellent downward visibility, two men scanned the oncoming traffic. Black balaclavas hid their faces. Holes allowed their eyes to shine in the gloom. A cellphone went off, sounding unnaturally loud, and one of the men reached into his pocket. He listened to the terse comment and slipped the cell back into his pocket. With a nod to his partner, he picked up the AK-47 assault rifle, suppression silencer mounted, and cocked the weapon, the snick of the slide absorbed by sounds of passing traffic.

He did not know who the targets were or why One wanted them eliminated; that wasn't his problem. He was a professional, content doing precision work. Worrying about the bigger picture only gave a man a headache. He'd been down that road before and it was the main reason why he left Metsada. It was better not to feel, not to think. In the end, it didn't matter. Everything was pointless, and taking out two more anonymous faces would not make it any saner. He only worried about reliability and exactness in carrying out his work. That was his sole satisfaction.

At least on this job, he was given time to properly prepare, something not always possible. Days before, he and his partner had driven back and forth along the highway, during daylight and at night, studying traffic flows, the roadway and the embankment that would provide cover and the necessary escape route. After choosing the shooting site, they'd lain in wait beneath a starry sky, watching, before he was satisfied. Ordinarily, he would never attempt such a job at night, at least not in this exposed position, but this one was within acceptable risk parameters.

The cab rounded the curve and approached a circle of bright roadway beneath the light pole. There were no cars on the other carriageway. Both men brought up their weapons and squinted through the telescopic sight.

"Three…two…one," the man with the cellphone called out softly and squeezed the trigger.

Carefully directed 710 meters per second rounds ripped through the rear end of a car that had just overtaken the cab, while another silent stream tore through the car behind the cab. A row of black holes appeared magically in the panels of both cars, but because there wasn't any noise of rifle fire, it took the drivers a few seconds to react before they slammed on the brakes. That gave the two men ample time to sight on the cab, now directly opposite them.

One stream stitched the length of the body. The other sprayed the exposed windows, sending safety glass flying. Expended rounds struck the median concrete barrier and whined into the night. The rounds did not glow or sparkle as they scattered, that only happened in the movies. Spent cartridges littered the grass around both shooters. They could see the three occupants jerk and shudder under the impact of multiple rounds. They kept firing until the twenty-round clips were empty, careful that no stray shots went over the barrier.

Out of control the cab swerved across two outer lanes before smashing against the barrier. Sparks showered the roadway as the left side of the vehicle skidded along the concrete. The cab finally came to rest. Behind it, cars screeched out of its way, brakes against the floor, tires smoking as they left black trails in their wake. Mercifully the traffic was light and no one got hurt. The occupants of the two vehicles hit first, shakily got out and inspected the peppered panels of their cars, looking around anxiously, waiting to be hit again.

On the carriageway going in the other direction, motorists saw stopped cars and naturally slowed down to gape. Despite blaring horns the ripple effect inevitably ground the traffic stream going toward the airport to a crawl. When they got there, it took the police only a few minutes to clear the sightseers and get them moving again.

Behind the embankment, the two men did not hang around admiring their handiwork. There was no gallery to provide applause. They scrambled down the grassy slope at the back and hurried toward a side road paralleling the highway at that point.

175

They climbed into a waiting sedan and surged off without showing any lights. On the highway behind them, they could hear a faint wail of sirens. The two men ripped off their balaclavas and grinned at each other like they'd pulled off some successful school mischief. For them it was a game, just a game.

* * *

Martin 'Snake' Brenner shoved the throttles of his aircraft to the stops and twin GE F414 turbofans roared at full military power, the holdback bar straining against the shuttle, keeping the trembling jet in place. The bow catapult officer calmly glanced down the track at the bow safety officer who still had his right hand up, thumb in the air announcing that the deck was clear. The signal light on the carrier's island superstructure turned green and the catapult shooter pressed the fire button. Below the hot humid flight deck, launch valves opened and high pressure steam slammed into the back of two catapult pistons, snapping the holdback bar retaining pin. The VFA-41 'Black Aces' F/A-18E rushed down the deck at more than 160 miles per hour and two seconds later it was in the air, trailing ribbons of vapor from the wingtips.

Brenner screamed with delight at the almost sexual rush he always got from a cat shot surge and slapped the gear handle. The wheels locked with a thump and covering panels closed to produce an unbroken aerodynamic surface. He trimmed the aircraft, set angle to eight degrees nose-up and held it as the Hornet accelerated. At 200 knots indicated air speed, he raised flaps and pulled back the stick. He glanced aft and nodded with satisfaction as his wingman clawed into the air with him, behind and on his left to cover his six. Both aircraft quickly punched through .8 Mach without any chatter on the radio as they climbed to their assigned altitude.

In the carrier's Primary Flight Control or Pre-Fly, about 140 feet above the deck, Captain Ulesky watched the Air Boss, Commander Chuck 'Yeager' Jones, launch the two Hornets and nod to his assistant, the Mini-Boss. The aircraft's twin exhausts belched tails of white fire as they pulled away. It was after 0900, but he already had a long morning, a long night, for that matter. No excitement right now, but you never let your guard down during air ops. Too many things waited to go wrong and a life could be lost. Jones was a good officer, but at 4.5 acres a carrier deck was an awfully large place and he could not keep an eye on everything at once. Still, should something go wrong, Ulesky would be ultimately responsible.

"Outer CAP launched, CAG," Jones announced after glancing at Ulesky. "Ready to launch Texaco in twenty minutes' time." The Air Boss was referring to a Super Hornet fitted with four external fuel tanks and a 'buddy store' tank, allowing it to refuel other aircraft in the air.

"Very well," Ulesky acknowledged and scanned the portside horizon, shrouded in low haze.

Somewhere over there was a looming wall of Iranian coastal mountains that were a bastion against foreign incursion. The threat axis was not the coast, but clusters of potent anti-ship missiles deployed on several islands like Abu Masa, Quesham and Sirri; something he was glad to leave in Brent Roberts' hands. Apart from destroyers *Higgins* and *Sampson* prowling off the port side, wrapped in hugging mist, the sea was empty. But he knew that over to starboard the other three DDGs of DESRON-23 were keeping vigil over *Nimitz* should Iran venture out with swarming patrol boats or hovercraft.

He wondered whether he would see any action today. He was hoping for it, but at the same time prayed it wouldn't happen. It was a contradiction, a peculiarity of military life. A warrior, Ulesky wanted to test himself and his aircraft against another warrior and his machine. His temperament sought such a confrontation and his training provided him the tools to carry it out. The savage in him demanded the rite of blood, while sanity pointed out that the blood could be his. The veneer of civilization that cloaked him was desperately thin, as with all men.

When this tour ended, *Nimitz* would be heading Stateside for some welcome R&R. And he could use a bit of recreation himself—of a female type. Like many career officers, he was divorced, demands of the service putting too much strain on a relationship, too much time away from home. Thankfully, there were no children, and he suspected that had been part of the problem. But like the old saw said, if the Navy wanted you to have a wife, they would have issued you one. It didn't make up for an empty bed at night.

Leveling off at 20,000 feet, 300 knots indicated, Brenner's ESM, Electronic Surveillance Module, threat receiver was quiet. Nobody targeting him—yet. He glanced at the Tactical Information Display in front of him and thumbed the mike button.

"Getting some side lobe from a 5N62 Square Pair and HQ-2 Guideline Tiger Song engagement radars."

Even though he was still out of threat range, Brenner was wary of SA-5 Gammon and Hawk missile batteries that ringed Bandar Abbas giving him the once-over. The SA-5 was not much of a threat one-on-one, but several at once crowding the sky around him could become uncomfortable. For now at least the ZSU-23/4 and ZSU-57/2 antiaircraft, or triple-A, sites were quiet, but he knew that they would wake up quickly enough should he venture closer to the coast, which he had no intention of doing. This was only a friendly looksee, no need to get riled.

"Copy that," Larry 'Wino' Sanders responded over the ICS, intercommunications system, in a lazy drawl.

This was routine, no sweat. They'd been doing this shit for a month now and Sanders was relaxed, but not so relaxed that he wasn't paying attention to his job.

"I've got the E-2C data link. Two bogies at 25,000, heading two-eight-zero. We're not being painted," Brenner said, checking his Horizontal Situation Display, HSD, and the AN/ASQ-228 ATFLIR (Advanced Targeting Forward Looking Infrared) sensor. The APG-79 AESA radar gave him a nice return on his HUD, heads-up display. His pulse began to quicken and his skin prickled as his body readied for possible action. This was more like it.

Sanders acknowledged with a click over his mike.

"Turning to two-eight-zero," Brenner announced. "Check master arm off." Friendly or not, he was not wading in with his ass trailing exposed.

Sanders clicked once and the two Hornets banked into a left turn, climbing to 30,000 feet to gain an energy position over the bogies should they want to play. Brenner wasn't about to let no raghead get close enough to *Nimitz* for a launch, let alone a visual. Carrying a slim AIM-9 heat seeking Sidewinder on each wingtip, two AIM-120 AMRAAM and two AIM-7 Sparrow radar-guided missiles slung on wing hardpoints, he had everything he needed to do business, except a target.

"Carpet, this is Raven," the patrolling E-2C Block II Hawkeye early warning, battle command and control aircraft called in.

Its job was to provide air and surface surveillance as well as strike and interceptor control. Modern carrier operations would be impossible without it. But slow and unarmed, should it come to a brawl, and despite covering fighters, they would be targets of choice for an enemy.

"Be advised bogies are identified as two F-5s, turning into you on zero-nine-five. Range, three-seven miles. You are 'go' to check them out. Signal is buster."

"Copy, Raven," Brenner acknowledged. "Got 'em painted. They are not radiating."

No missile lock, which was too bad, and they only sent him lousy F-5s. They could be sightseeing, but he kind of doubted it, not this close to the battle group. He had seen this type of maneuver before; dash out to provoke a reaction, then turn back

179

and run for home. Why couldn't they have sent him something interesting, like a MiG-29 Fulcrum? Now, that was a badass aircraft. Although a clunker compared to American technology, he wouldn't mind tangling with one to see what it could do, or mixing it with their new home-grown Saegeh bird, supposedly better than an F/A-18. That would be the day. But if it came to that, a cheap F-5 was still a kill and it all looked good in a fitness report.

Twenty-five miles off shore, Brenner and Sanders waited for the two F-5s to show their hand. After getting a hard-on in anticipation of splashing one, nothing happened. The F-5s hardly cleared the coast, their search radars going and turned north. Brenner was tempted to squirt a Sparrow just to hurry them along, CAG's warning or not.

Perhaps another day, guys.

"Carpet, this is Raven. Turn to one-eight-zero and resume outer CAP position, relieving two thirsty birds."

"Roger, Raven," Brenner acknowledged and clicked the ICS button. "We're bugging out, Wino. The gents don't seem to want to mess with us today."

"I'm not surprised. They must have heard Snake was in the neighborhood," was the dry comment.

"That's a rog." Brenner chuckled, threw the Hornet onto its wingtip and reefed into a tight right turn, grunting as the g's squeezed him into his seat. Sanders was right behind him as they rocketed away from the coast.

Ulesky listened to the radio chatter and shook his head. Brenner was a good stick and flew a Hornet like a second skin, but Snake better watch it or he would stomp on him. There was only so much slack available and Snake had used most of his up. In the air Brenner was a genius, but on deck, his casual attitude to discipline rankled some of the starched brass. Still, Ulesky imagined himself not all that different when he was driving F-14s, letting it all hang out. The plain fact was that naval aviators considered themselves top dogs and nobody was about to tell them different, CAG included. What Brenner needed was a shot at leading an element. Responsibility could steady him and make him fly straight.

Astern of the carrier, green shirts were checking the four arresting wires that stretched across the deck in preparation for aircraft landing. A kink or snag in any wire could be disastrous for the aircraft and crew on the deck if it happened to hook it and the wire broke. White shirts carried out final inspections and signaled the LSOs that the deck was clear.

Ulesky watched it all without consciously paying attention. He had spent a better part of ten hours in CVIC helping put together strike packages for Bandar Abbas and Chahbahar where the Iranians had their four Kilo-class diesel submarines, and he was bone weary. Intelligence teams provided most of the grunt work, and although the process was supported by complex computer systems, it required human input to correctly define specific targets, required weapons loads, strike composition, and most importantly, suppression of enemy air defenses, as both targets were heavily ringed with SAM batteries. CVIC was a damned computer center, filled with rows of consoles, large display LEDs and projection screens. He figured that one day computers would run everything; automated ships controlling automated aircraft that used smart weapons against intelligent defenses. No need for soldiers, just computer geeks who played ultra-sophisticated video games. It might not be a bad idea at that. But then, what of pride and honor?

Honor, Ulesky acknowledged resignedly, was something that had gone out of the warrior business a long time ago. And now, he was being cynical.

* * *

Mira opened the door for him. "Shalom. Good to see you

181

back, Mr. Irian."

"Nice to be back, except for the cold," he complained, flashed her a smile and walked through. Her eyes lingered on him for a moment, then with a glance at her boss, closed the door.

Lounging in his broad-backed chair, Namir nodded to Mira and extended an open hand at one of the empty couches.

"Take a seat," he ordered and waited for Matan to make himself comfortable. "You must be tough. I didn't expect you until some time after lunch, if at all."

"I couldn't sleep," Matan explained. "Too many things going on in my head. Sarah is at work and Admina is at school. I figured I might as well come in and annoy you rather than mope alone at home. But don't worry. Jet lag will catch up with me and I'll be out of your hair early."

Namir chuckled, but he wasn't fooled by Matan's easy banter. There were new tension lines around his eyes that betrayed inner turmoil. They were not obvious, but Namir knew this man better than most. It was inevitable and it came to all men who had to make life-changing decisions. Compared to Matan's previous ops, this was a quantum leap in scope and impact. He was not surprised to see circles under his eyes.

"I don't need to ask how things went. I've seen the TV. How about that!"

Matan scrutinized his boss. There was no regret, no remorse, only hard resolution borne of certainty and conviction in the righteousness of his cause. Where was the certainty of *his* convictions? Matan wondered whether his own doubts might be unwarranted after all. Sometimes it didn't pay to think too much.

"I've also seen the TV. The boys did a good job, and thankfully, it didn't cost too many lives."

"Always regrettable, especially in this case," Namir agreed heavily, not looking regretful, "but unavoidable."

Leaning back, Matan allowed himself a small smile. "Talking of lives, there was something else on TV, one particular item caught my eye, some sort of a roadside shooting. This time near the airport, just after midnight, I believe. Not long after I landed, as a matter of fact."

Namir sighed and shook his head, joining into the game. "Shabak must do something about those lawless marauders. They're getting bolder all the time. This time, it cost us two of our own, Ellis and Tabor. Would you believe it? What a coincidence. Hit about seven or eight times each, I understand."

"Most inconvenient," Matan sympathized, his face expressionless. "Promising men. We'll be taking the usual supportive steps with Ellis' family?"

"Of course. A posthumous medal and the usual citation. Same for Tabor. They deserve to be remembered."

"And the other, ah, inconvenience?"

"A heart attack. Incredible! It seems to take them younger every day, and the boy looked so fit. I always said it was the fast food."

Matan stared and they both chuckled. They had killed three men and were laughing about it. It was absurd really. Was life suddenly that cheap? Maybe it was relief that the operation was over. Was it?

"You're an evil and insensitive bastard, Namir," he offered with a shake of his head.

He reminded himself to replace the two TWIC badges into the box with the others, and wondered why that piece of trivia had popped into his head. His mind was going.

The Metsada director smirked and folded his arms across his chest. "Sometimes that's what the job calls for, my boy. No loose ends."

"You're right, of course. We must keep our eyes on the bigger picture. I hope the returns will be worth it."

"Nothing is certain until the dust settles. Until then, to an exemplary ops, Matan. Very well done."

"It seems to have gone off smoothly enough," Matan agreed

cautiously.

"Why the long face then?"

"There is always a random element, an overlooked detail, that could come back to haunt us. And you can bet the Americans will be thorough. That DHS conference was a convenient cover, but it also gave me a useful insight into how they operate and what we're up against. I'm probably uptight about nothing, but it's grinding me down."

"Then get your head out of your ass," Namir said firmly, his voice crisp. "This isn't like you. You're no good to me moping. Next, you'll be feeling sorry for yourself."

Matan grinned, but it was without humor. "I admit to some soul searching, but that's probably due to all the mileage. Those Atlantic flights, they give you too much time to think. And you told me enough times that in our business, thinking is an occupational disease."

"If I did say it, it is small of you to bring it up now. But seriously, we cannot spend time worrying about your damned random factor. If you stage-managed everything properly to cover yourself, we'll just have to wear the rest. To do otherwise is a waste of emotional energy. If something surfaces, no matter what it is, we'll deal with it then."

"You're right, of course. Lord! I cannot believe that it's only been a day," Matan mused, wanting to turn the conversation onto safer territory. "It's like I've been away a lifetime. Any reaction from Kameer and the government?"

"Our Director is sitting tight, but not altogether displeased at the prospect of America dishing it out to Iran. Sanvel is practically jumping up and down with glee."

"The man always did have a short fuse," Matan observed dryly.

Namir shook a finger at him. "That's no way to speak of a senior director."

Matan grinned. "I am suitably chastised."

"Glad to hear it. But I agree with you, and between the two of us, Kameer should get rid of the man. His judgments are too personal and overlaid with religious zeal. I don't trust a man who allows his personal bias to influence his professionalism."

"And Kameer?"

"What about him?"

"Come on, Namir! Don't patronize me," Matan said, irritated by the byplay.

"Testy, eh? For your information the Director *did* raise the similarity between the ops and your proposal. It was bound to happen."

"No one said that he wasn't smart."

"He can speculate all he wants, and that's about all he can do. As for the government, opinions are divided, as usual. Publicly, Sharron Ibrahim deplores the attack, of course, but secretly, I suspect that he wouldn't mind seeing Iran's nuclear threat pegged back a notch or two."

"The Americans haven't struck yet, you know," Matan reminded him. "If they do, it would eliminate just one of our problems."

"It's only a matter of time, my boy, and we tackle our problems as we see them. Leaving that package behind was an absolute masterstroke. With that evidence, I cannot see how President Walters can hold back. If Congress doesn't force him, public opinion certainly will. Besides, he *wants* to attack, or he would not have implemented sanctions of his own. How about that!"

Matan chewed his lower lip and nodded. "I guess. The events should unfold as we planned. You heard what happened at the UN?"

Namir snorted and shook his head. "I've got to give Al Zerkhani credit. Announcing open inspection of their facilities was a damn clever move. But it might be a case of too little, too late. There has been too much bad blood spilt for the gesture to mean much, not now. The tide of world opinion is against him."

"Perhaps, but it's got to set President Walters thinking."

"He'll think that the whole maneuver was staged to throw him off the track. I would. It's a case of believing the simplest hypothesis, and everything points to Iran. You made sure of that."

Matan had been telling himself the same thing and, of course, Namir was right. Why would the Americans think anything else? Set the wheels in motion and political inertia would do the rest. A path of least resistance…

"Anything from the Research Department about U.S. forces in the Gulf?"

"*Eisenhower* is sitting off Kharg Island with Bushehr right on the coast behind it, and *Nimitz* is parked off Bandar Abbas to clean up their navy. Both are conducting air and surface exercises. So far, the Iranians have not reacted with their usual provocative sallies or made any protests. They've got an Ilyushin Il-76 airborne early warning bird inland keeping an eye on proceedings, and two F-5s skirted the coast, but that's about it. Nobody is making any sudden moves."

"I don't blame them. What's the reaction on the street?"

"Uncertainty and confusion," Namir said promptly. "The hardliners are crowing, but most people out there, if you can believe the papers, are simply concerned, worrying where it will all end."

"I'm worried where it will all end myself," Matan quipped, sighed and stood up. "Thanks for the heads-up. I'll be at my desk, catching up on emails and stuff."

Namir waited for the door to close, then sat back and locked his fingers behind his head, pleased with himself. The hospital that treated Ronel's accident signed it off as simple cardiac failure—open-and-shut and his boys had taken care of the other two problems with their usual efficiency. Too bad about the cab driver, but that could not have been avoided. All in all, a neat piece of work, even if he said so himself. Nobody else would.

Rocking back and forth, the Metsada director pondered his

remaining problem and made a decision. For the moment, he would leave it alone. After all, there was such a thing as carrying paranoia too far. However, should the situation start to unravel, steps would be taken.

Chapter Seven

After a solid night's sleep, all of seven-and-a-half hours, long enough by his standards, Tom Meecham felt more kindly disposed toward his fellow human beings. Not that he was gushing over with virtue and magnanimous generosity. He still felt that most people would cheat, lie, steal and commit mayhem on each other if left to their own selfish and unrestrained devices. Despite his feel-good-at-the-world day, some semblance of normality had to be maintained. Nevertheless, a bright morning, clear skies lit with warm sunshine, no breeze, made his spirits soar. And he had not even thought about Malena, usually sitting across the breakfast table, prattling away about the usual little things that women prattle about.

He had not forgotten his craving for a bacon and egg sandwich either and was determined to indulge in one this morning. The sizzling bacon rashers smelled divine, guarded by two extra large farm eggs, while the percolator bubbled on the side, adding to the mix of enticing aromas. With some eggs he bought, it was hard to tell the difference between the yolk and the white. Chickens on drips, he mused sardonically. No wonder the eggs came out looking like jelly and smelled of fish. With the frying done, abandoning proper dining etiquette, he ate with undisguised relish, the toasted sandwich held in his hands, egg yolk dripping onto the plate.

Two cups of coffee later, he eased the Pontiac out of the garage and drove into a brand new day.

At 8 a.m., traffic was heavy along East TC Jester, crowding the I-160 on-ramp. Pretty soon it would be a parking lot. He kept on Ella Boulevard, avoiding the mess, coming into Pinegate

Drive the back way. Taking a rental house close to the Bureau office was done deliberately. Although removed from flashy restaurants and shopping conveniences, getting to and from work in minutes more than made up for it. It wasn't so bad in the morning when he was still fresh and relaxed, but at night, the thought of fighting other commuters for the same road space chilled him. He simply wanted to get home.

He drove into the FBI lot, parked in his spot and got his mind in gear. It was not like he could avoid thinking about Valero; the radio bulletins and TV channels made sure of that. But it was the same old stuff—Iran guilty as hell and when would the administration strike back? Iran had protested its innocence at the UN, of course, but it looked bad, and Al Jazeera claimed that its website had been illegally infiltrated with a bogus news page. Nobody believed either of them. Even the normally skeptical French and German media had stepped off their high moral ground and approved of an American measured response, whatever that meant. There was something to be said for old Rome where Caesar hustled aggrieved parties into the Coliseum and whoever walked out took all the spoils. Unfortunately, today's realpolitik did not allow for such a common-sense approach. Not that sense was common anyway, or he would be out of business.

Walking toward the main building, Tom reminded himself to call his contact at Cyber Division. Could they tell if those websites were indeed compromised? If they were, it would be nice to know by whom, but that would be crying for the moon. Never mind, one step at a time. First establish whether the sites *were* penetrated. As one techno geek once remarked, anything was possible on the Web. And if you knew what you were doing, it was untraceable. Wasn't science wonderful?

As suspected, his JTTF and FIG teams had drawn a blank, but it was still early days and they seemed to be taking the situation seriously. In a week's time, they would probably come out with a neat analysis stating why they couldn't analyze anything.

Spinning wheels, that was all. Tom held out his hopes with the CIA running down the George Bush Airport surveillance tapes against their database of known and suspected international terrorists. But even that was not a certainty. Too many people wanted to play dirty with Uncle Sam and most of them would not sit still for a CIA mug shot. Still, they could get lucky. However, there was considerable data to be processed and he did not expect a result anytime soon.

Discussing the mug scan with Mark Price, the NOC director told him that under his direction, the CIA and FBI were also running comparisons against domestic right-wing and extremist freedom fighter groups, just to cover all bases. Tom had not argued, but he didn't expect anything to turn up either. Well, it couldn't hurt. To him, Valero smelled like an international caper. Why would a domestic right-wing nut group hit an oil installation? Of course, it was always possible that he was wrong, and why not put all those nice Bureau computers to some use and keep them from rusting. But if Iran or some other unfriendly Middle Eastern group had carried this out, surely they would not be so foolish as to use known operatives. They must know that airport surveillance would tag them. Then again, experience told him that bad guys sometimes made the most childish mistakes.

Dr. Peters was practically dancing on the spot in front of Tom's office. Without bothering to hide a broad smile, Tom unlocked the door and walked in.

"Morning. I gather you found something interesting?"

Brian grabbed his arm and virtually dragged him into the office. With a suspicious stare around the floor, he closed the door.

"You'll like this," Brian gushed, hands waving. Tom walked behind his desk to his chair and sat down.

"You're not even giving me a chance to grab a cup of coffee," he protested mildly, amused by Brian's agitation.

"Never mind your coffee. This is important."

"I like enthusiasm, even when it is misplaced. Okay, spill it."

Now that he was actually with the senior agent, Peters was momentarily flustered. He snagged a visitor seat and sank into it. If he were wrong, his action could set off a chain of events that might be disastrous. He reviewed the facts in his mind and decided he was on solid ground. Scientific evidence rarely lied, when interpreted correctly, he reminded himself. It was the interpretation that usually undid one, but not this time.

"Remember that patch of sticky substance on the detonator casing? Well, I believe I found out what it was."

"And…"

"It's adhesive residue from a sticky label."

Tom frowned, completely thrown off the track. This was the big news? "You mean an ordinary office sticky label? You've lost me. What's the significance?"

"Ordinarily, none," Brian admitted with a small shrug. "But bear with me. I ran a scraping through a mass spectrograph to identify the components. You see, most pressure-sensitive adhesives use a blend of rubbery elastomer and low molecular weight tackifier resin. The tackifier is used primarily to modify the viscoelastic characteristics of the adhesive. Commercially, these are mainly solvent and water-borne acrylic emulsions. You with me so far?"

Tom nodded. He'd been around forensic technicians long enough to understand most of the parlance.

"I think so. These substances control the degree of stickiness?"

"Right. Simply put, they determine how well a label will adhere to a given surface, how long it will remain attached, and how easy it is to remove. The adhesive is supposed to remain permanently tacky, but variations in material composition and manufacture processes mean that there is a degree of disparity across brands. Now, most PSAs involve a base polymer such as natural rubber that's mixed with additives and tackifiers to produce the desired adhesion and peel value."

"The effort required to remove the label?"

"Right again. You need to realize that PSA performance can be modified by environmental conditions, particularly temperature. Too hot or too cold, and your sticky label won't stick, or it will bind permanently. So, manufacturers have played around with emulsion acrylics to improve adhesion and peel properties. One material that's being used is chitosan."

Tom looked blank. "Come again? It's been a while since I did chemistry, you know."

Brian grinned. "Stick with me for a while longer," he said and Tom rolled his eyes. "Chitosan is a relatively new development, traditionally used as a plant growth enhancer. The stuff is produced from chitin, the structural element in the exoskeleton of crustaceans such as crabs, shrimp and lobster. The material is also used in engineering water filtration applications. The latest such application is in medical bandages and homeostatic agents. But this is where things get interesting as far as we are concerned. Microencapsulated chitosan is now being used as an adhesive agent on sticky labels. The use is not widespread yet, but is gaining some exposure in Europe. Spectrographic analysis of our sample shows the presence of chitosan." Peters sat back and beamed, waiting for Meecham to make the connection.

Tom scratched his chin, then peered at the scientist and shook his head.

"I don't buy it. You stick a label on something and peel it off without expecting to leave behind any goo. I've done it. So why did our label, if it was a label, leave a residue?"

"It's simple, really," Brian said, relishing being a teacher again. "What's the internal cabin pressure of a passenger jetliner in flight?"

"Something like nine thousand feet, I understand."

"Right! The pressure drop isn't noticeable to people at rest, but it induces a subtle chemical change in certain organic bases—"

"Like chitosan," Mark said wryly as understanding dawned and Brian nodded.

"After ten or more hours in the air, it was enough to alter its peel value and leave a trace of tackifier on the control box."

"How come you know so much about this shit?" Tom complained accusingly.

"I had to bone up."

"Okay, I'll ask the obvious question. Where did this stuff come from?"

"Mediterranean. The base is made from crab shells, one of six species of Macropodia found in the area. There is one particular place where crab is extensively farmed for the domestic market, and this is the interesting bit…Israel."

"Christ!" Tom sat up with a jerk and stared as scenarios flashed through his head, all of them bad. Israel?

But what reason would they have to carry out sabotage in the United States? They were supposed to be allies, for crying out loud, and survived only by the grace of huge American economic and military subsidies. Talk about biting the hand that feeds you. It didn't make sense.

Peters sat there, looking pleased with himself. "I thought it would make your day."

"Maybe not. Are you sure it's crab?"

"Positive. There are traces of giant red shrimp—*Aristaeomorpha Foliacia*, also farmed by Israel. But that's probably a minor additive in the manufacturing process."

Tom gave him a nasty grin. "Thanks for the Latin lesson. Who else knows about this?"

"No one."

"Then keep it that way," Tom ordered sternly. "This is dynamite and you know it."

"I get it, all right. That's why I was hanging outside your door waiting for you to show up, and never mind the curious stares I got along the way. But before you ask the next question, there is only one manufacturer in Israel who produces commercial sticky labels from a chitosan emulsion—Manning Adar Industries, based in Haifa."

"How sure are you that this adhesive comes from an Israeli-made label?"

"I'm not, but all my evidence points that way. To nail it down, of course—"

"You want a real label to check against."

"Right." Brian looked hopeful. "Does this rate a transfer to Quantico?"

He had given up a university position to join the Bureau, and so far, he had not regretted the decision. However, to push his career further, he needed to be where the real action was, and Houston wasn't that place.

Tom sat back and chuckled. "I'll sign the slip myself. Man, you've really thrown me a curve." Shaking his head, he reached across the desk for his secure scramble phone, pressed the speaker button and punched in a private number. It took two rings.

"Mark Price."

"Mark, Meecham. Got a minute?"

"Shoot."

"Are you secure?"

"Go ahead."

"Brian has identified the adhesive on the control box."

"Say, that's real quick service. Does it tell us anything?"

"You won't believe it…Israel," Tom said and allowed himself a wry grin, knowing exactly what was going through the NOC director's head. This was going to cook Mark's day, he thought with relish. The silence stretched for several long seconds.

"Well, crap!" Mark said at last and heaved a weary sigh. "Is this information compartmented?"

Tom appreciated that Mark accepted his statement without querying the validity of the evidence. That took nerve.

"Only the three of us know, and I suggest that it should remain that way. For now, at least."

"Absolutely. If this got out…I don't even want to think about it." Tom heard a groan and a squeak of leather as Mark shifted in his seat. "Why in hell did you want to dump this on me just when I was starting to enjoy myself?"

"Just sharing the misery," Tom said and laughed. "There is more. This stuff isn't just any glue. To be absolutely sure that we *are* dealing with Israel, Brian needs a sample of plain office stickers made by Manning Adar Industries. Can you get the CIA Tel Aviv desk to send us some? Disguise it with some other stuff to make the request look innocuous."

Mark chuckled. "Asking Tel Aviv to send us office supplies is meant to sound innocuous?"

Tom had a chuckle himself. "I know. They'll think we are ready for the bunny hats."

"I would. Is Brian with you?"

"Right here, Mr. Price."

"Just Mark, and that was a damn good job, doc. Boy, you sure know how to spoil a fun day. These special labels, is anybody else making them?"

"China, Sweden and Norway are the main suppliers. But I don't want to start looking at them until I disprove Israel as the source."

"Makes sense. Hold on. Let me see what I can do about getting you a sample. This will be on speaker, so keep it zipped."

Tom heard numbers being punched into another phone, followed by ringing.

"Central Intelligence Agency, Director of National Clandestine Service, Rosslyn speaking. How may I help you?" she declared with crisp authority, designed to instantly intimidate any caller.

To Mark, she was no stranger, having run into her before: a cool, forbidding young lady who spurned all attempts at dates with dashing field operatives—maybe because she knew the work was not that dashing after all.

"Mark Price, Rosslyn, Director, National Operations Center, DHS. Please switch me to Mr. Zardwovsky."

"I know who you are, sir. But I'm afraid—"

"Ms. Rosslyn, you either put through my call or I'll be asking Raymond Grant why the CIA is not giving me its full cooperation in a matter of national security."

That obviously got through, for she took in a sharp breath and cleared her throat. "Ah, just a moment, sir." There was an empty time filled with Musak, followed by a click.

"Price, I heard you had wormed your way into DHS," Zardwovsky announced at length, his deep voice silky with loathing.

"You can't keep good talent down, but you certainly tried," Mark snapped with mutual animosity. It was childish, for the man was beneath contempt, simple chemistry. "You certainly did."

"Evidently not hard enough. You bullied yourself through Rosslyn, so what do you want?"

"I need you to call the Tel Aviv station desk and ask them to courier me samples of home-made and offshore manufactured office supplies using the fastest means available. I want pads, notebooks, sticky labels, stuff like that."

Tom suppressed a smile as Zardwovsky digested the seemingly asinine request.

"Ah, you also want party hats and candles?"

"Perhaps next time," Mark snapped.

"I don't know how you spend your days at DHS, Price, clearly not doing much, but over at Langley, we do real work. I don't have time to indulge in your practical gags. Now, if you will excuse me, I've got a report for the Director. No doubt you'll be hearing from Colin Forbes."

"Hold it, Zardwovsky!" Mark snarled, all pretence at civility lost. "I am making an official tasking order in my capacity as Director of NOC. You either carry it out or we'll see who'll be hearing from whom. You got that?"

"You're joking, right?"

"Never been more serious in my life."

"Why in hell do you want the stuff, anyway?"

"I'm running short and it's none of your damn business. I don't care how you do it, but I expect to see a package on my desk first thing in the morning, if not sooner," Mark snapped and cut the connection.

"I can see why you love the guy," Tom observed dryly.

"He is a balls polishing asshole, but we'll get our present tomorrow. Good enough, Brian?"

Peters nodded to Tom. "I am genuinely impressed, Mark. That's what I call cooperation."

"DHS aims to please. Do you want the stuff sent down to you?"

"No. I prefer to pick it up at your office, if you don't mind, and take it downtown to our labs. Now that I know what to look for, it should not take me long to verify the source. I'm sure you will want the results fast." He glanced at Tom who was wearing a bemused smile. "Ah, provided Mr. Meecham authorizes the flight. Sorry, Tom."

"Don't mind me, I just work here."

"Don't worry about costs," Mark interjected. "This one is on me. I'll have my Gulfstream pick you up from George Bush Domestic at 0600. My secretary will email Tom the details. How's that?"

"Good enough, and thanks," Peters deadpanned, impressed nonetheless, and relieved at not having to push through throngs of commuters or check-in queues—despite an early departure.

"Once you get it all sorted out, wrap it up nice and neat, and before we fly you back to Houston, I get to see a copy of all the paperwork."

"No problem."

"Excellent. While I've got you on the line, Tom, you got a minute?"

"Of course," Tom said and glanced at Brian, who hurriedly stood up.

"I shall see you tomorrow, Mr. Price."

"Until then," Mark replied.

Peters nodded to Tom and closed the office door with a soft click.

"Okay, Mark. Shoot."

"That was brilliant work by Brian. But if he is right, we've got ourselves a whole new ballgame, man. You know that."

"I know it, all right. Christ! Just when I was getting comfortable with Iran having done it."

"They still could have, you know. Anybody can buy a roll of labels over a counter."

"Yeah. Clever misdirection…if that's how it happened."

"That label, you know what I'm thinking?"

"Right with you. It could have been used to identify a presumably faulty pack, left there for us to find and draw the obvious conclusion."

"And possibly the wrong one. Makes you wonder who did what to whom and who got paid. This doesn't make your job any easier, Tom."

"On the contrary. Following a solid lead is right up my alley. No matter where the evidence leads. After that, it's your baby."

Mark gave a short barking laugh, but it was not with humor. "Thanks, I'll return the favor some day. But this particular baby lies squarely in the President's lap."

"And I'm sure he'll enjoy feeding it," Tom said with feeling, wearing a broad grin.

"You're nasty, did you know that?" Mark observed affably.

"Yep. It's been mentioned once or twice," Tom replied, comfortable with the idea. There was no parking room in the Bureau for soft guys, not if you wanted to be where the real work was done. "But listening to your exchange with Zardwovsky, I suspect that you might be cut from the same cloth."

"Count on it. He was my case officer once and almost got me killed. An ops in Libya. During the debrief, he tried to make it out like the whole thing was my fault. I guess we kind of stopped being chummy afterward."

"Yeah, it can work out like that. What do you plan to do now?"

Mark understood the question and did not play dumb. "I'll have to update Admiral Stone. He's the point man for the President and has to know. That will certainly mean bringing the Chief of Staff on board. There are ramifications to consider. After all, we don't want the President flushing the wrong guy now, do we?"

"This is starting to get out of hand, Mark. Too many people in the loop."

"Don't worry. I'll keep it bottled."

"I hope so. One more thing. It's early, I know, but did the CIA come up with anything from those airport tapes?"

"Well, crap! They've only been at it for a night. Have a heart, Tom."

"It's mortgaged, like the rest of me."

"Hah! You got anything else?"

"You'll be the first to know. Later, then," Tom said and switched off.

Staring at the dead phone, Mark sighed, rubbed his temples and shook his head. Israel? It hardly seemed possible. And if it *was* them, it would mean Metsada. They were the only ones with that type of barefaced gall and capability to pull off the Valero stunt. In his past life, he had tangled with the blacker side of Mossad and knew what they could do. Well, no use asking them for help now, at least not until he was sure they had nothing to do with it. But if the thing was compartmented, how could he tell? After a moment of introspection, he picked up the phone and punched in a number.

"Analysis," a bored voice answered after four rings. "Ian Shiloh."

"Ian, it's Mark."

There was an audible groan at that piece of cheery news. "Jesus, Mark! I've got a month's worth of tapes from IAH and more stuff is coming in from all over the place. This thing will take time. So, if you don't mind, do us both a fat favor. Put your feet on your desk, lean back and pretend to be thinking like the good public parasite that you are. I'll let you know if I come up with anything, okay?"

Mark laughed. Ian's unpretentious roughness was a cheerful change from the starched faces he normally saw. The National Imagery and Mapping Agency was initially tasked to provide skilled interpretation of photographic images obtained by high-flying aircraft and satellites. As surveillance technology expanded, so did its terms of reference, and now NIMA was responsible for interpretation of all photo and electronic image data.

While still spooking for the CIA, Mark had dealt with Ian on photo intelligence and analyses of threats for several missions, and found the elderly man a straight shooter, shunning all forms of subterfuge and office bullshit in every way, shape or form. Of course, that attitude had not endeared him to some, like Zardwovsky—chair polishers preferring to hear only good news that stroked their pinky-sized egos. That explained why Ian was still in Analysis instead of heading up a section of his own, but the man seemed content. He was fortunate.

"Well, crap! I love you too, but I wasn't going to rain on your shoes about those damned tapes."

"Oh? Then you're going to pee on me about something else, I'm sure. I know your kind, never happy." With that ventilation of spleen, Ian gave a resigned sigh. "Okay, what do you want? The sooner I get you out of my soup, the better I'll feel."

"My, eating raw bran again, eh?" Mark countered and gave a chuckle. "This should be an easy one for you. I want you to run a match for any Mossad operatives at George Bush, covering Saturday six a.m. to Monday six a.m.''

"Mossad, eh? Any particular reason or it's just your hate-the-Mossad-day again? I'm asking because that would eat into my time finding those Valero terrorists for you. Remember them? The bad guys all over the news?"

"I'm naturally nosy, Ian, and I enjoy annoying you."

"You got that right."

"And, Ian, get this going right away, and don't tell anybody what you're doing."

"That's easy. Nobody knows what I'm doing anyway."

"If anybody starts giving you a hard time, refer them to me."

"With pleasure."

"Call me—"

"As soon as I have anything. I know. But Mossad? Well, it's your money."

Mark could almost see Ian shaking his head with bemusement as he switched off. Ian bitched and moaned, but he got things done and his analyses were always right on the money, a good thing to have with your ass in a crack.

After replacing the receiver, Mark *did* feel like putting his feet on the desk, but that, of course, was out of the question. Still, he could dream about it. CIA held extensive files on many international operatives, including Mossad. Not all, but enough for the exercise to be useful if Peters' evidence turned out to mean something, and he could always get lucky. Nobody said that whoever pulled off Valero had to fly out of George Bush International, or fly out anywhere, for that matter. They could have taken a bus or Amtrak, but he didn't believe it. After the shit exploded, it was likely that all air services would be grounded and the bad guys would end up stuck in a country with everyone after them. No, they would fly out as quickly as possible, and the only airport that handled international flights was IAH. Then again, they *could* still be in the country. Stranger things had happened and he had done some of them himself as a field operative. The preposterous action sometimes worked best because it *was* preposterous and so unlikely. Always do the unpredictable, they told him at The Farm. The CIA trainers had told him many things, and not all of them turned out to be true.

Well, crap.

No use dallying any longer. He picked up the phone and pushed some keys, making sure the line was still scrambled. The response was immediate.

"Hi, Mark," Admiral Graham Stone answered. "Hardly a day's gone by and you're giving me a hard time already?"

"You know," Mark said with a smile, "you're the second one this morning to give me such a warm welcome. I guess I'll go and cry on Cottard's broad shoulders instead."

"You would. What's up? And no, the President is not about to blow the shit out of Iran, despite you guys finding that explosives package."

"I always thought Walters had a good head on his shoulders, because after I'm through with you, he'll need it."

"Something tells me I should have stayed in bed. Okay, son. Spill it."

"It could be Israel, Admiral."

"Shit! That would really make his day. Evidence?"

"That C-4 pack? FBI found traces of adhesive on the control box, but it's not your normal glue. Their forensic guy says the stuff was made in Israel. I asked the CIA to send us samples, mixed with other junk to throw them off the track. Zardwovsky thinks I should be locked up in a straightjacket, but that's okay as long as it keeps him from thinking along wrong lines."

"Agreed. Of course, it could all be a clever plant by the Iranians to throw us off the track."

"The thought had occurred to me, Admiral. That's why I asked the CIA analysis team to start looking for Mossad operatives who might have flown in or out of George Bush International during the weekend."

"That was good thinking," Stone acknowledged warmly and Mark preened.

He wished he had somebody like Stone running the CIA. They would not be in such a mess now and the Admiral had always run a tight ship. Well, life was unsympathetic even at the best of times and you had to surf the wave as it came along—mindful of the wipeout.

"When can you pin down this glue stuff?"

"Tomorrow, if the Tel Aviv desk comes across. As for tagging Mossad, it's a case of holding your breath and spinning the prayer wheels."

"Thanks for the heads-up, son. Even if unsubstantiated, the President will definitely want to know this. Talking of which, who else is in the loop here?"

"Tom Meecham and his forensic guy. It's contained."

"Meaning that you want the same thing at my end. Don't worry. I'll keep it tight. Have you talked to Forbes?"

"I planned on giving—"

"He doesn't have a need to know. Clear?"

Mark thought that one over and didn't like it. His boss wasn't going to like it either, but figured that Forbes would understand. He hoped so, or his bright new career could be in for a steep nosedive.

"Understood," he said reluctantly.

"I sympathize, Mark, and I apologize for putting you in a spot."

"No problem, Admiral. I'll live through it."

"I'll hear from you tomorrow, then."

"If not sooner," Mark said and replaced the receiver. He glanced at his wristwatch and grinned. It was only 9:30. What else could happen? His coffee cup was empty and he decided it was a good time for a refill.

When Price broke the connection, Stone frowned and tapped the desktop with strong fingertips. Still holding the receiver, he pressed the disconnect pin, waited for the dial tone and pushed an extension button.

"How's the morning, Graham?" the White House chief of staff queried cheerfully after a single ring.

"As a matter of fact, it's going pretty well. Can you snag the President for about half an hour? I've got something hot that both of you need to know."

Cottard did not ask what it was about. Right now, there was only one hot agenda item on their plate, but getting hold of the President was not going to be easy. The Corn Belt delegation was due; then there was the ethanol fuel lobby and the Senate Majority Leader wanted to chat. Well, he could field that one himself.

"His schedule is tight, but I'll see what I can do. Hold on."

Stone waited with the phone at his ear and resumed his finger drumming.

"You there? I'll be breaking a few hearts, but he'll see us at 10:15. It better be important, Admiral."

"It is."

"Care to give me a hint?" Cottard quipped and Stone chuckled.

"This is an open line, Manfred."

"It's a White House line!" Cottard protested in outrage.

"That's what I said."

"See you at 10:15."

Stone gave a small laugh, but he had been serious. He simply did not trust the integrity of White House internal comms. Some wiring was older than him. If what Price said was true and it got out prematurely, the president would have armed rioting on the front lawn. Which, of course, would make Iran very happy. And who could blame them? The whole thing was getting to be less and less fun. If he wanted fun, he should have stayed in the Navy. But that meant the Pentagon, as there were only so many sea duty command slots available, and even with rotation, far too many admirals waited for their chance to fill one. And most of them would be waiting in vain. No, he'd had his share of that fun and did not mind his new job at all.

He took a deep breath, still wishing for an occasional whiff of salt air and a sight of open seas, and then set his mouth. He had about half an hour to get his presentation sorted out and reminiscing wasn't going to cut the mustard. He pulled the PC keyboard toward him and accessed his special directory where he kept the various dark scenario files. He scrolled down the list and double-clicked one. When the file opened, he reached for his cup of strong Navy java and began reading. He preferred a medium roast, the grounds salted before brewing, of course. Just a pinch to take away the bitterness without scrambling the aroma. And contrary to popular belief, the coffee did not taste salty, unless you overdid it. He didn't worry too much about the taste. After all, it was Navy coffee, government issue. Some chiefs he knew made it so thick it felt chewy, a paint remover, but he preferred his a bit milder.

Staring vacantly at the flat screen, not seeing the words, Stone mulled over the summary. The brief didn't tell him anything new, reiterating the quagmire that was more or less a result of British empire building. But he knew that already. What irked him was that after having created the mess, they and everyone else were now looking at the United States to solve the problem, while making political mileage out of the failure of successive initiatives. If he were honest, and right now, he could not afford to be otherwise, past administrations giving only token attention to brokering an outcome that stood any chance of establishing a Palestinian State, or at least appeasing both parties. In reality the efforts merely reinforced the differences and irritated everybody. If it were not for the powerful Jewish lobby, would America have even bothered? Everybody coddling up to all those poor, suffering bloody Jews, not recognizing them for the predators they were. Instead of bombing Iran, they should bomb the Knesset.

When Stone thought of it in those terms, the idea of Israel committing a strike against America in order to force a response against Iran did not sound very far-fetched. Theoretically, anything was possible, but was it true?

He glanced at the digital readout of his desk clock and logged off the terminal. With easy strides, he walked out of his office and made his way through the crowded West Wing. Along the way, he received glances and nods of recognition, but it was merely distracted politeness. He stopped into Ms. Davies' domain, guardian of the White House chief of staff, and waited. A formidable young lady, she had no compunction about saying no even to a senior Cabinet member. She and Stone had reached an understanding. He would not bother Cottard unless he needed to. So far it was working.

Chapelle Davies looked up at his imposing form and flashed him a small smile. Stone considered himself fortunate for that token of acknowledgment. Most visitors only rated a frigid scowl.

"He is expecting you, Admiral," she said sweetly, got up and opened the door for him.

"Thanks," he said and walked through.

Cottard looked up, finished straightening a pile of papers on his cluttered desk, rubbed his nose and sighed.

"Ah, Graham, let's get this over with." He walked to a thickly lacquered natural wood door, knocked once and opened it wide. He stepped in without waiting for a response.

Samuel Walters glanced up as the two men walked into the Oval Office and stared pointedly at his national security advisor.

"You've ruined my morning, Admiral. It better be worth it."

Stone did not miss the fact that Walters had not used his first name. As far as he was concerned, the boss maintained an open-door policy with his senior staff and Stone wasn't about to back off because the president's schedule got bent around the edges.

"I think you'll find this useful, sir," he said and sat on the striped beige sofa set against the left wall. Cottard cast him a glance of warning.

"I did not mean to rub you the wrong way, Graham," Walters apologized. "It's just a bad time."

"Well, sir, it's about to get a whole lot worse. The FBI have come up with evidence which suggests that Israel could be behind the whole thing."

"Israel? Damnation! That's all I need," Walters snarled and gave a heavy sigh. "How solid is this?"

"It's not conclusive. They hope to nail it down one way or another by tomorrow."

"What tipped them off?" Cottard asked, looking shaken, unable to accept it. His mother was Jewish, for crying out loud. He realized that Stone would not bring this up unless he believed in the possibility.

Stone regarded Cottard with sympathy, aware of his dilemma. He knew that Cottard was not brought up as a Jew, his father being a devout Baptist, but understood the pain this would inflict on his mother if the allegation turned out to be true and it got out, which it would, of course.

"They found residue from an ordinary office label glue on the recovered timer box. The glue was made in Israel. The sticker could have been placed there to distinguish it from working packages—"

"And left as evidence to implicate Iran," Walters said savagely. "Damn sneaky, that."

"It is definitely a possibility, sir," Stone acknowledged. "To make sure that it *is* an Israeli-made label, Price is getting the CIA to send us a sample."

Cottard snorted. "I bet that went down well."

"I am sure it did," Stone agreed without humor. "However, this could still be a piece of clever misdirection. That's why Price is trying to ID any Mossad agents who might have been in Houston over the weekend, other than those at their consulate, of course."

Walters looked at him and frowned, his question clear.

"If this was carried out by Mossad, it would be a black ops, sir. They would want to keep it tight even from their own guys."

"Makes sense. So, all this could still be a cat and mouse game," Walters grated and shook his head. "As though the situation weren't complicated enough. What annoys me, if it *was* Israel, I can even understand why they might do it."

"Provoke us into a strike against Iran's nuclear installations," Cottard mused. "That's the only thing they're really afraid of right now. God, but that's clever."

"No, it's stupid!" Walters snapped. "I might not like what Iran is doing, but I never indicated that I would do something so drastic as to bomb them. Israel must know that exposure would sink them."

"Obviously they never expected the matter to surface," Stone said mildly. "That patch of glue was one of those random elements, a piece of plain bad luck. But until the FBI and Price produce corroborating evidence, all we have is simply another plausible, if disturbing, scenario."

Walters slammed his hand against the desk. "Disturbing is not the word for it. They were prepared to send the world's economy into a meltdown, not counting the political fallout in the region, merely to remove a potential security threat that could still be some five years off. If it's a threat at all."

Stone crossed his legs and studied the president. "Why are we treating this as a surprise?" he asked and Cottard stared. Walters looked predatory.

"You better explain that, Graham."

"Let's face some facts, Mr. President. America supports Israel because of misguided ideology and misplaced loyalty, and only to the extent that our support does not disrupt the flow of Arab oil. Those gymnastics caused us no end of grief with our Middle East policy. Even when the old Soviet Union was on the prowl, strategically, Israel wasn't on our threat board. Their governments have demonstrated time and again a willingness to exploit this one-sided relationship, provided the relationship did not compromise their own interests. You only need to look at their nuclear program, a blatant disregard of the Non-Proliferation Treaty, which they never bothered to sign, and their open trading of nuclear secrets and material with South Africa, France and Turkey. Mr. President, urged on by their powerful military machine, Israel has repeatedly shown a proclivity to turn on its allies for the sake of national expediency. Why wouldn't they do the same thing to us?

"If you want singular proof, the willingness to turn on us was vividly demonstrated in 1967 when they attacked the NSA SIGINT ship *Liberty*. After strafing her decks, they put two torpedoes into her, and then machine-gunned our sailors in life rafts. They later apologized, saying that *Liberty* was mistaken for an Egyptian troop carrier. Instead of kicking their butts, the Johnson administration covered up the matter for the sake of not upsetting the broader relationship between the two countries. What horseshit!"

Walters sighed, looking uncomfortable. "Not our finest hour exactly, was it?"

Stone forced a thin smile, disliking the idea of being patronized. "History can be a great teacher, Mr. President, provided you heed the lessons."

"And you're going to tell me that we ignored those lessons?" Walters asked equitably.

"I am, sir. The British practically invented Israel, when in 1917 they issued the Balfour Declaration, promising to set up a Jewish National Home in Palestine. They didn't do it in a sudden gush of altruism or sympathy for the Jews. They wanted control of Palestine and got it when the League of Nations later ratified the mandate. It turned out to be a Pandora's box that has haunted everybody ever since. Of course, the Palestinians were not very amused by the idea of losing their ancestral lands, but as a bunch of farmers and peasants they couldn't do too much about it at the time."

Walters raised his hand to forestall the flood of history. "If this is your intro into demonstrating Jewish ruthlessness when they turned on the British after WW II, I am aware of that salutary lesson, Graham."

"It is more than that, Mr. President. To a certain extent the Brits did it to themselves. When they started wooing Arab support as a bulwark against Germany and to protect their growing oil interests—"

"The Arabs demanded that Britain stop the influx of Jews into Palestine," Walters finished for him. "I know all that, Graham. I also know that in 1947 Britain resigned its mandate and the Arab League went into war with the Jews to prevent formation of Israel as a nation. They lost and in 1948 the UN recognized Israel. I've been to school. So, what's your point?"

"The relevant point, Mr. President, and the basis for ongoing conflict, instead of partitioning Palestine as they promised, to give both sides an independent country, the UN screwed the pooch. Denying them an identity as a people or their right to sovereignty, Israel forced over 700,000 Palestinians into Jordan, Lebanon and Syria. And Israel has been denying the Palestinians their identity ever since. I submit, sir, until they do so willingly or are forced into doing so, there will never be a settlement, no matter how many Camp Davids we hold. In my opinion, what they are doing to the Palestinians now is far worse than what Hitler did to them."

"That's pretty harsh, Graham," Walters mused, "but I understand what you're driving at. However, it's not that simple. I sincerely believe that Israel wants peace with the Palestinians and they would have achieved it if it weren't for the religious extremists in the Knesset."

"How does that make them any different from Iran's sectarian regime?" Stone queried.

"Mmm, yes. I hate it when you talk like that."

"Then take this on board as well, Mr. President. It may not be the Knesset that's the entire problem, but the influence of their military. They see themselves as the sole protector of Israel's existence, and so does the populace at large. It is not in the IDF's interest for Israel to be at peace."

"Okay, what's *your* solution?" Cottard demanded, stung by Stone's impartial dissection of Israel's psyche.

"We all know it, Manfred, but no one's been willing to bite the bullet. Israel must recognize Palestine's right to exist and relinquish the occupied territories."

"The Knesset would never allow it," Walters said firmly, "even if their government supported such a move."

"They would…if the alternative was withdrawal of American economic and military support," Stone said quietly.

"Congress would howl," Walters said promptly and shook his head. "The Jewish lobby holds half of them in their pocket."

"But if that lobby were discredited by what Mossad did at Valero?"

Walters raised a warning finger. "A hypothetical, and only if they in fact did carry out the attack on Valero, which is still by no means certain."

"Granted," Stone acknowledged.

Could it be as easy as that? It hardly seemed possible. Yet, the idea titillated his sense of irony. Instead of removing a perceived nuclear threat, Israel would in effect negate it while achieving a lasting peace, and perhaps ushering a level of stability into the region. God knows it could use it.

Cottard leaned forward. "Mr. President, if it turns out that Israel was responsible, *would* you cut them off?"

Walters frowned and tugged his chin. "I honestly don't know, Manfred. I really don't. But I would damn sure consider it—*if* they were responsible." He looked at Stone and grinned. "I have today and tomorrow to think about this, right?"

Stone nodded. "That's how it looks like, sir. Of course, if we are still only speculating, the idea of peace between Israel and the Palestinians could raise eyebrows of concern elsewhere."

"Yeah, I know," Walters mused. "Iran. We always come back to them, don't we? They are in a very strategic part of the world, oil rich and feeling their political muscle. The trouble in Iraq has given them a window to press old territorial claims and expand Shi'ia influence in the region. Peace could curtail that influence and they would want to do something about it."

"There is another dimension to Iran, Mr. President," Cottard said, glancing at Stone. "When Israel started working on its nu-clear program in the 1950s, we did nothing in clear violation of the Non-Proliferation Treaty. South Africa, India and Pakistan saw that and took note. As did Iran. When Iraq was building its reactor at Osirak, we again did nothing. And when Saddam Hus-sein employed chemical weapons against Iran during their eight-year war, we made token protests. In 2007 Israel bombed a Syrian reactor facility at Al Kibar and we pretended it didn't happen. From Iran's point of view, why bother with treaties when they are openly ignored or selectively enforced on the side of Western interests. To establish a credible defense posture, they needed to be self-reliant. We did nothing when Israel built their bomb, then screamed when Iran wanted to do the same thing for exactly the same reason. I cannot blame them for ignoring us or the IAEA."

Walters studied his two senior staffers and shook his head. "I can see that today is rub-my-face-in-it day."

Cottard grinned. "Mr. President—"

"It's okay, Manfred. I sometimes need to be reminded of the facts. What escapes me, why haven't past administrations acted on these same facts?" He looked at Graham. "You argued against my imposition of unilateral sanctions, as I recall. Was it because of what Manfred just said?"

"It was, sir," Stone said, his gaze level and unflinching.

Walters nodded and turned to Cottard. "Call President Al Zerkhani and advise him that the United States will lift its sanctions on immediate conclusion of the current crisis. If they're innocent, that is. I am yet to be convinced either way. But the note should reassure him that I am serious about reviewing our relationship despite the negative public rhetoric that might be going on right now. Got that?"

"Yes, sir. May I have a little leeway in how I express it?"

"Certainly."

"That's an excellent move, Mr. President," Stone said approvingly. "Finding that unexploded charge has put him in a difficult position. This should help."

"Mind you," Walters said sternly, "I am still prepared to blow his ass if the CIA cannot link Mossad with Houston."

"I am sure he knows that," Stone said dryly.

Walters grinned. "Your sarcasm has not gone unnoticed, Admiral, and one day there will be an accounting."

* * *

Brian Peters glanced around the well-appointed office, the fine leather furniture, original paintings, deep gray carpet, and nodded in appreciation. The open window plan provided lots of natural light and a great view of Washington. The smog was thrown in for free.

"So, this is where all my tax dollars went. I was wondering."

Mark nursed his cup of coffee, giving the FBI scientist a quick appraisal. The man obviously did not care much for authority and was not overawed by it. He had found his niche in life and seemed content. Mark wished he had such an attitude. Ambition can sometimes be a real drag, he mused and gave a mental shrug. Each to his own.

"Everything in moderation, Brian," he said without a trace of irony and sipped his coffee.

Brian grinned and nodded. "Obviously."

Mark reached into his desk drawer, pulled out a plain brown paper package and slid it onto his large, polished dark wood desk.

"Courtesy of our CIA brethren. I didn't ask how they got it here and I would advise you not to either."

"I'm just interested in the contents, Mr. Price," Brian said and picked up the sealed package. It was surprisingly heavy. He looked at Price and raised an eyebrow.

"I've got no idea what's in it. Could be C-4 for all I know."

"I didn't know the Department of Homeland Security had a sense of humor." Brian chuckled and tucked the package under his arm. Price grinned.

"When you're done—"

"You'll be the first to know."

"The Gulfstream will be waiting to fly you back."

"I appreciate that," Brian said with feeling. "Getting flight requisitions approved can be a major pain, especially when it is a matter of national security."

Mark laughed, knowing exactly what Peters was saying. "My pleasure."

Outside, the sky was smeared with patchy clouds, enough to create islands of cool shadow on the ground. The cab was already waiting for him. Brian fingered the charge voucher and climbed into the back seat. The cab driver confirmed his name, eased away from the curb and accelerated into the traffic stream toward downtown.

Brian settled back, lifted the package and tore open the seal, not paying attention to the scenery. He had been in Washington before. The only difference between DC and Houston was that Houston did not get as cold during winter. In summer, both places were unbearable. But if he had his pick, he would go for Washington. After all, this was where the big boys played, and his career wasn't going anywhere tucked away in Houston.

He peered into the package, surveying the contents: A4 and A5 notebooks, two boxes of circular sticky labels, red and green, a box of plain white square labels, yellow post-it pads in two sizes, a pack of bound windowless cream envelopes, a loose-leaf desktop calendar refill and an A4 diary book. He pulled out a box of circular labels and peered at the manufacturer ID—Manning Adar Industries—exactly what he wanted. The square labels were made in Shanghai, the box labeled in English and Cantonese. He replaced the plunder and sat back in the seat. For once, he appreciated the efficiency of a clandestine operation.

The approach to the J. Edgar Hoover Building along Pennsylvania Avenue was busy as always. The boulevard was full of Federal buildings housing a multitude of government departments. The cab approached East Street and the massive FBI building loomed ahead, taking up an entire city block. The whole beige-colored edifice, lined with uniform rows of square windows, had been poured out of concrete and was a butt of much ongoing criticism for looking more like a prison than a modern working environment. Not altogether modern though, having been more or less completed by 1974. Five stories tall, barred by two massive rectangular pillars at the front that supported a two-story box structure above the main building, certainly made it imposing if not aesthetic.

The cab pulled in opposite the entrance as another was driving off. Brian paid the driver, got out and walked through the wide glassed doorway into an open foyer. At the security desk, he showed his FBI badge, but still needed to sign in. Waiting for his visitor ID to be issued, an attending guard phoned Brian's contact. The guard put the phone down and handed over the ID.

"Dr. Riley will be down in a moment, Doctor."

"Thanks." Brian pinned on the badge and turned to face an alcove of elevators on his left. It did not take too long.

A tall, auburn-haired woman who looked to be in her mid-thirties, dressed in gray pants and a smart light brown jacket, walked out of the first elevator, spotted him as she turned and fixed on a smile. Up close, her warm brown eyes gave him a quick up and down look. He returned her scrutiny with a frank gaze. Her penetrating eyes were almost level with his, but she wore high heels, so that one didn't count.

"Dr. Peters? I am Patricia Riley, head of forensics. Welcome to Washington," she said pleasantly and stuck out a slim hand. Brian took it and squeezed lightly as the wheels of recognition clicked into place.

"Professor Riley? George Washington University?"

"In my past life," Pat admitted, pleased that Brian remembered.

"That's a hell of a record you have. But I thought you were at Quantico."

"I am, but it's my day out for catching up on stuff here."

"Just when I happen to be around?" Brian said with a small smile and she grinned back.

"Coincidence, Doctor."

"Thanks for meeting me anyway, and for allowing me to use your facilities."

"It's no trouble. After all, we are all on the same team. Do you need an assistant?"

"Half an hour at your spectrograph and I'll be out of your hair."

Her eyes twinkled and her mouth lifted in a small smile. "It must be something special that it cannot wait for you to get back to Houston."

"It is, Pat," Brian acknowledged, understanding her curiosity. These days the FBI did most of its serious work at the new Forensic Science Research and Training Center at the FBI Academy at Quantico, but for his needs the Hoover Building facilities were more than sufficient.

"I would love to share the secret, but then, it wouldn't be a secret."

Her eyes regarded him with undisguised amusement. "I can guess. Valero just had a bad night and you happened to want my lab. Of course, it could be mere happenstance, Dr. Peters."

Brian chuckled. "I hope to give you a heads-up once this blows over."

"I'll hold you to that, whatever 'this' might be," Pat said firmly and guided him to an open elevator.

On the second floor, the extensive laboratory facilities spanned most of the level. Specialized equipment and accumulated samples had all been moved to Quantico, taking the key personnel with it, but the layout here was still nonetheless impressive. The place had the usual smell of reagents and sharp chemicals, bubbling beakers, oddly twisted glass tubing and attentive white-coated technicians. The facility used to be open to the public and was a popular tourist attraction. After all, everyone wanted to see how the renowned FBI did business. But in 1999 the practice was stopped. Security paranoia had stepped in after the Oklahoma bombing and that was that. If anyone wanted to know how the FBI operated, all they had to do was visit any university lab.

Pat walked easily along the vinyl floor passage between two rows of test benches, her body fluid and undulating. She stopped before a large bench covered with electronic equipment and extended her left hand—no ring on finger.

"Your mass spectrograph. Unfortunately, I must attend a staff meeting and won't be able to see you out, but good luck with your investigation," she said and offered her hand. It felt cool and small and comfortable resting in his. Brian nodded and held it for a second longer than necessary.

"Thanks, Pat. I look forward to seeing you again."

She smiled broadly, her eyes lingering on him momentarily. "Are you moving to Washington?"

"I've applied for Quantico, but Beltrain, he's—"

"I know him," Pat said.

"He's sitting on my application."

"Let me see what I can do. We are short a section manager…"

"Hey! I didn't come here for a job."

"I would like to have you on the team," she said simply, her eyes steady.

"Well…"

"It's settled, then. You'll be hearing from me," she said briskly and walked off.

He looked on as she strode away, sure and confident in her bearing, before he pursed his lips and frowned. Time for business. The job was not going to get done by daydreaming. Still, he felt there had been a connection. And he *did* want to move to Washington.

Stop fantasizing, he chided himself.

A woman like that is committed and doesn't need a fawning middle-aged nobody drooling over her.

The machine was the same model type as his, not that a different box would present a problem. They all did the same thing, but setting up the test would be quicker. He pulled out a chair, its metal castors rattling, and sat down, then placed the brown package on the bench. He took out the box of round stickers and peeled off a label. Glancing about for a scalpel or knife, he pulled open the top bench drawer. Among the neatly arrayed tools, he picked out what looked like a scalpel. He scraped off some adhesive and fixed it onto the specimen plate. The plate slid into the spectrograph input slot and he selected the necessary settings from the LED menu.

The test itself took some four minutes, allowing for variation in source material. He naturally expected this label sample to be much purer and definitive. The printout slid out and he placed the page on the bench. A quick scan of the results confirmed his initial analysis. To make sure, he took out a copy of the original test from his inside jacket pocket, unfolded the paper and placed the sheet next to the new printout. With minor variations the key molecular breakdown spikes were identical. He stared at the new report for a few seconds, then shrugged. His job was done. What happened now was out of his hands. But he figured someone was in for a world of hurt.

He jabbed the print button for another copy, then pressed Reset to clear the printer buffer, and cleaned the specimen plate to prevent some nosy person, like Pat for instance, from repeating the test. Folding the two printouts in half, he glanced around, but apart from background conversation, no one seemed interested in what he was doing. He tucked the papers into his jacket and made his way toward the elevators.

It would be pleasant to share a coffee with Pat and discuss the job. Perhaps another time. Now, if Meecham was serious about signing that transfer…

In the lobby the security guard barely glanced up when Brian slid his visitor ID across the counter. A cab was about to pull out and he waved it down. The driver stopped beside him and Brian climbed into the back seat.

"Where to, buddy?" the Latino driver demanded, not really interested. It was just another fare.

"DHS offices, South Washington," Brian said and buckled up.

"You got it," the driver acknowledged and the cab moved smoothly into Pennsylvania Avenue. Brian pressed a button and the window whined shut, cutting out the noise and gasoline smells.

Mark Price kept him waiting two minutes, long enough to get rid of his current visitor. His secretary offered him coffee, but Brian declined. Secretaries were usually young and pretty, distracting attractions even when efficient. To him, she was nothing of the sort: elderly, running to bulk and her peppery brown hair had a permanent fright. But when she flashed him a dazzling smile, her face looked angelic. She must have been a knockout as a kid. Brian felt he could tell this woman anything and she would take away the ache.

A tall undertaker type, features severe and strained, walked out of Price's office and shot Brian a disapproving frown as he marched past. Price was standing in the doorway and cocked his head inside.

"Come on in."

Brian walked in, sat down and found the chair still warm from the previous occupant, which made him squirm.

Mark stepped quickly behind his desk and sprawled into a wide seat. "How's the traffic?"

"Noisy, but not bad for this time of day," Brian said easily. "It will get far worse as the day wears on and the Beltway fills up."

"Count on it. Okay. You got something for me?"

Brian placed the packet of samples on the floor, reached into his jacket and pulled out the folded papers. He selected the original test report, one copy of the new test and laid both pages side by side on Price's desk.

"A big something. The labels are the same. Check the right half of each printout."

Price leaned forward and studied the graph peaks and troughs with evident interest. "They seem the same," he mused and looked up. "This is absolutely solid?"

Brian nodded, not taking offense at Price's layman skepticism. "No mistake. The evidence is totally conclusive."

Mark glanced at the papers again and slid them closer to the right side of the desk. He sat back and regarded Peters with genuine warmth.

"You solved only part of my problem, Doctor, you know that. Both labels may have been made in Israel, but that doesn't connect the evidence to a guilty party."

"Agreed. What you want is a body, the men who planted the explosives. That may be a tough ask."

"Perhaps not," Mark observed, looking like a kid who had pulled off a particularly satisfying piece of naughtiness. "I've got the CIA scanning the IAH surveillance tapes for Mossad operatives."

Brian nodded in appreciation. "Not forgetting Iran in the meantime, of course. I'm still shaken by the idea that Israel could be behind this."

"I know what you mean. The President was not altogether thrilled by it either, but we've got to play it with the cards we're dealt."

Pursing his lips, Brian shook his head at the absurdity of the whole situation. "If it does turn out to be Israel, Mr. Price, it will be the shortest conspiracy run in history."

Mark nodded. "Three days. It does seem incredible."

"And all because of one lousy sticky label," Brian mused.

"If there is one thing I learned during my checkered career, doc, that it's always the most insignificant little item that screws up even the most carefully thought out operation."

"That certainly seems to have been the case here," Brian agreed, picked up his package and stood up. He might need the samples. "Tough luck, I guess. But my part in this sordid affair is done and again, my thanks for the use of your jet."

Mark rose, walked to Peters and held out his hand. "I'm the one to say thanks, Dr. Peters. If it were not for your professionalism, we might be bombing Iran right now. We still could, but at least we will be acting from knowledge."

Brian clasped the hand and looked directly into Price's dark eyes. "If it turns out to be Israel, I would hate to be in the President's shoes."

"You and me both." Mark opened the office door and peered at his secretary. "Mary, a car to Andrews for Dr. Peters."

"Already waiting, sir," she said brightly and looked directly at Peters. "At the main entrance, Doctor. And have a pleasant flight to Houston, sir."

"Thank you, Mary," Brian said and glanced at Price, who shrugged.

"I couldn't run NOC without her," he said simply and Mary chuckled.

"I am gratified by your confidence in me, sir."

Mark turned to Peters and hooked his thumb at her. "See? About that other matter, I'll let Tom know as soon as something comes in."

Brian nodded, glanced at Mary and walked out the office.

"A nice gentleman," Mary observed and Mark cocked his head.

"We could certainly use him here."

The phone rang and Mary picked up the handset from a terminal that would not be out of place at a phone exchange.

"Director, National Operations Center." She listened for a while, then nodded. "Just a moment, sir." She pressed a button that turned a steady yellow and replaced the handset. "Ian Shiloh for you, sir. Line two."

Mark beamed at her. "Outstanding!"

He hurried into his office, closed the door with a backhanded flip of his wrist and sat behind his desk. He reached for one of the phones and pressed the line two button.

"What's up, Ian?"

"You always did have a good nose for intelligence, Mark," Ian admitted ruefully, not wasting time on preliminaries. "I found three faces for you."

"You didn't spend the night on this, did you?" Mark demanded sternly.

"Aw, hell, a little missed sleep won't hurt me. Besides, I got the impression you wanted this done in a hurry."

"I did, but—"

"No buts, Mark. You want to hear what I've got or don't you?"

Mark sighed. It was no use arguing with Ian and both of them knew it. "I give up. Shoot."

"You'll like this. Two are known couriers and they've been

here a number of times. The third guy is Matan Irian, number three at Metsada."

Mark let out a soft whistle. "Irian? Now, that's very interesting."

"I'm being eaten up with curiosity, but I know better than to pry," Ian said in a wistful voice.

"Keep your cool and all shall be revealed," Mark told him crisply. "No one's been snooping around your work?"

"I've had the whole analysis lab to myself."

"Excellent. Time stamps?"

"I've got several shots of Irian at the airport between 2115 and 2150. The other two are from 2025 onward. They could have departed on the same flight."

"Courier me the shots, will you? Then you can go and get some sleep. You've earned it big time. And don't talk about this with anyone."

"Right. What about all that other data? Not interested?"

"Keep looking at it for another day, but I've got what I wanted."

"Ah, keep up appearances, is that it?"

"Something like that. And, Ian? Thanks."

"You'll get your stuff in an hour. Want the usual soft copy?"

"The same."

"Don't be a stranger," Ian said and broke the connection.

Mark clasped his hands behind his back and leaned into his seat. Irian, eh? Not really a field operative, more a case officer and stage manager. Well, crap! The man must have gotten tired handling an office and decided to handle something more challenging. The only question he had, did Irian carry this out on his own initiative or did Namir Bethan pull the strings? Probably the latter. Valero was not like popping a foreign operative or some geriatric Nazi.

Ian's information put him ahead of the curve, but he wasn't home yet. He reached across the desk, picked up a phone and pressed a dialup number.

"Meecham," the now familiar voice responded.

"Hi, Tom. Can you talk?"

"Go ahead. I'm secure."

"It's my turn to return a favor. Peters confirmed that the label was made by Adar Manning."

"So, things are beginning to stack up," Tom replied with pleasure.

"You've got no idea how high. My CIA photo analyst identified three Israeli operatives transiting out of Houston some time after ten p.m. on Sunday."

"Christ! So it's the Israelis. I can't believe it."

"It's suggestive, all right," Mark agreed, "but we're not done yet. I've got a job for you."

"Go for it."

"I'll send you names and shots of all three operatives, but what I want is a check with Immigration at LaGuardia, Newark, JFK and Ronald Reagan at DC to establish entry and departure. Houston is your pivot point."

"Any special reason for picking New York and Washington?"

"New York is the hub for all Tel Aviv flights. One of the men is a senior Metsada case officer. If he planned and executed the ops, which I suspect is the case, he would want it smooth and transparent. No loose ends. None of that infiltration and false passports shit. That only works in the movies. He would be open and above board, working behind an impenetrable cover, and he will be totally official. The fact that Valero happened to suffer a minor mishap while he was around, well, that's just tough titties."

"Sounds like a real hardass," Tom observed.

"A consummate professional," Mark assured him. "There won't be any mistakes in his wake."

"Everyone makes a mistake, Mark. The label, remember? Every crime scene has something that links the perpetrator to the deed."

Mark had to smile. "Not always, Tom, or I'd be enjoying different scenery right now."

Tom laughed. "Doesn't mean a thing. The break you got was that the other side simply couldn't cut it."

"As much as I hate to admit it, you make a good point. In Matan Irian's case—"

"That's our guy?"

"That's him. Anyway, in his case, he either did not realize the implication of the label, or his boys forgot to wipe down the control box."

"Bears out my point about mistakes," Tom said with clear satisfaction. "Okay, I'll play the devil's advocate. Even though it looks bad for this Irian guy, there is nothing to connect him or his men with Valero."

"You're annoyingly correct, of course. That's why I'll have to keep digging. While your men are nosing around the airports, check if Irian or the two couriers happened to rent a car. If they did and we can find it—"

"Peters can pull it apart to see if it was anywhere near Valero."

"That's the idea. A long shot at best, I admit, but we need to establish a chain of evidence. Once you find out when Irian came to Houston, we can start work on recreating his movement profile. That goes for the other two as well."

"What we have is a terrific leg up, Mark, but we are still missing that smoking gun."

"A good detective, which you're supposed to be, should realize a case is a mosaic of big and little pieces. Today, we scored two big ones."

"Sarcasm doesn't become you, and I'm too thick-skinned for that remark to cut any ice."

"Well, crap! I'll just have to try harder. But seriously, Tom, this is not your ordinary case and no one here is going to court. That gives us more options. Besides, going through the courts can be such a tangled and messy business. Throw in hair-splitting lawyers and the outcome is by no means always certain. The CIA has developed a much more effective and direct means to deal with people who piss us off."

Tom gave a short laugh. "I'm glad you're on our side, but the President will still want a clear evidence trail before he starts shooting at someone."

"You got that right. And this is where I'll be calling my pal Zardwovsky."

"More stickers?"

Mark chuckled. "Not quite, you evil bastard. Call me when you have something."

"Don't think that it's been fun, because it hasn't," Tom remarked and switched off.

Humming softly, feeling mellow, Mark figured he had good reason to be pleased. It wasn't all wrapped up, far from it, but he had solid lines of investigation going, which was a huge break. All the Valero fires were out and the massive cleanup had already started. Another Valero worker had died from his injuries, but the others were still managing to hang in there despite substantial third-degree burns.

The Environment Protection Agency had given Valero some unwarranted grief before Mark stepped in to quash the EPA nit-picking bureaucrat. On the political front the president could have bowed to pressure and acted on reflex, plunging the entire world into turmoil. But he resisted, insisting on evidence, regardless of the cost to his popularity. Polls already showed him down six points. The masses were baying for blood and not interested in who got whacked. There was probably blood to be spilled before this ended, but he hoped the real villains would be the ones spilling it.

"Just hold on, Mr. President, and we'll get you out of this looking like a hero," he mumbled to himself and reached for the phone.

"Central Intelligence—"

"Ms. Rosslyn, it's Mark Price."

"Ah, just a moment, sir. I'll put you through."

"Thank you. And, Ms. Rosslyn?"

"Yes, sir?"

"You're doing a good job there."

"Why, thank you, sir." There was a click, followed by about thirty seconds of mindless music.

"What is it this time, Price?" Zardwovsky demanded gruffly. "Cutlery?"

Mark grinned. The man was a genuine asshole. All in all, he was glad to be out of Langley. Had he stayed, he would probably be up on a murder rap.

"And a good morning to you too. I wanted to say thanks for the package." That clearly confused Zardwovsky, because Mark only heard heavy breathing.

"I'll pass that along. Anything else?"

"I've got something and it's not cutlery. I need you to ask the Tel Aviv desk for a report on anything unusual that might have gone down at Mossad over the last week or so."

"Unusual how?"

"If I knew, I wouldn't be asking. Tell them to cover everything: births, deaths, marriages, staff turnover, disappearances, everything."

"Why this sudden interest in the Mossad, Price? If this is connected to Valero, are you holding evidence the Company should know?"

"I can't tell you, and I'm not being cagey."

"All right, I'll buy it," Zardwovsky said after a moment of silence.

"As soon as you can, okay?"

"Email good enough?"

"Good enough," Mark agreed and put the phone down. He hated dealing with the worm, but he could not afford to jeopardize the investigation because he had lost professional objectivity.

A knock on his door made him look up. "Come in."

Mary walked in with a steaming cup in her hand and Mark beamed.

"Mary, you're a mind reader and a treasure," he declared and she flashed him a smile as she placed the cup on his desk.

"Not a mind reader, Mr. Price, or you'd be in trouble."

"I'll settle for treasure, then," he said and took a grateful sip. "You always know the right thing to do at the right time."

"Thank you, sir. Will there be anything else? Buns? I've got some fresh ones."

Mark shook his head. "Not right now. What's my schedule look like?"

"You have a meeting with Mr. Forbes at 11:30, a Mr. Russell from the National Security Agency at one p.m. and Elaine Coopers from the Director, National Intelligence office at 2:30."

"Thanks, Mary."

"Very good, sir," she murmured and walked out.

Mark took another sip and picked up the phone.

"Morning Mark," Stone said pleasantly. "What's new?"

"A better than average morning, Admiral. The FBI have confirmed that the sticky label was made in Israel and the CIA have given us three Metsada faces at George Bush on Sunday night."

"Shit! What a tangled web we weave…"

"Except that this one is unraveling fast."

"What are you doing to confirm Mossad involvement?"

"Meecham is getting Immigration details on all three and I've asked Zardwovsky for anything unusual that might have happened at Mossad."

"Why would you want to know something like that?"

"I was one of those sneaky undercover bastards myself not too long ago, Admiral. I know how these things are run. On an ops like Valero, you would want to sweep up after you."

"Lose the evidence trail?"

"That's it."

Stone sighed. "Makes sense. I'll have to update Cottard and the President, Mark."

"I understand."

"Always exciting talking to you," Stone said and Mark grinned.

"When I left Langley, I never expected to be washing dirty laundry again."

"It never stops, son. You handled this well," Stone added and Mark raised an eyebrow.

"Meecham and Zardwovsky did all the work."

"But you pointed them in the right direction and that's where it matters."

"I'll take that in the spirit it was given," Mark growled. Stone laughed and switched off.

Sitting back, Mark wondered whether Stone had a point. Well, crap! If the national security advisor wanted to dish out brownie points, he was not about to throw them back in his face.

Chapter Eight

"Closing to twelve miles," Snake announced, pushing his Hornet parallel to the Iranian coastline. As usual the skies were clear, crossed by jetliner contrails, the Gulf hidden by sea mist. In the east it was already getting dark, enough for him to be able to see the sparkle of lights from a multitude of oil platforms cluttering the Gulf. Soon, he would be in evening goo and trapping, hopefully early enough to catch some sliders for dinner.

A sharp *deedle...deedle...deedle* 'you are dead' missile lock warning chirped in his ears, coming from the two F-5s tailing them. They've been doing this gag for the last twenty minutes; close on the Hornets, light off their targeting radars and after about a minute, pull back. Now they were closing again. Snake wished that they'd make up their mind, cook or clean.

Wino clicked his mike in acknowledgment and gained some altitude, still covering his partner's six. Playing tag with targeting radar was an old Iranian game, but still uncomfortable when you were on the receiving end of a potential shot up the tail pipe. No telling what one of those ragheads was liable to do. Totally unpredictable, and that's what made them so dangerous, even though they were driving obsolete crates. The airframes may be old, but their missiles were state of the art Russian variants.

"Carpet, this is Raven." The now familiar lush voice from the E-2C Hawkeye controller suddenly broke the tension. "You are authorized to arm, but do not engage your targeting radar. Maintain flight level 220."

"Roger, Raven," Snake confirmed, not liking it at all, as he held at 22,000 feet, regardless of the fact that the E-2C junior controller's voice sent his hormones sizzling.

His instincts screamed at him to turn into the F-5s and light them up, honoring the threat. See how they liked a *deedle...deedle* in their damn ears, but that would not go down well with Raven or CAG. Having a choice between an IR Aphid in his face or CAG, he would take the Russian missile any day. But dragging his ass in front of those F-5 Tigers, pussycats really, felt a touch breezy. He fervently hoped the honey in the E-2C knew her shit. He had in fact met her yesterday, a good-looking broad, but her radar was firmly locked on a lieutenant commander in Engineering. Snake had seen the tall, taciturn guy and had no wish to be the object of his displeasure. Well, you can't win them all, and they cannot shoot you for fantasizing a little.

After three days of continuous ops, prowling up and down the godforsaken Iranian coastline, he wanted action. All they had to show for the gallons of burned avgas were the same two lousy F-5s giving them the once-over. Why not exchange email addresses! And still no MiG-29s. He figured that those creampuffs back in Pentagon would hang on some balls and let VFA-41 do real business for a change. That's why they were out here, and he wasn't getting any younger. The Hornet drifted down a tad and he automatically corrected. The lady said flight level 220, didn't she? Well, that's what she would get.

"Carpet, this is Raven. Be advised bogies are closing on your position. Maintain your status."

"Ah, Raven, we are kind of hanging our butts out here, you know."

"Maintain your status, Carpet!" The crisp no-nonsense order came from the senior male controller.

"Copy, Raven," Snake acknowledged, his ass suddenly very itchy, wishing he could change places with that controller.

"Carpet, bogies closing on you at six miles...four...two..."

"Wino, you getting any side lobe from those guys?" Snake demanded, forcing himself to stay calm. If the Tigers wanted to play, they would have made their move by now, he hoped.

"They are not radiating, Snake."

Not good. Not good. The F-5s did not need to radiate to squirt off a heat seeker.

"Carpet, bogies now at your position."

"Roger, that."

Snake turned his head left, then right and spotted the sleek twin-engine bird easing next to his starboard wingtip. Man, he never expected a close encounter of this kind. The Iranian driver looked at him, his face hidden behind a tinted black visor, and unexpectedly saluted. Startled and the last thing he expected, Snake made a sketchy salute in return.

"Wino, you believe that shit?"

"His pal is in my lap, but they're not doing anything," Snake's wingman announced, bemused rather than worried.

The F-5 waggled its wings and fell away to port. The other joined him and they headed off toward the coast. Snake watched them go, noting the white war shot missiles slung under their wings.

"Well, if that don't beat all," he said when the bogies vanished into low haze.

"Carpet, turn to heading one-one-five for Texaco."

"Roger, Raven." Snake automatically checked his fuel state, a bit low, and glanced back to check that Wino was still at his six.

He reefed the Hornet into a gentle starboard turn. Adrenalin was still pumping and he could sense himself coming down off a high. Wino followed and they headed toward an afternoon sky. All in all, not a bad day at the office.

Down in CVIC, Ulesky and Admiral Vincent had followed the entire episode on large tactical LED screens. One of them had been the E-2C's real-time radar repeater. When the F-5s pulled away, Ulesky glanced at Vincent and frowned.

"What do you make of that, Admiral?"

Vincent's eyebrows twitched and he pulled at his chin. It was certainly a most unusual and uncharacteristic maneuver closing in on the F/A-18s.

"Not sure, CAG. It's more than just their boys having a bit of harmless fun. Good in-flight discipline, though. And that goes for your element as well."

"It couldn't have been comfortable for Snake and Wino, that's all I got to say, sir," Ulesky said flatly. He had felt Snake's tension as the Hornets waited to see what the F-5s would do. But Snake had held his cool and that was good.

"I know," Vincent said moodily, still trying to figure the angles. "One wrong move by anybody and we could be in a shooting scenario."

"What's the matter with NAVCENT?" Ulesky demanded doggedly. "Give us an ATO or pull us back, or sure as Sunday, someone is going to blink. And what's the President waiting for? An engraved invitation from the Ayatollah? The proof is there!"

"It's not that easy, Captain. Washington probably doesn't have all the facts yet and they've got to be sure."

"How many facts does it take?" Ulesky demanded and snorted. When he thought about it, he realized that obviously the proof was not all there, or the president would have let them off the leash already.

"They will tell us when they're ready," Vincent said soothingly. "Until then, you might be right about pulling back a little to ease the tension on everybody."

"A change of scenery would be good, Admiral. Things are getting a little too comfortable for both sides."

"I'll move the carrier group closer to the Strait. That should give your boys a new patch of sea and desert to admire," Vincent offered with a small smile.

"When I started out, I thought we'd be mixing it up by now, but this waiting for the shoe to drop is a major pain."

"I was here when we invaded Iraq the second time around," Vincent mused. "We flew sorties, but there wasn't that sense of impending danger that we have now. Those things felt more like bomb practice runs and were about as exciting. After years of grinding them down the Iraqis didn't own anything much in a way of an air force to throw at us. After we took out their SAM sites, we controlled the skies. With the Iranians though, we are in a different ballgame."

Ulesky studied the Admiral, trying to fathom the thinking that went on behind those clear eyes. At flag level, the world must seem a very complicated place. Why would anyone want to take on such baggage? Yet, Ulesky knew that if promotion were ever offered him, he would take a swing at it. You don't refuse duty. Should he ever reach that point of indecision, he hoped that he would have enough sense to hand in his wings before he hashed it up or cost someone their life because he was an incompetent.

He contented himself with the thought that for now at least, such decisions were way above his pay grade, and felt an unaccountable flood of relief. But if that moment ever came his way, could he change the course of the world? He looked into the admiral's eyes and nodded.

"I guess we'll have to trust the President and hope he makes the right call," Ulesky said quietly. Vincent smiled and patted him on the shoulder.

"You are judged by how you wield power when the situation is falling apart around you, Captain. Not how you look in your dress whites."

Ulesky straightened. "Admiral, sir, CVW-11 is ready for you to command."

"In that case, Captain, pull in your CAP and stand by for a change of course."

"Aye aye, sir!"

* * *

Mark Price waited for the Secret Service to check him in and issue a visitor pass. He had been at the White House a number of times and was always amazed by the place. There probably wasn't another executive building like it anywhere. The building itself was not intimidating. In fact, it had an old style Southern grandeur and charm that reminded him of cotton fields, stately carriages…and slaves. But the weight of history, brief as it was, that surrounded the structure and the sheer power it exuded by being the core of Western democracy, *that* was intimidating.

"Here you go, Mr. Price," the Secret Service agent said pleasantly and handed over the pass.

"Thanks." Mark pinned it on and walked through the sensor portal. Around him, staffers were going about with whatever they were doing: hurrying, standing in corridors conducting impromptu meetings, all the while filling the background with sounds of voices and footsteps to the shrilling of telephones.

He strode purposefully down the West Wing corridor, past glass-partitioned cubicles and paused before Graham Stone's office. He knocked and entered. Stone's secretary looked up and smiled.

"Good morning, Mr. Price. The Admiral is waiting for you, sir. Would you like a coffee?"

"I could use one, thanks. Black, one sugar," Mark said, walked to the only door there and opened it. Stone finished picking at his keyboard, surrounded by stacks of open folders, and waved a hand.

"Pull up a chair, my boy."

Mark glanced briefly at the sparse interior: a tropical island seascape on the wall behind the desk, a rough oil painting of a battleship on another, a watercolor of an elderly blond woman, which Mark figured was the Admiral's wife, and a hanging temperature/barometer gauge. A dark wood credenza crowded with books, DVDs, magazines, files and the inevitable bound reports churned out by the bureaucracy, filled part of the left wall. On a stand beside it hung a flat TV and a DVD player. Mark guessed ungraciously that the national security advisor liked to play an odd naval action movie in his spare time. He closed the door behind him and sat in one of two soft chairs.

Stone pushed back the keyboard, cleared away some open folders and sat back. Wearing a satisfied smile, he gave a short exhale.

"This must be good or you wouldn't be here," he observed, waiting for his visitor to make the first move.

"Not all of it is good, Admiral."

There was a knock and the secretary walked in, bearing a mug of coffee.

"Thank you," Mark said and took a sip. It was strong, but the taste wasn't all bad—for government issue.

The secretary nodded to Stone and shut the door after her.

"Navy java," Stone remarked with obvious relish, watching Mark's expression. "A bit different, don't you think?"

"It's not a bad way to discourage repeat visitors," Mark pointed out as he placed the mug on the desk. "I need your help."

Stone glared. "After rubbishing my coffee, you want my help? You've got nerve. Okay, spill it."

"I can't close off Valero with the information Tom Meecham and the CIA have given us, and NSA and the DNI have drawn a blank. I half expected it, but they've drawn zip *everywhere*! No emails, cellphone or ordinary landline calls with even a hint about Valero. A complete blank. In my experience there is *always* something there if you dig deep enough. It is conceivable that NSA could still come up with something. After all, it's only been three days, but frankly, we are only spinning our prayer wheels."

"What have you got so far?"

"On Sunday night, all three Mossad operatives, and they're Metsada by the way, flew out at 2225 from George Bush International on an Air France flight AF31 bound for Paris. Last week, Matan Irian, the man I'm interested in, and who I suspect planned the whole deal, attended the DHS symposium on antiterrorism. Now, that took gall. He spent Friday at the Israeli embassy, then flew down to Houston and spent time at their consulate. The other two flew into Houston the next afternoon."

"What was their cover? Just idle curiosity. Not that it matters a damn now."

"Couriers. Both have pulled that gag before. All legal and above board. They presumably spent Sunday sightseeing and just happened to take the same flight to Paris. There is nothing to suggest that the three of them were ever together."

Stone gave a short laugh. "Your frustration is showing, Mark."

"Well, crap! It's also tinged with admiration. If we ignore the C-4 package and the label, although suggestive as hell, all we have is a stack of tantalizing suppositions. If the President wants to bomb somebody in a hurry, he might as well toss a coin." Mark reached for the mug and took a long pull.

"And you can stretch the available evidence only so far. I can see why you'd be frustrated," Stone mused and rubbed his chin. "Let's for the moment speculate that it is Israel. If this Irian guy planned the ops, it was certainly a brilliant example of the type: clean, completely open with no evidence trail. You got to hand it to him."

"What I would like to hand him is that C-4 with a working timer," Mark snapped and Stone grinned broadly. "To complete the domestic picture, Meecham touched base with the FBI Cyber Division about those websites. The bottom line, if you know what you're doing, you can get in and out of almost any site without leaving a footprint. They did some snooping of their own and came up empty. According to Cyber, those websites were set up for public consumption anyway, and did not hold anything sensitive. Security was rudimentary at best."

Stone nodded. "I know. This morning the MOIS chief himself called Cottard apologizing for not being able to give us anything."

"No kidding?"

"Serious. On the other hand, if the Iranians themselves pulled off Valero, there wouldn't be a trail in any case. And if this Irian guy was the mastermind, Metsada would have used their best." Stone looked speculatively at the NOC director. Price was clearly annoyed, but he hadn't come over to cry on somebody's shoulder. "You said 'domestic picture'. I take it this is leading up to something?"

Mark took another sip. After a while the taste didn't seem so bad. He fixed on a grin and nodded.

"You got it, Admiral. For my money, I would say Iran is off the hook."

"Oh?"

"Remember my request for something unusual happening at Mossad? Well, the CIA came up with two interesting items. The stuff was buried amongst a lot of trivia, but I knew what to look for."

"Go on before I expire from curiosity," Stone prompted roughly and Mark chuckled.

"I ought to make you sweat for it. The first item that caught my attention was the death of a Web specialist from their Technology Department on Monday morning their time. Wrapped his car around a light pole—an apparent heart attack according to the papers. The teasing bit is that the incident took place some forty minutes after Valero went up."

"You have a devious and torturous mind there, Mark, but I can see where you're going with this. You think that he was the one who penetrated the websites?"

"A good bet, Admiral. The other item was a newspaper report of a roadside shooting incident near Ben-Gurion airport at about one twenty the same night."

"Let me guess. Our two couriers?"

"The same."

"Connecting the dots, you're saying that Irian took steps to make sure the ops remained black?"

"In a case like this, that's what I would do if I were in his shoes. And what is more, I have done just that more than once myself."

Stone winced and raised his left arm. "I don't want to know!" He glared and drummed his fingers against the desk. "You've dug up an awful lot of good material, but like you said, it's simply speculation. I cannot take this to the President. Unless you can nail down this Irian guy—"

"If Namir Bethan hasn't done that for us already," Mark added dryly and Stone shrugged.

"That would definitely be it, then. Okay, you vented your spleen. What do you want me to do?"

Mark took a deep breath and looked squarely at Stone. "We must have solid proof, a confession. To get it, I want to go to Tel Aviv, nab Matan Irian and persuade him to tell us what exactly he was doing in Houston. That's the only way I know how to finish this, Admiral."

Stone raised an eyebrow in astonishment. The idea was outrageous, of course, but he admired the boy's balls. He leaned forward and cocked his head.

"Let me get this straight. You're asking my permission to kidnap a senior operative of a supposedly friendly intelligence service that belongs to a supposedly friendly country, and give him a shot of babble juice. Is that what you're asking?"

"That's it," Mark said firmly, allowing no room for misunderstanding.

"That's what I thought you said. Son, if I let you do this and Irian was in fact simply sightseeing, there would be hell to pay. We'd both be out of a job, more likely in some minimum-security prison somewhere. The United States would be faced with major international embarrassment and we'd have Israel pissed at us. Not to mention Iran laughing their bloody heads off."

"Why do you think I came to see you? I am right about Israel, Admiral, and what's more, you agree with me. If I'm wrong, we can still roll over Iran."

"Ah, shit! I am only supposed to be the National Security Advisor. The operative word here is *advisor*."

"Sometimes you must do, rather than just talk," Mark deadpanned and Stone looked sharply at him.

"I believe the Navy was too hasty abolishing the lash, because you would easily rate a dozen for that remark. What's more, I would lay them on you myself, you scoundrel."

"Those were the good old days, all right," Mark agreed with a grin.

Stone shook his head and sighed. "Seriously, Mark, this is a risky business, no matter what the outcome."

"So is crossing Pennsylvania Avenue, Admiral. You've got to be able to tell the President which country to hit with no qualifiers. If we don't do this and play it safe, we'll cream the wrong bastards and Mossad would have pulled a fast one on us—again."

"Yeah, you're right. The other question I'm sure you would want to ask Irian is, who ordered the mission."

"And he will know," Mark confirmed.

"And if it was Sharron Ibrahim?"

"Then this could get even uglier."

"You got that right. Presumably, you don't want the CIA desk involved?"

"I don't want to, but I need a car and a driver who knows his way around Tel Aviv. It would be embarrassing to end up in Jerusalem because I didn't know where the hell I was going," Matan said dryly and Stone nodded. "I will want Matan Irian's residential address, of course. To throw him off, I'll ask Zardwovsky to supply addresses of every Metsada operative they have on file."

"You're using up an awful lot of goodwill with Zardwovsky, son."

Stone clicked his tongue and took a deep breath. Well, it had been a nice career. But like the boy said, sometimes you just have to wade in and do it. As the NSA, he held broad powers, mostly defined by the person who occupied the office, as the position was not accountable to Congress. It all depended on how much an individual president allowed the NSA to have his head. In his case, Walters had given Stone a degree of slack, only because he had usually been right. Then again, if this turned out to be a wrong call, there was always the lecture circuit.

"Okay. You have my authorization."

Mark nodded in appreciation, knowing what it cost the national security advisor. He hoped the trust would not be betrayed.

"Thank you. I'll be taking Tom Meecham with me. We owe him that."

"Covering your ass, eh? Okay, I guess we do owe him," Stone growled and glared. "Now get out of here before I change my mind and get the Secret Service to lock you up. Maybe they should lock up both of us!"

* * *

Tom ate up the distance with long, easy strides, feeling more than a little exposed on the open tarmac. The sleek Gulfstream V with its T tail and twin rear engines did not look big and he wondered whether he should have packed extra cans of gas instead of shirts. He could not see how the thing could reach the coast, let alone Tel Aviv in a single hop. But it certainly could. With a maximum range of some 7,500 miles, Tel Aviv was definitely within its reach.

An F-16 taxied onto the north-south East Perimeter active runway, walled it to the stops and accelerated. All too quickly, it lifted, gear folding away and went almost vertical. The sound of its passage boomed across Andrews Air Force Base in rolling thunder. Opposite the runway a neat row of F-16s and EA-6B Prowlers lined the apron. Tankers and smaller craft cluttered the tarmac on the 1st Street side. Hangars and repair shops clustered around both runways. 'Follow Me' vehicles wandered aimlessly along the taxiways. The air smelled of Jet A-1, which made Tom think of civilian airports, jostling crowds and long check-in queues. He could not see any of the Air Force One 747s, although he knew that they were based here. The F-16 was only a black speck in the northern sky as he looked away. He had seen airports, of course, but this was the first time he had been on the other side of the gate, and only one thing spoiled his enjoyment of the experience.

"I can't believe you did this to me," he complained petulantly to the tall figure matching his strides. "I actually lied to Beltrain. Really lied! He thinks I'm in Washington. With you!"

Mark grinned at him, not breaking his stride. "You *are* with me. It just won't be in Washington."

"That makes me feel a whole lot better."

"Cheer up, Tom. If this works out, they'll be pinning medals on you."

"And if it doesn't?"

"Well, crap. We'll still have the Gulfstream. Where would you like to retire?"

"Christ!"

They boarded the sleek executive jet, clambering up four steps. A pert Air Force attendant smiled at them as they entered the luxurious cabin, her long blond hair tucked away beneath a blue cap.

"Nice to see you again, Mr. Price. Your first flight, Mr. Meecham?"

"My first in something as fancy as this," Tom agreed as he surveyed the wide cream leather chairs, solid wood paneling and tastefully designed small tables fitted between the seats. His eyes strayed to the bar cabinet at the rear with its row of bottles filled with various colored liquids.

"Tom, meet Nancy," Mark gushed. "She'll be looking after us for the duration."

"Air Force?" Tom queried and raised a quizzical eyebrow, admiring her form as they shook hands. She did not seem to notice, or ignored the scrutiny.

"Just on international hops. Makes some things simpler," Mark explained without elaborating.

Nancy smiled again, her almond eyes bright, and extended a slim arm at the seats. "If you gentlemen would please strap in, we'll be on our way. Flight time to Tel Aviv will be ten-and-a-half hours and we are scheduled to land at 0430 local time. Refreshments and snacks will be served once we clear the coast."

She retracted the steps and dogged the hatch. With a glance in their direction, she walked into the open cockpit and closed the door after her. Tom's eyes lingered on her tightly filled skirt and sighed, wondering if he had a chance with two flashy pilots on board as competition. Probably not. Then again…

They stowed their bags and Tom sank into a wide first-class seat, facing aft. He grinned as the soft padding molded itself around him, much to the relief of his butt.

"I could get used to this," he murmured softly and reached for the seatbelt. Clipping it, he looked at Mark across the table. "Will Nancy be okay? It doesn't look all that spacious up front. Of course, she could be after more comfortable seating," he deadpanned.

Mark glared and raised a finger. "And you got a dirty mind. Nancy is a nice kid. Get it? She likes to be up front when they take off and land. Besides, there is a fully serviced rear cabin when she gets tired of their company."

"I never even laid a finger on her," Tom protested his innocence as the two Rolls-Royce turbofans spooled up. *A fully serviced cabin, eh?*

The Gulfstream V began rolling along the taxiway that ran parallel to the 1st Street runway. As the aircraft bumped over uneven concrete joins, he felt strange, like something was missing. Then he figured it out. There was none of that annoying pre-flight safety instruction crap that always preceded a commercial flight. As though any of that bullshit would actually help someone in a genuine emergency.

Taking a sharp left turn the Gulfstream took the central taxiway across the first runway, turned left again onto the second runway and immediately accelerated, making him strain against the seatbelt. The engines whined at full power, but their location at the tail and superb insulation meant the noise was actually quite soft. The wingtips came up as the airflow strengthened and the nose pitched up. There was a thump as the gear sagged down the wells and they were airborne. The flaps wound in and the aircraft turned east. According to his watch, it was just on 9:55. Two flights in the same day and probably a quick turnover as well. And he couldn't put this on his frequent flier card either. Christ!

Nancy emerged and twitched her smile into place. "Would you gentlemen care for a drink?"

"Wild Turkey on the rocks if you have it," Tom ordered, unclipping his belt. The thought of all those dreary long miles there and back had unsettled him.

"Chivas Regal for me, Nancy," Mark asked pleasantly. She nodded and moved toward the bar.

Tom worked his jaw until his ears popped, and suddenly everything was louder, including the clinking of glasses and ice. The jet shuddered as it pushed through mild turbulence and steadied. The pervasive background hum of engines filled every space, but he was fast learning to ignore it. Nancy walked toward them carrying a tray with their drinks. She placed them on the small table between them, together with a bowl of mixed nuts.

"Thank you," Tom said and she flashed him a smile.

"You're welcome, sir." She walked back toward the rear and Tom took a sip. The bourbon was smooth and he figured at least eighteen years old. Apparently the Air Force brass believed in having only the best. Cooking smells drifted in the air as Nancy brought a tray of hot finger tidbits, two small plates and napkins.

"Lunch will be served in about two hours. In the meantime, should you need anything, please buzz."

Tom watched her walk to the rear cabin and turned to Mark. "You're right. She is a nice kid." He took another pull out of his tumbler. "Okay, what's the plan? You sort of kept me hanging last night. 'You want to go to Tel Aviv?', that's all the man said."

Mark grinned, sat back and crossed his legs. "It worked, didn't it? Anyway, this is how I see it. There'll be an embassy car to meet us at the airport. We drive to Matan Irian's place, address courtesy of Zardwovsky, and grab him. Irian won't know what happened. Most of these things are done either in broad daylight or when somebody is leaving work. I should know."

"This car bit. Sounds familiar," Tom remarked with a grin and chuckled.

"Well, crap. Why not play the same gag on them, eh?"

"I like it. When you say 'we', you meant the two of us?"

"And our driver," Mark confirmed. Tom lifted his head and rolled his eyes.

"I can't tell you how much I'm looking forward to this."

Mark laughed. "Look at it this way. Where else would you have a chance to fly in an executive jet and get to see the Holy Land, all at Uncle Sugar's expense?"

"It's not the Holy Land," Tom muttered. "It's the holier-than-thou land!"

"It does seem like that sometime, doesn't it?"

"What about hardware?"

"Everything is in my bag, including a couple of silencers, which I hope we won't be needing."

"You seem to have covered it all. And if Zardwovsky decides to have us tailed?"

Mark smiled, but there was a cold glint in his eyes. "I learned an odd trick or two in my shadowy past that should take care of such distractions. And no doubt you know some angles yourself."

"One or two," Tom drawled.

"I told Zardwovsky if he plants a bug on the car or driver, I'll find out eventually. He won't be a happy chappy."

Tom grinned, liking it. It had been a while since he was last in the field, and a first for him on foreign soil. It seemed the trip would be a first in more ways than one. He understood Mark's reasoning for not involving the CIA more than absolutely necessary, especially Zardwovsky. He'd had dealings with them himself and didn't particularly care for their attitude or style. But when he agreed to accompany Mark, he figured they would *have* to get them in the loop. It never occurred to him that Mark would try this stunt alone, until he remembered who the NOC director was. Or more exactly, who he had been. And Tom understood why he had been invited. Mark wanted a backup. After all, how many men does it take to snatch a body?

He noticed Mark looking at him with a speculative expression.

"I can see the wheels turning," Mark said, wearing a broad smile.

"They finished turning. And don't worry. I'm not mad at you for not spilling it all yesterday when you asked me on this hair-brained jaunt. I wouldn't have missed it for anything."

"Glad to hear it. Seriously, Tom, I don't know whom I'd rather have."

"Like you said. If we don't get shot, we'll be heroes." Standing up, Tom picked up Mark's tumbler and made his way to the bar. He fixed refills for both of them and relaxed into his seat again. Taking a sip, he studied the NOC director.

"How in the world did you happen to end up working for the CIA, of all places?"

Mark gave a sour grin. "More easily than you might think. I was at Columbia U doing the usual things that boys do: football, chasing girls, football, and if there was any time left, do some studying. I was an economics major, but I loved physics. Don't that beat all? The problem was, physics was a lot of work and I was far too busy—"

"I know. Football and chasing girls," Tom finished for him.

"Well, crap! A guy had to have his priorities straight. Anyway, in the middle of my final year, I attended one of those recruiting drives all the big corps indulge in. But there were two other out-fits there."

"The FBI and the CIA," Tom added with an understanding nod.

"It never occurred to me to work for the government. The pay is lousy and if you didn't end up shuffling paperwork, you could get shot or captured and tortured. Not much fun. My plan was to land a fat-paying job with some bank or Wall Street trading outfit. But what the hell! I took their brochures just to see what spin they were pushing. A CIA recruiter saw me leafing through one and looked me over. He gave me a phony fatherly smile that made me want to run, until I saw his eyes—empty and cold. They were eyes of death and it made my skin crawl.

"'You thinking of joining up, son?' he asked me. I shook my head, gave him a short laugh and replaced the brochure.

"'No way', I told him. 'I prefer my skin in one piece.'

"He smiled his fatherly smile and nodded. 'You know, it's funny, but that's exactly what I said.'

"'What changed your mind?' I asked him out of curiosity, making polite conversation. What struck me is what the recruiter said next. He said, 'If you believe in it, you can make a difference. Think about it.' With that, he simply walked off."

Mark sat there, lost in memories, his tumbler sitting in the palm of his hand. Then he chuckled.

"It was a corny line, freshman psychology, but I couldn't get it out of my mind. I guess it made an impact, because I quit foot-ball and cut down on chasing girls. I had not reformed *that* much. Before I graduated, they held another one of those recruiting drives and that CIA man was there again. He remembered me when I walked up to him. Without saying anything, he pulled out a set of papers and handed them over. And you know what? They were already filled out.

"'You don't need to sign anything now,' he said, looking at me like I was a slab of prize salmon. 'Come to The Farm and make up your own mind.' They paid for the flight to DC and all." Mark gave a wan smile and shrugged. "Maybe it was psychology after all, but it worked and I joined up. I've been through some scary shit along the way, but I wasn't bored. I like to think that I made a difference, even though the pay was lousy." He took another sip and looked at Tom. "How about you? What made you pick the Bureau?"

"Except for a few minor details, they snagged me in exactly the same way. I was living in Seattle studying accounting and business law. It was a pure con job and I regretted joining a dozen times, but I'm still with the Bureau. Maybe one day they'll give me a branch somewhere in Nebraska and I'll go quietly to pieces."

Mark chuckled. "I just don't see you in that picture."

"Yeah. Nebraska would be a hard sell after hopping around in a luxury jet. What about you?"

"I like DHS, at least the operational arm of it. The rest is padding and dead wood—bureaucrats shuffling paper and generating reports on reports. If I can believe Walters' campaign rhetoric, he'll carve up DHS and throw the fat into the fire. At least I hope he will."

"Or he'll make it a Bureau Division. Wouldn't that be something? We already have the necessary infrastructure in place."

"Could happen," Mark said, not believing it. Still…God and governments move in mysterious ways.

Lunch was a culinary luxury that matched the aircraft's interior: two different entrées, one hot, the other cold, with a light Chablis to go with it. That was followed by a delicious vegetable soup, a butter-soft fillet mignon accompanied by a smooth Sauvignon. Dessert was a creamy baked cheesecake, and it wasn't Sara

Lee. With a fine brandy afterward, Tom appreciated how the rich and the movers lived, at least while they were in the air.

Sipping his brandy, he mulled over what to do next. He would probably not get a chance to sleep much once they hit Tel Aviv and decided on a nap.

Nancy made up two bunks at the rear and dimmed the lights. Tom's gaze lingered on her as she retired to the rear cabin. Following his look, Mark pointed a finger at him.

"Don't even think it!"

Tom laughed and stood up. "Can't shoot a man for dreaming. Don't wait up for me, mother."

"Like I said, she's a nice kid."

Tom waved at him and walked toward the bunks. He slipped out of his clothes, crawled into the makeshift bed and pulled the covers around him with a satisfied sigh. Apart from the background hum of engines, almost soothing, he could be at home.

Despite comfortable surroundings and the lingering aftertaste of brandy in his mouth, he found it difficult to let go. For some reason, he kept seeing twisting flames and billowing black smoke churning in tortured agony as it climbed above the Valero refinery. The image changed and he saw Houston enveloped in towering fire. In the background was a silhouette of Washington's Capitol building.

Three days after Iran supposedly struck Valero, the president had still refrained from lashing out, to the consternation of most media and the public at large. Despite a bank of enormous popularity, the polls showed him at only fifty-three percent approval, a full sixteen points down from a week ago. Placard-waving protesters had started to picket the White House along Pennsylvania Avenue, demanding that the president do the right thing. The tabloids were out of control as usual and the Fox channel always on the edge with extreme views, all the while claiming to be the people's voice. But papers like *The New York Times* and *The Washington Post* presented more balanced and measured commentary.

They did not know any details of the FBI and CIA investigations, of course, and realized that a knee-jerk reaction without full facts could lead the United States down the same path it took when it attacked Iraq without solid evidence to back up its decision. Still, the delay in responding invariably raised a host of new questions and wild speculation.

What *was* the evidence that prevented the President from unleashing hell on Iran, the papers kept asking? And why wouldn't the White House disclose it? When all else failed, they dragged out the old chestnut about the people's right to know. Tom knew the president was not holding out on them, exactly. He could truthfully say that the investigation was still under way, and when he had all the facts, he would act. Besides, there was enough footage from *Ike* and *Nimitz* carrying out flight operations in the Gulf demonstrating his resolve. As always the media wanted to see blood and gore, good for ratings, but for now, they had to be satisfied with salivating at the bowl.

After a while, he drifted off to sleep.

Mark glanced at Tom's sleeping form, took a sip of whiskey and sat back. The engines hummed to him. He envied the younger man's casual attitude and apparent indifference to the possible consequences should his plan misfire. A lot could go wrong with the snatch and he did not relish the prospect of having to explain himself to Mossad or the Israeli police. And what if Matan Irian had actually been in Houston just to visit his consulate? He should have directed Zardwowsky to grab Irian and let him take the heat if things went sour, but that would have been passing the buck and everyone would know it.

Perhaps Tom was right not to dwell on it too much. Mark finished his whiskey, got up and made his way down the aisle. Both of them would have an early day, and banking some sleep was not a bad idea.

* * *

Coming in off the Mediterranean coast, the Gulfstream V turned on final for a roughly east-west approach to Ben-Gurion. Tel Aviv blazed beneath them, somehow looking small after Washington's sprawl, but still a sight as it hugged the black coastline. Wings rocking, the aircraft sank, and with a rush, was over the runway. It seemed to hover for a moment, then touched down smoothly and the pilot immediately put the engines into reverse thrust. Through the window, Tom could see domestic and international aircraft clustered around Terminal 3 spokes.

An airport at night is depressing. There is hardly anybody about. All the shops and conveniences are closed and people who happen to be about tend to look at each other suspiciously, wondering what the hell they're doing here at this time of night. Footsteps echoed forlornly on marble floors or hard carpets. Tom would rather wait at a train station than a terminal at night.

As a United States military aircraft the Israeli Immigration and Customs officers met them when the Gulfstream taxied off the active runway and rolled to a stop in front of a maintenance hangar on the eastern side of the passenger terminal. It was 4:36 a.m. Mark held a diplomatic passport and was immune from search. Even though an FBI officer, Tom was effectively still a civilian, and he figured the Israeli officials were probably more interested in getting back to bed than searching for contraband. He felt like that himself. Although he slept well, it was not the same thing as being in your own bed. Eventually, they stamped his passport and left after an exchange of pleasantries.

There was the usual smell of jet fuel and lubricant in the air as they alighted. It was silent outside, silent and crisp. Tied to a terminal spoke, a Continental Airlines 747 had all its cabin lights on. Nav lights blinked above the cockpit and wingtips. A luggage train rolled to its side while a fuel truck sat beneath the port wing. Looking about curiously, Tom pulled his windbreaker closer about him and stared accusingly at Mark.

"I thought it would be warm around here this time of year."

"Not at night," Mark replied cheerfully, searching the open hangar. Apart from benches along the walls, spare jet engines and stacked crates, the place was empty. "Our driver seems to be lost," he murmured.

Just then, a short figure dressed in black jeans and a dark blue corduroy jacket, emerged from the gloom beside the hangar and slowly walked toward them, favoring his left leg. The thin figure, all bones and loose skin, showed little expression as he took in the Gulfstream, turbines slowly spooling down. A white scar ran down the left side of the elongated face. He stopped and gave Mark and Tom a suspicious once-over.

"Mr. Price?" the man asked harshly, his voice mangled like it rolled in a barrel.

"That's me," Mark said curiously and waited.

"You can call me Stan." He reached into his jacket pocket and extracted an envelope. "The information you wanted, sir."

"Thanks for meeting us this early…Stan." Mark could not see 'Stan' fitting this skeletal frame, but kept his peace. It was none of his business what the guy chose to call himself. It was probably a cover name anyway.

"Don't mention it," Stan rasped and wheezed. "I've done some stranger things in my day than this."

Mark smiled and nodded. "I don't doubt it."

"When you're ready, sir, I'll be in the car outside the gate." Stan turned abruptly and ambled off.

Mark watched him disappear around the hangar, then tore open the envelope and extracted a single sheet of paper. A quick scan down the page and he nodded.

"Okay, let's get out of here."

Standing in the doorway, Nancy gave the retreating figure a curious glance, then wished them luck and climbed back into the aircraft to prepare for the return leg. The pilots were still in the cockpit, presumably doing pre-flight checks with the tower. Bag in hand, Mark walked after the driver. The embassy car stood parked outside a heavy chain-link fence side gate, engine running, vapor trailing from the exhaust pipe. He gave the heavy white Merc a quick scan for visible markings, making sure it did not bear an official number plate. A guard stepped out of his cubicle, saluted and held the gate open for them. In the east, the sky was tinged deep purple. Pausing beside the back door of the sedan, Mark glanced up. There was no cloud and the lesser stars had already fled under the mild glare of a pale half-moon. He took a deep breath, held it for a second, and exhaled. He opened the door and slid in, his face tingling from the crisp air.

Once everyone was in and belted up, Stan peered at Mark.

"Where to, sir?" he rasped without expression. He could be ordering pizza for all the emotion he showed.

"Eleven Unklus Street, Bavli," Mark said, positioning the bag between his legs.

Stan looked blank, the map of Tel Aviv scrolling through his head. He finally nodded and backed the car into the service road, heading for Highway 1. The dashboard digital clock read 5:20.

They drove in silence, Tel Aviv bright on their left, twinkling prettily in the pre-dawn glow. Ayalon Highway had enough cars going both ways to keep it from feeling empty, but it would build up soon as commuters made their way into the city for the day. Headlights coming the other way stabbed into darkness. Mark had never been to Israel and he gazed with interest at the semi-arid environment, as much as he could see of it in the gloom. He wasn't religious, but the sense of turbulent centuries that had stamped this land was an almost palpable blanket permeating the very air. The tragedy was, that turbulence still molded this country, seemingly without an end in sight. He could easily believe Armageddon starting here, opposing hordes crying out the same plea to heaven. Perhaps God should wipe the slate clean and have a go at a new and perhaps better beginning. But with free will, even God could not be certain it would be better second time around.

He stared out the car window, taking it all in, listening to the whisper of tires and the drone of the engine. An occasional lone car overtook them with a muted rush, hurrying toward an empty appointment.

Stan turned into Rokach Boulevard, crossed the Yarkon River and got onto Haifa Road. It was getting lighter and Mark felt a familiar tingle down his back as he readied himself for action. It had been some time since he felt the thrill of naked danger, but this time, he did not welcome it. It was not like the old days when he knew his enemy and the world was relatively black and white. Now, the endless shades of gray merely complicated and confused, but there was no turning back. Time only had a one-way door.

Looking about in the gathering dawn, applying a bit of imagination, he could be in any suburb back home. Town planners can only do so much with streets, houses and driveways, but they had not done it here. Most of the houses were blocky, flat-roofed double-story structures made from the same uniform milky sandstone. Behind brick fences, trees, bushes and palms sprinkled a few small front yards. The lots were tiny and houses clustered together along curvy streets. Light poles cast yellow circles on the road below.

Stan slowed, turned left and accelerated. At the next T intersection, he turned right and drove slowly, checking the numbers.

"Coming up to number eleven on our right, sir," he said, not slowing down.

Mark looked sharply right, craning his head back as the car made its way down the street. The house was almost indistinguishable from its neighbors, the inevitable television antenna and satellite dish clawing at a pale sky. There was a single upstairs light showing. Early risers, maybe? Well, he'd been there himself.

"Make a turn and park a couple of houses before number eleven," Mark ordered quietly.

"You got it."

When they eased close to the curb and stopped, Mark checked his watch: 6:10. He sat back and composed himself. Now, it was simply a matter of waiting. His only worry was that Irian might have taken a day off or gone on a holiday. He was certain that the Tel Aviv CIA desk held detailed movement information on all senior Mossad personnel, but at a risk of being compromised, that was one thing he had not been willing to request. He figured he had pushed his luck with Zardwovsky far enough.

He dragged his bag off the floor and placed it on his lap. Jerking back the zipper, he opened the sides and handed Tom a Browning Hi-Power nine millimeter fitted with a slim silencer. In case they had to shoot, Mark did not want the local authorities pointed in the right direction by using an American caliber weapon. Tom pulled out the clip and checked the slide, then chambered a round and slid the handgun into his jacket pocket, ignoring the curious stare from Stan's reflection in the rear-view mirror. It wasn't a comfortable fit, but he would not need to wear it for long.

Mark repeated the procedure. Reaching into the bag again, he lifted out a slim black plastic case and opened it. The thin syringe was half-filled with a clear yellow fluid. Replacing the case, he rummaged inside and extracted a thin credit card-sized recorder. That also went back into the bag. Looking up, he saw Tom studying him with interest.

"Just making sure," he said defensively and Tom smiled.

"Don't mind me."

Shaking his head, Mark eased the bag to the front seat, leaned back and breathed steadily. Several cars passed them going both ways, factory workers probably, but these days it was hard to tell. Sunshine at last broke through high branches, splashing houses with a yellow glow that deepened the shadows. Colors looked alive and vibrant. The wind had died down and everything was still, also waiting. He could hear an odd twitter of birds fighting for possession over a favorite perch among the branches. A solitary jogger in bright blue boxer shorts and green T-shirt ambled down the sidewalk without giving them a glance. Time dragged and Mark resisted the temptation to look at the dashboard digital clock.

At 7:15 the garage door at number eleven began to roll up, showing a dull red Audi sedan. White vapor shot from the tailpipe as the car revved.

"Cut him off!" Mark snapped as soon as he saw the lone male figure in the driver's seat and his heart began to pick up.

In a fluid motion, Stan started the engine and covered the distance to Irian's driveway just as the red car backed through the sidewalk. Stan brought the Merc to a stop with a jerk, blocking the driveway, the car facing the wrong way down the street. The Audi was hardly moving and stopped immediately.

Matan was instantly aware of the car behind him as it slid to a stop. If he was thinking of anything, it was breakfast and conversation with Sarah about taking time off and going away, just the two of them. Both needed to renew and replenish the closeness that had started to fade around the edges. The last thing he expected was some young fool learning to drive blocking him. He opened the door, got out and pointed up the street.

"You idiot! Get out of the damned way. And you're on the wrong side of the road, moron!"

It was only then that he noticed the driver and two large men sitting in the rear. His professional alarms went off with a clang and he paled, sensing something bad was about to happen. He vaguely thought about running, but it was far too late. You cannot outrun a bullet, if that's what they intended. The idea died as the two men moved.

Mark glanced at Tom and both opened their doors. He only had to take one step to stand before the Mossad agent. Moving close, making sure his movement could not be seen from the houses around him, Mark eased out the Browning and jammed the silencer against Irian's chest, his eyes hard as they bored into the other man. Irian seemed to grasp the situation immediately and stood still. With a jerk of his head, Mark indicated at the open rear door. Irian nodded, glanced at his house hoping to glimpse Sarah, then stepped to the car, crouched and got in. Mark slammed the door shut, pushed the handgun into his jacket and yanked open the front door. Tom was already sliding into the back seat, his weapon pointed unwaveringly at their quarry. Mark pushed the bag to the floor, slid into the front seat and pulled the door shut.

Stan immediately eased the Merc away from the curb and accelerated without leaving rubber on the road, heading across to the right side of the street. Behind them, the Audi still had its left door open, engine running. Stan turned left at the T intersection, pulled a right at the next street and headed for Haifa Road. The snatch had taken perhaps thirty seconds.

Nobody said a word and their guest seemed resigned to the inevitable. When Mark turned, gun in hand, the Mossad agent returned his gaze without blinking. Mark took a glance at the long face, dark complexion, square jaw, mahogany eyes sunk deep into the skull, and sensed a hardened professional. This man had faced death before and knew how to handle himself, but Mark expected nothing else. The cold-blooded execution of Valero left little room for extraneous emotion. He kept his weapon steady. There would be no cheap heroics from this man, but he was not about to make things easy either.

"American?" Matan asked, but only got stony silence in return.

A humorless smile touched his face and he sat back trying to relax, ignoring the figure beside him. The men could be Namir's, but he sensed not. There was something about their movements and clothing that marked them as foreigners. Americans, then. In a way, he would have preferred Namir's hit squad, wondering how he was burned. The ops had been flawless! Clearly not, otherwise these men would not be here. It didn't matter, not now. Nothing mattered, not for him anyway. His only concern was for Sarah and Admina. His innocent Admina, shamed by a father she worshiped. He wondered if she would ever understand and be able to forgive him. Would Sarah? The thought of losing her, losing both of them, cut deep.

Lord, anything else but that.

When Stan crossed the Yarkon River bridge, Mark touched his shoulder and indicated with his left hand to pull over. Stan immediately slowed and eased the Merc to the shoulder. With a glance at Mark, he opened the door and got out. The door clicked shut and he slowly walked down the road a few paces. The car rocked slightly every time a car passed them. Mark laid the Browning on his lap, reached for his bag, pulled out the recorder and switched it on.

"My name is Mark Price, Director, National Operations Center, Department of Homeland Security. With me is Thomas Meecham, Supervising Special Agent, FBI, Houston. Our prisoner is Matan Irian, Special Operations Division, Mossad. Mr. Irian has been detained for questioning regarding possible Mossad involvement in sabotage of the Valero Texas City Refinery."

He switched off the recorder and reached into the bag again. He took out the plastic case, opened it and held up the syringe. He turned and looked meaningfully at Irian.

"Is this necessary?"

Matan's eyes flickered at the naked needle before returning to study Mark. The American would get what he came for, with or without his cooperation. There was no point playing the tough guy. This was tying up a loose end on their part, albeit an important one. He could lie, but they would probably sense it and there was always that needle.

"Ask your questions, Mr. Price. I shall not resist," he said heavily without irony. Looking at the operation objectively, if he were Namir, he would have cleaned up *every* loose end. Some-times, that's what it took.

"Very well." Mark nodded, put away the syringe and switched on the recorder. "Mr. Irian is not under duress and is cooperating voluntarily. Please state if you had any involvement with the Valero incident."

"I did."

"In what capacity?"

"I once prepared a scenario paper for an attack against Gal-veston oil platforms, making it appear the attack was carried out by Iran."

"What was the objective of that scenario?"

"To trigger a response by the United States against Iran's ura-nium enrichment facilities and the Bushehr reactor, removing a strategic threat against Israel and neutralizing an extremist Shi'ia regime in the region."

"What was your specific involvement with Valero?"

"Under direction of Namir Bethan, Director, Special Opera-tions Division, I planned and stage managed the sabotage of the Valero complex."

"Was this action known to the Israeli government or the Prime Minister?"

"No. The operation was totally black."

Hesitating, Mark clicked on the safety and slid the Browning into the bag. He lifted his head and stared hard at his prisoner.

"Why?"

"I have already answered that question, Mr. Price."

"We are supposed to be allies!"

Matan gave a sad smile. "Israel has no allies, only acquaint-ances of opportunity. Surely you must realize that?"

"Well, crap! It's nice to know for sure. Without American sup-port, your country would not exist."

"Eliminating threats to our survival can take on many forms, not all of them strictly honorable or ethical. We all do it. You do it. But when *you* overstep the mark, everybody simply grumbles. What else can they do? Despite the noble words of the Nuclear Non-Proliferation Treaty, America and the world stood by and did nothing while India, Pakistan, South Africa and now Iran, engaged their nuclear programs. Surrounded by hostile Arab nations, we were left with a simple choice. Do nothing or act."

"You certainly acted when you built your own nuclear arsenal, noble words notwithstanding," Mark replied dryly and Matan smiled, ignoring the bitter irony of the situation,

"True. And I guess we all embarked down that road for the most honorable of reasons, at least as far as our respective citizens were concerned. India and Pakistan's nuclear capability is of concern, but they are not a threat as they lack a delivery system to reach us. Iran represents a clear and present danger. We waited for America, our ally, to act and remove this threat. It turned out to be a lonely and doomed vigil as you were preoccupied pursuing your own interests. In the end, some of us could wait no longer. Our government is locked in factional power in-fighting and has lost the ability to make hard decisions."

"So you decided for them."

Matan searched Mark's face, looking for understanding perhaps? For sympathy? There was nothing, not even revulsion. Would that have eased his conscience? But his conscience was already burning without having to be prompted by someone else.

"What do you want me to say? That I'm sorry for the destruction? Sorry for the lives lost? Yes, but I believed in what I did. I still do."

"You don't have to justify anything, Mr. Irian," Mark said gravely, not interested in the man's excuses. "You told me everything I need." He switched off the recorder and shoved it into the bag.

"If you don't mind telling me," Matan ventured, somehow relieved that it had ended, "as one professional to another, what gave me away? I thought I covered everything."

"You did, but for one small detail," Mark said and glanced at Tom.

"The label," Tom murmured with a cold grin.

Matan raised his eyes in puzzlement, not understanding.

"When we recovered the planted package, a label that had been fixed to the detonator box left some adhesive residue. Whoever removed the sticker forgot to wipe down the box. I am surmising that one of your couriers—"

"You know about them as well?"

"And how they died, yes. Once we found out about the label, the rest was easy. As I was saying, one of your couriers probably brought the explosives with him. I was told that at an equivalent pressure of nine thousand feet, normal for an airliner, a slight chemical reaction can be triggered in some organic substances."

"Such as our adhesive," Matan finished with a wry shake of his head. He could hardly believe that such an insignificant piece of evidence could have undone the entire mission. It was always the little things.

"The sticky label that was used had an organic base that made it more prone to an altitude-induced reaction. In this case, enough to leave minute traces on the control box. And this particular label is made at only one place."

"You must have a very good forensic scientist," Matan murmured with admiration. He had been right to fear American technology and ingenuity. Who could have foreseen this development? You couldn't know everything, yet you had to, and he had warned Tabor and Ellis to wipe down the casing. Well, they paid for their mistake. And how would he pay for his?

Tom did not say anything. He didn't have to. The fact that Irian was here spoke of Brian's effectiveness.

Matan looked at Mark. "And what now, Mr. Price?"

"As far as you are concerned, nothing."

"After what I have done, you will simply let me go?"

"More or less. I have what I came for."

261

Matan thought that over and nodded. "I understand. Mine was not an ordinary criminal act, and bringing me to trial would be pointless. Your presence here demonstrates that. Can you at least tell me what will happen to my country?"

"If it were up to me," Mark rasped harshly, "it would be something drastic. But it's not up to me. President Walters will make that call."

Matan's eyes were pleading as he regarded his captor. "You might as well kill me now and save my government the trouble of shooting me."

"Frankly, Mister, that's your problem. And I won't be the one giving you an easy way out."

"I'm thinking of my family, Mr. Price."

"You should have thought of them before you coldly contemplated the death of innocent Americans, and Iranians, had your plan worked."

Matan sagged and something, some spark of vitality, seemed to die in his eyes. He could sense it go. There was nowhere for him to flee, to hide, and there was nowhere for Israel to hide either. He and his country would suffer when America brought the full weight of its anger to bear, and he wondered who would suffer most. And it had been such a good plan, hadn't it?

Looking at him, for a moment, Mark felt sorry for the man. Noblest of intentions? With millions of lives lost throughout history on that altar of hypocrisy, his conscience was clear. The Mossad did not have to do it like this. Israel didn't have to do it like this! He reached into his bag, rummaged about and lifted a small plastic bottle. He unscrewed the top, took out two pills and held them up.

"These will knock you out for about two hours."

"Sufficient time for you to get away," Matan said matter-of-factly and took the pills. He put both in his mouth and swallowed, hoping they were cyanide. "I might have bungled my mission,

Mr. Price, but Iran's nuclear program is still a threat to my country and the region. America must know that."

Mark slowly shook his head. "That's where you're wrong, Mr. Irian. The only threat a nuclear Iran poses is to the power and influence of your military, not your people. You are a military officer and so is Namir Bethan. When planning your operation, you should have asked yourselves this question. Would you have chosen the same option had you been civilians?"

Matan's eyes widened in shock, then slowly closed as darkness fell and he slumped against the window. His last thought was that he had not only betrayed his country, he had betrayed himself as well. Leaving the Army had been a coward's way out after all.

Chapter Nine

Light blue, clear of cloud, the sky looked soft and inviting, promising a fine day. Listening to Tchaikovsky's stirring strands of *Capricio Italien*, following the traffic stream to Herzliya, for once Namir Bethan was not enjoying his music, even though it was one of his favorite pieces. Sunlight created sharp contrasts among houses and looming office blocks, and some drivers still had their headlights on. A few would forget to switch them off and be annoyingly surprised at the end of the day when all they wanted was to get home. He eased the black BMW into Harav Kook Street, his brow knitted with concern.

It was inaction on the part of America that worried him. Four days since Valero was hit and they were still sitting on their hands. It was both frustrating and alarming. Frustrating that President Walters had not acted despite overwhelming evidence that Iran was responsible, and alarming in its implication. What could be stopping the American president from acting? Clearly, it had to be something important enough for him to ignore mounting pressure from Congress and the public at large.

He had seen the growing picket lines in front of the White House on TV and the increasingly acerbic newspaper commentary, all of it progressively more critical of the administration's failure to act. To Namir, it meant only one thing. The FBI or the CIA, probably the former, as the CIA did not dabble in domestic investigations, or at least it wasn't supposed to, must have uncovered some lead that they were running down, causing the president to stay his hand. It couldn't be anything else. If true, there was still a slim window of opportunity within which to act and remove the last threat to his operation. To delay longer would be to invite disaster, and he may have delayed too long already, all because of sentimentality. And he thought he was beyond such foolishness.

He was turning into Shival Hekochavim when his cellphone went off with a shrill. There were only a select few who knew his number and none of them would call unless compelled by dire need. He eased the BMW to the curb and stopped, read the caller's name on the screen and punched the call button on the dashboard-mounted phone.

"Sarah, an unexpected surprise," he said crisply and waited, puzzled that she would be calling.

"Namir, something's happened to Matan! You must—"

"Hold on, Sarah. Take it easy. Tell me what happened."

"They took him!" she cried with a wrenching sob, anguish clear in her panicked voice.

"Who took him?"

"I don't know! He was leaving for work at his usual time. There was nothing out of the ordinary. It was only when Admina looked out the front window and saw a car blocking Matan's Audi that she called me. At first, I thought he had an accident, but when I looked out, his car was just standing there, door open, engine running. It was then that I saw a white Mercedes saloon accelerating down the street. I couldn't see which way it turned at the intersection. By the time I rushed out it was gone. Namir, you've got to help me!"

Listening to Sarah's frantic voice, Namir grew cold. Matan had enemies, they all did, but which one of them would pick this particular moment to do something about it? And if it was the Americans? His heart skipped a beat at the thought. Still, he could not afford to ignore the awful possibility, however unpalatable.

"Sarah, listen to me—"

"They've hurt him. I just know it!" She broke into uncontrolled sobs.

Namir knew that she liked to be in control, but this was understandably a harrowing moment, a lingering fear that had at last surfaced—for both of them.

"Sarah! Take hold of yourself. You're not helping matters by getting hysterical." He heard two loud sniffs and her breathing slowed.

"You're right," she said slowly, her voice calmer. "I'm sorry. It's just…"

"It's hard, I know, but you've got to concentrate. Now tell me. How many people in the other car?"

There was a moment of silence. "I saw two men in the back seat. I couldn't tell if there was anyone at the front."

"That's good, Sarah. Did you see any markings on the car? Anything that might have caught your eye?"

"It was a white car, that's all I saw. I don't remember anything else. It all happened so quickly."

"I understand. Did you see the number plate? Do you remember any lettering?"

"Not really. I only saw a glimpse as it sped away, but they looked ordinary."

Namir pursed his lips. It had been a long shot anyway. Diplomatic license plates carried a country designation. It would have helped.

"That's okay. Leave it with me for now and I'll call you when I have something."

"I'm worried, Namir. This was always at the back of my mind, but I never though—"

"Just hang in there. We'll find him."

"I didn't want to call the police—"

"Don't! Leave everything to me, okay?"

"Thank you, Namir. You're a real friend."

"I'll call you." He switched off and leaned back against the seat, thinking it through. *Damn!*

Hamas could have taken him, but they had not bothered Mossad before. Besides, their style was to spray their target with bullets, not stoop to kidnapping. Well, if it wasn't an enemy, it had to be a friend. No use hiding from what he instinctively knew had happened. The thought did not give him any comfort. He leaned forward and dialed. It took three rings.

"David Ben Gillon," a gruff voice responded.

"It's Namir, David. I've got a problem."

"That's the only time you ever call," Gillon, head of Shabak's Non-Arab Affairs Department, complained somewhat peevishly. "Or when you want me to haul your ass out of some sticky predicament. Do you know what time it is? Not all of us get up with the sun, you know."

"If you will just shut up for a moment," Namir snapped, not in the mood for banter. "This is serious. How about that!"

"And a shalom to you too," Gillon added, then sighed. "Okay, what do you want?"

"Somebody snatched Matan Irian as he was leaving for work. Sarah thinks they got away in a white Mercedes saloon. No identity profile."

"Tell her to call the police, Namir."

"Very funny. I think it was the CIA."

"The CIA? What would they want with Matan?"

"I want you to call Ben-Gurion airport security and tell them to detain every U.S. national for questioning. I also want you to stop all aircraft from departing, commercial and private, until we get to the bottom of this."

"You've got to be shitting me," Gillon declared flatly. "I don't have authority to delay commercial flights without cause, not without ministerial approval."

"Then get it!"

"Ignoring your foul temper, what makes you think they would fly him out? He could be anywhere."

"That's right, he could. But if he's on the ground, you have time to mount a proper search."

There was a moment of tense silence. "Okay, Namir. Let me see what I can do. But the CIA?"

"Thanks, David. I mean it. Shalom."

Cutting the connection, he sighed and rubbed his eyes. He should have acted sooner. He told himself countless times that in his business, there was no room for distracting sentimentality. And what does he do? On the most important ops of his life, he allowed sentiment to cloud his professional judgment. And now, he could very well reap the reward for his folly.

If the Americans were indeed the ones who took Matan, they probably had all the information they wanted already. They wouldn't be wasting time with fancy maneuvers, not in a potentially hostile environment. Against modern drugs, Matan wouldn't stand a chance. Of course, drugs might not have been used at all. Faced with the inevitable, he would probably cooperate and Namir wouldn't blame him at all. Contrary to movie images of a gutsy hero who keeps his mouth shut in spite of everything, that just doesn't work. In real life *everybody* breaks under physical or drug-induced persuasion.

Namir did not believe Matan would be hurt; there wasn't much point to it, unless the kidnappers were sadists—always possible. The options available to the Americans were limited. They might take Matan Stateside, or leave him in some gutter alive or dead while they made their getaway on the ground. He did not consider it likely, but it was possible. No, they would fly out, quick and simple; that's what he would do. Could David really bottle up Ben-Gurion? By the time he worked his way through the chain of government bureaucracy and obtained the necessary clearances, probably not. Everybody was still asleep. Still, it was worth a shot. The Americans might *not* have interrogated Matan yet, and if they did, they might not have communicated with Washington. Both hopes were thread-slim possibilities, but possibilities nonetheless. And if he could exploit this window…

He punched the recall number button and waited.

"Namir, I just finished talking to you. I'm good, but not that good!"

"David, please check with Ben-Gurion tower and ask them if they have any American government or military aircraft scheduled for departure. Please hurry."

"Hang on. I'll call them on another line." There was a click and thick silence.

Namir looked out, taking in the sunny surrounds. The sunshine did nothing to lift his spirits. His fingers drummed impatiently against the steering wheel. Jaron would be getting worried by now that he hadn't shown up at his usual time. The thought raised a fleeting smile.

"You there?"

"What've you got, David?"

"An American Air Force Gulfstream V landed at 0432 and is cleared for immediate unscheduled departure."

Namir allowed himself a grim nod of satisfaction. "That's our bird. I want you to stop it taking off. I don't care what you do. Shoot out a tire or throw a rock at it. Just stop it!"

Gillon gave a fruity laugh. "I like your sense of humor, Namir, especially this early in the morning. You want me to detain an authorized American military aircraft? What do I tell security?"

"I don't give a damn what you tell them. Just do it!"

"Namir, we've known each other for a while, too long for bullshit. I know Matan is your friend, but what you're asking for cannot be done."

"Call the Prime Minister—"

"It's no good. I have to follow procedure, you know that."

Namir pounded his palm against the steering wheel. "Damn it all, David. There isn't *time* for procedure."

Gillon cleared his throat. "What's going on, Namir? This is not a simple snatch at all, is it?"

"No, it's not. We are talking national security here, David."

"Listen to me, Namir. Even if I called the PM, he will want details and I cannot give him any. He would have me shot for disturbing his breakfast. Then he would have *you* shot. It's an American military flight!"

"You don't have to call anyone and we both know it. You'd be acting under my authority."

"I'm sorry, my friend, I really am, but that's not good enough."

Namir was about to send him a searing blast, but refrained. That wouldn't get him anywhere and he would needlessly alienate a valuable ally. And if he looked at it from David's point of view, without additional facts, his request would sound somewhat extreme to say the least. He took a deep breath and let it out in a long sigh. Things were falling apart and it was his fault.

"Forget the whole thing, David," he said wearily, resigned to whatever the fates now had in store for him…and for Israel.

"If Matan is still on the ground, I'll find him. No hard feelings?"

"None, honestly. I was out of line."

"Later, then. Shalom."

Namir squinted hard at the cellphone and punched in another call. He had resources of his own, but was there enough time to do the job? There was only one way of finding out. He should have acted sooner. Stupid!

"Yes, sir?" a soft, guttural voice answered almost immediately.

"American Gulfstream V at Ben-Gurion Airport. Prevent departure. Urgent immediate."

The line went dead.

He almost smiled as he made the next call. At the rate he was raking up calls, he would be taking his lunch in the car.

"Special Operations Division, Mossad. Mira Dayon."

"Hello, Mira. It's Bethan."

"Shalom, Mr. Bethan. What can I do for you, sir?"

"Someone's taken Matan Irian in front of his house this

morning."

"How terrible!" Mira sounded genuinely shocked.

"Shabak has instigated a search, but I want you to contact David Ben Gillon and offer him our help: manpower, information, anything."

"Of course, sir. Right away. Will you be coming in?"

"Ten minutes. I'm just down the street."

"Very good, sir. Can I ask how Sarah is taking it?"

"Badly, as you can expect. I'll fill you in when I get into the office."

She switched off and he nodded. Capable girl; should go far. He would transfer her immediately while he still held some influence. and the move would give her career a leg-up. No need to drag her down when the scandal broke, and he was realistic enough to realize that it would break. What then? Should he run or brazen it out? He had several contingency plans in place and he needed to make up his mind quickly which one to follow.

Driven by sheer habit, he started the car and eased the BMW away from the curb.

* * *

Stan slowed and stopped the Merc opposite the little guard-house. The security man stepped out and looked at them with disinterest. His only thought was finishing his shift and getting home.

Mark patted Stan on the shoulder and hooked his thumb at Irian. "When he wakes, leave him near a bus station or something. I don't need to tell you not to get caught."

"Piece of cake, Mr. Price," Stan rasped confidently.

"No offense, Stan, but you don't discuss this with anyone. And I mean anyone," Mark added firmly, staring into the man's eyes.

A lazy grin lit Stan's face. "I wouldn't have missed it for anything, sir, and this should make me the center of attention for a change."

Mark nodded, glanced at Tom and gathered his bag. He climbed out of the car without looking at Irian's slumped form and pushed the door shut. With determined strides, he marched toward the open side gate. Tom got out and hurried after him.

"Good morning, gentlemen," the guard said politely, remembering them.

"Shalom," Mark said and walked through the gate, not bothering with his passport.

The Gulfstream was already lined up, its engines idling, ready to taxi. As Mark and Tom approached, the door opened and Nancy lowered the steps. They climbed aboard and she immediately buttoned up, looking crisp and pressed like she'd had a good night's sleep in her bed.

"We are cleared for direct departure, sir," she told Mark. "If you would please be seated, we'll be on our way. Our arrival time at Andrews is scheduled for 1450, but we are expecting some headwinds."

Mark took his old seat, buckled in and allowed himself to relax. All the planning and careful preparation had paid off. They came in quickly, executed the job with a minimum of fuss, and were now about to get away clean. That's what he called a perfect ops. A glance at his watch showed 8:22. The engines spooled up and the aircraft began moving. They waited two minutes on the taxiway as an Air France Airbus came down with puffs of gray smoke from its rear tires. Cleared, the Gulfstream rolled to the active runway, wound up both engines and surged. Mark felt a rush as the concrete blurred beside him. Terminal 3 on his right, with parked aircraft clustered around the spokes, suddenly looked small, like a kid's toy set. The wings lifted and the Gulfstream powered into the eastern sky. As they gained altitude the aircraft banked and steadied on a westerly course. Nancy appeared from the cockpit, her usual warm smile firmly fixed.

"No sightseeing?" she inquired, her eyes quizzical as they traveled over the two men.

"We saw all the right sights, Nancy," Tom assured her, admiring her form.

"Your visit a success, then?"

"Entirely."

"In that case, a drink…coffee?"

"A coffee would be terrific," Mark said with a rush and Tom nodded.

"The same for me."

"Excellent."

Mark unbuckled and retrieved his bag. He pulled out the recorder, rewound the tape and shoved the unit into his coat pocket. A delicious smell of freshly ground coffee wafted from the rear, mixed with odors of warming snacks. Nancy brought a tray and laid out the small table with a carafe of coffee, cups and accompanying add-ons. She also unloaded a platter of assorted hot tidbits. Tom reached for one and popped it in his mouth. Chewing, he nodded in appreciation.

"Thanks, Nancy. If we can have a moment alone, please?" Mark asked and she immediately straightened.

"Of course, sir. I shall be up front if you want anything."

While Mark fiddled with the encrypted telephone, Tom poured them both a coffee. After dialing, Mark pressed the speaker button and looked up.

"Graham Stone," a sleepy voice answered after five rings. "And I hope you've got a good reason for doing this to me."

Mark hated to wake the national security advisor at 1:45 in the morning, but the admiral would be more than pissed if he didn't.

"Mark Price, sir. My apologies for the early call, but you must hear this." He dug the recorder out of his pocket. "Are you secure?"

"Yes. Where are you now, son?"

"We just took off from Ben-Gurion."

"And?"

"It was a Metsada black ops, Admiral. As we suspected, Matan Irian planned and stage-managed the whole thing. Namir Bethan authorized the operation. It's all on tape. Can you record?"

"Just say when."

"Coming through now." Mark pressed the recorder against the speaker pickup and pressed the Play button. He sat back, picked up his cup and nodded to Tom in thanks.

Tom sipped his coffee, holding the cup in both hands, allowing its soothing warmth to relax him. It felt strange listening to a conversation that happened just over an hour ago, reliving every moment, images crowding his mind. It felt more like a lifetime of conflicting impressions and emotions. What a way to see the Holy Land. Not that he had seen much of it. Nonetheless, the Arabic flavor of the landscape and architecture were pronounced. He would not have minded a day or two strolling about. After this, he wondered whether the Israeli government would ever allow him to return. Probably would; then pound him. Anyway, the documentaries did it better. But it wasn't the same thing as being there.

When the tape finished, Mark pocketed the recorder.

"Well, this definitely lets Iran off the hook," Stone remarked, fully awake, his mind evaluating options the president might take in response, and the possible strategic impact on Israel.

None of them looked good. Of course, President Walters could issue a 'naughty boy' slap to Prime Minister Ibrahim, but he doubted it. The president was a former fighter pilot and would not hesitate to move in on the guy's six and shoot. Still, that was some time ago and Walters was now a politician, having to be mindful of the 'big picture'. How many times was *that* used as an excuse to do nothing.

"Outstanding performance, my boy. Is Mr. Meecham with

you?"

"I'm here, sir," Tom answered politely.

"I cannot congratulate you enough and the work done by your team, son."

"Just doing my job, sir, but I cannot say it hasn't been fun."

Stone chuckled. "For everybody, I am sure. Did you two have any trouble?"

"Everything went smoothly, Admiral, and nobody got hurt," Mark said.

"Good. This Matan Irian sounds like a cold sort of a fish."

"I'm sure it will get plenty hot for him once he wakes up."

"No sympathy?"

"If it were up to me, Admiral, I would have shot him."

"Yeah. See me when you land, both of you," Stone ordered and cut the connection.

Mark sat back, deep in thought, then smiled at Tom and raised his cup in a salute. "To our noble selves. There are damn few of us left."

They clicked cups and Tom laughed. "Christ! I haven't heard that one in a while."

"My mind's a junkyard," Mark said comfortably and sagged into his seat. "We're done, but this is where things get very interesting."

"Especially for Israel," Tom agreed.

* * *

A dark sedan pulled up outside the airport perimeter fence. The two occupants slowly scanned the taxiways and the main runway. Nothing was moving and there was no sign of the Gulfstream. In the bright clear sunshine, there was not much chance of missing an aircraft out in the open. The front seat passenger tapped the driver's shoulder and pointed east. The driver squinted and leaned forward. Perhaps two kilometers away the elegant twin-engine executive jet was banking left into a long turn. They watched it dwindle into a black speck as it headed west.

The driver glanced at his partner, saying nothing. They had missed their target by perhaps two minutes. There was no expression on his hard face or steel gray eyes. He dealt with reality as it was dished out. Moping over what might have been was an exercise in futility and a waste of energy. In a long string of operations, failure was a statistical certainty. He wasn't making excuses either. The call from One gave them only moments to get ready, check equipment and head off. Morning traffic was an unavoidable factor and he had not dared speed. Getting caught for a traffic violation would be an immediate show gasper. It was simple. Circumstances conspired to delay them and the target had flown—literally.

He dragged out his cellphone and punched a recall number.

"Yes?" a gruff voice answered after two rings.

"Mission failed," the driver said coldly and cut contact. There was no need for explanations, not to One. The job was either done or it wasn't. Dissecting a dead horse would not bring it back to life.

Pocketing the cellphone, he started the engine and glanced at his partner.

"Coffee?"

The other shrugged. "Why not? There isn't much else to do."

A touch of gas and the car moved smoothly toward the terminal.

* * *

The national security advisor replaced the receiver, exhaled sharply and rubbed his face with both hands. His eyes felt gummy and sore. After a long evening at the White House, a string of long evenings, he only managed to catch two hours of sleep. The fact that he was a sailor who stood countless night watches did not help; he had not stood a watch in decades. Despite telling himself that he needed to slow down, after all, there were only so many hours available in a day, he was still at it, burning it from both ends. He glanced at the bedside electronic clock: 2:15 a.m. The green numbers stared back indifferently, the seconds remorselessly marching on.

"You can rest when you're dead," he told himself grumpily, and that might not be all that far off. Well, if his night was ruined, he might as well share the misery. He picked up the receiver and pressed a dialup button, deriving a certain sardonic satisfaction at what he was about to do.

It took several forlorn rings.

"Graham! Do you have any idea what it's like getting up right now?" an aggrieved voice demanded petulantly. "If you've got insomnia, take a pill, for Crissake!"

"If it's any consolation, Manfred, I've been up longer than you."

"It is not. You want to tell me why you called me at this ungodly hour or maybe you just missed hearing my voice?"

"Is your line secure?"

"Go ahead."

"Price confirmed the attack on Valero was a Mossad black ops. I've got it all on tape."

"Shit! Who sanctioned it?"

"No one. The Metsada director apparently did it all by himself."

There was a prolonged sigh at the other end. "Okay. I guess it was worth waking up for that, but not by much. I don't believe the President will be too thrilled when I tell him that it's Israel after all. What a mess. How soon can you come in?"

"Give me forty-five minutes."

"We'll see him at three thirty. Bring the tape," Cottard ordered and switched off.

Stone threw back the lightweight bed-cover with a grunt and got up. He switched on the main bedroom lights and stepped into his home office. Flicking on the light switch, he walked to the desk and opened the top drawer. Rummaging around, he took out a blank USB memory stick. He plugged it into a front port of his PC communications station and tapped the Enter key to wake the machine. Accessing the encrypted messages directory, he highlighted Price's download, set 'Decrypt' and dragged the file into the USB's root directory. When the copy process finished, he activated Media Player and selected USB input. Price's voice came through clearly. He nodded, unplugged the USB and left it on the desk.

A quick shower and two fried eggs on toast, accompanied by a cup of strong black coffee, woke him up more fully. He switched everything off, retrieved the USB and locked up. The drive to the White House from his Georgetown terrace residence was easy, hardly anybody about. Street poles cast milky shadows on the tree-lined road, making the surrounding stately old houses even darker, somehow forbidding. The Secret Service car kept a discreet, but close distance behind him. The traffic got heavier when he entered Pennsylvania Avenue, but still flowed smoothly. Downtown was a blaze of lights, all the buildings and monuments fully lit, and his spirits lifted. He could see the floodlit Washington Monument pushing into a black sky, its anti-collision red light winking on the point. He suppressed a yawn.

He swiped his badge against the security sensor and hurried through the semi-dark West Wing. Several owl staffers looked up in surprise as he walked past glass cubicles, no doubt raising a wave of wild speculation at the sight of the national security advisor in this early. He paused outside the deputy chief of staff secretary's office where a percolator maintained a perpetual supply of what was generously called coffee. He poured himself a mug of tarry mess, added sugar, and walked toward his office. Footsteps behind him made him glance over his shoulder.

Cottard strode past him, pointing toward the Oval Office. "He's waiting for us."

Stone shrugged and walked after the chief of staff, mug in hand.

Walters was sitting behind his desk, clad in black jeans, brown flannel shirt and a beige corduroy windbreaker. He looked shaved and manicured. Stone wondered how long that manicure would last today. A correctly dressed steward was pouring coffee into a white porcelain cup with a gold lip border. He handed it to the president, nodded to the new arrivals and silently padded out. Cottard filled a cup and sat down on the sofa.

Walters noted Stone's mug and gave a sardonic smile. "My coffee not good enough for you anymore, Graham?" he chided, looking pointedly at the carafe on the small table set between two beige sofas. A tray of sweet pastries completed the tableau.

"You grab your coffee while you can, sir. Learned that one in the Navy."

"So I heard. That's why the Air Force looks after its men so much better, but it brings back memories. I wouldn't mind strapping on an F/A-18 right now, or an F-16. The only thing you had to worry about was not screwing the pooch. What about you, Graham? Want to con a battle group again?"

"It was fun, but that part of my life is behind me now. I'm conning a big enough ship now, Mr. President."

"You can say that again, for both of us. Okay, make yourselves comfortable and let's get this done. Details, Graham, but get your Danish pastry first."

"Thank you, Mr. President."

Stone eased himself onto a sofa facing the president, took a sip of coffee and reached for an apricot Danish. He took two big bites, nodded in appreciation and looked up.

"Price followed a hunch and had the CIA look for Mossad operatives flying out of Houston last Sunday night. They identified three. One of them was Matan Irian, a senior case officer in

Metsada. Yesterday, I gave Price permission to go to Tel Aviv, nail Irian and make him tell all." He reached into his pocket and placed the USB stick on the coffee table. "It's all there, Mr. President."

"Bastards," Walters murmured and shook his head. "You took a lot on yourself, Graham," he added, studying the hardened admiral.

The man returned his gaze without looking away. Walters had nothing to gripe about. He picked Stone because he was smart, levelheaded and able to make decisions that mattered without running to anybody for permission—provided they turned out to be the right decisions. So far, he had always been right.

"The payback was worth it, sir."

"Evidently. Manfred tells me that Sharron Ibrahim wasn't involved," Walters said. "Is that right?"

"That's the story. Of course, Irian could be protecting Ibrahim's ass, but I don't think so. No matter how much Ibrahim wanted to take out Iran's nuclear facilities, he would not want to do it like this. He would send in an air strike package."

"Agreed. The arrogant bastard would have done exactly that."

Barely into his term, Walters had tangled with the wily Israeli prime minister, and the experience left both men hugely dissatisfied. Seeing him as young and inexperienced, Ibrahim urged him to immediately strike at Iran's nuclear facilities, claiming a favorable response from the international community. Walters was not convinced of the need for a military response, advising a diplomatic solution, which embittered Ibrahim and cooled the relationship between them, especially after Walters warned Israel against taking unilateral action. The way he saw it, Ibrahim was quick to advocate others to take action, but seemed coy to act himself when compliance with the Roadmap was raised.

The president stirred himself and looked searchingly at his senior staff. "What are my options?"

"Remember that scenario I proposed, Mr. President?" Stone

prompted softly and waited.

"You think it could work despite all the obvious obstacles?"

"Needs some polishing, certainly, but yes, sir. It could be made to work and it is high time that we acted."

"Manfred?"

"If you forced something like that on Ibrahim, his government would fall, Mr. President," Cottard said immediately.

"When this breaks, his government will fall anyway," Walters added pointedly.

"As may be, but any Israeli government trying to push through such a plan would fall. They are stuck with the fact that right-wing orthodox parties hold the balance of power. The major parties might be willing to talk, but they're hamstrung and won't risk a vote of no confidence."

"Yeah. People will do much stay in power, even if it prolongs misery," Walters mused and his jaw firmed. "It's going to be bloody either way, but I feel that we have reached a pivotal point where this just might be possible. If that means a shakeup of how their Knesset works, so be it."

"It is definitely worth pursuing, sir," Stone affirmed. "And we might not get another opportunity like this for some time, if at all."

"What about Congress? I've got control of both Houses, but will they support me? I may be the President, but they have their own agenda and doing the right thing is not always a priority for them."

"Ignore the Congress, Mr. President," Stone interjected firmly. "Lay it out before the people. My guess is they will support you, and Congress won't have a choice but to go along."

"And if they don't?"

Stone shrugged. "That's politics, Mr. President. But you would have shown yourself to be a cool statesman, not bending under pressure when you know you're right. Having urged you to lash out at Iran, everybody will be eating crow, even Congress.

I'd say you would have a blank check to do just about anything."

Walters was wearing a broad grin. "And they would make me pay for it later, Graham. Okay, Manfred. Let's hear your slant on this."

"I must agree with Graham, Mr. President. You have a singular opportunity to make a major shift in the administration's Middle East policy. Of course, the old Hamas and Hezbollah hard-liners are still an influence and would have to be dealt with, but if you forced Israel into major concessions, you would take the wind out of their sails, so to speak. Everyone on both sides is just damn tired of this conflict, and you stand a fair chance of doing something positive about it."

Walters stared at nothing in particular, his eyes lost in a vision of a peaceful Middle East. Manfred was a romantic if he thought that centuries of prejudice, hate, suspicion and resentment could be swept away with a presidential edict. There were simply too many entrenched, vested interests on all sides for the idea to work. Iran seeking to expand its regional influence, Syria struggling to reestablish control over Lebanon, and Israel hating everybody while nodding before the Wailing Wall seeking supplication for victory over its enemies. Too many men enjoyed power gained and sustained by ongoing conflict to suddenly give it up voluntarily—even for peace. Without power, those men would be nothing. Once such a man acquires a taste for power, he would invariably strive to keep it, whatever the cost or pain to others. Thus were born dictators and autocrats. And the worst ones of all fought under the banner of God.

But if he didn't at least make an effort, how would people judge him, not only as a man, but supposedly as leader of the free world? Was freedom only the province of America? Weren't others entitled to the same opportunities? The founding fathers laid out the foundations for a nation based on the noblest of ideals: the right to dignity of every individual. Surely, that must apply to all mankind? Why should he withhold that right from others simply because supporting a repressive regime guaranteed a grudging flow of oil, or maintained an illusory bulwark against communism, terrorism or growing geopolitical influence merely to sustain America's economic and political advantage? Do as I say, not as I do, was a bankrupt policy of expedience for too long, that only succeeded in alienating everybody and diminished respect for America as an honest broker. A shift in policy did not necessarily mean turning the other cheek, but it could herald turning over a new leaf.

Walters glanced at the eagle engraved in the great seal before his desk and wondered whether he was worthy to stand before that noble bird and raise his voice in a cry for justice. He slowly turned his head and fixed his eyes on his chief of staff.

"Call the Chairman of the Joint Chiefs. Have him withdraw the *Eisenhower* and *Nimitz* carrier groups to their normal cruising positions. And if General Jason McDonald gives you any lip, fire his ass. Next, I want the Israeli Ambassador here. I want her around when I call Sharron Ibrahim. Then get me President Al Zerkhani. After you've done all that, call in all the senior staff."

"Already alerted, Mr. President," Cottard announced formally and stood up. "Don't start a war without me."

Stone pointed at the USB. "We'll want a player that can take this."

"I'll get a staffer to bring something in," Cottard said and walked across the Oval Office to a door that led to his office.

Allowing himself a moment of distraction, Walters got up and ambled to a sofa opposite Stone. He sat down and poured himself a fresh cup. Stone picked another Danish and dug in.

"These are good," he remarked between bites. "Where do you get them?"

"They bake them right here," Walters said with a smug smile and helped himself to one. Taking out a chunk, he nodded. "Not bad, are they?"

"Whoever made these would make a fortune on the outside,"

Stone added meditatively between bites and Walters chuckled.

"But he wouldn't have the perks."

"There is that."

Walters looked warmly at his national security advisor. "Mark Price did well. As did the FBI."

"Thomas Meecham, sir. I told both of them to see me when they got to Andrews. I was hoping you could have a word with them."

"Absolutely. Outstanding work. When are they due in?"

"Sometime around three o'clock."

"Two Atlantic crossings in one day. They'll be beat."

"The Gulfstream V Price uses is comfortable, Mr. President."

"Still…of course you know the risk you took with Price?"

Stone immediately shook his head. "Not for a moment, sir. He was an extremely capable CIA operative. I checked his file. If it weren't for Zardwovsky and Grant, he would still be doing good work there. Colin Forbes is lucky to have him."

"Another good man," Walters agreed with a thoughtful nod.

"Price has a nose for intelligence and trusts his instincts. Given the information supplied by Meecham, it was easy to connect the dots."

"But he did more than that," Walters added. "He was prepared to finish it himself instead of simply dumping it on you. I like that in a man. If you think you're right, go for it. Don't put a buck down each way." He allowed himself a small smile. "And that's what you did too."

"Thank you, sir."

"I'd give you another medal, but you already have all the good ones. For what's it worth, you have the thanks of your President."

"Better than any medal, sir."

"But I'm not going to thank you for dumping me into this mess. Here I was, looking forward to doing some of the fun things for a year or so that new presidents indulge in without having to worry about foreign policy too much. And then this shit comes along."

"There's no justice, is there?" Stone remarked equitably.

Walters wagged a finger at him, then slapped his thigh. "I forgot to tell Manfred to call Tanner. My SecState should be here when I talk to Ibrahim."

"Larry will not be too pleased when he learns that you've kept him in the dark. He's already sore that you've been talking to President Al Zerkhani without his permission."

"He'll grumble, but he'll take it on the chin. I will announce policy and he'll grumble some more, then he'll make it work." Cottard walked in and Walters raised a hand in exasperation. "I should have told you—"

"Tanner is on his way, Mr. President," Cottard remarked dryly and Walters cocked his head at Stone.

"See why I put up with him?"

"Somebody's got to run things around here," Cottard said easily and rubbed the underside of his nose. He sat down and selected a pastry.

"Not much longer, not with that attitude. Everything arranged?"

"McDonald wanted to know why we were pulling back the carriers, but I shut him up. Hannakah did not appreciate being dragged out of bed because the President could not tell the time. Her words."

"She can complain all she wants as long as she drags her ass in here," Walters growled with total lack of sympathy. "Okay, let's get President Al Zerkhani on the line," he said briskly, walked back behind his desk and sprawled into his seat.

Cottard reached into his pocket and took out a yellow post-it sticker. The outer office was lit, but the support staff were yet to arrive. He leaned across the *Resolute* desk, pressed the speaker button and punched in the call, reading the numbers off the post-it sticker. There was some clicking as the international exchanges talked to each other. After three rings a polite male voice said something in Farsi.

"President Samuel Walters on the line for President Al Zerkhani," Cottard interrupted and sat on the sofa.

There was a moment of poignant silence, presumably while the voice got over his shock. "Just a moment, sir." More silence, probably to allow time for some running around by the flunkeys. There was a click and the now familiar voice of Zerkhani's translator came on.

"President Walters?" the translator queried politely.

"Good morning, sir," Walters answered immediately, looking forward to talking with the Iranian president again. Bearing gifts always came easy.

"A pleasant surprise, Mr. President. Is there anything I can do for you, sir?"

"It's what I can do for you. We have identified the responsible party for the attack on Valero."

Muffled voices came from the other end at this development.

"I am relieved to hear that, and gratified that justice will hopefully be meted out to those who deserve it. May I ask who they were?"

"I regret I cannot reveal that information now and I hope you will forgive me for that. However, in a few hours you will know, as will everyone else. Given the identity of the party, I need to consult with them before announcing America's response."

"I understand, sir, and I am not offended. I am thankful that the perpetrators were identified so promptly, and grateful to you for showing courage in staying your hand where a lesser man would have acted out of ingrained bias."

"Thank you, Mr. President."

"I fear that I know the identity of the perpetrator already and why the attack was carried out, but I shall not take advantage of the situation to seek a hollow political victory."

"I appreciate that very much, sir. Premature disclosure could compromise developments which I hope will benefit everyone in the region." Walters paused to gather his thoughts. "This has been a difficult time for both of us, President Al Zerkhani, and I wish to express my admiration for your handling of this matter, and the restraint shown by your military forces."

"It would have been counterproductive in the extreme to act in any other way. Given the circumstances, I understand that you had to act as you did, positioning your naval forces in the Gulf."

"I have already initiated withdrawal of my carrier battle groups to their normal patrol positions, sir."

Walters waited until another hurried conference finished.

"This is indeed welcome news and will greatly ease the handling of my domestic position," the translator announced, and Walters felt a smile twitch at the corner of his mouth.

It could not have been comfortable for Zerkhani, standing idly by with street demonstrations in Tehran while *Ike* and *Nimitz* paraded off the Iranian coast, spoiling for trouble. Well, this is where he made amends, embarking on a course of action which he was certain would not be met with unanimous approval, at home or abroad.

"Mr. President, your country and the entire Middle East has endured injustice from foreign powers, including the United States. I am not pretending that it is in my hands to right all the wrongs of history, but I am prepared to take a step along a path that will hopefully lead to a mutually beneficial future. As promised in my previous communiqué, the United States UN Ambassador will today announce the lifting of American trade sanctions and will urge the lifting of general UN sanctions now in place. He will also announce an offer to open a dialogue between our two countries for the purpose of normalizing relations. With your permission, I will direct Secretary of State Tanner to explore and agree to a mutually acceptable agenda with your government to form a basis for an initial round of bilateral talks. During this time, I would like to maintain direct dialogue with you in order to resolve any diplomatic sticking points that might arise between our respective delegations as a result of possible misunderstandings."

The silence was almost loud as the Iranian leader, and presumably one or two of his senior advisors, digested this most unusual announcement and proposal. Walters was certain that no one in the West had ever spoken to them in such terms. Certainly no one in any previous administration had done so. If Zerkhani harbored suspicions, given the track record between them, Walters could hardly blame him. He did not expect that they would be embracing each other anytime soon, too much distrust and suspicion on both sides prevented that, but he was prepared to undertake a cautious reappraisal. President Bush's Axis of Evil statement still hung over them like a dark blanket, which Walters wanted to tear down promptly.

"President Walters?"

"I am here, sir."

"Forgive me this moment of inattention, sir. Your words have caught me by surprise and the impact of their portent will take time to be evaluated fully. However, I can say this with genuine feeling. Throughout this tragic episode, and with your words now, you have held an open hand to me and my country, asking for nothing. Now, you hold out your hand again, not bearing a sword, but with an offer of respect. Mr. President, if your words are genuine, I am willing to extend you an open hand in return.

"As you said, the past has left Iran with deep wounds, which only time can remove. The lifting of your sanctions is a significant first step in that process. I shall consult with my government your offer to open negotiations, which I trust will lead to a positive outcome. In the meantime, Mr. President, I thank you for your call and I look forward to witnessing the eventual resolution of difficulties you now face with your, ah, other party. Walk with God, sir."

"Thank you for your understanding, sir," Walters said and the line went dead. He punched the speaker button, gave a deep sigh and sat back.

Cottard ventured a wan smile and shook his head. "You've taken a fairly large bite there, Mr. President. But can you swallow it?"

"I like your vote of confidence, Manfred. It gives me courage to go on," Walters said amiably and his eyes wandered to Stone. "Graham? Any beefs?"

"The objective is ambitious and has a raft of problems to overcome, but in the long term it is doable. More importantly, it is honorable. I'm not saying that we'll be exchanging ambassadors by the weekend, but perhaps one day we will. Our delegation will need to be chosen carefully, sir. We don't want ingrained prejudices poisoning the whole thing from the outset."

"I realize that, Graham. Tanner will handle it. Damnation! Where is that man?"

"Mr. President, what will you tell Prime Minister Ibrahim?" Cottard asked and Walters raised his right hand, palm open.

"Wait until Tanner—"

There was a knock and Walters' secretary opened the door. "Good morning, Mr. President. The Secretary of State is here, sir."

"Unice! What in the world are you doing here?" Walters demanded in genuine surprise.

"My job, sir."

Walters shook his head and waved her away. "Send him in."

SecState was an imposing figure. Tall, impeccably dressed in a dark blue worsted, thick brown hair combed straight back, his round face testified to a comfortable life. It was the eyes that demanded attention. Icy blue, they gave nothing away and saw everything, like digital cameras. A former Boeing executive and ambassador to China in a previous administration, Tanner's competence was obvious. When he made a statement on international affairs, that's how it was, leaving little room for disagreement. That tended to rub some people the wrong way, but Tanner was a skilled politician and could couch his delivery without offering direct offense, but not brooking dissent either. His views sometimes clashed with Walters', but it was more in the nature of a patient teacher instructing an irascible student. With Tanner in the room, there was no doubting as to who was the teacher. The secretary of state did not always agree with him and wasn't bashful at saying so, but when Walters made a decision, Tanner accepted it with grace and carried it out with detached efficiency.

He marched into the Oval Office like a man with a mission, nodded to Cottard and Stone, and stopped on the great seal.

"What's going on that Manfred had to drag me out here in the middle of the night? Not even with a by your leave. Well?"

Walters glanced at Unice. She immediately closed the heavy door. "Sit down, Larry, and pour yourself a cup of coffee."

Wearing the sulky look of a spoiled child, Tanner grasped an easy chair, swung it around to face the three men and lowered his bulk. He did not bother with the coffee.

"Okay, I'm sitting down. Satisfied?"

"It's Valero," Walters said patiently and Tanner lifted his eyebrows.

"The FBI nailed the bastards? And this couldn't wait until morning?" He shot Cottard a vitriolic glance. "We'll talk about this later, Manfred," he said and turned to the president. "I suppose you'll be committing to a strike then? Not that those Iranian ragheads didn't have it coming."

"It's not Iran," Walters said, hating to burst Larry's bubble of enthusiasm.

"Excuse me? But all the evidence—"

"Was planted," Walters finished for him, enjoying Larry's moment of confusion. It was not every day that he got to pull one on SecState.

"Planted?" Tanner waited and glared. "Well? Are you going to tell me by whom or am I supposed to consult a psychic?"

"I don't know why I put up with your insolence, Larry. If I

had any sense, I'd fire your ass."

Tanner gave a nasty grin. "You need me to tell you how to shape your foreign policy. Well, who was it?"

Walters shook his head. "One day you'll go too far. It was a Mossad black ops."

"What? It can't be! Israel wouldn't dare."

"We've got it all on tape. Confession from a senior Metsada operative who carried it out."

"Ah, shit!" Tanner sagged into his seat, looking unbearably tired. "Stupid, stupid. What are you going to do?"

"I pulled back *Ike* and *Nimitz* and I've asked President Al Zerkhani to consider opening a first round of bilateral talks as a prelude to normalizing relations."

Tanner leaned forward and raised a finger. "Wait a minute. You actually talked to him? I cannot believe you did this without me, Mr. President."

"You'll have enough on your plate managing the process. And I want these talks to succeed. Is that clear?"

Tanner nodded, albeit reluctantly. "If we cannot trust Israel, I guess we've got to look for other friends, is that it?"

"Israel is not buried yet and Iran will not be exactly a friend. Not anytime soon, but at least we can make a start."

"I'm not arguing and there could be many advantages for everybody with a half-friendly Iran. But it won't be easy to bring the Ayatollahs to our side, though," Tanner mused, tilted his head and snorted. "Israel...unbelievable. I guess Ibrahim's government is dead. Still, you can almost sympathize why they did it."

"No, I can't, Larry," Walters snapped sharply. "I can understand, but I cannot sympathize at all. There were other ways of going about this, and I'm not letting Ibrahim off the hook because Mossad acted behind his back. They are his personal thugs."

"That's cutting it a bit strong, but okay, you're mad as hell. What next?"

"When Hannakah gets here, I'll be calling Ibrahim and give him the bad news."

"Which is?"

"You'll find out when he does."

Tanner sat up and shook his head. "I know that look. Mr. President, whatever's on your mind, we've got to talk about it, now! I am your Secretary of State. I cannot advise you if you don't tell me things."

"I know all that, but this is one of those times when I get to be presidential and act without having my decisions discussed."

"We're not talking about enacting sanctions against Rumania. This is Israel!"

"Yes, it is. But it's my call, Larry, and if it turns out bad, I'll take the heat."

"Mr. President, I did not mean to imply—"

"I know. You want to protect my ass. I appreciate it, but this one is mine."

Tanner was unhappy that Walters had gone out to play on his own, but not that unhappy to resign or get himself fired by swimming upstream. He was not thrilled at being kept in the dark, but events sometimes happen even when he was not around. Middle Eastern politics had always been thorny ground for American administrations and he did not want his brand new president getting caught out in a major policy gaffe first thing into his term. But Walters was knowledgeable and always cut to the heart of any issue. Besides, exercising executive privilege was his right. He comforted himself with the thought that should Walters stumble, he would still be there to catch him. Resigning himself to the inevitable, he got up, poured himself coffee and grinned.

"Okay, you win. And I'm gonna love watching you wipe that smug, superior expression off Hannakah's face."

"One more thing, Larry. Manfred will be in touch with your office. I want you to assign Middle East experts to give me a series of orientation sessions about the region: history, culture, politics, religion, the works. I want somebody here starting tomorrow."

Tanner shot Cottard a stony look and nodded. This was not exactly a revelation, but he wasn't altogether displeased. It was about time the U.S. took the Arabs seriously.

"I'll get it set up."

There was a knock and Unice stood there, holding a portable CD player. Walters stood up and motioned her to come in.

"On my desk, please. When the Israeli Ambassador shows up, let her straight in. Then give me three minutes and call Prime Minister Sharron Ibrahim."

"Very good, sir." She placed the player on the *Resolute* desk and walked out.

Walters checked the back to make sure it had a USB port. He glanced at Manfred, who picked up the memory stick and held it out. Walters plugged it in, switched on the player and stared at the small LED screen. He selected 'External Device Input' and pressed Play. When Price's voice came through, he pressed Stop.

He looked up at the expressionless faces before him and frowned. "Just making sure the damn thing works," he said, daring anyone to say something, and sat in his leather chair.

"Of course, sir," Cottard ventured politely.

Another knock interrupted whatever Stone was about to say. Unice opened the door wide to reveal a strikingly handsome woman. She was slim, of medium height, rusty hair cut short, a black pearl choker adorning her neck. A simple brown business jacket and matching trousers completed the ensemble. The men got to their feet and her dark eyes traveled imperiously over them like a queen over her subjects.

"President Walters," she said coolly with a slight accent, walked to his desk and held out her manicured hand.

Walters stood and grasped it, but did not smile. "Thank you

for coming so promptly, Madam Ambassador. You know everybody here," he said and extended an open hand at a seat.

"Gentlemen." She nodded and everyone shuffled as they resumed their seats.

"Would you care for some coffee, Lucila?" Walters offered and Hannakah shook her head, conscious of the chilly atmosphere in the room and wondered what was so important that the president had to call her to his office this early.

"No thank you, sir. What is it you wanted to see me about?"

Walters sat down, leaned forward and clasped his hands over the desk. It was not her words, but the way she said them and her general attitude that tended to rankle. They reflected Israel as it was today: confident, haughty, dismissive of international opinion, yet demanding unconditional recognition and support for its flawed policies. Like Israel, Hannakah needed a reality check.

"There is no easy way to do this, Madam Ambassador, so I will talk plainly. We have evidence that a Metsada black ops team made the attack on the Valero Texas City Refinery."

Hannakah inhaled sharply and went white. To her credit, she did not look away, but maintained eye contact with Walters.

"Metsada…I think I'll take that coffee after all," she said breathlessly, her assured demeanor instantly transformed to one of fearful foreboding.

Cottard immediately stood up and poured her a cup. He placed it on a saucer and held it to her. She sat down and took a sip, her hand steady. Nonetheless, the cup made a small rattle as she put it back on the saucer.

"Mr. President—"

"There is nothing to say, Lucila," Walters said softly. "You are here simply as a witness when I talk to Prime Minister Ibrahim."

"May I ask what you intend doing?"

His phone went off and he pressed the speaker button. "Yes, Unice?"

"The Prime Minister of Israel on line two, sir."

"Put him through."

"President Walters?"

"Good morning, Prime Minister. Thank you for taking this call."

"Always a pleasure, Mr. President," Ibrahim said in clear, but nasal English.

"I wish that I were calling under more pleasant circumstances—"

"What is it you wish to tell me, Mr. President?" Ibrahim interrupted and Walters frowned at this impertinence.

Hannakah squirmed in her seat and had the grace to blush.

"I want to tell you, Prime Minister, that it was not Iran who carried out the attack on Valero, but Mossad."

"Mossad? Impossible! If this is an attempt to smear—"

"Prime Minister, please listen to this," Walters said calmly and pressed the Play button on the CD player.

There was stony silence as the recording was played out to its inexorable end. Hannakah looked visibly shaken and fought to keep her emotions under control, her eyes pleading with him.

To Walters, it was an age-old question. How far should government responsibility extend for actions of its administrative apparatus? There was also an age-old answer—totally. Unfortunately, realpolitik seldom enforced that responsibility in practice. Scapegoats, deserving or not, invariably bore the resulting fallout. This time, he was prepared to see that responsibility went all the way. No country under any circumstances could ever again presume to do what Israel had done, officially or otherwise.

When the recording ended, he pressed the Stop button and allowed a few moments of silence to linger over everybody.

"Mr. President…this is…monstrous!" Ibrahim choked, clearly shocked. "To think that Mossad would not only dare to contemplate such an act, but to actually carry it out, contrary to the policy and wishes of my government, is intolerable." He cleared his throat, then said briskly, "Naturally, the matter will be fully investigated and you have my word that the guilty will be prosecuted to the full extent of the law. Furthermore, I offer my sincerest condolences to the innocent who have suffered as a result of this barbaric act. Any compensation you deem appropriate, sir, including damage reparations, will be fully met."

"And how do you intend to meet those reparations, Prime Minister? Deduction from the four billion in our annual economic aid package?" Walters demanded coldly, irritated at Ibrahim's casual acceptance of the whole thing as though a mere apology could make up for what had been done.

"I wish you would clarify that, Mr. President, as I don't like what you are implying."

"Let me explain what I don't like, Prime Minister. Your government and your predecessors have urged America to take military action to neutralize Iran's nuclear program. That is on record. And you personally were less than satisfied at my refusal to do so. That is also on record. I suggest, sir, that your sole concern was not the perceived threat against Israel, but the loss of your unilateral capability to threaten nuclear retaliation against your Arab neighbors. A nuclear Iran would force you into a course of action that Israel has avoided for decades, namely the creation of a Palestinian state, because peace would undermine the power and influence of your military establishment."

"Mr. President, I cannot believe that you could have such a simple view of what is a very complex problem. Surely, you have better advisors than that."

"If Israel genuinely wanted peace, you would have removed all the settlements from the occupied territories as per the Roadmap, and withdraw from Gaza and the West Bank."

"And leave Israel open to attack by Hamas and another Intifada? Surely, Mr. President, you cannot be that naive?"

"Prime Minister, Israel's occupation of Gaza and the West Bank is based on the premise that the Arab world refuses to acknowledge your right to exist. I suggest that your refusal to acknowledge the right of the Palestinian people to exist is in no way different, perpetuating the conflict. What Mossad did was not an act by zealots, but an act set against a culmination of inconsistent policies of opportunism followed by successive Israeli governments. Mossad would not have acted had you exercised due diligence and control over an apparatus for which you are directly responsible."

"Do I understand that you're holding me personally accountable?"

"The Mossad Director reports to the Office of the Prime Minister, sir."

"And what do you propose I do to atone for this unfortunate incident, Mr. President?"

"It is what I intend doing, Prime Minister. What you do will be up to you."

"Mr. President, I apologized and offered compensation. What more do you expect from me?"

"A great deal, Prime Minister. The action of your intelligence service came close to initiating hostilities between America and Iran to further your agenda, perhaps serving your own unspoken objective. They acted, ignoring the potential loss of innocent life on both sides and the political and economic fallout for the world and the entire Middle East that would ensue.

"This morning, the American Ambassador to the United Nations will formally denounce Israel's act and seek an official apology, including reparations. He shall demand immediate arrest and prosecution of Namir Bethan and Matan Irian, and any other party found to be involved in the Valero plot. He shall announce a cessation of all economic and military aid to Israel and demand your withdrawal from Gaza and the West Bank, including dismantlement of all illegal Jewish settlements in the occupied territories as required by the Roadmap. Moreover, he shall demand that Israel formally acknowledges the establishment of a Palestinian state, comprising the Gaza and the West Bank under existing borders. The United States of America will seek a UN resolution to codify these demands, and if necessary, to be enforced by United Nations forces…my forces. I shall also take steps to immediately expel all known Mossad operatives from your Embassy and Consulates. Is that all clear, Prime Minister?"

Ibrahim gave a short, derisive laugh. "That was quite a list, Mr. President. I can hardly believe your naivety that Israel would accept or carry out your ill-advised demands, or that you would seek a UN mandate to enforce them. Even if I were personally predisposed to acknowledge the substance of your demands, I would not survive long enough to implement them. As for withdrawing your support, you must know that it will be a gesture of limited impact. We are a prosperous country."

"I am pleased to hear, Prime Minister, that Israel no longer requires our support. I shall therefore instruct Treasury and the Secretary of Defense to suspend all such support forthwith."

There was a slight pause, followed by Ibrahim clearing his throat again. "Do I understand that by suspension of military support—"

"Means exactly that. Suspension and withdrawal of all monetary, material and personnel support, including all weapons procurement programs, current and pending."

"Mr. President, you cannot be serious. Our defense posture is reliant on American equipment and ancillary logistics. Removal of that support would leave us open to immediate aggression. This is not only morally indefensible, but legally suspect. We have contracts!"

"My understanding, Prime Minister, was that it would be a gesture of little impact."

"Ah, I didn't exactly mean that, sir." Ibrahim's voice suddenly changed tone and became pleading. "I must protest this, Mr. President."

"And how do you intend to implement your protest, Prime

Minister? An attack on Galveston Roads perhaps?"

"Sir, that is a dishonorable assertion."

"Prime Minister, you heard what the United States intends doing, and you dismissed me as naive and simplistic. That, of course, is your privilege. If on reflection you find this administration's position having some merit, I am always available for discussion. In the meantime, I wish you good day, sir."

"Wait!" Ibrahim cried out. "What you're demanding is impossible. You must understand that my government is a coalition. If I announced even a moderate support for your demands, the Kadima Party would be thrown out of office. A new government would face an identical problem if it tried to comply, and we would have a constitutional crisis, a development not in anyone's interest."

"On the contrary, Prime Minister. It would be in the interest of your people and all Palestinians. What the Knesset lacks is will and moral courage to correct an injustice perpetrated and sustained under an illusory ideal of self-preservation."

"President Walters, Israel will have a civil war on its hands!"

"What you're faced with is not war, Prime Minister, but lack of faith in your own people. Your people are weary of living in an armed camp. If you extended your hand to them with honesty, hiding nothing, you might be surprised at their depth of understanding and preparedness to step in a new direction and face the obstacles placed in their way. You must be aware of vested interests, within and outside Israel, who will resist genuine reform because to do otherwise, they would lose their *raison d'être*. They will do almost anything to hold onto power, whether religious, military or political, even if it means annihilation of everything and everybody around them. Are you prepared to walk that line, sir?"

"Mr. President, ignoring your veiled slur on my character, if you embark on this course of action, you will be opening the gates of chaos and embittering a longstanding friend."

"Friends don't murder each other's innocents, Prime Minister, or incite to war."

"You're punishing my government and my country for an act carried out by renegades. I implore you to reconsider, sir!"

"I have reconsidered. I reconsidered the intransigent position of your government and found it wanting. I reconsidered the reactionary blindness of Hamas and found them wanting. I look at Syria and Iran and see a resurgence of old ambitions and territorial aspirations, brought about by arbitrary carving up of their countries by World War I victors. I see what the old European colonial powers have done to the Middle East and I have reconsidered. Prime Minister, today you face a choice. Continue to maintain an injustice as evil as any perpetrated against the Jews during centuries of Diaspora, or address it. We are all men under God, deserving of dignity and recognition to live in peace. Withhold not good from them to whom it is due, when it is in the power of thine hand to do it. Proverbs 3:27."

For a long minute, silence echoed loud in the Oval Office. Walters turned his head and looked at Hannakah. Her eyes were wide in puzzlement and something else, wonderment? There was a similar expression on Tanner's face. Graham and Manfred simply nodded to him in encouragement.

"President Walters," Ibrahim said at length, subdued and reflective, "I offer you my unreserved apology for considering you simple and naive. You are clearly neither, sir, but with all due respect, I am forced to say that you're nonetheless idealistic. I acknowledge that without noble goals to pursue and strive for, our lives are but hollow mockeries and shallow expressions of personal gratification. Unfortunately, however noble your demands, I live in a real world, which imposes real limitations. History has inertia, sir, whose course cannot be easily diverted simply by demanding it."

"Prime Minister, if you have the will to act, you can do so. My course of action is not without risk either. But perhaps between the two of us, we can overcome that inertia, not of history, but the entrenched vested interests of a select few whose goals are mere personal gratification. Extend your hand and the world will embrace it. Any time you wish to consult, my line is open. I await the announcement of your government's position, sir." Walters reached for the keypad and cut the connection, then looked at Hannakah.

"Madam Ambassador, I regret having dragged you out here like this, but as you now realize, it was not for a frivolous reason."

Hannakah stood up and smoothed down her jacket. "I can see that now. Mr. President, is there anything I can say or do to make you reconsider?"

"To what end, Lucila? Should I be satisfied with a mere apology and pretend that it's business as usual? There must be an end to what Israel is doing. There will be pain as in any birth, but there is also joy when new life is delivered into the world. I aim to see that new life is brought to the Palestinians…and to Israel. If you will excuse me now…"

Hannakah was about to say something, changed her mind and gave a small bow. "Mr. President…gentlemen."

Cottard got up and escorted her to the door. When he returned to his seat, Tanner crossed his legs and gazed at Walters with penetrating frankness.

"I am genuinely impressed, Mr. President. That was some performance."

"You didn't think I had it in me, did you?"

"Frankly, no. You almost had me convinced, and that's a hard sell at the best of times, but yours is a doomed hope. You will get the Palestinian National Authority excited, but unless there is a revolution, Hamas will still remain a problem to be dealt with. I wouldn't hold my breath with Ibrahim, though. He's a hardboiled pragmatist with only one item on his agenda sheet—staying in power. You may not care much for him, but he's right about the Knesset. The moment Prichard starts talking, if Ibrahim dares to say anything supportive, they will boot out his ass and the entire Kadima Party with him. Nobody will act. The way the Knesset is stacked up, they *can't* act!"

"The people might," Walters said, not in the least distracted by Larry's dash of cold water.

The secretary of state shrugged. "Miracles do happen, but I wouldn't bet my house on it."

Walters leaned forward, his eyes pinning Larry to his seat. "It is Israel who has to bet not only their house, but the entire country. If they don't, they have already lost. For as sure as hell, I'm not going to sit in this office spouting empty rhetoric of past administrations, then pat myself on the back for solving the Palestinian problem. Bush and Clinton trod down that path and the only thing they achieved was to embitter everybody when they failed to follow up on their promises. I am not discounting genuine grievances held by both sides or the problems everyone will face, but I am backing my play with real action, not just words. The ball is now firmly in Ibrahim's court. If he fails to hit it, I'll go there and pick up the damned thing myself. And if Syria or Iran don't want to play, *Ike* and *Nimitz* are still on station."

"What if Israel folds, Mr. President?" Tanner demanded, not dodging the issue.

"Sooner or later they must bet. I will not offer them an easy way out. And if anybody thinks that this is a golden opportunity to even out some overdue scores, I'll bomb their ass. Prichard needs to spell that out in no uncertain terms. I want him at the UN at nine o'clock reciting chapter and verse to the entire General Assembly, at least to those who are there. The rest will just have to read about it in the papers. You'll square away the Security Council later today."

"You wouldn't consider making a personal pitch to the networks, would you?" Tanner prompted hopefully.

Walters immediately shook his head. "You make sure that Prichard is thoroughly briefed. He is a good orator and I don't want to steal his thunder."

"If I may say so, Mr. President, you're not a bad orator your-self. Bringing Ibrahim around was no mean feat," Stone offered, seeing the President in a new light.

It *had* been a good performance. He still might not agree with all of Walters' policies, but there was an undeniable depth of con-viction that only now has become forcefully apparent to him. But he should have known; he should have. Even if this venture failed, the president had raised the bar of expectation and given everybody firm goals to aim for. Shuttle diplomacy would no longer be enough, or acceptable.

"The arrogant bastard was simply pissing in my face," Walters growled. "The only reason he stopped was when he suddenly re-alized that I was withdrawing our military and economic support. You were right to remind me, Graham, that America's relation-ship with Israel is a one-way street going in their direction. If they didn't need us, they would have dumped us. Well, I've had enough of that shit. He can go to the French and the Brits for his planes and tanks."

"Oh, he'll do it," Tanner said. "Or at least he'll try."

"You meant it when you said you will expel their Mossad op-eratives?" Cottard asked, liking it, and rubbed his nose.

Those 'Trade Attachés' had meddled in commercial and secu-rity espionage far too often. But the speed with which the drama had evolved was nonetheless somewhat startling, despite Ibra-him's predictable reaction.

"Absolutely. You and Larry get going on that after he finishes briefing Prichard. Issue notices telling them they are now *persona non grata* and they've got twenty-four hours to get out or I'll have the FBI crate them off."

Tanner passed a hand through his hair. "Well, it looks like my office will be busy for a while. If that is all, Mr. President, I'll call Prichard and give him the word."

"When you're done with him, bring him to me," Walters ordered. "I want to make sure he has the right slant on everything."

"You don't trust me, eh?" Tanner complained, vastly amused.

"This has to be done right, Larry, and I don't give a toss if anybody's feelings get ruffled in the process," the President of the United States answered coldly.

Chapter Ten

Matan's eyes fluttered open as awareness stirred his senses into life. An onrush of bright light forced him to squeeze them shut in pain. A wave of mild dizziness and disorientation sent his stomach trembling. After a moment, it all steadied down and he opened his eyes fully. The world came rushing in: traffic, people everywhere, a car horn here and there, buildings and noises, and a face looking at him wearing a quizzical smile. A face he vaguely remembered.

"You okay?" the elongated face wheezed with detached interest.

It was then that Matan realized where he was and why. The jolt of memories made him sit up and he nodded.

"I think so. How long have I been out?" he managed to croak and cleared his throat.

Stan glanced at his watch. "Two hours and ten minutes. As for your next question, you're at the Savidor central railway station. If you feel up to it, you're free to go."

"And that's it?" His eyes probed the CIA man's expressionless features.

"If it were up to me, Mister, I would shoot you, but Mr. Price said to let you go. And I did not want to upset the man over a piece of shit like you. As for the rest of it, that'll be up to your government."

Matan had nothing to say. What could he say? He opened the door and eased himself out. The Merc immediately pulled away and accelerated into the traffic, taking his past with it. Standing on the sidewalk, surrounded by strangers hurrying around him, he looked up and stared forlornly into the depths of a clear blue

Stefan Vučak

sky. The sun felt warm and soothing on his cheeks and the air smelled clean and fresh. It should have been a day where being alive was joyful, but he felt dejected, alone and abandoned. There seemed little for him to be joyful about. He might as well be dead. Just then, his world did not look such a bright place at all.

He remembered the last thought he had before oblivion overwhelmed him. Did he really betray himself or was that merely a momentary emotion brought about by the unusual circumstances? If he were honest with himself, and right now seemed to be a good time for it, it was probably a bit of both. Was Price right when he said that, as military officers, he and Namir were predisposed to seek a force-oriented solution? Force was the result of failed diplomacy. Didn't somebody say that? With Hezbollah and Hamas, there had never been any diplomacy, only reaction and counter-reaction. That had always been the case and that's how life is lived with the Arabs.

What disturbed him was a realization that the Israeli military indeed held a stranglehold over the executive arm of government and the Knesset. He personally knew generals who exerted enormous influence over the legislature, but it was something he kept buried, preferring to accept it as another fact of life. In that case, what Namir had done was clearly a result of dissatisfaction with the parliamentary process, its powers and constraints. Namir thought that he was in a superior position to decide what was in Israel's best interest. Having the resources to implement his unilateral decision, he acted and Matan had followed willingly. He planned it! A startling comprehension flashed into his mind. They should have hit Bushehr themselves, international backlash notwithstanding. Metsada had the means and the men. Too late now and it was no use blaming it on good intentions either. Hell was paved with those. Somebody also said that.

Matan straightened and some sparkle returned to his eyes. He had fought hard battles before, shooting and office kinds, and always won. Valero may have been fought in a different arena, but the objectives were the same—defeat your enemy. America might not end up bombing Iran, but perhaps his action could stir them into a policy change that may well achieve the same objective. And wasn't that what counted? But at what price to Israel? That part of the future was now for others to write. His future, he would write himself.

With renewed determination, he patted the pocket on the right side of his jacket and reached for the cellphone. Scrolling down a list of preset numbers, he selected one. It took two rings.

"Hello, Namir?" Sarah's anxious voice sent a tremble through his heart.

He could hardly imagine what the past three hours were like for her; a fear always at the back of her mind, but never actually voiced, and now suddenly realized.

"It's me, Sarah," he answered softly and swallowed hard. At this moment, he was prepared to endure hell as long as after everything was done, she did not go away from him. He would not want to live then, not without her.

"Oh, Matan! I was so worried, darling. Are you all right?"

"I'm fine, sweetie. They didn't hurt me."

"Where are you?"

"Outside Savidor station. Can you pick me up?"

"I'll be right there, silly. Don't go away. Oh, it's so good to hear your voice. I was beside myself with worry."

"Sarah, no matter what happens, remember always that I love you."

"Matan! What's going on? Are you in some kind of danger?"

"I'll tell you everything when you get here," he said tenderly and switched off. He selected another number and pressed the call button.

"Where are you, Matan?" Namir asked with concern, but there was steel in his voice.

"The Americans know everything," Matan said simply and waited.

Although unlikely now, the Metsada director could still be tempted to remove his one remaining loose end, and Matan was no longer prepared to go out like that. Whatever waited for him, he would face it. The silence seemed to stretch on forever, but it could only have been an instant. Time flowed in slow motion and he felt calm, almost at peace, but he knew that to be illusory. It was always calm in the eye of a storm.

"Sarah told me what happened. I suppose I can call off Shabak now. Did they hurt you?"

"They were professionals."

"Where are you?" Namir demanded again.

"Outside, looking at a blue sky, waiting for my life to end."

Namir gave a sour chuckle. "You're giving up on me? Is that it?"

"I need to do some thinking right now, Namir. You probably want to do a bit of that yourself. But I am far from giving up, on you or myself."

"We'll tough it out, my boy."

"I'll come in a bit later…when I'm through thinking."

"No matter what, we did the right thing."

"Right or wrong, it's out of our hands now," Matan said phlegmatically and switched off. He meant what he said about not giving up. This was simply another battle to be planned, coordinated and executed. And he did not need a sand table to do it.

Pocketing the phone, he looked around and spotted an empty bench along the sidewalk, one of several placed in front of the station. He walked slowly toward it, not minding the people hurrying to get into the station or fleeing out of it. An elderly Muslim woman, dressed in a traditional black *burqa*, strode past him and heaved two bulging bags of groceries onto the bench and sat down between them. When he paused, she glared at him, daring him to say anything.

Yesterday, such rudeness would have irritated him. Now, it

was trivia, beneath his consideration. What would be achieved by arguing with her? It would be a pointless exercise in futility. If she considered her action a moral victory, he would not deprive her of the pleasure. There was another empty bench farther on and he made his way toward it. The woman seemed annoyed that he didn't try and make something out of it. Poetic justice perhaps.

Matan sat down, crossed his legs and waited, allowing the cacophony of sounds to wash over him, through him. The sunshine was pleasant and his senses seemed to sharpen, take on an edge he hadn't felt for some time. In fact, since the day Sarah agreed to marry him and when he witnessed his daughter's birth. Both events were miracles. Only yesterday, issues that seemed of paramount significance suddenly paled into irrelevancy. His mortgage, the rising cost of living, Admina's education expenses, his career; it meant nothing. They were fleeting, transitory things, the fairy floss of life. The love he had for Sarah, the desire for Admina to become a responsible, caring woman, honor, these were things worth striving for. The honor part might be a bit tainted right now, but he hoped to redeem that—as long as Sarah didn't leave him. He could face everything else, but a world without her in it would be a bleak and shallow thing.

The red Audi passed him by a few meters before Sarah managed a sudden stop. A car behind her barely swerved out of the way, horn blaring. She jumped out and ran toward him, leaving the car door open. It slowly closed after her. He stood up and she was in his arms, her hot cheek against his, her body trembling with almost silent sobs.

"I thought I would never see you again," she murmured into his ear between sobs. He cupped her face between his hands and stared into her sparkling eyes.

"I shall never leave you," he whispered and brought his mouth to her lips. She moved against him and her tongue was a velvety dance of exquisite sweetness. He pulled back and brushed her hair with his fingers. "Let's pick a coffee shop. I've got lots to tell you."

"What's going on, Matan? Who were those men that took you?"

"Where's Admina?"

"At school. There was no reason for her to moon about the house."

He held her hand and walked to the car, oblivious to the stares around them. She offered that he drive, but he shook his head and sat in the front passenger seat. He did not want to concentrate on anything and there was still a certain lethargy about him, probably a lingering aftereffect from the drug. After a searching glance at his face, she pulled away from the curb. There were lots of corner coffee and takeaway joints along the strip fronting the railway station, including McDonald's, Burger King and Kentucky Fried. It was one American cancer that seemed to have no cure. Matan paid little attention as Sarah parked outside Starbucks. They got out and walked inside. The smell of roasted coffee, powdered chocolate and cinnamon permeated the air. There were enough people in there to make two more anonymous. Nobody gave them a glance.

He picked a small square table near the window and sat down. The traffic outside were blurry images and muted noises. A pretty teenager, chewing gum, her black hair tied back in a ponytail, wearing a lime-green uniform, walked toward them, pen and pad ready.

"What will you have?"

"A flat white for me and a long black for her," Matan said absently.

The kid scribbled, nodded and walked back behind the counter where two other girls were filling takeaway orders and working the coffee machines. The cash register clanged as money was exchanged.

He lifted his head and his stomach suddenly filled with nervous flutters. Reaching for Sarah's hand, he placed it in his. With his thumb, he slowly stroked her cool, smooth skin. He should have done this a long time ago when they were alone, talking or watching TV or simply walking down the street. He hoped he hadn't left it too late.

"Sarah…"

Her eyes regarded him, waiting. Then… "What is it, Matan?" When he didn't say anything, she leaned toward him, her features stern. "If you don't tell me what's going on, I'll scream," she whispered fiercely.

He gave a fleeting smile. "That trip to Washington? It wasn't just any trip. There was more to it than just the conference."

"Who is she?" she demanded with a grin that was only half-humorous. "You were doing her in the shower, is that it?"

"It wasn't like that," he said with a shake of his head and a small smile. He paused and his face turned hard. "It's Valero."

"The American refinery? What about it?"

Matan gave a long exhale. "I was the one who headed the Metsada black ops team, and the Americans found out. They were the ones who took me this morning," he said with a rush and his heart hammered loud in his ears.

She went ashen and pulled back her hand. For long seconds, she stared at him, not saying anything. Then she took a deep breath, poured herself a glass of water from the standing pitcher and took several gulps. She placed the glass on the table and held it between her hands. With a nervous little smile, she brushed back a lock of hair with a flutter of fingers.

"Goodness! You certainly know how to shock a person."

"Sarah—"

"You and Namir wanted America to attack Iran?"

"Iran's nuclear facilities are a threat to our very existence," Matan said, trying to justify himself, but now it sounded hollow even to him. "Ibrahim's government refused to act. America and the UN refused to act. This was the only way to do something about it."

The waitress brought their coffees and left the bill on the table. Matan took a sip. It was too hot and too bitter.

"Was it the only way?" Sarah demanded, not touching her cup.

"In hindsight, perhaps not, but that's the way we did it."

"But to attack America! They are keeping our country alive."

"We are keeping our country alive. America may protect us from the Arabs, but it's to further their own interests, not ours."

"I cannot argue with you. You know more about this than I do. What will they do now?"

There was no accusation in her voice, no recrimination, only concern. That might change, but he hoped not. He so desperately wanted her to understand.

"I don't know. Whatever it is, it won't be comfortable for us. Ibrahim's government will probably fall when the news breaks. There will be an outcry from the Arabs, of course, and probably a UN resolution condemning us."

"Another resolution," Sarah snorted, met his eyes then giggled. Matan simply stared at her and gave an ironic chuckle himself. It was absurd really. Another resolution…

She took a sip of her coffee, winced and pushed the cup to one side. "What will happen to you?"

"I don't know. I will probably be arrested, as will Namir. Doron Kameer could lose his job and that little shit Sanvel would get his big chance to step into Kameer's shoes."

"That wasn't what I meant."

Matan nodded. "I know, sweetie. A trial, prison, who knows? And it might not be that at all. There are many powerful people in the Knesset and the IDF who would be on my side. Whatever happens, it is certainly the end of my career in Mossad." His face softened and he reached for her hand. "Will you be at my side? Now that you know, can you still love me? Nothing else matters. It never did."

She placed her free hand on his and squeezed. "Always. I

don't understand everything and I'm not sure what you did was right, but I do know one thing. Your decision could not have been an easy one. I know you. You were restless and moody for some time, and now, I know why. You're kind and generous and you did what you thought was right. Others can judge the legality of it. I am with you, no matter what."

Matan blinked to clear the sting in his eyes and a weight lifted off his shoulders. He had been a fool to doubt her. After a moment, he lifted her hand and kissed it.

"It doesn't matter what others think," he whispered and cleared his throat. "I only care about you." His brow knitted with concern. "This will be hard on Admina."

"Perhaps, but she is our daughter and she has character. She will handle it."

"I only hope that she can forgive me."

"We'll talk to her," she said comfortably and patted his hand. "What now?"

He threw some change on the table and stood up. "I must face it. Let's get out of here."

Sarah drove them home, a ten-minute run. In the driveway, she parked the car leaving the engine running, got out and stood there, waiting. After a moment, he unbuckled and climbed out. He walked to her and opened his arms. She hugged him, her head against his neck.

"Just come back to me. That's all I want," she whispered and her eyes filled, shining with tears. "That's all I ever wanted."

He kissed her, a tender fleeting touch, then pulled away. He got in and buckled up. Glancing back, he reversed and eased the Audi forward. A last glance, a last wave, and he accelerated down the street.

* * *

Prime Minister Sharron Ibrahim slammed down the phone,

313

seething with rage. He not only patronized the president of the United States, fatally as it turned out, but the younger man had humbled him, exposing him as arrogant and condescending. The fact that it was all true was beside the point. No one liked to have his nose rubbed in truth. To add insult to injustice, the president had dared quote Proverbs to him. Never mind that the saying was apt, how very apt. He was lectured to like a schoolboy who had missed an easy one.

Damn Mossad!

With an angry shove, he pushed back his leather chair and stood up, his spacious office suddenly too small. Everything was crowding in on him. The wall-building program along the West Bank had turned into a propaganda disaster, and grabbing Palestinian land along the way was an even bigger disaster, and so stupid. Never mind that he inherited the program from a previous administration. He should have dismantled the thing, but now it had a momentum of its own and like a runaway juggernaut, there was no stopping it. Hamas suicide bombings were on the rise again and Shabak seemed powerless to end them. With expanding suburbia, people were complaining about inadequate public transport. The balance of trade continued to worsen and the cost of energy seemed to have a steady upward curve, paralleling the cost of living. And the Army, always demanding an increase in appropriations: more aircraft, missiles, tanks, men. The list was without end despite evidence that they had enough inventory to wipe out all the Arab countries around them.

He turned to stand before the large rectangular window that overlooked Jerusalem and clasped his hands behind his back. His eyes traveled down Ruppin Street to the Interior and Finance Ministry buildings, identical slabs of yellow sandstone and unbroken rows of reflective windows. They finally rested on the flat-roofed, colonnade-walled Knesset. An imposing structure that attracted constant streams of tourists, yet filled with so much discord and bitterness, a nation tearing itself apart.

President Walters *was* naive if he thought that Israel could accede to his demands. Americans, with their secular state and clear separation of powers, simply did not comprehend the enormous influence and control the orthodox parties exerted over the Knesset. With their unshakeable hold on the balance of power in any coalition, they effectively dictated what a government could and could not do. And they *had* to be in any coalition since no single party held enough seats to form a majority. It had always been that way and there was no getting around it, a millstone around everyone's neck that frustrated and thwarted progress. The problem, of course, Israel was not a single people with a unified voice, but a conglomeration of disparate populations gathered from the world over, each with their own voice, ideology, and agenda. It was a miracle that anything did manage to get done.

He could just see the Dome of the Rock, sunlight glinting off its polished golden covering. So much history crying out there, crying for release, an end. Could President Walters be right when he essentially accused Israel of maintaining the status quo? There was no end to settlement expansion, a cause of irritation for everybody and a slow poison that derailed any attempt to take even a marginal step forward. Dismantling them would entail a huge effort, politically and logistically. Housing needed to be found for the displaced, jobs, compensation and a new lifestyle. All the while the settlers would be kicking and screaming, literally, as they were dragged off and there would be protest marches and breast-beating, mixed with invective and condemnation from every side. How dare he remove people from their God-given land?

Of course, it was not God-given at all. It was won by conquest and lost through more conquest. But the Torah said that this was God's land and for many, that was enough. Conveniently, no one stopped to consider that men wrote the Torah to codify the disparate beliefs and practices of scattered tribes and city-states of ancient Israel and Judah, some 400 years BCE. That did not matter to the eighteen orthodox political parties in the Knesset. As far as they were concerned, this was God's land and there was no room in it for the non-believers—of whatever persuasion.

Past prime ministers *had* dismantled settlements, but they were token gestures to appease the international community and achieved nothing. There was the inevitable furor when it happened, but that too had died down as everybody settled back to the demands of their daily lives. Could he do it and have the job done once and for all? It could be achieved, of course. All it took was courage and will. He needed both, and he was uncertain that he had that resolve.

There was no arguing the right or the wrong of it. Israel was in violation of several UN resolutions for not removing the settlements. The move would certainly engender international support and earn him considerable goodwill, including goodwill from the Palestinians and Arabs in general. At home, he would face a storm, but that would be from a hardline minority. Would the majority of people support him as Walters alluded? It was possible, but a thin thread to hang his career on, if he had one left at all. Withdrawing from Gaza and the West Bank was simply issuing an order to the generals.

There was Hamas to contend with and stopping ongoing attacks on Israeli soil, but America would help.

Could he count on pressure from the Palestinians themselves to stop rocket and suicide attacks when they saw genuine progress and a demonstrated desire by Israel to achieve, if not exactly peace, at least a wary coexistence? It was possible. What about declaring a Palestinian state? Just words on paper, but words that held enormous implication for everybody. It was perhaps his best weapon to bring over the Palestinians. Nonetheless, compared to removing the settlers, that one would be easy. Hezbollah could be a headache. After gaining veto power over the Lebanon government, they were becoming an increasing nuisance and another mess to sort out. Would they continue to seek Israel's destruction even if Palestine was created as a sovereign country? Perhaps, but at least the problem would be reduced to a single front and he would enjoy international support.

Too complicated…too complicated.

Staring at the city that had witnessed so much, suffered so much, could he really end it? His name would go down in history forever as a visionary and peacemaker, admittedly forced into it by circumstances, but there nonetheless. His name would go down anyway as the man who attacked America. The fact that it was Mossad would be lost in the fine print. Was he being simplistic and naive, the accusation he had thrown at President Walters, or merely caught up in a cycle of events he was unable or unwilling to break? Peace might not necessarily be in Syria's and Iran's best interest, but he was happy for America to field that one, if Walters meant what he said. After blowing up one of their refineries, he would be asking an awful lot from them. Surely, a peaceful Middle East was in their interest as well.

If he did nothing, his political career was effectively ended. It was probably dead in any case, but at least he would be shot for trying to do something positive—a legacy any successive government would have to deal with and a solution no nearer in sight if he did nothing. How desperate was he to hold on to power if the cost was simply more misery? Pushed into it, he had reached a cusp and it was time to decide. He had until four o'clock to resolve a problem that's been festering since the '50s. Yet, it wasn't as though he didn't know what needed to be done.

Fish or cut bait.

He turned, sat down, unutterably weary, and reached for the phone. He hesitated briefly, then pressed a button that held a particular preset number. The pickup was almost immediate.

"Mr. Prime Minister," Doron Kameer answered politely. "Good morning, sir. Is there something I can do for you?"

"Yes, there is. We have a situation. I want you to take Namir

Bethan and Matan Irian into immediate custody, and I want the three of you in my office ten minutes after that."

"Ah, that's a highly unusual request, Prime Minister."

"It is unusual, but it's not a request. The two of them ran a black ops to attack Valero."

"You can't be serious, Prime Minister!"

"On your way over, you can ask Bethan to explain it to you."

"I still can't believe it."

"My office. Now."

He replaced the phone and touched another button. It would take Kameer a little while to drive up from Tel Aviv, more than enough time to take care of his next piece of business, he hoped. He steeled himself, knowing that if he took this step, there would be no turning back—for anybody. Right now the price of one career seemed a bargain if he could do some lasting good for his country. Of course, many would not see it in the same glowing light, but there were always people like that. There were always the dissenters, the pessimists and the defeatists who crowed their protests from a fence while enjoying the freedoms bought by the blood of others. And he was tired of fighting the same old battles over and over again. Tired to his very soul. As Israel was tired at having its people blown up by fanatics whose only objective was to perpetuate the bloodshed.

There must be an end, one way or another. He was rationalizing, preparing himself to step into the abyss without knowing what lay at the bottom.

"Abdon Sayar," a smooth, cultured voice answered after three rings, the Harvard accent clearly distinguishable behind his Hebrew.

"Abdon, it's Sharron," he said, suppressing an irritating feeling of inadequacy whenever he confronted the man, and cleared his throat.

It was nothing specific, just that Abdon held an aura of sophistication, power and accomplishment that made Ibrahim seem provincial. But Abdon was in opposition, so he couldn't be as smart as his image projected. It wouldn't be so bad if the man didn't *look* so regal.

"Well, an unexpected surprise, Prime Minister. How is that dry cough of yours?"

"The cough is doing fine, thanks. Abdon, we must talk. Are you available to come over?"

"What's up? You're not thinking of resigning, are you?" Sayar gave a short laugh at his own joke.

"Please! This is serious."

Sayar was silent for several seconds. "Tell me now and I'll let you know if we can talk."

Ibrahim held little love for the Avoda leader, but this was too important for hollow maneuvering and partisan byplays. And if he had to deal with anybody, he did not want to do it with the Likud Party. Besides power, what more could he lose? He'd had a good run and his legacy would not be without some honor. Miriam at least, would be pleased to have him home permanently. But he had not achieved peace yet, he reminded himself with brutal honesty. There were still formidable obstacles to overcome.

"Are you secure and alone?" he said, swallowing his bile, and his pride.

"Yes, to both."

"When I'm through, don't attempt to make political mileage out of this, Abdon. Believe me, it's not going to work. Not this time."

"What's on your mind, Sharron?"

"How long have we known each other?" Ibrahim demanded.

There was a pause before Sayar answered, "About nine years."

"In those nine years, have I ever thrown you a curve?"

"Well, apart from the usual inter-party sparring, you always played fair, for a Kadima bastard."

"Okay, then listen to this." Ibrahim paused, took a deep

breath and exhaled. Without trying to soften it, he quickly sketched the situation and outlined the American demands.

"At nine o'clock New York time, that's four p.m. here, the American UN Ambassador will announce the President's position. I don't have to tell you what will happen then."

"The Knesset will call for a vote of no confidence and I will become the next Prime Minister," Sayar said instantly, not without some relish at the prospect.

"You may end up as Prime Minister, and you're welcome to it, but then you'll also have to deal with the American demands. And this time, I don't believe they will allow the problem to be buried in another round of photo ops and diplomatic talks. President Walters will want us to act and act promptly, or he will take action unilaterally. Of course, you don't have to do anything, but when you run down military logistics and our aircraft start falling out of the sky, a domestic economy in crisis and your country shunned by the world's community, you might be willing to reconsider."

"Damn it, Sharron! How could you let Mossad get away with such chicanery?"

"The same way Avoda did when you were last in government. Mossad has become a loose cannon and it's time something serious was done to rein them in, by me or by you. And right now, I don't particularly give a toss. They are a boil we should have lanced long ago."

"The American President is naive if he thinks we'll carry out his demands," Sayar said dismissively, "and he can keep his military support."

"That's pretty much what I told him, but it won't wash, Abdon."

"Planes and tanks we can get from anybody and they'll be eager to sell."

"But we don't have the fiscal position to rearm and retrain. Not right now. And when this breaks, the international money markets may not be all that keen to extend us credit. This will be a singular opportunity for them to get back at us and I don't think they will pass it up. Think it through."

There was a moment of silence. "Walters would actually allow the Arabs to attack us without doing anything?"

"Perhaps not, but with our country at stake, can we take that chance?"

"He wouldn't dare! We own half the Congress. They would impeach him!"

"Congress won't have a say if he rallies the people behind him. They want to bomb someone over Valero, and right now, they might not care if we are on the receiving end."

"And he means to expel all our special Trade Attachés?"

"Wouldn't you? Once this breaks, other countries will follow suit."

"We still have the ultimate deterrent," Sayar said quietly.

"Yes, we do, but are you prepared to start Armageddon? For that's what it would be. We'd have a solution, because both sides of the problem would have been eliminated. Do you really want that?"

"Damn Mossad!" Sayar said at length.

"Yeah, that's exactly what I said."

"What do you have in mind?"

"I need your support. Frankly, it galls me to be placed in this position, and you're free to gloat, but I am thinking of Israel's future, and we're on a short fuse. The harsh truth is that this is simply too big for either of us. If I try to implement the President's demands alone, Knesset would murder me. But it could be done…if we are united."

"Let me get this straight. You are proposing that we form a new coalition government, bypassing the orthodox zealots?"

"That is exactly what I am proposing, Abdon. It would remove a major obstacle that's always hampered previous attempts at a settlement."

"With you as Prime Minster and the Kadima Party as the senior partner?" Sayar did not exactly sneer, but his disdain was clear in his voice.

Ibrahim gave a long sigh, disappointed that Abdon was still playing politics. "I frankly don't give a damn who is PM. Don't you get it yet what is going on? If we don't handle this just right, Israel will end up on the international pariah list. It still might, besieged by Arabs and abandoned by America. We have a window of opportunity to make a positive stride to end a strife that has divided and embittered our people for almost sixty years, and which is bleeding our economy of resources badly needed for civil works, health and education, to name a few. The IDF might not like what we are doing, but they exist to serve us, not the other way around."

"I wish somebody would get around to telling them that," Sayar said dryly and snorted. "You paint a bleak picture, Sharron, and I agree with much of what you said. But you know as well as I do that selling this to my Labor Party colleagues won't be easy. And you, my misguided friend, face the same dilemma with the Kadima."

"That's why we must talk and present a united front," Ibrahim countered hotly. "If you want to talk politics and be coldly brutal about it, the Knesset members are in it for power and will want to hold onto their seats. Those who are compelled by their party or personal convictions will resign in protest, and others, more tractable to our ideas, seeing this as an opportunity to gain more power, will fill their place. If our two parties stand together, there will be no power spill or a need to hold an election. By the time an election is called, the unrest will have died down when people see genuine progress being made."

"You hope. On the other hand, we could have riots on our hands," Sayar suggested. "But I agree with your assessment about the Knesset. What if the Army forces the issue and opposes our program?"

"Then we'll either have dictatorship or a revolution. Either way, it would be the end of Israel as we know it."

"All this because of Mossad!" Sayar said and snorted with contempt. "May they roast in hell. But Sharron, it's one thing to declare a Palestinian state and tell the world that we're pulling out of the territories and abandoning the settlements, and another to actually do it. If we look at each issue one at a time, what about borders? Are we talking 1967 or current borders? And we don't want to forget the problem we created for ourselves by building that wall on the West Bank."

"And the land we appropriated while doing it," Ibrahim agreed. "Walters stipulated current borders and we'll take it from there."

"What about refugee repatriation? When Israel was created, we displaced hundreds of thousands of Palestinians. They cannot all come back, and Hamas will be sure to raise a stink over that. There simply isn't enough ground to hold them even if they had somewhere to live. There is no infrastructure, housing or industry."

"We can help, but we can't hold their hand, dammit! They want independence, we'll give it to them, but the rest they'll have to tackle themselves."

"There is one problem that could derail everything," Sayar said soberly.

"The settlements, I know. We can clear out isolated pockets, but East Jerusalem is far too heavily built up to abandon. We'll have to draw the border around it, and Hamas and the Palestinian National Authority will simply have to lump it. I am prepared to be pushed only so far."

"You genuinely believe this could work?"

"I believe it's the only way we can get it done."

"Okay, let's say I can convince my party. What about portfolios? How would you divide that? The Labor Party will not accept token ministerial posts. If we are going to share, everything must be on the table."

"Everything will be on the table, and I mean that. I will do anything to make this work. If you want to be the PM, it's yours. But if you don't believe in this, or you want to play partisan games, tell me right now. I don't want to waste any more of my time."

"You're a bastard, Prime Minister. You would win no matter what I do and you know it."

"It's not about me, you idiot! Can't you get that through your thick head?"

"I get it, all right. Okay, we'll talk. There is much to work out and we don't have the time for details. Are you free now?"

"I'm not, but there is nothing more important on my plate right now."

"Ten minutes, then. By the way, what do you intend doing about Bethan and Irian?"

"We'll have to do something. What pisses me off though, is not so much what they did, but that they failed to get away with it, damn it!"

"Agreed. And Sharron? Thanks for being honest with me."

"Forget it. Shalom."

* * *

Feeling like a man going to the gallows, Matan was escorted into the Prime Minister's inner office by two burly security guards. Staffers gaped at them, wondering what was going on. Inside, he was surprised to see Abdon Sayar, leader of the Labor Party opposition, seated before the wide solid wood desk. Perhaps the wheeling and dealing had already begun. The office was comfortable without being ostentatious, and the tasteful decor did not distract from the occupants inside. Matan always wanted to meet the acclaimed and sometimes derided prime minister, but not under these circumstances. He stood there and waited for fates to pronounce judgment.

When he drove in to work, two agents were already waiting. They were apologetic and polite, but left no room for argument as they escorted him to Kameer's office. What he saw surprised him. Instead of a frigid reception, Doron and Namir were seated around the conference table sipping coffee. The situation was cordial, but the conversation that followed was less so. No one said much during the drive to Jerusalem.

Ibrahim nodded to the escort and the two security men faded, closing the door after them with a soft click. He did not offer his three visitors a seat. Face expressionless, he glanced at Sayar, then looked at Bethan with a mixture of disappointment and regret.

"As a result of your meddling, Director, the full weight of President Walters' fury has now been unleashed against Israel, which may plunge this country into civil unrest. You will understand when you hear the American demands announced at the UN later today. I don't need to ask why you did what you did. You thought that your understanding of international politics was superior to mine and you had no faith in the policies of your government. Simply put, you knew better than anybody what was the right course to take for this country, and in your schoolboy version of diplomacy, implemented your impetuous decision. Had you succeeded, you might have had sufficient reason for self-congratulation. But as with such things, you failed and plunged Israel into turmoil. However well intentioned, your misguided act has gotten you more than you bargained for. Perhaps more than anyone bargained for. To survive the aftermath, the Kadima and Labor Parties are now in coalition, with Abdon Sayar as Prime Minister. This is not official yet, but it will be soon." He turned to Sayar. "Do you wish to add anything?"

Sayar shook his head. "You're simply echoing my own thoughts."

Ibrahim nodded and fixed his eyes on Kameer. "I want your resignation, effective immediately. Perhaps there was no way for you to intercept this, but the fact that one of your departments could mount such an operation under your nose is inexcusable. You can delegate authority, but you cannot delegate responsibility. And that goes all the way up. We both lost control and are now paying the same penalty," he said and looked at Bethan again.

"As for you, Director, if you want to make policy, seek a seat in the Knesset! You're subject to the freedoms and constraints that govern this country, and they are not to be discarded or ignored when you find them personally inconvenient. If you don't like them, you should campaign to have them changed using the mechanisms available for that purpose. Do you understand what I am saying?"

Bethan straightened and looked steadily at the Prime Minister. What could he say? In the end, there was nothing more he could say. It had all been said already.

"I understand perfectly, sir, and I regret the fallout of my actions, on you and on Israel."

"We may all regret the fallout of your actions, but you will have time to reflect on your methods and actions as a guest of the Ayalon Penitentiary," Ibrahim announced with a hard glare, then shifted his gaze to Irian.

"I have studied your record, Colonel. You had a brilliant career in the Army and chalked up some outstanding achievements during your stay in Mossad. You discarded one career because of moral qualms and the other by following what you must have known was an illegal order. We all understand the threat Iran's nuclear program holds for Israel, but that does not mean we're prepared to take unilateral action to remove it like we did with Iraq's reactor at Osirak. This is not 1981. Loyalty is a fine thing when directed properly."

Matan knew all right, and didn't attempt to evade responsibility. He wondered what Ayalon would be like.

"I have nothing to say in my defense, sir, and I stand ready to accept what arrogance and presumption has brought me."

"You are correct, there is nothing to say." Ibrahim looked at Sayar who nodded. "Mr. Irian, you will be dragged through inevitable hearings and some will demand your head. But I believe that you are an honorable man who does not deserve to suffer the full weight of the law. You have probably inflicted enough punishment on yourself already, a far more important outcome. I am skating on thin ice here, but in the final analysis, you were following an order. This country has serious problems to overcome and Prime Minister Sayar will need all the capable men he can find to overcome them. You are therefore free to go, sir."

Matan stood there stunned, unable to comprehend that he would actually be allowed to walk away from the carnage of his making. Could this be happening and dare he hope?

"Sir…I am overwhelmed, but I stand guilty with Director Bethan."

Sayar smiled, but it was without humor. "Putting you in jail would be an easy solution, Colonel. Sorting out the mess you helped create may be a more fitting punishment. We will have to deal with Iran's nuclear threat, but it will not be through clandestine or military means. At least not while I am Prime Minister. The command structure of our defense force has become dangerously reactionary, as have the responses of our intelligence services, which Mossad demonstrated so vividly. Your particular insight into both problems and how I should deal with them will be valuable. My office shall be in touch, Colonel."

In shock and the realization that he still had an honorable future, held him immobile for several seconds.

"Sir, when America learns—"

Sayar raised his hand. "You can leave America to me. I will not see a valuable man sacrificed for the sake of shallow political expediency. America will have punished us enough."

Matan slowly looked at his mentor. "Namir…"

The Metsada director nodded fondly. "Don't worry about me,

my boy. They did the right thing, for me and for you. You go home to Sarah and patch things up. How about that!"

Still stunned, Matan faced the two prime ministers and gave a small bow.

"Gentlemen…"

He turned and walked out. Slowly, a sense of euphoria enveloped him and his step suddenly had a light spring to it. He did not feel cleansed, but he felt that he had been given a chance to atone—he was on probation. Several staffers gave him curious stares as he marched down the wide expanse of gray carpet that separated two glass-walled cubicles of the prime minister's outer office. Outside, the security guard straightened when Matan closed the door behind him.

"Sir, I was instructed to take you anywhere you wanted to go."

Matan gave him a long look, then nodded. "If I can have a moment, please."

"Of course, sir. I shall be by the elevator," the guard said and walked off.

Palms sweaty with excitement, stomach fluttering, Matan dragged out his cellphone and pressed a recall number.

"Hello? Matan, is that you?" Sarah's nervous voice clearly conveyed her agitation and concern.

"Hi, sweetie. You're not going to believe this. The Prime Minister has let me go!"

"Let you go? What are you talking about?"

Matan laughed, he couldn't help it as his bubbling spirits demanded release. "Not only that, he's got a job for me."

"I don't understand."

"I don't understand it either, but I'll see you in a while and explain everything. Love you."

"Oh, Matan! You'll be my death yet. Please hurry."

He switched off and walked quickly toward a bank of three elevators. The guard pressed the down button.

"Take me home," Matan ordered, looking forward to a new

beginning.

* * *

Mark finished pouring his second cup of coffee and stirred in half a teaspoon of sugar. Enticing smells of hot croissants, jam, bacon and eggs filled the cabin. A nap had restored some of his vigor, but all the flying had nevertheless started to become somewhat wearisome. Right now, he only wanted to get home, take a long shower and crawl into his large bed. But that was still many dreary hours off.

The phone jangled next to his elbow and he picked it up.

"National Security Advisor on the line, sir," Nancy announced from the cockpit.

Mark's eyebrows twitched in surprise. What would Stone want with him at this hour? He placed his palm against the pickup and glanced at Tom.

"It's Stone."

Holding a cup, Tom shrugged. At 30,000 feet, there wasn't much that Stone or anybody else could do to him. At least by the time he got back to Houston, he wouldn't have to explain himself to Beltrain, he hoped. He did not exactly lie about his trip to see Price, but Beltrain could end up being miffed. Christ! Why worry about it.

"Put him through," Mark said and pressed the speaker button so that Tom could hear.

"Hello, Mark?"

"Right here, Admiral."

"Hope I didn't catch you at a bad moment."

"Just finishing up on a late breakfast."

"Good. You might be interested in watching CNN at nine o'clock our time, son. Prichard is going to make an announcement to the UN."

"At nine o'clock in the morning?"

Stone gave a short barking laugh. "I know. Most of those guys will still be tucking into their caviar and toast. But the UN and the networks were alerted and the General Assembly should not be completely empty."

"Did the President read the riot act to the Israelis?"

"He certainly did. It was a good performance, my boy. Even Tanner was impressed. But I won't spill the beans on Prichard. Watch the TV."

"I'll do that, Admiral."

"Don't forget. My office when you land."

"Got it."

"Enjoy your flight, son," Stone said and switched off.

Mark replaced the phone and took a sip of coffee. A glance at one of the three clocks mounted on the left front bulkhead showed eight minutes to nine.

"What do you think is going on?" Tom ventured and took a bite out of a jam-filled croissant.

Now he knew why the food was so good on board. There had to be some compensation for being cooped up in a flying beer can for twenty hours, albeit a comfortable one.

"I guess Prichard will hang Israel out to dry. At least I hope so. Sons of bitches."

Tom peered at Mark and grinned. "You don't care for them much, do you?"

"The intelligence community thinks that Mossad is a pretty sharp outfit with some smart operators. Perhaps it is, but I haven't seen any of them. The ones I met were pretty much full of themselves and felt that they could go anywhere and do anything simply because they were Jews and everybody was supposed to feel sorry for them. Fucking bastards! Bringing them and Israel down a peg or two will be a healthy thing."

"Christ! I'm glad you didn't hold back," Tom said and laughed.

Mark smiled, then broke into a few chuckles himself. "Well,

crap! I didn't want you to get the wrong picture," he said and reached for the phone. "Nancy, can we have CNN on the big screen please?"

Nancy emerged from the cockpit, smiled at them and pulled back a hinged painting mounted on the right bulkhead, behind which stood a 36" LED screen. Using the remote, she switched it on. It was probably satellite reception because the picture was sharp and clear. She changed channels from a movie to CNN and held the remote to Mark. He shook his head and pointed at a seat.

"You're welcome to stay, Nancy. Our UN Ambassador is about to address the General Assembly."

"Is this about that dreadful attack on the Valero refinery?"

"It certainly is."

"I assume you know who did it?"

Mark nodded. "Tom and his team did all the work."

She flashed Tom a sunny smile. "Outstanding. Can you tell me who it was?"

"That would spoil the surprise," Tom said grinning at her and wondered again if he dare ask her out. But she was in Washington and he was at the steamy ass end of nowhere. Still, she can only say no, and if he didn't ask, he would never know.

She glanced at Mark. "If you're sure that I would not be intruding?"

"Since you played an indirect part in our investigation, it is the least we can do."

After a brief hesitation, she nodded and took a seat next to Tom on the other side of the aisle. She pressed a black button on the armrest and swiveled the seat forward. Watching her, Tom did the same and she beamed at him.

In a swirl of color, the CNN logo splashed across the screen, accompanied by the usual music. When the picture cleared, the camera focused on the two principal anchors.

"Good morning. This is CNN nine o'clock news, live from New York

center. Your hosts, Ralph White and Sharyl Knight."

Arranging his face, Ralph fixed on a smile. *"Welcome to this special broadcast from the United Nations General Assembly, where the American Ambassador is about to make a statement regarding the tragic incident at the Valero Texas City Refinery last Sunday night."* He turned to his sidekick, starched smile firmly in place. *"Sharyl, do we have any information regarding the substance of Ambassador Prichard's announcement?"*

"That's the strange thing, Ralph," she said, looking cool and sophisticated. *"Usually the White House provides us with a brief, but not this time. It all sounds very mysterious,"* she continued breathlessly, allowing a touch of excitement to creep into her voice. *"We see on our screens that Ambassador Prichard is about to make his address. This early, the grand hall is barely half full as members were caught flat-footed. We are switching to the General Assembly chamber now. Stay tuned."*

Prichard looked distinguished and stately as he made the preliminary statements. Despite the microphone pickup, his full-bodied voice carried well. Pausing for effect, his eyes flickered at the Iranian ambassador.

"At two a.m. last Sunday, a series of explosions rocked the Valero Texas City Refinery in Houston, causing loss of life and considerable damage. Initial evidence pointed to Iran as the perpetrators of this unprovoked attack on the United States, namely Web pages posted on Iranian and Al Jazeera sites proclaiming responsibility. On Monday morning, FBI investigators located an unexploded device of Iranian manufacture. On that evidence the President immediately ordered two carrier battle groups stationed in the Persian Gulf to position themselves off the Iranian coast in readiness to carry out a counterstrike."

After a measured look around the Assembly, Prichard grasped the sides of the lectern.

"This is not news. What is news is that after being manipulated to execute a strike against Iran, the FBI and the Department of Homeland Security successfully tracked down the real perpetrators. It was not Iran, but Israel's intelligence service, the Mossad!" His voice was thunder and his

outstretched arm pointed at the Israeli ambassador, an accusation from God.

Nancy gasped and placed her hand before her mouth, reflecting the consternation and shock that swept through the chamber, which Prichard allowed to run its natural course. When the Assembly chamber settled down, he looked at the members with an imperious gaze.

"Had the United States acted in haste as many urged us to do, we would be facing a different world today, a far more troubled world. However, President Walters' unwavering determination to identify the responsible party before acting has averted global disaster. Acknowledging Iran's cooperation during this crisis, the administration has invited President Al Zerkhani to a series of bilateral talks designed to normalize relations and take steps to undo some of the injustices that Iran has suffered, firstly at the hands of old European colonial powers, and of late, from America itself. The President is hopeful that these talks can succeed if there is good will on both sides. After allowing IAEA inspectors into the country, I want to announce an immediate lifting of U.S. trade sanctions against Iran and urge the UN to do the same."

Then he turned and faced the Israeli ambassador. *"The United States expresses severe disappointment that Israel has chosen to act as it did, and condemns in the strongest terms possible, action by Israel's security service that carried out this cowardly attack against a longstanding friend and ally. The fact that the Israeli government was unaware of Mossad's treachery in no way absolves Prime Minister Ibrahim. The United States demands a formal apology from Israel, compensation for the injured and those killed, and reparations for the damage done to the Valero refinery. America also demands the arrest and prosecution of all Mossad operatives responsible for the planning and execution of this attack. But that is not enough. Not for the first time, Israel has shown itself willing to attack a friend in pursuit of its singular interests. This time, it was done at its peril.*

"Following the First World War, the Middle East has been a cauldron of turbulence and strife, which has left ruin and misery in its wake, not only for Israel, but the Palestinian people as well. This has to end now, whatever

the effort it might take. The United States demands immediate dismantle-
ment of all settlements in the Gaza Strip and the West Bank in accordance
with the Roadmap. We demand that Israel withdraws fully from the occupied
territories and that it declares the establishment of a Palestinian state, com-
prising of the two territories defined under current borders.

"Due to extensive settlement building in East Jerusalem, it is recognized
that total withdrawal there will not be possible. Israel and the Palestinian
National Authority are to enter into immediate negotiations and agree on a
new border within thirty days, or a border will be imposed on them. To enforce
its demands, the United States is seeking a resolution to compel Israel to
comply, with force if necessary.

"Here and now, the United States is making a promise to the Palestinian
and Israeli people that we stand ready to implement a lasting peace in the
Middle East. We don't pretend that the road ahead will be easy, but with
cooperation and understanding, we will overcome entrenched ideologies and
vested interests of those on both sides for whom peace is a threat, not a goal
to be achieved. Hamas and Hezbollah, including their supporters, stand
warned that America will respond with force should any party seize this
moment to exercise aggression against Israel."

Casting a glance at the Secretary General sitting on the po-
dium behind him, Prichard slowly walked back to his seat with
all the dignity of an outraged father at a wayward offspring. There
was silence in the great chamber as everyone digested the aston-
ishing development. They could not believe that Mossad had
come close to dragging America into a war with Iran. What else
had they done that remained a buried secret? Then, to everybody's surprise, the Iranian ambassador stood up and began to
clap. After a slight hesitation, the Syrian ambassador joined him.
As members rose, the chamber began to resound to a standing
ovation, which became more energetic as dignity was shed at the
prospect of witnessing a historic moment and a determined
America finally assuming positive leadership.

If carried out, Mark realized that the United States had in a
single announcement laid down a framework that could achieve

a lasting settlement. If successful, the implications were enormous and far-reaching for the entire region, including the geopolitical landscape.

"Well, crap!" He chuckled and shook his head in wonder. "Walters actually went and done it."

"But will Israel carry out the demands?" Tom mused and sipped at his coffee. Nancy's eyes were huge when she turned to look at him.

"It hardly seems possible that Mossad would really do something so horrible."

"Well, I guess the day of reckoning has come," Tom said affably.

The Secretary General banged his gavel to restore calm, but the underlying ripple of whispers took longer to die down.

"The Ambassador for Israel," he declared and waited.

Several members booed as the smallish man stood up, not prepared to take the lectern. When he looked up, there was no bravado or defiance in his stance, only grim determination to carry out an unpleasant task.

"I wish to announce to the Assembly that under Prime Minister Abdon Sayar, Israel has a new coalition government. I stand before all of you, offering Israel's unreserved apology to the United States for the hurt caused to its citizens and damage done to a valued ally and hopefully, still a friend. Compensation and reparations will be fully met.

"Israel announces that it will immediately commence dismantlement of all settlements in the occupied territories. Moreover, the standing infrastructure and housing will remain. It will be up to the Palestinian National Authority to decide how they will be distributed and used by its people. Israel also announces the withdrawal of all forces from the territories. At this time, Israel also wishes to announce the formal recognition of the Gaza Strip and the West Bank as a sovereign Palestinian state within the definition of existing borders. Israel would welcome an opportunity to engage in bilateral talks to resolve the East Jerusalem border, Customs, security, transit rights and trade issues." The Ambassador paused and cast his eyes around

the Assembly floor. *"Given what has transpired, we have no right or expectation, but we are asking the international community for its patience and understanding while our country moves through a troubling transition, which hopefully, will lead to a lasting peace for all."*

Stunned silence followed the ambassador's deceptively simple declaration as he sat down. Almost as one, everyone stood up, clapped and cheered, perhaps not as enthusiastically as for the American ambassador, but vigorously enough, buoyed by the prospect of finally seeing a resolution to a conflict that had torn Palestine apart for decades.

Nancy smiled gleefully at Tom and clapped. "Unbelievable! Can it really happen? Peace at last?" Her eyes were round with wonder. "It was you, wasn't it?"

"Mark organized it all," Tom said. "I was just another hired hand."

"I am certain it was not all that simple," she said coyly and something new appeared in her eyes. A dazzle of hero worship?

Tom had seen that look before and didn't trust it. After an evening out, the dazzle usually wore off. Still, a night out opened possibilities for other nights, and who knows where that might lead.

Mark nodded to Nancy and she switched off the screen. "Israel is faced with a complex transition, but they just might pull it off if everyone is prepared to cooperate. Before we get overly sympathetic, we need to remember that they created this mess themselves. On that note, we should celebrate to a successful mission. May all Israeli problems be thorny ones," he declared comfortably and Tom grinned.

"Now you're talking. The usual for us and pour one for yourself, Nancy."

"Oh, I couldn't do that, sir," she said firmly. "Not while on duty."

"Maybe when you're not on duty?" Tom asked, suddenly feeling self-conscious, which was ridiculous. He had dated women before.

She gave him a secretive smile. "Perhaps."

* * *

Looking like it was hovering, the Gulfstream drifted over the outer marker, then with a rush, shot over the East Perimeter runway and touched down in a puff of gray smoke from the skidding tires. Slowing rapidly under reverse thrust the aircraft reached the end of the runway and moved onto the taxiway. Afternoon sunshine streamed into the cabin as the twin engines wound down, the aircraft shuddering over uneven concrete joints.

When it stopped, Nancy emerged from the cockpit looking crisp and fresh, opened the front hatch and lowered the steps. Tom had already unbuckled and retrieved his overnight bag. With a glance at Mark, he walked toward the hatch.

"I hope to see you again soon...sir," Nancy murmured, her eyes challenging him, reinforced by a whiff of a go-for-the-kill perfume.

He paused, uncertain whether to start something. Christ! He still had Malena on his mind. He locked eyes with Nancy and smiled slowly. Hero worship or not...

"I would like that. Until then..."

Standing on the apron before the open hangar, he dropped his bag and looked around. Air Force ratings moved inside, working on uncovered engines and servicing another Gulfstream. They did not seem to be interested in the new arrival. Nothing stirred on the two open runways. The air smelled of avgas and pollution. A brown haze hung over Washington and his nose crinkled with distaste. Compared to Israel, this was another world. Familiar, yet alien, and he felt out of place. Too much flying and the shifting time zones were catching up with him. He felt bone tired, his body clock totally scrambled. What he needed was a solid workout and a five-mile run to re-oil the machinery.

337

Mark said something to Nancy, who nodded, smiled and disappeared inside. He stepped off the aircraft and strolled toward Tom, stopped and stretched his arms.

"Man! What I wouldn't give for a good massage."

"Just what I was thinking. Do we have to see Stone?" Tom moaned, shoulders drooping. "Couldn't this wait until I've had two days of sleep?"

Mark grinned, commiserating. "Brace up, I am sure you'll survive the experience," he said easily, giving Tom a speculative stare. "Don't start something with Nancy unless you mean to finish it, okay? Like I said, she's a nice kid. I wouldn't want to come after you if things didn't work out."

"Christ! What are you? Her mother?"

"Just protecting her from prowling wolves," Mark said and started walking toward his car.

Tom shook his head, picked up his bag and walked after him. It wasn't as if he was after a piece of patch…exactly. And besides, Nancy was a big girl, able to make up her own mind about things. Wasn't she?

It took them some forty minutes to reach Pennsylvania Avenue, the Capitol building looming bright in the setting light. The traffic had not been bad going in, but it was a different story in the car park that made up the opposite lanes. Tom felt little sympathy for drivers fighting their way home, enduring the crush with resigned patience or seething frustration—not after spending twenty-one hours in the air. He still needed to get back to Houston. The prospect did nothing to cheer him up.

Mark drove through the White House Executive Drive entrance and parked in the reserved visitors slot. The Secret Service checked them in and let them loose. Tired or not, this was Tom's first ever visit and he made the most of it. He did not exactly drag his feet, but didn't rush either as he followed Mark, observing the bustle and noises of a government in action.

Mark paused outside Stone's office and waited for Tom to

catch up, hoping that Stone wasn't about to conduct a postmortem session. After two Atlantic crossings, he was totally exhausted and the prospect of a lengthy debrief did not exactly fill him with enthusiasm.

Tom caught up and gave Mark a challenging stare. "What?"

"Nothing," Mark said with an indulgent smile and opened the door, not holding Tom's understandable curiosity against him, remembering his own first visit.

Stone's secretary looked up and nodded. "Good afternoon, gentlemen. The Admiral will be with you in a moment."

Just then, Stone emerged out of his private office, his eyes lighting up when he saw the two men.

"Ah, the prodigal son returns. Hi, Mark. Welcome back to the real world," he said and stuck out a hand to Tom, measuring him with a glance. "You must be Meecham. Mark has spoken of you."

"I hope not all of it bad, sir," Tom said easily as they shook hands, liking the older man instantly.

Stone laughed. The boy was confident and carried himself with authority. Under different circumstances, he would have made an excellent naval officer. Well, working for the FBI wasn't a bad job either.

"From Mark, it's always bad, son. Come, let's get this done." Stone cocked his head at his secretary. "Let Cottard know that we're on our way."

"Very good, sir," she said and picked up a phone.

Stone opened the door and led them out. With strong determined strides, he made his way to the chief of staff's office, not looking at the distractions around him. Curious eyes followed the trio, leaving a ripple of gossip in their wake.

Chapelle Davies looked up as they entered and nodded at the closed door on their left.

"You can go right in, Admiral."

With a small nod, Stone walked to the door and opened it. Cottard waved him in, a phone at his ear.

339

"Right! First thing in the morning." He replaced the phone and frowned. "Damned National Rifle Association. Sometimes I want to shoot them." He eased himself around the desk to stand before them. "Mr. Meecham, Mr. Price, I am Manfred Cottard. Welcome to the White House," he said, getting the names right, and glanced at Stone. "So, they are the ones who caused all this grief for Israel?"

"I'd like to believe they brought it on themselves," Stone said in a dry voice and Cottard chuckled.

"You got that right." He looked them over and gave a conspiratorial smile, relishing what was about to happen. "Okay, I believe we're about ready."

He knocked once on a wide polished door, opened it and walked through. Stone gave his two protégés a nasty grin and followed. Tom and Mark exchanged puzzled glances and small shrugs. This walking from office to office was getting mysterious. But there was no mystery when they strode into the Oval Office and found President Walters beaming at them from a sofa. Tom suddenly felt self-conscious and shot Mark an accusing stare. Mark lifted his eyebrows and gave a minute shake of his head as if to say that he knew nothing about it.

Walters stood up. "Hi, Graham. Any reaction from the Israeli media?"

"Nothing definitive yet, sir."

"Damnation! Probably still digesting the news, but I'm sure they'll have plenty to say in their evening edition. Okay, Manfred, make the introductions."

"Mr. President, I would like you to meet Mark Price, Director, National Operations Center."

Walters immediately offered his hand. "A genuine pleasure, Mr. Price. An outstanding piece of work."

Mark cleared his throat as they shook hands. "Thank you, Mr. President. That means a lot coming from you."

"Nonsense! You deserve it, and lots more. We need to talk,

Mr. Price. I want to hear your views about chopping up the DHS. Manfred will call your office."

Mark blinked. "That's flattering, Mr. President, but perhaps Mr. Forbes—"

Walters waved his hand. "He'll get his chance, but I want some down-to-earth input." With that, he looked at Tom.

"FBI Supervising Special Agent, Tom Meecham, Mr. President," Cottard announced.

"Mr. Meecham." Walters extended his hand and smiled with genuine warmth. As they shook hands, the president lightly clapped Tom on the shoulder. "First-class detective work, Mr. Meecham. Just four days. Unbelievable."

"I had a great team behind me, Mr. President, and we've had some breaks," Tom said, fast losing his awe, trying hard not to stare around the office. Walters may be the president, but he was still only a man. Well, almost.

"A great team is nothing without a good leader, Mr. Meecham. You two have done this country an inestimable service. Without your diligence and professionalism, the United States might have been forced into a war with Iran. We could still end up in a war, but it will not be with Iran." Walters nodded and looked at Cottard. "All the preparations made?"

"Everything is ready, Mr. President."

"Good. You two," Walters pointed at Mark and Tom, "need to be here tomorrow at eleven a.m. for a presentation of well-earned citations; an expression of thanks from your President. Mr. Meecham, that means you will not be flying back to Houston today, but I trust being guest of the United States government for the night will make up for any inconvenience. Manfred will give you the details. And if you're concerned about squaring this with Mr. Beltrain, don't be. Director Marshal has been updated."

"Thank you, Mr. President. I was wondering how to explain all this to my boss," Tom said.

Things were piling up fast and he needed a moment to come

up for air. But being guest of the government could mean many things, not always pleasant. However, the prospect of not having to endure three more hours or so in the air and a long drive home sounded pretty good right now.

"It's settled, then," Walters said firmly and glanced at his national security advisor. "Good enough for you, Graham?"

"It will do for a start, sir," Stone answered with a mischievous twinkle in his eyes.

Walters grinned and turned to his guests. "Tomorrow at eleven, then," he said in dismissal.

"Thank you, Mr. President," Cottard said and ushered everyone back to his office.

Once inside, he sat down behind his desk. "Tom, I'll have a Secret Service car take you to the JW Marriott Hotel for the night and pick you up in the morning at ten thirty. That suits you?"

"Sounds good to me, sir." From what Tom heard, Marriott was a classy joint and he wasn't about to complain. He wondered if Nancy would care to have dinner with him, and Mark probably had her number.

"Good. Mark, I'm afraid you'll have to make your own way over."

"No problem."

"But to show you that the administration does have a heart, albeit dime-sized, I'll have an escort clear a path for you going home."

Mark nodded in surprise. "That's very generous of you, sir."

"It's the least we can do."

Outside Cottard's office, Mark and Tom exchanged smiles and big high fives.

Epilogue

Beneath the pitiless glare of a noonday sun burning from a clear sky, a meandering Persian ibex stopped and lay panting in the scant shade provided by a clump of thorn-cushions. Dwarf shrub and sagebrush dotted the gully between shallow valleys bordered by an endless sea of rolling yellow sand dunes and expanse of pea-gravel flats.

A lonely rutted road wound its way along the valley floor of the Dasht-e-Lut southern Iranian plateau. Topping a rise, a cluster of tin-covered huts baked in the heat. A kilometer farther on, the road ended at what looked like a dilapidated oil derrick. Two Pasdaran military trucks streaked with grime left a thin trail of dust as they drove away from the skeletal tower.

Silence lay thick over the parched land, like it too had given up under the relentless heat. The air twisted and shimmered in the distance, making it impossible to tell where the desert ended and the sky began. A dust devil swirled briefly across the flowing sands and vanished in the haze.

The two trucks stopped near the largest hut and four men emerged wearing traditional *keffiyehs*. With a glance at the distant tower, they moved inside. Some six minutes later, a low rumble made the ground quiver and birds lifted out of the brush, chirping in alarm.

With a puff of dust, the ground beneath the tower gave way in a round depression. The rumble grew to a subdued roar and an intense flash of light cast harsh shadows across the dunes. A circular shockwave rippled across the dunes. Fine sand drifted into the sky, dissipating quickly in the light breeze. The birds circled and slowly settled back into the brush. When the dust cleared, there was no sign of the tower within the bowl left in the ground.

In their 35,780-kilometer geosynchronous orbits above the blue and white crescent, in the three GPS satellites, part of the Integrated Operational Nuclear Detection System, arrays of photodiode sensors detected a millisecond burst of intense light coming from the Iranian plateau. Immediately, other sensors recorded a low level electromagnetic pulse. Onboard computers analyzed the data and sent a microwave transmission to NORAD's Operations Center buried deep within Cheyenne Mountain, Colorado, and the U.S. Strategic Command, Command Center at Offutt Air Force Base, Nebraska.

In the underground command post, affectionately known as the molehole, the senior controller read the FLASH message from the computer and automatically routed it to the National Military Command Center in Washington DC.

When the message reached Manfred Cottard, he leaned back in his chair and locked his hands behind his head, deep in thought. After a time, he slowly picked up the printout, got up and walked into the Oval Office.

About the author

Stefan Vučak has written eight Shadow Gods Saga sci-fi novels and six contemporary political drama books. He started writing science fiction while still in college, but didn't get published until 2001. His *Cry of Eagles* won the coveted Readers' Favorite silver medal award, and his *All the Evils* was the prestigious Eric Hoffer contest finalist and Readers' Favorite silver medal winner. *Strike for Honor* won the gold medal.

Stefan leveraged a successful career in the Information Technology industry, which took him to the Middle East working on cellphone systems. He applied his IT discipline to create realistic storylines for his books. Writing has been a road of discovery, helping him broaden his horizons. He also spends time as an editor and book reviewer. Stefan lives in Melbourne, Australia.

To learn more about Stefan, visit his:
Website: www.stefanvucak.com
Facebook: www.facebook.com/StefanVucakAuthor
Twitter: @stefanvucak

Shadow Gods books by Stefan Vučak

In the Shadow of Death
An extraterrestrial craft is discovered in an ancient Mayan pyramid and the knowledge throws Earth into social and political turmoil. As a new agent in the Diplomatic Branch, First Scout Terrllss-rr is tasked to destroy the craft before international tension throws Earth into open conflict.

Against the Gods of Shadow
Facing economic sabotage by Palean raiders, Pizgor pleads for help from the Serrll government. Second Scout Terrllss-rr is tasked to find the raider base and expose Palean's duplicity. Terr is forced to battle a Fleet ship that leaves them both badly damaged and leads Terr to confront forces that threaten to destabilize the Serrll itself.

A Whisper from Shadow
An extraterrestrial craft is discovered in an ancient Mayan pyramid and the knowledge throws Earth into social and political turmoil. As a new agent in the Diplomatic Branch, First Scout Terrllss-rr is tasked to destroy the craft before international tension throws Earth into open conflict.

Shadow Masters
With his mission on Earth completed, Fist Scout Terrllss-rr is returning home, only to be intercepted by an Orieli Technic Union survey ship. The encounter sends ripples of consternation throughout the Serrll Combine. In an attempt to establish a link between a raider network and the AUP Provisional Committee, Terr's cover is compromised. To extricate himself, he has to raise the hand of Death.

Immortal in Shadow
On his way to a prison planet, Tanard, a renegade Fleet officer, escapes and vows vengeance. He is recruited by an extremist Palean group to raid Kaleen worlds. First Scout Terrllss-rr must find the secret base that is supporting him before the Wanderers rise up and unleash Death's wrath on the Serrll.

With Shadow and Thunder
The Orieli are caught in an interstellar war and now they are about to drag the Serrll Combine into it. Betrayed by his Wanderer brother Dharaklin, First Scout Terrllss-rr crashes to Earth in a sabotaged ship. He now has a whole world after the secrets he holds.

Through the Valley of Shadow
Bent on revenge, Terrllss-rr pursues his Anar'on brother to the fabled world of the Wanderers—and face judgment by the god of Death. On their frontier, the Serrll Combine is plunged into a savage encounter with a Kran invader, showing them a glimpse of a dark future.

Guardians of Shadow
Having destroyed a Kran invader, Terr, Teena and his brother Dharaklin, head for Orieli space where they will begin their cultural exchange mission. In a devastating Kran attack, Teena is taken and Terr seeks to rescue her. To win a war that threatens to consume the Orieli and the Serrll Combine, the fabled Wanderers must march against the Krans wielding the hand of Death.

Other books by Stefan Vučak

Cry of Eagles
2011 Reader's Favorite silver medal winner

Iran's nuclear capability represents a clear national threat to Israel, but the United States and Europe do nothing. A Mossad black ops team sabotages a refinery complex in Galveston, plants evidence that incriminates Iran, confident that an enraged America will strike back in retaliation. But the Mossad team makes one small mistake, which the FBI exploits to uncover the plot before America vents its wrath on Iran and plunges the world into political and economic turmoil. An award-winning thriller that will leave you at the edge of your seat.

All the Evils
2013 Eric Hoffer finalist
2013 Readers' Favorite silver medal winner

A researcher in the Secret Vatican Archives uncovers a papyrus that claims Jesus was John the Baptist's disciple and the second Messiah. To prevent the tractate from becoming public, the Vatican secret service engages an assassin to silence anyone who has knowledge of the papyrus. It is up to an FBI agent to unravel a series of murders and prevent the assassin from killing him.

Towers of Darkness
A Wyoming mineworker discovers a human hand bone embedded in a forty million year-old coal seam. An anthropologist, Larry Krafter is sent to recover the bone and unearths a human skull. Instead of receiving acclaim when he publishes his discovery, vested establishment interests seek to discredit him, using murder to do it.

Strike for Honor
2013 Readers' Favorite gold medal winner

In a joint exercise with the Korean navy, Admiral Pacino's son is one of the casualties from a North Korean missile strike. Enraged that the President is more interested in appeasing the North Koreans, forgetting the lost American lives, Pacino decides to make a statement by bombing military facilities in both Koreas. His court-martial puts American foreign policy under public scrutiny.

Proportional Response
2015 Readers' Favorite finalist

The Chinese populist faction, the Tuanpai, plan to trigger a global disaster that will devastate America. In the aftermath, the FBI identifies China as the culprit, but don't know if this was a rogue operation or a government plot. Fearful of American retaliation, China invites U.S. investigators to find that proof. Under a cloud of mutual suspicion, America readies itself for a military confrontation. A mind-bending expose of international politics!

Legitimate Power
What happens when a person living on the outskirts of Jerusalem digs up two ossuaries and finds a strange crystal the size of a smartphone able to repair itself when scratched and turns into a perfect mirror under laser light? When the crystal is put on the shadow gem market, suspecting that it is not natural, an American collector buys it, wanting to tap into its hidden potential. When the Israelis learn what it is, they want it back…as do the Chinese…as does the American government, which sets off a race to get it, no matter what the cost in shattered lives.

Lifeliners

When everybody is against them, it is tough being a lifeliner, as Nash Bannon found out. Lifeliners are ordinary people…almost. They can draw energy from another person; they live longer and are smarter. Scientists claim that Western high-pressure living and growing sterility in developed countries has triggered the rise of lifeliners, and *homo sapiens* will replaced by *homo renata* within ten generations. So, what's not to like about lifeliners?

CPSIA information can be obtained
at www.ICGtesting.com
Printed in the USA
BVHW031347150319
542769BV00001B/44/P

9 780648 473114